# THE RADIANCE OF THE MOON

# ALSO BY ASHLEY WORRELL

## THE HEBRIDEAN SHIELD SERIES

*The Radiance of the Moon*

*The Splendor of Fire (Fall 2024)*

*The Speed of Lightning (Spring 2025)*

*To learn more about this nine book series please visit:*

*www.byashleyworrell.com*

# The RADIANCE OF THE MOON

ASHLEY WORRELL

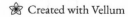

*For Rachel*
*Who walked me beside me to the abbey.*

# CONTENTS

Prologue 1

Chapter 1 9
*Rathmullan, Ireland - March 15, 1383*

Chapter 2 15
*Council of the Isles - April 16, 1383*

Chapter 3 27
*Lochbuie Oighreachd - June 1, 1383*

Chapter 4 35
*Duart Oighreachd - June 1, 1383*

Chapter 5 46
*Lochbuie Oighreachd - June 18, 1383*

Chapter 6 56
*Lochbuie Oighreachd - June 19, 1383*

Chapter 7 61
*Lochbuie Oighreachd - June 19, 1383*

Chapter 8 72
*Lochbuie Oighreachd - June 20, 1383*

Chapter 9 79
*Duart Oighreachd - July 29, 1383*

Chapter 10 90
*Lochbuie Oighreachd - July 30, 1383*

Chapter 11 101
*Lochbuie Oighreachd - August 5, 1383*

Chapter 12 112
*Lochbuie Oighreachd - August 7, 1383*

Chapter 13 119
*Duart Oighreachd - August 15, 1383*

Chapter 14 131
*Lochbuie Oighreachd - August 16, 1383*

Chapter 15 143
*Duart Oighreachd - August 16, 1383*

Chapter 16 149
*Duart Oighreachd - September 10, 1383*

Chapter 17 154
*Duart Oighreachd - September 10, 1383*

Chapter 18 157
*Duart Oighreachd - September 10, 1383*

Chapter 19 163
*Duart Oighreachd - September 10, 1383*

Chapter 20 171
*Duart Oighreachd - September 13, 1383*

Chapter 21 182
*Duart Oighreachd - September 13, 1383*

Chapter 22 188
*Lochbuie Oighreachd - October 8, 1383*

Chapter 23 195
*Lochbuie Oighreachd - October 8, 1383*

Chapter 24 203
*Lochbuie Oighreachd - October 9, 1383*

Chapter 25 208
*Lochbuie Oighreachd - October 10, 1383*

Chapter 26 219
*Lochbuie Oighreachd - October 24, 1383*

Chapter 27 230
*Lochbuie Oighreachd - October 25, 1383*

Chapter 28 236
*Duart Oighreachd - October 25, 1383*

Chapter 29 244
*Duart Oighreachd - October 26, 1383*

Chapter 30 253
*Duart Oighreachd - October 26, 1383*

Chapter 31 264
*Lochbuie Oighreachd - November 22, 1383*

Chapter 32 271
*Lochbuie Oighreachd - November 29, 1383*

Chapter 33 278
*Lochbuie Oighreachd - November 22, 1383*

Chapter 34 283
*Lochbuie Oighreachd - November 30, 1383*

Chapter 35 286
*Lochbuie Oighreachd - December 2, 1383*

Chapter 36 289
*Isle of Scarba - December 2, 1383*

Chapter 37 293
*Knockvologan, Mull - December 3, 1383*

Chapter 38                                                    302
*Lochindorb Castle - December 16, 1383*

Chapter 39                                                    310
*Lochindorb Castle - December 16, 1383*

Chapter 40                                                    315
*Lochindorb Castle - December 16, 1383*

Chapter 41                                                    324
*MacKenzie Oighreachd- December 22, 1383*

Epilogue                                                      327


Notes                                                         331
Dear Reader                                                   337
Acknowledgments                                               339
About the Author                                              341

# The Council of the Isles

King John of Islay

**Royal MacDonald Sons**
Tànaiste Donald MacDonald of Dounarwyse
John Mór MacDonald of Dunnyveg
Ranald MacDonald of Garmoran
Alastair MacDonald of Keppoch

**Nobles of the Kingdom of the Isles**
Chief Iain MacLeod of Dunvegan
Chief Lachlan MacLean of Duart
Chief Robert MacLeod of Harris

**Thanes of the Kingdom of the Isles**
Chief Niall MacKinnon of Skye
Chief Brodie MacNeil of Barra
Chief Ewan MacFie of Colonsay

**Great Men of Royal Blood of the Kingdom of the Isles**
Chieftain Angus MacKay of Sanaigmore
Chieftain Týr MacLean of Jura
Chieftain Hector MacLean of Lochbuie

**Holy Order of the Kingdom of the Isles**
Fingon MacKinnon, Abbot of Iona
Paul O'Gallagher, Bishop of the Isles

# Noble Clans of the Isles

### Clan MacLeod
Chief Iain MacLeod of Dunvegan
Lady Eilidh MacLeod of Dunvegan
Chief Robert MacLeod of Harris
Lady Agnes MacLeod of Harris

### Clan MacLean of Duart
Chief Lachlan MacLean of Duart
Lady Mhairi (MacDonald) MacLean of Duart
Tànaiste Hector MacLean, the Younger, of Duart
John MacLean of Duart
Lachlan MacLean, the Younger, of Duart
Neil MacLean of Duart
Somerled MacLean of Duart

### Clan MacLean of Lochbuie
Chieftain Hector MacLean of Lochbuie

### Clan MacLean of Jura
Chieftain Týr MacLean of Jura
Lady Mariota MacLean of Jura
Tànaiste Calum MacLean of Jura

### Clan MacKinnon
Chief Niall MacKinnon of Skye
Dowager Lady Malvina MacKinnon of Skye
Fingon MacKinnon, Abbot of Iona
Lady Elspeth MacKinnon of Skye
Léonid MacKinnon of Calais

"In all things take the shield of faith, wherewith you may be able to extinguish all the fiery arrows of the most wicked one."

— Ephesians 6:16

# Prologue

## Isle of Iona - May 15, 1378

He wasn't supposed to be here. Deep throbbing pounded the right side of his head, soon replaced by stomach-clenching nausea as the ship dipped down and pitched back up. His head lay on bare wood, and crates surrounded him. With the feeling of sitting up out of his own grave, Hector pushed himself to a seated position. How had he gotten from a tavern on the River Lune to a merchant vessel?

Daylight cracked through an eye-level knot in the wood, blinding him and sending sharp stabs of pain through his forehead. He raised a hand to block the light. His fist still clenched the bottle, a trickle of whisky sloshing around the bottom. As he brought the bottle to his lips, the early morning tremors caused half the precious liquid to run down his face and neck. In desperation he mopped his face and licked what he could from his fingers, every drop needed to keep the memories away. It would not be enough.

Unable to stand upright, he crawled across the rough wooden floor of his berth and up the stairs to the main deck. Sound and light clamped vise-like at his temples, prompting him to lurch to the ship's rail and heave into the sea.

Resting his forehead on his arm, he tried to reconcile the rocking of the boat and the spinning of the world around him.

"What's the matter with you?" A boy unloading crates on the gangway below gaped at him. He spoke in Hector's native tongue, but it took him several moments to remember the words he'd not used in eight years.

"Seasickness."

The young lad moved crates from the forecastle to the ramp. "Get off the ship then. It's giving you the boak."

The lad's command of Gaelic slang gave Hector an idea of his whereabouts. "Is this the Rhins of Galloway?"[1]

The young dockworker looked at him as if he were daft. "The Isles. You're on Iona."[2]

*No, no, no.* He couldn't be in the Isles. "How?"

The boy shrugged and walked down the ramp back toward the shore. With great effort, Hector tried to focus his eyes. Across the mile-wide Sound of Iona, he glimpsed the jutting green hills of Mull. Home. Longing and shame took up residence side by side. Connection to people and places that reminded him of who he was, and who he wasn't anymore.

A stiff wind kicked up off the sea, and he shivered. No, he wasn't shivering. The tremor had started again. Involuntary shaking began in his head, then spread down his extremities. He needed more whisky, and he needed it now.

Putting one unsteady foot in front of the other, he walked a crooked path down the gangway. He recalled a flourishing market at the dock's end where islanders stopped to trade on their way to the abbey. The potent Islay whisky his father bought there by the barrel called to his battered soul, the broken vow to never end up like his da filling him with embarrassment.

Trekking the path beside the crystal sea, his sword's weight caused him to sway every few feet on wobbly legs. Bits and pieces of his last night in England stirred in his thickened memory.

It started as it always did. Just one drink. One drink to take the edge off the guilt, and the memories he yearned to leave behind. One drink became two, two became three, three became four. Around his fourth drink the man seated at the table next to him in the tavern started a quarrel with him.

Pain radiated through his bruised knuckles, and he wiggled them. What sparked the altercation? Groping through the darkness of drunken memory, he could recall the man starting the argument, and how he'd finished it. Not until after the fight did he discover the man was the local constable.

Rather than face the consequences, Hector had slipped away into the night. Heading for the dockside he found a merchant pulling up anchor and threw coin at the man, then stumbled aboard. The destination was irrelevant. All that mattered was that it was departing.

A fresh swell of nausea sent him to the side of a squat stone structure to retch into the bushes.

"Hector MacLean, is that you?"

Brushing away the sweaty curls that clung to his forehead, Hector lifted his head, recognizing the voice of his uncle. He rubbed his sour mouth on the back of his sleeve and suppressed another urge to be sick.

Pádraig's familiar round face creased with wrinkles, and his hair had aged to silver, but his affectionate brown eyes remained the same. Longing to run into the arms of the man who had been closer to him than his own father battled with the desire to run away before Pádraig glimpsed the sinner he'd become.

"Pádraig."

Despite the stench of whisky and sickness, Pádraig closed the gap between them and pulled him into his chest. Cradling Hector like a beloved child, he placed a hand on the back of his head and began to praise God. Love conquered Hector's resistance, and he moored himself to Pádraig, tightening his arms around him. In an instant, eight years of separation vanished as if it were the day after the most harrowing night of his life. How could Pádraig embrace him? Why wasn't he angry?

Pádraig's voice broke. "Why did you leave?"

Hector buried his face in his shoulder. "I couldnae face you after what I did. I never meant to harm him. I only wanted Da to stop hurting me."

"I know, lad, I know." Pádraig pulled away and looked deep into his eyes. "We could have found a way through. We're your family. Where've you been?"

"France, Iberia, Ireland, England. I ran and kept running."

Pádraig put a hand to Hector's scarred cheek but didn't mention the disfigurement it caused him. "Look at you, you're nearly thirty."

Hector unfolded his giant frame from around Pádraig's short, round body. Blinding pain rang through his head, and he wobbled, still shaky on his feet. The refreshment of his uncle's forgiveness couldn't keep the anguish of war from seizing his mind. An overwhelming feeling of dread piled upon him like a stone cairn, breathlessness crushing his lungs.

Pádraig's all-seeing eye raked over his disheveled appearance. "You look like a right mess."

Sweat ran down Hector's face and collected in his mustache. "Aye. Seasick."

Pádraig raised a gray eyebrow. "You're shaking, lad. And you smell like whisky."

Hector adjusted his black leather cuirass[3] and noticed the stain down his front. In another life, he would've died rather than see the look of disappointment on his uncle's face. But with no spirits in his system to numb the memories, the nightmare delusions of battle would soon descend. There was no choice but to ask for his help securing a drink.

"Do ye ken where I can get some *uisge-beatha*? I tho' there was a market near the dock."[4]

It'd been years since he used the Gaelic term for whisky. Uisge-beatha, the Water of Life. Fitting, since it had become a central part of his life, necessary for everything.

Pádraig's face carried a look of bafflement. "It's the Lord's day. Our day of prayer. You used to be devout."

Two days of drinking aboard ship blurred together. Dismay washed over him. It wasn't Saturday, it was Sunday. The market was closed. Iona was a holy site, so there was no tavern to even have a flagon of ale.

"That was a long time ago. Before Pontvallain."[5] Pounding roared in his ears—the rhythmic beat of hooves. Clouds formed before his eyes on the horizon indicating an enemy force advancing toward them. He forced his eyes shut. *It isn't real. There are no riders or clouds of dust. You can forget the memories. You only need a drink.*

Trying and failing to keep the note of desperation out of his voice, Hector pleaded with his uncle. "I've got to have a drink. Do you have a flask? Anything, please."

Without a drink he relived that terrible day. He could see the men, hear the voices, and smell the death as vividly as if it were happening all over again. Drink was the only thing that kept it at bay.

Pádraig's eyebrows knit together in concern. "My father was at Bannockburn. The intensity of that battle weighed on him his whole life. He could never bring himself to discuss it. Nearly drank himself into an early grave."[6]

The din of a battle long over, but as palpable as if it were happening again grew in his mind, threatening to drown out Pádraig's voice. *It isn't real.*

Pádraig continued to explain, unaware of the fear pumping in Hector's heart. "The whisky eventually failed, but God never did. When he turned to prayer instead of drink, Bannockburn couldn't touch him anymore."

Pádraig's solution made his terror recede like a nightlight in a darkened room. Could prayer really achieve that?

Longing for surrender sprang from his heart. He dangled from the tattered strand of his choices, wishing he could give up, but terrified to let go. Arms burning, he held on, scared of the fall that would break his will but may save his life.

"I havenae prayed in years."

Pádraig walked away in the abbey's direction. "I can tell."

Unable to decide if he was ready to face God or if he should charter a boat to take him toward more whisky, Hector paused on the narrow road. The storehouse of his mind seized upon his hesitation, and he plunged into the thick of battle. Screams rent the surrounding air; his hands locked around a man's throat as he tried to protect the young soldier next to him.

Struggling to stay in the present, Hector forced himself to cry for help. "Wait—"

Pádraig slowed and looked at him wide-eyed. Desperate to stay ahead of his past, Hector staggered toward the abbey, the steady presence of his uncle giving him the courage he needed to try.

They passed the nunnery and moved toward the church. Iona Abbey waited at the crest of a vivid green hill, keeping watch over the sound. Wind ruffled the tall grass, a small reminder of what was real. *Don't stop. Keep moving.*

A vision of a rider, sword raised, appeared in his path. Hector squeezed his eyes shut, feeling the darkness roll over him. *God, please...* Opening his eyes, Pádraig was again by his side, guiding him toward the abbey. Tremors vibrated through his body, shifting the crushing weight of fear all around him. *You're not mad. Talk. Stay in the present.*

Hector's voice shook. "Is my brother well?"

"Aye, he's chief of the MacLeans now. Married the king of the Isles' youngest daughter. Four sons, and she's about to give birth to their fifth child. They named their oldest Young Hector."

"Hector?" The warm comfort of long-denied brotherly affection broke his heart. He was the only other person who'd survived their father and understood the pain of his childhood.

"His life isn't the same without you by his side. Lachlan's made inquiries for years trying to find you. He heard you'd taken work as a mercenary on the continent. We pray each night that you return to us. That you know we've forgiven you."

Lachlan forgave him. After everything he'd done.

"I tho' it was better for everyone if I left. It's sheer coincidence that I'm even back here. I was trying to outrun another mistake."

"What's important is you're here now. You must go to him."

What would he say, standing on Lachlan's doorstep? His brother had become the chief God wanted him to be, and Hector had become a rotten drunk like their father. How would he react when he found out Hector had done nothing to deserve the honor of having his firstborn child named after him?

Remorse pinched his chest, and his voice caught in his throat. "I cannae go home."

Pádraig stopped in front of the abbey church steps. "The Lord has brought you back where you belong. Go in, lad. I'll be here waiting when you're done. You've come this far."

Arms trembling, Hector longed to let go, but his hands gripped tight to his will. How could he do it without a drink?

Screams of the wounded came to life around him, the sound of dying more real than the sound of Pádraig's voice, drowning out everything life giving. Thirst for whisky parched his dry throat, and his body cried out for relief. *It isn't real.*

Putting one foot in front of the other, he approached the door. Heart pounding, he wrenched it open and rushed inside.

The cool stillness of the stone abbey was a stark contrast to his sweating palms and racing heart. The distant sound of plainsong echoed from the nearby chancel, "Veni Creator Spiritus." Come, Creator Spirit.

Lingering at the door, he braced for the visions to overtake him. Nothing happened. Glowing candles beckoned from the front of the sanctuary, inviting him to come closer.

Hector wet his finger in the font and genuflected, recognizing Father, Son, and Holy Ghost. Astonished, he held his hand out in front of him. It was steady as stone. Clarity of mind had replaced the thick fog of drink. Comfort replaced throbbing pain.

On legs strengthened by the nearness of peace, he crossed the narthex and passed into the nave. A simple stone altar anchored the sanctuary, a silver cross its only adornment.

The turmoil that burdened his shoulders eased as the Savior of the world took the yoke beside him. In the same way the presence of God made the ground beneath the burning bush holy, he had the distinct feeling that he was now standing on holy ground. He removed his boots, then his sword. Arms outstretched, he placed his battle-scarred sword on the altar and knelt before the cross, relinquishing his fight.

"Jesus, are you there?"

*What are you running from?*

His voice became a heavy whisper. "Myself."

If only he could change his past and be like his brother, a man who hadn't wasted his life. What could he possibly say to God to explain the darkness of his choices? Longing to yield to sovereign will overwhelmed him, but he was scared to let go, knowing how unworthy of redemption he was.

*You can't change your past. Trust Me with your future. I will light the way.*

Hector collapsed to the cold stone floor and covered his head, ashamed. "I'll do anything you tell me. I'll go wherever you send me. Tell me how to fix the mess I've made."

*Be still. Stop fighting. The battle is already won.*

Stillness was foreign to him. Victory without having to fight, impossible. If he wasn't a warrior, who was he? "I dinnae know who I am."

*I know who you are, and I know the plans I have for you.*

Tears stung his eyes. Plans? Why would God give him anything? Confession sprang to his lips. "I've been trying to make things right, but I've made them even worse, taking on the traits of a man I swore I'd never be. Drinking helps me forget, but it's stolen my life away. I'm a miserable sinner, wasting all the opportunities I've ever had. I have nothing to offer you."

*Give me your heart. I will make it brand new.*

"Lord, if you are willing..."

*I will catch you, don't be afraid.*

Hector loosened his fingers and let go of his will, plummeting backward into the unknown. "Save me."

# CHAPTER 1

## RATHMULLAN, IRELAND - MARCH 15, 1383

Cara swiped her tears and placed her hand on her husband's icy, immovable face. She concentrated on the stillness of his chest, expecting it to rise and fall. He'd been dead two days and the silence in the cottage was overpowering. An emptiness permeated every corner of the room.

Outside the cottage window, the clouds had taken on a purplish color, and the dawn breeze stirred the window covering outward. Fresh wind off Lough Swilly cooled her wet cheeks and helped her regain her composure. It was almost time to take his body to the burial ground.

A jackdaw landed on the open window. The soot-colored bird cocked its head, studying her in the candlelight. It ruffled its silvery wings and squawked. Her mother would have said the jackdaw was an omen, a thief of joy and scavenger of hope. Yet she knew better. An absence of conflict never present in their home had settled in, and while she'd tried to love Duncan, she was thankful he could never hurt her again. Her tears were not tears of grief, but of relief and thankfulness that God had delivered her.

The reflection looking back at her from the bowl of rosewater was familiar, but the woman inside—a stranger. To earn praise from him, she'd quenched everything about herself that he despised. Who was she now that he was gone?

Duncan's face, etched with a permanent frown, showed the depth of his disappointment in her as he passed on to the next life. Crossing his wrists, she tucked the burial linen around his arms and chest, carefully securing it around his broken neck. She dipped the comb in rosewater and ran it through his hair, then plaited it close to his scalp, preparing him for the face covering.

As she cradled his head in her lap, she smoothed her fingers over his face as she did in the beginning before he had grown to regret his choice of wife. No voice raised. No hand pushed her away. Hollow desire for what should have been clawed at her heart. Even in his worst moments she'd wanted to love him, wanted to believe he would change. Now she knew with certainty he never would.

A tear dripped off her nose onto his. The abrasive, wax-soaked linen scratched against her skin as she wound it around his head, swaddling him in a shroud of unanswered questions. Would he still be alive if they'd not fought? How would their lives have been different if she never married him at all? Her gaze lingered on the once strong body, now hidden beneath the burial cloth. Things would never be different for them.

A small knock sounded at the door and scared the ominous jackdaw away. Cara attempted to wipe away her tears, but the sight of her mother-in-law on her doorstep, her safe place to hide, made her drop all pretenses.

"My sweet girl." Margaret's cool fingers soothed her as she caressed the tender bruise on Cara's jaw.

Cara roped her arms around her and tried to impart the same comfort. They had both survived. "I should be comforting you."

"My dearest, there is nothing that can take away my pain. Duncan is gone. I have no one left."

Cara took Margaret's hand in hers. "Not as long as I am here."

Margaret gazed upon her only child, clothed for his burial, and wiped fresh tears away. She tightened her grip in Cara's hand, then leaned down and kissed the top of Duncan's head. Things would never be different between them, either.

"Thank you for covering him. I couldn't have borne it."

Cara nodded and tried to breathe through her blocked nose. "I failed him in the only way that mattered, at least this I could do."

Two days ago, Margaret had come from her adjoining cottage as soon as she heard Duncan's raised voice and arrived just before he stormed out. He was angry Cara wouldn't leave for the Iona nunnery, angry that she refused to leave Margaret. Cornering Cara at the edge of the table, he leaned over her, screaming and yelling into her face. Chastising her for the one quality she longed to change most, and for her selfishness. When his fist connected with her jaw, he shattered her will. She agreed to go at dawn's light.

Pushing past his mother he fled into the night. Back to his leman[1]. Into the darkness. Onto the horse that would lose its shoe. Over the cliff to the rocks below.

Cara picked up the bowl of rosewater and emptied it out the front door. "Eve was over last night when they brought his body. They've given her the cottages and all their contents. We must vacate this evening. Bringing my father's loom is not an option. It's hers now."

Eve, the woman who Duncan had put her aside for, had come to claim her son's inheritance.

Margaret's hand covered her mouth. "No, Cara. It's your livelihood. It's all you have left of your father."

"Eve's baby, he looked just like..." She almost couldn't bring herself to say it. "Duncan." The room swayed as a sudden burst of faintness broke over her.

"Take a deep breath." Margaret steadied her, taking the bowl from her shaking hands, and rested Cara's head once more on her shoulder. Cara drew in a reluctant breath through her mouth to hold back her tears. "There's nothing that can be done to change our lot. You will marry again."

Cara scoffed. "I cannot conceive children. I need to accept that. No man wants a barren wife."

"Dinnae speak words of discouragement about your life, Cara. You are a treasure. You will make some man a wonderful wife. A kind man, one that will see everything I do."

Cara wiped angry tears away, frustrated that her body could not do something Eve's could. "Ten years of trying without a hint of conception. What else can I believe? I cannot bear disappointing another husband month after month."

Margaret rubbed soothing hands down her back. "Aren't there children in need of love from mothers of the heart desperate to provide it? Why, look at me."

"You had Duncan."

"Losing an abusive child before he can change is more painful than having no children. He became a version of his father, yet worse in every way. He never loved me, Cara."

A surge of guilt hit her remembering the times Margaret had tried to shield her but encountered the same violence. "I know."

"I prayed for God to help me reach him so that he would change. I never saw it happen, but do you know what did?"

Cara shook her head.

"God sent me you instead. A daughter to love, to nourish, to treasure, and who came to faith just listening to me babble stories while she weaved. He gave me a friend and the child I always longed for. God knows who we need and who needs us."

Like the humble Scottish thistle, Margaret had found a way to survive in the harshest of conditions. Unassuming but robust, she was able to root herself in faith and tolerate times of hardship.

As soon as Duncan left each day, Margaret came next door. While Cara weaved, Margaret talked, recounting stories from the Scriptures. It was the first time Cara had learned the names Gideon, Abigail, and Ruth, and the first time she had learned the fruits of the Spirit and the many parables Jesus told. What Duncan broke down each night, Margaret faithfully rebuilt each day, refusing to allow Cara to wither away in the decade she had been her daughter-in-law.

Margaret took a deep breath. "A mother knows when to love and a mother knows when to let go. You must go home to your family."

A wave of alarm rushed through her. Cara could never return to a life without God, to a life without the woman who had shown her the way. "No, Margaret. What will become of you?"

Margaret's face bore a look of complete despondency, as if every ounce of joy was taken away from her. "Eve has clarified that I am no' welcome near their child. There is nothing here for me. I will go home to the Isles, to my clan and my brother and sister."

Being parted from Margaret was unthinkable. Cara wrapped her arms around her mother-in-law and cinched her tight. For so long, they had taken refuge in each other, protected each other, and learned from each other. They couldn't be separated.

"You're not sending me away from you. Do you hear me? I will not go back. I'm going with you."

"Cara, I would only be a burden to you. You must return to your family."

She looked deeply into Margaret's eyes, remembering the words of Ruth, a woman who, like Cara, loved her mother-in-law as a daughter of the heart. "You're my only family. Where you go, I go. Your people will become my people, and your land will be my land. There is no future apart from you. I'll not hear another word about it."

Margaret's eyebrows knit together. "How will you afford your journey? I've only enough for one passage to Mull."

Cara slid the thick band of gold from her hand. "It's all I have left."

A knock sounded at the door and they both jumped. Margaret's gaze dropped to Duncan's lifeless body on the rush-covered floor.

Cara replaced the ring on her finger. "'Tis time to go."

Margaret dropped beside Duncan, her tears forming spots on his linen-covered cheeks as she kissed them. "I love you, my dear boy. God be merciful to you."

Taking her trembling shoulders under her hands, Cara helped her to her feet. "Ready?"

Margaret wiped her eyes and nodded.

Heart thudding as though she had just sprinted for miles, Cara opened the door and admitted the six members of the MacSweeney guard who would take Duncan to his final resting place. Together, they carried him out onto the road and hoisted him on their shoulders.

Every familiar bit of her life from the last ten years was now being carried away from her, and for a moment Cara thought she might be sick. Somehow her feet found a steady rhythm behind the guard as three keening women fell into step behind her. Margaret's hand tightened around hers.

Having not led keening[2] since her father had died ten years earlier, the words strangled in her throat, choked away by thankfulness so powerful it drained her strength. The words of mourning she needed to sing felt more like praise. Her steps faltered, but Margaret held her up. "I've got you, lass."

Misting rain began and clung to her eyelashes, mixing with tears of profound relief and uncertainty for her future. *God, please don't leave me.*

A salty breeze swept in from the coast behind her and lifted her veil. The clouds began to break, and sun warmed her back. With the sun and wind behind her, a rainbow appeared on the horizon, just over the burial ground. A promise of mercy and goodness that would follow her, and abide with her, all the days of her life.

Thanking God, she took a deep, misting breath into her lungs and began the first lilting notes.

# CHAPTER 2

## COUNCIL OF THE ISLES - APRIL 16, 1383

Torrential rain battered the old black brat looped around Hector's head and shoulders as he crossed the island ahead of this quarter's council meeting. Cold rivulets of water soaked into his beard, and he shivered against a bracing eastern wind. Juggling three warm pasties beneath his heavy brat, he cut between a row of small shacks heading for the burial ground where his contingent of guard had drawn humble, and some might say squat, clan accommodations.

A man in a hooded cloak stepped from between two shacks and gave him a yellow-toothed smile. "Laird MacLean?"

Laird. It had been almost five years since God had saved his life, and four since King John had given him control of Lochbuie, and he still hadn't gotten used to the title.

"Aye?"

"I tho' that was you. Big as a monster just as they say."

Hector squinted at the man, trying to place him, but came up short. "Aye."

"Nice brooch you have there. Rare-like. Mark of a chieftain."

Hector dared not drop his gaze to his shoulder where the amethyst brooch marked his status as a member of the king's council and chieftain of Lochbuie. Instead, he kept his senses alert and his mind a step ahead of the robbery that he was certain was about to happen.

Two men crept into the street, and the sound of footfalls issued from behind him. The yellow-toothed man drew a dagger and extended it between them motioning toward Hector's brat.

"Drop whatever is in your hands and put them out."

An empty stomach of more concern than facing a few brigands, a sinking feeling of regret settled over him—he would have to abandon the lamb pasties. Hector realized the man behind him blocked his exit back to the market, and with it any hope of enjoying a warm meal before the council meeting.

With a grunt he threw the pasties to the rain-soaked ground and raised his hands. "Now you've made me ruin my supper."

The yellow-toothed man waved his dagger at the man lurking behind Hector. "Brooch."

Homing in on the sounds of movement behind him, battle training kicking in, he was ready for the fight. As soon as the man behind him touched his shoulder, he twisted, throwing his fist forward into the man's shoulder, then deflected two quick punches. Trapping one arm and then another, he compressed the man's range of control and drove his head up into his jaw.

The first thief went slack, and a blond man stepped forward making a grab for the brooch. The two men behind Hector began pulling backward on his brat. The sound of ripping fabric met his ears as the yellow-toothed man stabbed forward with the dagger and missed, tangling the blade in the heavy wool.

Hector drove forward creating space between himself and the weapon. Pulling against the weight of the men, he dodged two incoming punches from the blond man, catching the man's arm and slamming his fist into his rat-like face sending him flying backward.

Twisting out of the brat, Hector heard the brooch skitter across the pebbled walkway.

A man in a hooded cloak the color of wine burst from between two shacks and Hector saw a flash of silver as the hooded stranger drew his sword and aimed it at the yellow-toothed man, guarding Hector's back as they each faced off against the two remaining thieves.

16

The red-haired brigand in front of Hector charged forward releasing a series of blows to his side. Hector snaked his hands beneath the man's arms and maneuvered them upward until they were caught in an embrace. Hector began to tighten his arms, crushing and squeezing, the red-haired man crying out as his hips became unsettled. Crashing down on top of him, Hector trapped the man between his legs and released his fist into the man's face over and over until his eyes rolled back.

Getting to his feet, Hector saw that the hooded stranger had taken down the yellow-toothed man who lay with his arms outstretched over his head, the dagger laying six feet away. Chest heaving, Hector picked up the ivory-hilted dagger and secured it in his boot. The man was unconscious, but not dead, a thin red mark beginning to form across his face. The sort of mark a man earned when he met with the dull edge of a French estoc.[1] Hector's eyes shot to the stranger.

The hooded man made a slow stroll over to the amethyst brooch and picked it up, turning it in his grasp and walking it back to him. The man's olive fingers held it out, and Hector took it, looking into a face he hadn't seen since his last night in France.

His heart dropped, unable to believe his eyes. "MacKinnon."

Léo's eyes traveled over the deep scar upon Hector's cheek. "MacLean."

The same lanky frame, waves of brown hair, and beard worn in the French style. Léo MacKinnon, now five years older since the day they'd last seen each other in Calais.

Hector winced. It'd been the occasion of Léo's wedding, and he'd arrived drunk, made a speech he couldn't remember, and vomited on the chapel stairs. He'd left for England that night, humiliated that he couldn't control his drinking for even one day, the most important day in Léo's life.

Léo's face remained stoic. "I suppose I should say Laird MacLean now."

Hector fumbled with his muddy brat and threw it over his shoulders, releasing a yelp as a wave of cold water ran down his back. A smirk touched the corner of Léo's mouth, and Hector tried to train his face into a look of authority. "Laird of Lochbuie for four years now."

Léo's tone remained impassive. "I've heard. Though I must say I'm curious to know what kind of men King John passed over to select you as the most qualified chieftain."

The remark stung but was not undeserved. That he was once the most unsuitable choice to lead the Lochbuie clan territory was an obvious fact. When the king asked Hector to lead a contingent of caterans to dispense with the corrupt MacFadyen chieftain, neither one of them had thought he'd be taking his place. But the people respected him, listened to him, and had been eager to pledge their fealty to him. And so, King John had decided to allow him the chieftainship for a short time, until a new leader could be found.

Against all expectations, he'd brought the neglected backwater to the southwest of his brother's territory on Mull into a time of peace and prosperity, and four years on, he was still Laird of Lochbuie in title, if not in land charter.

Something in Léo's eyes became stormy the longer they stared at each other, and Hector remembered his wife's tears of embarrassment as she stood on the chapel stairs. "About Théa...I want to say how sorry I am that I..."

Léo turned on his heel. "I've got to get inside. *Bon après-midi.*"[2]

Hector watched him walk away, the familiar guilt that accompanied a night of heavy drinking cloaking around him. He looked at the men groaning and coming to around him and headed in the direction of the burial ground.

Calum and Murdoch exited their leaky shack and looked at him expectantly.

Murdoch's brow furrowed. "I tho' you were at the market getting pasties."

"I got into a scuffle with some brigands interested in my brooch and had to drop them in a puddle."

Murdoch's eyebrows shot up. "The pasties or the brigands?"

"Both."

Calum MacLean, the commander of the Lochbuie guard, held his plaid over his head, the tattooed wolfhound peeking out along his arm and onto his ink-darkened fingers. "Are they loony? I'd target auld Brodie MacNeil if I wanted a brooch, not the man who looks like he ate Brodie MacNeil."

Murdoch MacFadyen, the master of the Lochbuie bowman, leapt between puddles and hurried ahead of them, shivering. "How many were there?"

"Four."

Murdoch scoffed. "And you handled all of them by yourself? Seems like a lot even for you."

Léo's stormy brown eyes skewered his thoughts. "Someone helped, took out one of them."

Calum wiped water from his face. "Someone you know?"

"Aye."

The two men looked at each other. Calum pressed. "Who was it?"

They ducked inside the arched stone doorway of the council building and Hector squeezed rain from his sopping black plaits and beard. "A *camarade* I fought with in France."[3]

Inside, the council chambers glowed with torchlight and a fire that roared from the center of the stone gallery. Angus MacKay, the chieftain of the MacKays of Islay, motioned to Hector from their usual table.

He held out his soaking brat to Calum, who took it, his gray eyes wincing.

Self-conscious, Hector peeled his sopping tunic away from himself. "Do I look that disheveled?"

"You look like a *beithir*[4] monster that just chased his prey into a loch."

Hector forced a smile to the side of his face that worked, and Calum shivered.

Murdoch crossed his arms. "You best stick to frowning. You look aff your heid when you smile."

Hector rolled his eyes and headed for the front of the gallery. "See you when we're adjourned."

Making an effort to fluff his beard and shake out his sodden tunic, he made his way to the chieftain's table, grateful for the warmth provided by the open hearth beside it.

Angus rose and took his hand, returning his firm shake. "I dinnae ken if I'd see you here or if you'd washed away in the flood. By the looks of it you almost did."

"Aye. We drew the cottage nearest the burial ground this gathering. It's a fair walk."

Angus raised an eyebrow, his quiet voice lifting with amusement. "Still taking that auld pile? I tho' you'd take an accommodation with your brother this gathering. You had the greatest harvest out of all the chiefs and chieftains last year. From what I heard, King John did a jig when your coin arrived in December."

Hector chuckled and settled onto the bench beside Calum's father, Týr MacLean. His broad shoulders forced Angus and Týr apart, and he tried to act like he belonged. It was his sixteenth council meeting, but he still felt out of place due to his size and his reputation. The room was stuffed with tables of councilors, and he said a silent prayer to get through another meeting without embarrassing himself or his brother.

At the first table sat the four royal MacDonald sons. At the second, the three noble island chiefs, including his brother, and friend Iain MacLeod. At the third table sat the lesser island chiefs not connected to the MacDonalds by blood or marriage—including Léo MacKinnon sitting in his brother Niall's seat. Unusual.

Hector sat at the fourth table, consisting of the chieftains holding lands on behalf of the king but who had not yet had their lands chartered to them as chiefs.

At the other sixteen tables sat leaders from among the island clans as well as highland chiefs from the Morvern Peninsula, Oban, and the Strath on the Scottish mainland. Though these men were not given a vote, their presence was essential for the deliberation of council matters. High Chief David MacKenzie tossed him a wave, and Hector raised a return wave jamming his arm into Týr.

Týr hung off the side of the bench. "You're soakin' me through with that wet tunic."

Hector squeezed his arms together the best he could but still took up a space meant for three men. "Sorry."

The rich, resonant sound of the dord[5] echoed through the gallery and the Council of the Isles was called to order, every noble rising to their feet. The doors opened at the end of the gallery, and John, King of the Isles, entered and walked through the center of the gathering.

Dressed in his symbolic robes of white and a shining bascinet helmet crowned with eagle feathers, John took his seat at the front of the gathering, settling his foot upon the coronation stone. Sounds of screeching wood benches against the stone floors echoed through the gallery and the councilors took their seats.

John nodded to the gathered assembly. "Men of the Isles, I thank you for coming to Findlugan with little notice. As you are aware, the problem of Alexander Stewart has been growing since his marriage to Euphemia of Ross last July."

A rumble of disquiet erupted around the room, and his heart sank. Alexander Stewart, the Wolf of Badenoch, the son of the King of Scotland. Thanks to his father's patronage and a vile band of caterans, Alexander had been granted, coerced, or stolen land from half a dozen highland chiefs. He was now the effective ruler of the highlands, and by the sound of it, he was setting his sights south.

"The transfer of Euphemia's estates has now been completed, and lordships on the isles of Skye and Lewis have been affirmed by the Scottish king."

Murmurs grew into outraged growls. What they'd feared since Alexander had been spotted in Euphemia's company last April had come to pass. The Wolf of Badenoch, once only a threat to the clans on the Scottish mainland, had now become a threat to the Isles as well.

Brodie MacNeil got to his feet; his tone outraged. "For years we've watched without retaliation as Scotland has increased their overlordship over the Isles. What right do they have to give away Isles land? When will we assert our independence on these matters? I say the time is now."

Around Brodie, men drummed their fists in agreement. Lachlan's eyes found Hector's from across the room, and he brushed a finger over his nose. Their signal for Hector to speak on behalf of clan MacLean. They'd known Brodie was to petition for the war the MacLeans opposed at this meeting, and as a lower-level chieftain, Hector could voice their dissent with fewer repercussions than Lachlan.

Hector got to his feet. "While I agree that the Wolf is not a man to be swept aside, and that Scotland shouldnae be allowed to rule any part of the Isles, an assertion of independence from the mainland will mean only one certainty, and that is war."

A smaller group of councilors drummed their fists on the table in support of his words.

Brodie squinted at him through his cloudy blue eye. "Is that Hector MacLean?"

Hector raised his voice so the half-blind and half-deaf man could hear him. "Aye."

"The man who became a celebrated mercenary under Guesclin, winning territory back for Charles V piece by bloody piece in only four years? A warrior of such distinction he was honored by the French court?"

A ripple of ayes sounded around the room, and Hector straightened his back, knowing what was coming. Men who loved the idea of noble fighting but who'd never faced the harsh nature of war often made an attack on character if you didn't support them.

Brodie continued his tirade. "Am I to understand you are willing to fight for your own benefit but not for the benefit of our homeland? I can assure you that the MacNeils are ready to send the cur back to Scotland not just for our good, but the good of the Isles entire."

Thumping began all around him and Hector waited for the men to settle before speaking. "My fealty lies with King John and to the people of Lochbuie. It is because of the great trust they have placed in me as chieftain, and for the benefit of their safety, that I urge restraint. There may be a time to assert our independence, but the Wolf should be approached with caution. A swift defeat in battle will only increase Scotland's holdings in the Isles." Stomping and thumping began at the table of chieftains and picked up in smatterings around the room.

King John raised his hand for silence. "Your strategy in taking Lochbuie from Laird MacFadyen was effective. I am certain that if I called upon you to lead our forces you would do so with great skill."

Sweat pricked the back of Hector's neck despite the chill that raced up his spine. The thought of leading a zealous group of untried island chiefs against the Wolf's caterans made his blood run cold. Raids and cattle reiving could not compare to the brutal horror of battle.

John continued. "But you make a fair argument. May I take it that you would be willing to assist in alternative means of securing peace for the Isles to demonstrate your loyalty?"

Lachlan made an almost imperceptible nod. An uneasy pit formed in his stomach.

"Aye." The word of agreement came out like a question.

John nodded. "Good." He gestured to Léo, who stood. Hector's heart sank like a stone into a bottomless well. "I am told you are well acquainted with Niall MacKinnon's half-brother Léo."

Léo gave a curt nod and did not make eye contact with Hector. "*Oui*. Hector and I fought beside each other for seven years. He saved my life at Pontvallain."

The king looked astounded. "He saved your life?"

"Oui. Twice that day. I was a foolish lad. Abandoned by my brothers in France and stupid enough to follow my uncle into battle against the English. He was an old man and killed swiftly. Hector killed the knight who was about to end me, then threw me out of the path of a cavalry-man, taking a sword meant for my neck to the side of his face."

All eyes went to the jagged swipe along Hector's cheek now covered in part by his black beard.

Hector shifted and focused on a fissure in the stone floor as the dark memories of battle threatened to form on the recesses of his mind. His hands around a man's throat. The rider with the raised sword galloping toward him. The searing pain of injury. Fear knotting in his gut that he would not be able to save Léo and himself from the hell of war.

John cleared his throat. "I summoned Léo here as a favor to the Isles. As you will have noticed, Chief MacKinnon is not in attendance. Given Léo's position he may be very useful to us."

Whispers circled the room. Léo, the product of his father's illicit relationship with a French noblewoman, couldn't have been more different from the legitimate MacKinnon children. Where the natural MacKinnon offspring were cold, calculating, and selfish, Léo was amiable, measured, and brave. After that grisly day at Pontvallain they'd been battle bonded closer than brothers, becoming the family they'd both lost.

That bond, and the way they fought as one unit, was the reason they'd been selected for Guesclin's command. Guesclin had been so impressed by Léo's skill, manner, and strategy, that he'd personally seen to his training at the Sorbonne during their year of peace in 1375. It was the year that Léo caught the attention of Charles V and become a *marmouset*[6] and part of his private counsel. It was also the year that Hector had lost himself entirely to drink.

After eight years conquering the French court Léo was wealthier and more powerful than anyone in the room—including King John. A fact that could not have been lost on the king, nor Léo's brothers.

The king continued. "The MacKinnons have hosted Alexander Stewart at Dun Ringill several times over the past few months, seeking an alliance to alleviate the financial burdens their clan is suffering."

Hector fidgeted. "What have you in mind? For Léo and me to lead your forces into Skye?"

John chuckled. "No. My desire, with the consent of this body of councilors, is to strengthen our bonds with the MacKinnons and create more reasons to secure their fealty. They're a formidable fighting contingent, best kept as allies."

Léo cleared his throat twice. A habit he'd picked up to steady his nerves when walking into battle. Not a good sign.

John continued. "When I selected you to take over Lochbuie, it was at much protestation from Niall MacKinnon."

Was that the plan? Hector frowned. The thought of giving Lochbuie to Niall rankled. From the corner of his eye, he saw Calum and Murdoch shift forward in their seats.

Hector ventured a guess. "You wish to give Niall the chieftainship of Lochbuie to increase his holdings on Mull?"

Mutterings began all over the room and John once more raised his hands for silence. "I assure you no one wants that. Thanks to your brother's careful strategy, I believe we have come to an arrangement agreeable to all."

Léo cleared his throat twice again. Hector was beginning to get the feeling that this arrangement would be agreeable to everyone in the Isles except him since his brother failed to mention this furtive scheme.

Lachlan took a deep breath and began to explain. "Léo and I have begun the work of securing a marriage negotiation between yourself and Elspeth MacKinnon. Her bride-price will solve the problem of the MacKinnons' dwindling treasury, and you'll inherit more land on Mull as part of her tocher. It's a perfect incentive to secure their loyalty and to hinder the Wolf's conquest of the Isles without resorting to war."[7]

Hoots of delight sounded around the room and Hector swayed. Elspeth MacKinnon, Léo's half-sister. Twenty-seven, the widow of an elderly low-level laird, and so beautiful it almost hurt your eyes to look at her, akin to staring into the sun. Bred for nobility, she'd been educated with private tutors and had been running the MacKinnon estate, Dun Ringill, with the assistance of her mother for two years.

The king was presenting him with the most eligible bride in the Isles and more land. A burble of unease cramped his stomach. There was but one problem... While he felt no particular way about Elspeth, she couldn't stand him. Or most men of the Isles.

When the room quieted down, Hector spoke. "I thank you for your consideration of me for this noble task. But is there one more qualified than I? Iain MacLeod perhaps? I am certain Niall would like to increase his connection to holdings on Skye."

Iain narrowed his eyes at him and gave a slight shake of his head and the room erupted into laughter. Unlike most men on the council who were dazzled by her obvious beauty, Iain hated Elspeth with an intense passion. They'd gotten into a screaming match after the last Harvest Games at Duart when she'd insulted his clan and his thick brogue as he'd tried wooing her.

John waited for the laughter to die down. "A clever jest."

Hector tried to look as though he wasn't concerned. "I wasnae jesting."

Brodie's fist collided with the table. "You see? He's been presented with the most beautiful bride in all the Isles and Scotland, and he refuses to take her. He has no fealty to his family, no fealty to these Isles. The only thing the lad is loyal to is his drink, from what I've heard."

Lachlan shot to his feet. "Shut yer gob!"

John raised his hands, and the room became silent once more. "We all know Hector's past, but we also know how hard he's worked to care for his clan. His lands, the care taken with his people, and his protection of the sea lanes for trade and communication speaks to the man he is, not the man he was."

John's green eyes pierced Hector's, and he put a finger on the arm of his chair. "If you agree, I can promise you that the charter for Lochbuie will be granted to you on the day of your marriage along with twenty merks of additional land on Mull, Morvern, Arran, and Jura."[8]

Hector's mouth hung open. That much land was greater than what he'd given to Lachlan on the event of Lachlan's marriage to his own daughter, a sure sign of the importance of this mission.

"Further, if you are successful in keeping the threat of the Wolf to a minimum, either by peaceful means or...other means, you will be added to the MacDonald clan as if you were one of my sons-in-law. A noble chief."

Murdoch and Calum had gotten to their feet across from a gobsmacked Brodie MacNeil. It meant a security and stability for Lochbuie not known in over twenty-five years. More income to support their numbers. A place of respect in the Kingdom of the Isles.

"Will you agree?"

Hector swallowed, then nodded. "Aye."

Drumming began all around him and men got to their feet to slap his back in congratulations. John raised his hands and shouted for order.

"Excellent. There is but one stipulation that has been made by the MacKinnon clan before they consent to begin marriage negotiations. Due to your history, they have requested that Léo come to Lochbuie for the summer to ensure that you are a changed man. Léo will be looking over your stewardship of Lochbuie, the cultivation of your lands, your accounts. All a formality, of course, since I've seen these things firsthand and am satisfied."

Léo's brown eyes met Hector's and he saw the deep resentment that swam in their depths. "We still feel that before we turn over such a prize, we must know she will receive a husband worthy of her."

Hector nodded. "I understand and consent to these terms."

The room erupted and Lachlan strode over to him, pulling him into his embrace and dropping his voice so only he could hear. "Thank you, brother. You're saving us from war."

Hector clamped his shoulder. Lachlan had never asked him for one favor in the thirty-four years they'd been brothers. That he could aid him in this request should feel like a relief after all that Lachlan had done to help him. So why then did it feel as if he had already let him down?

# CHAPTER 3

## LOCHBUIE OIGHREACHD - JUNE 1, 1383

Sun warmed Cara's back as the bìrlinn[1] sailed into the harbor at
Lochbuie. Skin crawling inside her leine[2], she had never been so
grateful to spot land. For the last three days she had fantasized
about a steaming pot of water and a cake of soap to wash away the sweat
and dirt that clung to her. For three nights Margaret and she had slept in
the open bìrlinn, accompanying a merchant and a few seamen as they
traveled their normal trading route around the coast of Ireland, the Isle
of Man, and Galloway. And that was nothing in comparison to the two-
and-a-half months of sleeping rough while they waited for the oceans to
become safe for crossing.

After arriving on Islay early that morning they'd met Father Timothy, the parish priest for the southern Isles, who'd offered them safe
passage into Mull. Father Timothy smiled as Margaret's face took in the
familiar sight of her native land. "Does it look the same as you remember, mistress?"

"From a distance, aye, it looks exactly as I remember." Margaret
wiped a tear at the corner of her eye. "I didn't think I'd ever be seeing
home again."

Wonder filled Cara as the natural beauty of the isle grew larger. Situ-
ated at the end of a wide sea inlet and framed by rocky moss-covered

cliffs, it was as if they had entered a new world. Rolling green mountains bowed down around the stony shore, and flocks of birds dipped along funnels of air. A dolphin sailed through the bìrlinn's wake and arced over the water before racing back beneath the boat, exposing its white belly.

As the laird's guard rowed toward a wide galley slip, a crumbling stone keep greeted them from beyond sturdier-looking barmkin[3] walls. Margaret gave a little hop like an excited child. "I see the walls. They look better than I remember."

Father Timothy held onto his cap as the breeze whipped off the water. "That will be thanks to Laird MacLean."

The guards on the dock signaled to the bìrlinn and the men aboard signaled back. Cara felt a bubble of hope float to the top of her chest. When she'd moved to Rathmullan ten years earlier, she'd been a lass of eighteen and full of trepidation. Now, at twenty-eight, life was beginning again without the same apprehension or inexperience. This time, perhaps things would be different.

The guards caught the rope and pulled the bìrlinn in, securing it to the dock. Father Timothy climbed out and greeted two guards, one blond and one brown-haired and mustached. The blond man winked at her. Blush warmed her cheeks, and she tightened her kerchief.

The mustached man held up his hand in greeting. "What have you brought us, Father Tim? Two fine doves?"

Father Timothy helped them onto the shore. "This is Margaret MacFadyen and Cara O'Ballevan. Margaret is returning to the clan after the death of her son, God rest his soul, and Cara was—is, her daughter-in-law."

The young blond man put out his hand darkened by ink marks, and Cara took it and dipped a curtsy.

"Pleasure to meet you. I'm Calum MacLean, and this is Murdoch MacFadyen." Murdoch took hold of Margaret's trunk and nodded in greeting.

Cara smiled. "Pleased to meet you."

Murdoch grinned back. "An Irish lass. That beautiful lilt does me in."

The instinct to hide behind Margaret was strong, but she reminded herself that hiding from such attentions was no longer necessary. Duncan could no longer harm her.

Murdoch hefted Margaret's trunk over his shoulder. "Margaret MacFadyen, would you be the sister of Ursula and Malcolm? I feel as if I've heard you mentioned before. You've a Saxon name."

Margaret smiled. "Our mother was Saxon. Are my brother and sister well?"

"Aye ma'am. Although..." Murdoch's voice trailed off.

Father Timothy offered his arm to Margaret. "Malcolm passed away last summer, mistress, my condolences." Margaret's joy had been quickly dashed. Cara's heart broke for her.

"I should have expected. After thirty years..." Margaret's voice wobbled. "Malcolm would have been seventy-two this year."

Calum picked up Cara's trunk, and she followed him down the dock. "Malcolm and Ursula are very dear to our clan. Ursula has healed me many times."

"Is she well?" Margaret asked, her tone wary.

"Aye, madam, she is well. I believe she may be a bit lonely since Malcolm passed."

The jingling sound of crotal bells[4] caused Cara to look up just in time to step out of the path of a pony and cart carrying fine furniture away from the barmkin walls.

"What happened to the old tower keep?" Margaret asked, watching the rush of people as they carried supplies down the crumbling stairs of the castle.

Father Timothy shook his head. "It's being taken down in part. It isn't habitable. The laird is making ready for a new bride."

Calum dropped her trunk into a pony cart. "Let's hope it's looking better than this before Elspeth arrives. The laird will need an intervention from God to make the keep livable. She's a woman of fine tastes. No' that Dun Ringill is much better to look at."

"The new laird is marrying?" Margaret asked.

Father Timothy gave Murdoch an indecipherable look. "That's the hope. The lady is visiting at Duart Castle until harvest with the laird's brother and wife. She is to be the honored guest at banquet tonight."

29

Margaret eyed the dilapidated keep, narrowing her eyes. "Is he a good laird?"

Murdoch's expression was sober as he loaded Margaret's trunk into the pony cart. "He wasn't supposed to be laird, but he saved our people. Auld Laird MacFadyen had almost starved us to death. Sickness took my whole family that winter, they were so weak. The same happened in almost every household. The day he took Lochbuie, Laird MacLean broke open the granary and stopped the law of poaching. For the first time in years, we ate like kings. He's restored order, fixed what was failing. Aye. He's an exceptional laird."

Cara looked at the decaying keep and the workers scattering about doing their laird's work and handling his things with great care. Whoever this new laird was it was evident that the MacLeans and the MacFadyens wanted him to succeed.

Murdoch shook his head. "God protect him trying to court a MacKinnon."

Margaret made a sound of understanding and Cara raised her eyebrows at her. "Och lass, you'll learn it soon enough. The MacKinnons are a sordid lot. Respectable on the surface, but poisonous beneath."

Calum looked besotted. "Aye, but Elspeth MacKinnon is beautiful. And accomplished."

Murdoch refused to agree. "A beautiful, poisonous flower."

———

At the edge of a sandy beach a row of cottages came into view. Father Timothy halted his pony and helped them down onto the path.

"Ursula and Malcolm let your parents' croft be reclaimed by the laird years ago." He gestured to wild fields of flowers rising in places to five feet tall. "She grows herbs and flowers now, useful for healing. Raises bees as well. Her honey is the best in the Isles, and she makes a fair living off it."

Margaret's hands wrung. "Och, I hope she's happy to see us. Imagine living in the auld sheepcote."

A winding path cut through the tall flowers and herbs, and a converted stone sheepcote with rough-looking thatch appeared. At the far end of the garden clearing lay dozens of bee skeps. Before they could approach the door, it swung open, revealing a woman as skinny as Margaret with a halo of gray curls that framed a pretty face.

"Margaret? Margaret, is it really you?"

Unable to control her excitement, Margaret squealed and tore toward her sister, throwing her arms around her. "Ursula!" The two sisters dissolved into laughter and sobs as Margaret put her hands to Ursula's cheeks. "Look how old you've gotten!"

Ursula laughed and hiccuped. "Me? Look how old you are. Though you look just the same! I cannae believe it, how are you here?" She pulled away and looked into Margaret's identical gray eyes, placing her hand on her cheek. The knowledge that only something quite terrible could have brought her sister home seemed to dawn on her and she dropped her jovial tone. "Oh Margaret, was it Hugh?"

Margaret's eyes spilled over with tears. "Hugh died eleven years ago. It was Duncan, our son, only a few months ago."

Ursula wrapped her arms around Margaret, in the way only sisters could comfort, and held her for long minutes.

"Oh, but I am forgetting myself." Margaret put her arm out toward Cara. "Ursula, this is Cara, my daughter-in-law."

In the same way Margaret had been quick to welcome her to Rathmullan ten years earlier, Ursula hurried over and embraced her, her bony frame squeezing all breath from her lungs. "You are both here to stay?"

"Aye, to stay," Cara answered.

Ursula released her and gestured to the slightly lopsided door. "Bring their things right in here, I have more than enough room."

They followed Ursula, but both froze in the doorway. Half divided for sheltering a long-gone herd, and half modest accommodation for a shepherd's family, the sheep half of the cottage had long fallen into disrepair and a hole in the roof shone daylight onto the dirty floor.

Looking appalled, neat and tidy Margaret gawped at the hundreds of drying herbs and flowers that hung from the rafters, the smell pleasant and calming, but bits of leaves and seed scattered across the stone floor.

Cara tried to find something nice to say about her new home. "It's large."

A mink jumped down into the cottage and buried a bird egg among the piles of dried debris. Noticing their staring he lifted his head and examined them before resuming his excavation.

"That's auld Fluffy," said Ursula tossing him a piece of fish.

Margaret continued to stare horrified as the fish smeared an oily track across the untidy stone floor. Fluffy shoved the fish into his cheeks waggling his patchy, not at all fluffy, tail.

Margaret tried to speak. "Ursula..."

The balding mink climbed up Ursula's apron and rested upon her shoulder, stuffing tiny handfuls of fish into his cheeks.

Margaret spluttered. "There's a mink in your house."

Ursula chuckled. "Aye."

Margaret put her hands to her cheeks. "There's a hole in the roof."

"Aye."

"There's no' supposed to be a hole in the roof."

"But if I have the roof patched how will Fluffy get in?"

Margaret shook her head and tried again. "He should be in the woods. Where are the sheep?"

Ursula waved her off. "I sold the flock to the MacLeans ages ago. They're over on the other side of the standing stones in far nicer pastures. They get such a lovely mountain breeze now."

Margaret wasn't closing her mouth.

Father Timothy cleared his throat. "If you change your mind about needing the roof patched now that Margaret and Cara have come to stay, I can let the laird know about the repair."

"Bosh. Margaret dinnae mind Fluffy."

At the sight of Margaret's now permanently shocked expression, Cara nearly burst out laughing. Out of respect for Ursula she placed a hand over her mouth and managed to hold onto her composure.

Margaret was a meticulous housekeeper and could not live in such conditions. If it weren't so humorous, she herself would be horrified at the thought of the three of them adapting their living conditions to accommodate a weasel.

Cara cleared her throat and placed a hand on Ursula's shoulder, careful to avoid the mink snuggling against her neck. "Perhaps we can train, em—Fluffy, to come through the window?"

Margaret gawped at her. "Through the window?"

Ursula placed a finger to her cheek and considered the suggestion. "I suppose we could."

"Perhaps a trail of fish may lead him to his new entry way?"

"She's never come through the window before," Ursula hesitated. "I cannae lose my Fluffy dear."

As if it understood, the mink cuddled closer against Ursula's neck and rubbed its face in her nest of gray curls. Margaret squeaked.

Cara licked her dry lips and tried to humor her. "Look how clever Fluffy is. I've never seen such an intelligent mink. Have you, Margaret?"

Margaret swallowed. "I suppose he is a rather clever thing."

"Fluffy is a lass," Ursula sniffed, rubbing Fluffy's head with one finger. "Helped her with her litter of kits last spring. Made her home right there in the corner, and she come back ever since." Ursula beamed with such pride Cara didn't have the heart to tell her how repulsive the thought of rooming with a weasel was.

She placed a steadying hand in Margaret's as the balding mink blinked at her. "Aye, a pretty lass at that. It's only that winter will be here in short order. T'would be so much warmer if we could patch the roof."

A stone hearth sat at the end of the sheepcote. To have an efficient fireplace to heat the home and carry the smoke away was a luxury Cara had never known before. Even with that luxury, it would be an enormous challenge to keep the large sheepcote warm enough in the long winter to come.

"Last winter *was* terribly cold. All right then. I wouldnae want you two to freeze on account of us." They'd won the all-important battle of the roof, but the way that Ursula had referred to Fluffy and herself as "us" made Cara certain the mink wars were only beginning.

Father Timothy pushed Margaret's trunk through a pile of leaves. "I'll tell the laird and we will have you thatched as soon as we can."

Margaret's shoulders drooped. "Do you have any coin, Ursula? Cara and I dinnae have funds left to pay for a repair."

Father Timothy chuckled. "Doesnae work like that around here anymore. All the buildings belong to the laird, and he sees it as his duty to keep them in good repair."

Ursula nodded. "If you're needing funds though, I'm sure Pádraig can let you help with the harvest. It won't pay a large wage, but you won't go hungry."

A strange look came over Margaret's face. "Pádraig MacLean?"

Ursula gave her a wink. "Aye, he's the new *fear-taic* under Laird MacLean. He manages the land, and rents, and the cottage properties."

Margaret gave a sigh of relief. "You can trust him, Cara. Pádraig is a good man. I'm sure if you go to him this afternoon seeking work, he'll take care of you."

Reassurance swept over her. Beyond getting to Mull, she'd worried the entire journey about how she would support not only herself, but also her mother-in-law once she arrived. Without her weaving equipment it would require menial labor, and as a woman and an outsider she wasn't certain she'd be able to procure work.

Father Timothy nodded. "Aye, his cottage is on the other side of the rocky outcropping we passed to get to Laggan. If I would've known you knew him, we could have stopped for you to get reacquainted."

Margaret paled. "I'm sure Cara will do just fine on her own."

Cara exhaled with relief. "Thank you, I will see to it." A family, a home, and work. The Lord was with her.

# CHAPTER 4

## DUART OIGHREACHD - JUNE 1, 1383

He didn't want to marry Elspeth MacKinnon. The thought tumbled over and over through Hector's mind on the ride from Lochbuie to Duart. After six weeks of cudgeling his brains to think of an alternative plan to keep the MacKinnons from making things worse he'd come up empty. Elspeth, and her hefty bride-price, together with the additional lands from King John was the only way to ensure Niall MacKinnon would be vested enough in the Isles to keep the Wolf out of them.

For six weeks Hector had fasted and prayed, begging the Lord to make his future wife humble and measured. A woman of wisdom and a peacemaker. He cringed. It was a miracle only the Lord could work in Elspeth's heart.

Were he an ordinary man he could make his living by boat or land in blessed anonymity. He could choose his bride for himself or remain alone. But he wasn't an ordinary man. Like it or not, God had given him the role of chieftain. *I don't know how, Lord, but light the way. Everything feels wrong.*

Ghoustie galloped over the fields toward the bright walls of the keep, and he perched in the saddle. The seat of the Duart MacLeans and the seat of the Lochbuie MacLeans were worlds apart. Set high upon the cliffs over the Sound of Mull, Duart Castle was an impregnable and dignified clan seat. By contrast, years of neglect and dampness had crumbled his own keep, Moy Castle, years before its time.

Besides the problem of Elspeth's heart making her an unsuitable choice for his bride, there was the issue of her vanity. To convince her to live in such an outmoded keep would take Léo, Hector, and Lachlan's efforts combined.

A young groom met him in the courtyard and Hector handed him Ghoustie's reins. "He'll need a good brush down." The boy nodded. "Did the visitors arrive from Skye?"

A dreamy look came over the young man's face and the word came out in a sigh. "Aye."

He chuckled. "That bonny?"

The lad smirked and rubbed Ghoustie under the forelock. "Aye. That bonny." Unease mounted atop his shoulders. He wasn't sure he liked the idea of his wife inspiring such looks in every man and boy in Scotland and the Isles.

Ascending the stairs with haste, Hector hurried into the keep hoping his family hadn't gone in without him. To his relief, his five nephews waited in the long gallery, their parents having not yet joined them. At once the youngest boys—Neil, Young Lachlan, and Somerled—squealed their greetings and began climbing him like a tree.

"Uncle Hector, has your face always looked so glum?" Somerled asked climbing Hector's long legs and swinging onto his back.

"Aye lad, but I reckon it became glummer once my cheek was mangled. That side of my face always wants to frown."

"I think it's ace," said Young Hector, the eldest, and most interested in his former life as a warrior. As always, he worried that his namesake was too intrigued by the mystery of war and by the slaps on the back men paid him for the brutal things he'd done.

"It didnae feel ace at the time."

"What did it feel like?" Neil asked, pushing up Hector's front using his sword belt as a toehold.

"It felt like my cheek had nearly been sliced off. I dinnae know."

"It hurt?" Young Lachlan asked, slithering up his arm as if it were a rope.

"Aye it hurt," said Young John from the corner of the gallery, arms crossed. He was the second-born, and sometimes overlooked, child. Young John most resembled Hector's own personality, looks, and stature, already outgrowing his eldest brother as they stood together by the door to the hall.

Neil climbed onto Hector's shoulders and raised his fists over his head. "I made it tae the top first!"

Hector jumped up and down. "Did you now?" Somerled squealed and hung onto the back of his neck. "Let's hope you dinnae get bucked off."

Hector jumped, pranced, and whirled in a circle. The three youngest boys flew off and into various furniture. They giggled until their small voices became nothing more than a series of clicks and gasps.

"Enough of that, boys. It's time to go to supper," Mhairi said, entering the room and restoring order to the raucous group.

Lachlan followed close behind and put his hand on Hector's shoulder, a glint in his eye. "Ready to see your bride?"

Mhairi approached Hector and kissed his jagged cheek, picking white bits of plaster from his brat. "You're in a state."

"Shoulders got wedged on my way down the stairs at Moy. Useful for stopping people from coming into the keep, but annoying if you're an overgrown giant."

"Bend down." She picked more white plaster from his plait. "How've you managed to get it in your hair?"

"Knocked my head on the low ceiling trying to get my shoulders free. I've no' got a chance, have I?"

Mhairi laughed. "I dinnae ken. I think I've fixed you proper now."

Hector straightened his leather cuirass and lifted his chin toward Lachlan. "The lovesick groom in the courtyard tells me they arrived this morning?"

Lachlan took Mhairi's arm. "Aye, and you're in for it. She's even more beautiful than the last time you saw her in the fall."

"Looks aren't important to me. Let's hope they aren't to her."

37

Lachlan pursed his lips and winced. "I'm no' sure that will be the case. She asked me if you still looked like the beithir at the midday meal."

All five boys burst into laughter at the obvious similarities between his appearance and the legendary monster.

Hector rumbled with deep laughter, not offended in the slightest, then trained his face into mock seriousness. "How can she say that? I'm no' venomous." The boys giggled harder, and Hector winked at them.

Lachlan shrugged. "Apparently you look venomous to Elspeth."

Hector's dark looks and towering height had served him well with the ladies in his younger years, but surviving dozens of battles had given him a permanent look of ferocity.

As the family lined up outside the great hall, Hector muttered to his brother over the sounds of the clan, "What did you tell her? Put in a good word for me?"

"I was honest of course. I told her you looked worse."

Hector couldn't argue with the truth. He felt every bit of his near thirty-five years of hard living in each muscle of his body.

"How was Léo?"

"Quiet. I think a bit annoyed he had to disrupt his life at the French court to escort his sister to Mull. I'm no' sure he feels any loyalty to the MacKinnons. As far as he is concerned, this is a foreign land."

After seven years of battle-bonded life together, he knew that wasn't true. The acceptance of his half-brothers was something Léo had desired since he was a lad, though he did his best to pretend he didn't care.

"I'm surprised he came after the way we parted in Calais."

"You mean the way you abandoned him?"

A familiar pang of regret for past mistakes caused him to shift from one foot to the other. "Do you think he's holding a grudge?"

Lachlan lifted a shoulder. "I dinnae think so. He seemed to agree that the alliance was necessary between us and his brothers to protect the Isles from the Wolf."

The piper struck up the MacLean march and Lachlan guided Mhairi into the hall, their boys taking their spots behind them. Hector tousled Somerled's blond feathery hair before falling in line and following them dutifully to the dais.

Preferring the homey suppers the Lochbuies hosted in their crofts and cottages to formal feasts, Hector squirmed. At Duart, he was obliged to sit at the high table, where the entire clan watched him eat. Which, due to his size, gave him the feeling of a chained bear in a menagerie being gawped at during feeding time. He took his seat beside Lachlan, appreciating that his knees and thighs did not wedge against the table as they did at Moy. A servant whom he did not recognize filled each cup with claret and Hector placed his hand over his cup.

In a firm, low voice he tried to convey to the man that he could not drink the claret. "Not. Mine. Water only."

The man's eyes went wide, and for one horrible moment he thought the servant was about to cry. He tried to transfigure his face into something approaching friendly, but had a feeling the best he achieved was threatening. Gulping, the man retreated in search of the water jug.

Impatience filled his chest. He just wanted to get the meal over with. "Where is she?"

Lachlan shrugged. "Mhairi says the lass knows how to make an impression. I expect she'll be here soon."

The servant returned with the water jug, and Hector grunted in what he thought was thanks as the man tilted the jug over his cup, pottery chattering against pottery. A runnel of water sloshed over the top of the cup and painted a gray stain across the spotless linen. Prickled, the servant mopped at the stain with his sleeve.

Hector caught the man's hand. "It's fine. A little water doesnae bother me."

Tears filled the servant's eyes and he hurried away.

*Saints.* Why was that always the effect he had on people? Sighing, he drank from his cup, surveying the room for the promised woman of his dreams, feeling a bit like he was waiting for an executioner. "She is still here, correct?"

Mhairi rolled her eyes as if it should be obvious she would take so long. "Of course, you daftie. It's sweet that you're so nervous to meet her."

The piper struck a slow air as Léo MacKinnon appeared in the doorway of the hall, his sister on his arm. Every man in the room rose to their feet and removed their bonnets. Elspeth MacKinnon was as regal as a queen, mink-colored hair, full lips, a shapely figure. Her satin gown spilled over her, its color like the wing of the goldcrest. The men bowed to her as she made her way to the dais. Léo paused before them and extended his hand to present the exquisite prize.

Elspeth swept into a deep curtsy and raised her chin, lifting her long-lashed eyes to Hector. "My laird."

He swallowed, not immune to a beauty obvious to his rapidly weakening self-control. Diverting his thoughts, he clasped Léo's hand and gave him a firm shake. A good sign. Perhaps all was forgiven between them. "Léo, good to see you again."

Léo nodded, and smiled at the scores of clanswomen who were whispering and giggling in his direction. Unlike Hector who resembled something beastie, there was a refined quality to Léo's features thanks in no small part to his French mother.

An awkward pause rose, and Hector tried to fill it. "What's it been, five years since I left?"

"Six." A note of something bitter tinged his voice.

That's right. Six, not five. The haze of his final three years in France blurred together in his memory. "My mistake. Those last two years were...I'm a different man now," he said, trying to plug the leak in his memory with a finger of explanation.

"So I've heard," Léo said in a clipped voice, picking up his chalice of claret.

"How is Théa?"

Pain shadowed Léo's features, and he knew at once he had tread with irreverence onto hallowed ground.

"She died two years ago."

A memory of gentle Théa came to mind, her bluebell-colored eyes and dark hair. Fresh shame cloaked him. She'd died and he hadn't apologized to her.

"Léo, I'm so sorry."

"Let's not talk about it."

When no further invitation to converse was extended, he leaned over and decided to try talking to Elspeth, his throat dry for a numbing swallow of claret. "I'm pleased to see you again, Elspeth."

Elspeth gave him a breezy laugh and a dazzling smile. "Thank you,

Laird MacLean. I'm not sure where my brother's manners are. He's been tight lipped since arriving in Skye a few weeks ago and won't tell me how you know each other so well. He only says I need to be careful."

Hector looked at Léo. "Careful?"

"He seems to think that you may be careless with me."

Léo rolled his eyes and brought the claret to his lips. "Show discretion."

Drinking an unsatisfying swallow of warm water, Hector steeled himself. "Your brother has every right to warn you."

Elspeth raised a perfect eyebrow and dropped her voice to a husky whisper. "Are you dangerous?"

"Deadly," Léo said, tone flat.

Conversation came to a screeching halt. Mentally, he switched his shield into his dominant hand. "In another life."

Léo parried. "You only have one life. What we've done is always a part of us, even if we think we've changed."

*Touché.*[1]

Mhairi put down her glass and her face seemed to weigh what to say to help the situation as she often could. "How did you two meet?"

Hector grimaced.

Léo spoke rapid Gaelic into his cup. "My brothers tricked me into visiting my mother's family and Niall abandoned me there. Elspeth probably doesn't remember much."

Boredom crossed Elspeth's face. "Only that one day you were home, and then you weren't."

A grumble cramped Hector's stomach, and he began to pray. His family didn't know how terrible the circumstances of their meeting were, and he wanted to leave it that way.

Léo met his eye and began a flat dispensation of facts. "My uncle Arnoul took me as his squire into the battle of Pontvallain. The man was too old to be anywhere near a battlefield, but stories of his exploits with King David of Scotland made me desire the glory of knighthood. I was eager to follow him into battle." Young Hector sat up in his seat and leaned forward, hanging on the battle tale and Hector braced.

"Arnoul was cut down beneath the walls of the Château de la Faigne, overpowered easily by younger English soldiers. I stood there

41

and fought like I'd been taught by my father, but I was seventeen, and green, and bested after only a few minutes. Just as an English soldier brought his sword down toward my skull, Hector tackled the man and disarmed him. They were locked in close quarters fighting. He strangled the man to death with his bare hands." Young Hector's face went pale.

"I stood there, frozen, unable to move, terrified out of my mind. Another knight came galloping toward us just as Hector choked the life out of my attacker. He threw me behind him at the last second, taking the man's sword to the left side of his face." All eyes again went to his scar. By the looks on their faces, its appearance was no longer humorous to his young nephews.

Léo continued. "It was our first taste of battle. He was only four years older than me, but he protected me throughout the rest of the day... hell on earth." Léo took a deep drink of wine. "Heavy casualties that day. The English were wiped out."

Lachlan shifted beside Elspeth. Mhairi bit her lip. Elspeth's eyes stared at the sickle-shaped scar that mangled him badly from chin to cheek. A faint look of disgust crossed her face before it became serene again. She'd been quick to hide her feelings, but he'd seen them all the same.

Léo made a sound of contempt. "You'd think that after that terrifying experience I would've learned to stay away from conflict. But no. I wanted to prove to Hector I wasn't a weakling."

Hector released a heavy breath. He'd allowed Léo to follow him back to camp after the battle, silent and dazed. Innocence stolen by the brutality of what he had just witnessed. Léo stayed in his tent for days, collecting himself.

Léo finished his claret and motioned for more. "It was the way you transformed once the battle got close enough. I'd always wanted to see a berserker in action, and I did that day. He had a bloodlust. Fought like fury, agile like a cat, ruthless and deadly like an adder."[2]

"As I say, that was another time," Hector said, attempting to steer the conversation away from his past.

Elspeth placed a hand on his forearm. "What brought you back to the Isles?"

Lachlan smiled. "I did."

"You missed your brother?"

"Far from it. Gold brought him here, not Lachlan." Léo took a deep drink from his cup then motioned to the servant to return with the claret a third time.

A feeling of thunder began to grow on the edges of his temper. In another time, in another place, he would've known how to deal with a tipsy Léo MacKinnon. He placed his hand over Léo's cup. "You dinnae want more."

Léo stared at him, clearly on the edge of insulting him. Hector returned the stare, unafraid. He wasn't the man he used to be. Cowed, Léo looked away.

Hector turned to Elspeth and dropped all pretense. "Despite what you've said, I know your brother has already apprised you of how I became Laird of Lochbuie, and my past, because I know your brother as well as I know myself. I also suppose he told you why you are here and what roles we all must play in this."

"He may have mentioned..." Elspeth's voice trailed off.

"Léo, if there is something you'd like to say to me I suggest you say it like a man. Otherwise, it would be rude to our hosts to continue this."

Léo looked serious. "Aye, I suppose you're right. We all have a part to play."

Elspeth leaned close to Hector, her tone now warm, the cloying smell of rose making him want to sneeze. "Léo told me you made a vast fortune as a mercenary. Is your keep finer than Duart?"

Hector choked on his water, and it spurted out his nose, between his fingers, and onto an unsuspecting Elspeth. Mhairi handed him a linen cloth, aghast. He mopped his face and beard and patted Elspeth's arm apologizing.

"I can do it!" She snatched the cloth away from him.

"My keep. Moy," he stalled. "It's..."

"Bucolic," Mhairi helped.

Elspeth put the cloth down and examined her ruined sleeve and he got the feeling that it was costing an enormous effort on her part to make it through this meal. "How nice."

His palms began to sweat. "It does need some renovation, but that is on course to be completed by the end of the harvest."

"Have you plans to expand?"

"No." Judging by the expression on her face, it was not the answer she was hoping for.

"There's certainly no more peaceful coastline than Lochbuie," said Mhairi. "Beautiful white sand beaches, a freshwater loch behind Moy, and a tall and diverse wood surrounding the inlet." Mhairi had side-stepped the problem of his crumbling pile by talking up the beauty of the land itself.

"It's true," Hector agreed without a hint of deception. "Ben Buie is just over the horizon as well. The land is what makes the estate so valuable, and its position on the sea lanes."

Elspeth looked wooden. "How fortunate. How many rooms does your keep have? Moy, was it?"

"Ten." Only two were livable, only one was comfortable, and the upper two floors needed replacing altogether.

"A start. But so few."

A start? Hector had to bite down on his tongue to keep from laughing. Compared to the crofts and cottages around Lochbuie that were one- or two-room affairs shared with livestock, Moy was still luxurious even as it crumbled.

Reading his expression, Elspeth lifted her chin and began to converse with Léo in French. Her demeanor sweet, but her words poisonous. She began to complain, first about Hector's size, his appearance, his dishonesty about Moy. Fair enough, he thought. Léo looked at Hector with alarm and attempted to interrupt her rant but she continued unabated.

She did not want to wed an overgrown giant. Again, he thought, fair enough. She looked around the hall. Duart, she said, was an excuse for Mhairi to show off her poor taste and garish things.

"*Ç'est assez*," Hector said firmly.[3] Elspeth had the decency to look somewhat ashamed. "Yes," he said in perfect French. "I understood exactly what you said. Now if you're done insulting us, maybe we can be friends."

Mhairi smiled at Hector, unaware of the fiery barbs that Elspeth had just lobbed in her direction. "You speak such lovely French."

Lachlan gestured to his sons. "Uncle Hector was always the clever lad."

Léo inclined his head to Hector and spoke in French. "My apologies for our rudeness. Perhaps we need to start again."

Hector looked at the trickle of wine at the bottom of Léo's chalice. God help him, this was going to take a miracle.

# CHAPTER 5

## LOCHBUIE OIGHREACHD · JUNE 18, 1383

C ara's arms burned and shook as she struggled to keep pace, turning the barley with a hayfork. Ahead of her, the scythe man cut the barley with a rhythmic swish, creating a neat swathe on the left side of the lazybed.[1] She had pursued him along the stretch of lazybed since the sun had risen and he'd not slowed down or taken a break since midday.

Like an Egyptian taskmaster monitoring his Israelite slave, the boy behind her urged her to move quicker. "Get moving *Èireannach*. We'll be here all night if you dinnae move faster."[2]

Refusing to give him the satisfaction of a reaction, Cara kept up her rapid pace. The boy followed her, spreading bracken over the turned barley to ward off vermin and dampness. The boy moved with the practiced speed of someone who'd been working in these fields his whole life, and he released a noise of displeasure as he again came to a halt waiting for her to finish. Sweat beaded at her upper lip and her arms struggled to do her task half as well as the others. Repressing her agitation, she determined not to be defeated by the task and kept working.

Two weeks had gone by since they had arrived on Mull, and aside from Pádraig, the overseer of the barley fields, the villagers demonstrated no willingness to accept her. For ten days she was always the last one to finish her row. The children had begun to draw lots, and the one with the shortest straw was forced to work with her.

Today, Cara worked with Donal MacFadyen, a boy with hair that shone like a flame and a temper that was just as hot. "Hurry, you lazy Èireannach!"

Reaching the end of her patience, Cara hefted her fork and rounded on him. "If you don't pipe down, I'll fork you through, you wee scunner."

The boy pinched his lips and narrowed his eyes. "Maw, the Èireannach threatened me…"

A large woman from the next lazybed dropped her fork and marched over to her, hands on hips. Knees like jelly, Cara took two wobbling steps backward.

Donal crossed his arms. "She said she was going to fork me through, just for doing my job."

"Fork my son, will you?" The woman climbed over her lazybed and advanced on her, delivering a slap so hard it reverberated in her ears. Hopeless defeat tightened in her chest, but she lifted her chin and resolved not to cry, as she'd learned to do with Duncan.

Pádraig's voice called across the fields. "What's going on over there?"

Responsibility for Margaret overcame the anger in her heart, and Cara waved him off. It didn't matter what the boy said or did, she needed to make it through the day. "I'm sorry, Donal."

The boy doubled over laughing at her, and his mother spat on her. "Go back to Ireland."

She wiped the woman's saliva from her cheek and took a deep, shuddering breath. Resuming her work, she picked up the fork and began turning, wishing she was at her loom, doing work that came easily to her. She pushed the memory away. It would do no good to look back.

"That's more like it, Èireannach. All you needed was a man to bring you to heel," Donal said, spreading bracken behind her. The set down from a boy that could have been her child almost sent her over the edge. Almost. Standing strong, she refused to feel the sting of rejection for a second time in her life. Her hard work would be rewarded with acceptance.

A few hours later, when the sun was almost gone in the darkening sky and she still hadn't reached the end of the row, Cara walked back to where Donal was, deciding she needed to make peace with the boy. "Go home, I'll spread the bracken after I finish turning. I apologize for yelling at you, I'm still new at this."

The boy looked at her like she had sprouted a second head and made no move to accept her olive branch. What was wrong with these island devils? Why was it so hard to accept an apology?

After long moments he threw his fork to the ground. "Fine."

Without bothering to return his equipment or look back, he sprinted in the direction of home.

Loneliness weighed down her heart and soul despite her efforts to pretend that it didn't. Here she was, standing in a field in a foreign land, alone and unwanted, failing at this new life. Crouching in the dirt she spread the flake of bracken Donal abandoned, lifting a silent prayer from her broken heart. *Jesus, help me. Help me to find my way. Will I ever have someone who will love me just as I am? I'm so lonely, God. Please, take this pain away. Send someone to help me.*

Around her, crickets began their evening song as she worked her way slowly down the row. Tears stung her eyes as she wiped dirt from her hands, looked up into the sky, and stood awed.

A full moon, radiant with pink hue, illuminated the heavens. A glow of rose-colored light brightened the dark barley field around her. Hundreds of stars winked in the sky, beckoning her to surrender the loneliness of a land not her own, a people not her own, and a dialect not her own, into the Lord's hands.

The words of a psalm came to mind, and she began to sing the words into the vast void of night. "Who heals the broken in heart and binds up their bruises? Who determines the number of stars and calls them all by name? Great is our Lord. Great is His Power. His wisdom cannot be numbered. The Lord lifts up the meek and brings the wicked down to the ground. Sing, you, to the Lord with praise..."

She knelt to the ground taking the fronds of bracken, spreading it lovingly over the barley and continued to sing to the one who could make her burden light.

"An Irish lass."

Startled, she turned, finding a giant standing right behind her.

Piercing blue eyes glowed from the hard angles of his face. A scar marred one cheek, carving down into a dark beard. Scared out of her wits, she took a step back and fell over the lazybed on her backside, breath disappearing from her lungs.

The giant's face contorted into shock, and he knelt beside her to help her up. "I'm sorry, I didnae mean to scare you. I tho' I saw someone out here still working, and then I heard your song. I won't hurt you; I only came to see if you needed help."

Trying to recover her senses, she put a hand over her thudding heart, unsure if she should trust him. He gave her a lopsided grin, his eyes shining with amusement. Her mouth opened and closed, and she tried to remember words, any words. She began to speak in Irish before remembering where she was and repeating herself in Scottish. "By the saints. You scared the life out of me."

Extending a hand to her, his growling voice became a warm, soothing rumble of laughter. She placed her shaking hand in his enormous paw, and he pulled her up in one quick motion. How tall was he? She rose just above his elbow. When he didn't release her hand, she stared at him in awkward silence, knowing she should say something, but words still came into her brain mixed in two dialects.

"I'm Cara."

"I'm Hector." His half smile was so wide it looked as if it might escape off the left side of his face. Staring at her hand still clenched in his bouncing grip, he cleared his throat and let it go. "Your voice is pure. Enchanting."

Embarrassed, she adjusted the linen cloth around her head, searching for something to do with herself. "Thank you. I didn't real-realize I had an audience." Her voice caught in her throat, and she tried not to be intimidated by his resemblance to Margaret's stories of Samson. The man seemed nearly seven feet tall, his body strong, and his hair a feral mass of long black curls.

He crossed muscled arms over his broad chest and looked out over the empty field. "The other workers left you to finish by yourself?"

The empty fields around them made her realize how ridiculous she must seem working by the light of the moon. "I'm new. They don't know me yet. Once they do, I'm sure someone will help me."

"They shouldnae leave you out here by yourself. Does Pádraig know you're here?"

"I expect so. I'm not as fast or strong as the others. I've finished late every night for days. I try to get the equipment back to the granary before it's locked for the night. Sometimes Pádraig forgets I'm still here. If he locks it before I make it there, I roll it home and bring it back in the morning. — I'll get stronger; I just need time."

Arms still crossed, he took in every chattering word as she spoke in a nervous blather, eyes combing her from toes to head. "Why dinnae I help you finish?"

Her tongue stilled its chattering. The long row stretched on before her, and humiliation washed over her afresh that it had taken her so long to finish. Now a strange man would have to help make up for her deficiency. Yet, there was kindness in his icy blue eyes. "All right, then."

Hector picked up a hayfork without further comment and hefted most of the contents of the handcart, dusting the bed with flake and working at a pace that would've made Donal proud. She followed him, rustling the bracken to make sure the barley was concealed beneath its cover.

"Where are you from in Ireland, Cara?" It was the first time someone had called her more than Èireannach.

"Buncrana, originally. Come here by way of Rathmullan."

"*Dhún na nGall*," he said in her dialect.[3]

"That's right. Donegal."

He switched into effortless and perfect Irish. "Beautiful country. I took work there six years ago with the O'Dohertys." The familiar sound of her own language unfurled around her like a warm blanket and brought a fresh wave of emotion to her eyes that she blinked away.

"Why didn't you stay?"

A flicker of something crossed his face, but he continued after a bare moment. "I found other work in England."

"You're a traveler then?"

"Cateran, gallowglass, routier..."

That accounted for his large size and muscled frame. "A hired warrior."

"Aye."

"And here I thought with your height you'd be very useful hanging tapestries." A deep, hearty chuckle rewarded her with a sense of pride that she'd made him laugh. Silence fell between them and she felt his eyes on her again.

"Is your husband a member of this clan?"

Her hands stopped over the bracken, and her heart pinched. "No." Warmth drained out of her. "How did you know I was married?"

"You wrap your hair with linen, but arenae wearing a ring. I dinnae mean to intrude. I only want to be sure he won't be cross I'm helping you. If you think he'll be irritated, you can go, and I'll finish this."

As an unmarried woman she was under no obligation to cover her hair, but after so many years of disguising herself to please Duncan it felt sinful to be without it. Indeed, if Duncan could see a man speaking to her, he would have made her pay dearly for her disloyalty. "He died almost three months ago. I suppose it's a habit to cover it."

Hector paused at the end of the row and turned back to help her finish spreading the bracken. Crouching beside her, his hands moved beside hers with a careful grace she had not expected of their size. His voice came out low and tender. "I'm sorry."

She swallowed and steadied herself against his kindness, then dusted her hands and rose, picking up her hayfork. "Thank you."

Hector moved to follow her. "Toss it in the handcart, I'll see you home and come back and put it away later."

Trepidation rose. "These are the laird's fields. I wouldn't want anything to happen to his tools. I appreciate your help, but you can go. I can put these things away. It's my responsibility."

The half-smile crept back up his left cheek and he smoothed his hand over his coiled, inky hair. "I know the laird. It wouldnae please him to know that you're out here alone in the dark, worrying over his belongings instead of your safety. Besides, you look done in."

All her strength vanished in an instant as the hard day's labor caught up with her. She was tempted to take him up on the offer, but the thought of being held responsible for any missing equipment prevented her from agreeing. She picked up both hayforks. "If you push the handcart, I'll carry these. It doesn't feel right for me to leave them here without his approval. It's only a few minutes' walk to the granary."

The half-smile lifted higher on the undamaged side of his face. "All right. Put them in the handcart at least."

Her arms ached, but she ignored her fatigue. "If I carry them, they won't clatter around. I don't want them to be damaged. I don't mind." Before he could say anything else, she turned and headed for the granary.

The steady squeaking of the wooden handcart protested behind her. "Are you always this resistant to help?"

"The clan is burdened enough by my being here. I'm sorry you've had to take time out of your day to help me correct my short-comings."

The moonrise continued to glow with vibrant light and painted shades of purple, pink, and blue over the distant sea loch. Spreading across the fields, it illuminated her shoulders and she smiled at the strange glow. It brought another verse to mind. "From the rising of the sun until the going down of the same, the name of the Lord is worthy of praise. Thank you, Lord, for this day."

"Amen."

She looked back at him. "You believe?"

He shrugged. "I do. Don't most people?"

The hayforks began to grow heavy in her hands and she hefted them over each shoulder. "Most people say they do, but don't live like they believe in Him."

He was quiet.

"I'm sorry. Have I offended you?"

That half-smile lifted again. "You apologize too much. I agree with you. I was such a man once."

"But no longer?" Stepping into the road they headed up the hill toward the granary.

"I'm trying to be a man who lives like he believes." She liked that answer. He lifted his chin. "I can tell by what I've seen here that you believe."

"I do. It's difficult sometimes. I feel so insignificant."

Handcart squeaking, he closed the space between them in a few strides. "What makes you think you're insignificant?"

Unexpected grief clutched at her chest. How to boil down ten years of misery to this stranger? She deflected the question. "My father never thought so. He told me I was different, special."

He walked silent beside her and seemed attuned to her words, so she carried on. "My mother died when I was small, my father when I was twelve. I became an unwanted burden to my aunt and uncle. I took a hand-fasted marriage to get away." A bitter laugh escaped her. "I was a burden to my husband as well." Embarrassment flooded her as she realized she had shared too much. "I'm sorry I'm blatherin'. I shouldn't have said that."

He was quiet for long moments, and she feared she had made him uncomfortable.

"You are significant, Cara."

She tried to laugh it off. "You wouldn't know, would you?"

"There are things only you can speak, a path that only you can walk, people only you can touch. Dinnae diminish your worth." A strange intimacy coming from a near stranger, but words she needed to hear.

Pádraig bellowed greetings from the top of the hill, and Hector hollered greetings back in Scottish before switching once more to Irish. "Put your forks in the handcart, I'll be right back. Dinnae go anywhere."

Cara watched him jog up the hill and hand off the tools to Pádraig. They spoke for a few minutes, and Pádraig seemed to be motioning at her. Anxiousness formed in her stomach, and she hoped Pádraig wasn't too upset at the late hour of her return. The two men shook hands before Hector turned and jogged back down the hill. "I'll see you home. Do you live far?"

"I live out by Laggan Sands. I won't make you walk me. It's too far out of the way."

"Nonsense. You're no' walking home by yourself in the dark." Hector whistled and waited. Out of the field, a silvery destrier trotted forward and dipped his head. Heart pounding, she hid behind Hector.

He looked over his shoulder. "What's the matter?"

She cowered behind his muscled back. "That horse is huge. I can walk. It's not that far."

His voice became piteous. "Now dinnae say it like that, you'll hurt his feelings."

The horse turned his silver neck toward her and tossed his head up and down as if he concurred. Hector raised his arm and gently pulled her by the wrist, tucking her against his side. Solid and steady beside her, he took her hand in his and put it on the horse's shoulder. "This is his spot. It's called the withers. Give him a scratch here. That's right. He's robust but if you're relaxed, he will be."

"What's his name?"

"Ghoustie."

Ghoustie stretched the long crest of muscle in his neck and wiggled his lips, enjoying her long nails. Hector chuckled and removed his hand from hers and stepped away.

"He's verra fond of a long, flattering *goood lad* when you get to know him."

She mimicked the deep tone of his voice and spoke in Scottish. "Goood lad, Ghoustie."

Ghoustie inclined his neck toward her and gave her two eyes the same eerie blue color as Hector's. She extended her hand, and he nuzzled her palm for a few seconds, neck relaxed.

"Ah, he likes you."

"You're certain he'll accept a stranger riding him?"

"Aye. He's my special lad. Brave when he needs to be and docile with those I trust."

She relented. "All right."

"I'll give you a boost."

He knelt beside her, and two large hands braced around the skin of her calf, his thumb brushing over the raised white scar and raw memory. She jumped backward, fright suddenly taking over her senses, and almost fell into the dirt. Concern knit his dark angled brows together.

"I'm sorry." She brushed her palms over her face, pressing down the emotion at her eyes. He wasn't going to hurt her. Feeling skittish, she let out a sigh and placed a hand on his rock-hard shoulder.

His frost-colored eyes looked to her for permission. "Ready?"

She nodded and his warm hands came around her calf once more, lifting her with little effort into the saddle.

He clicked his tongue and Ghoustie followed him up the road toward town. "Where do you live in Laggan?"

She hesitated. "Ursula MacFadyen's sheepcote." Ursula, she'd learned, had the reputation of being batty. Which, to be honest, she was a little. She waited for him to make a comment about her kin.

"Ursula. I havenae met her, but I've heard she is a remarkable healer. I didnae know she had any Irish relatives."

Nervous words burbled out of her. "Aye, she has a sister, and me. Her sister was—is my mother-in-law. My mother-in-law is a MacFadyen. Not Irish. Scottish." Hector nodded and did not press her for more information. No man wanted to hear unasked-for details.

Grateful for the ride after a long day, and having found a friend, Cara held her tongue and enjoyed the stillness of the two-mile walk along the shoreline as they headed toward Laggan. The gloom of the terrible day had been punctuated by the glow of radiant moonlight— she was significant.

Every few minutes, Hector turned and looked up at her, and when he did, her heart leapt with girlish infatuation. There was something about the man. He looked forbidding but hadn't overlooked her.

His frosted blue eyes pierced through the darkness of night as he looked up at her again. Their eyes met this time, and she held his gaze, wondering what he might see in her, and if he guessed what she recognized in him.

Hector paused in front of the lane that led to Ursula's sheepcote. After steadying the horse, he wrapped his massive hands around her waist and eased her down. In a rush of reckless gratitude, she touched her fingertips to his neck and pulled his face gently down. Heart acting of its own volition, she touched her lips to his scarred cheek and kissed him in appreciation for his words, his care, and his protection.

"Thank you, Hector. The kindness you've shown me is—I'm so grateful for your help. If I can ever repay you for this, please don't hesitate to ask." She motioned to his homespun tunic. "I'm a weaver by trade. Or I was before I left Ireland. I had to leave my loom behind in Rathmullan. If you ever need something mended? Or sewn? Saints. I haven't even asked if you have a wife—if she wouldn't mind, that is. I could sew for either of you...I'm blatherin' again."

"Aye," he said with a wink, removing his hands which had lingered too long on her waist. He backed up a few paces, but his aqua eyes never left hers. "And no, I dinnae have a wife."

# CHAPTER 6

## LOCHBUIE OIGHREACHD - JUNE 19, 1383

Hector touched his scarred cheek for the sixth time that morning as he made his way to Pádraig's cottage, hoping the man was awake. He'd woken long before dawn, thinking about Cara, unable to forget her mossy green eyes and the feel of her diminutive frame as it tucked against his own. And unable to forget that he was supposed to secure a marriage alliance with a woman who hadn't ignited a tenth of what he felt for the small Irish lass.

Haunted by the lack of control in his heart, he had lain awake in bed thinking of the sound of her voice and of her song, so much like a lullaby. Knowing there were several more hours before dawn, but unable to sleep, he went running along the path to Glenbyre. The run had done little to quell his energy and left him filled with questions. After taking a pre-dawn bowl of porridge, he gave up trying to resist thoughts of her and decided to seek Pádraig out and see what he knew about her.

Pádraig's stone cottage lay on the edge of the arable fields just a short walk from where he had met Cara the night before. Hector spied a rush light at the window and knocked on the damp oak door.

Wide-eyed, Pádraig smoothed a hand over his gray beard as he opened the door. "Hector. What brings you here so early?"

Hector brushed past him and into the cottage. "I wanted to talk to you about the woman who lingered in the fields last evening."

Everything in Pádraig's cottage was clean, laying at precise right angles. His house reflected the ordered wisdom that Hector had sought all his life.

Pádraig sat down across from him at the pine table, his only furnishing in the front room. "I ken what you're going to say, Hec. I want to assure you that the woman only needs a bit of time and she'll be as strong and fast as the others on the field. She's an unusual woman with a good heart."

Hector opened his mouth to protest, but Pádraig raised his hands in front of him as if he were coaxing a frightened pony. "I ken, I should assign workers to her for help, and I offered, but the woman refused. She doesnae want anyone to be made to work with her, she wants to win them over on her own. Give her a chance. I dinnae want to send her away. She needs my help."

Hector shook his head. "I didnae come to tell you to get rid of her. I wanted to find out who she is and how she came to be staying with our clan."

Pádraig's brown eyes studied him, and Hector knew he was trying to puzzle out his motives for coming at such an early hour. Pádraig poured warm cider into two cups from the jug beside him and handed one to him. "Cara is a good lass. The first to arrive every morning, the last to leave every night. She arrived here a few weeks ago with her mother-in-law, Margaret. Margaret used to be a part of the MacFadyen clan thirty-odd years ago." Pádraig sipped his cider and stared into the peat fire. "Gorgeous woman, and for some reason she was in love with me."

Hector paused, the cup of cider halfway to his lips. "You had a flame before you married Morág?"

Pádraig smiled. "Aye. It was a long time ago. I was part of the MacLeans of Craignure, a wild bunch back in those days thanks to your Da. Her father didn't like us, tho' we were too wild for his eldest daughter. But she loved me all the same. Waited for me to make up my mind to marry her, but I wanted to be ready. Three years she waited for me, and then one Michaelmas at the Harvest Games, Hugh MacSweeney entered the sheaf toss and caught her eye. They married three weeks later."

Never had he witnessed a look of such longing on Pádraig's face. "Ah, but I never forgot her. You never forget your first love. Perhaps that's why Margaret sent her daughter-in-law to me for work. Cara asked me for a job so that she could support them both. Girl's a weaver by trade, but there was trouble in Ireland when her husband died, and her loom went with her household."

Hector's ears perked up. "What sort of trouble?"

"I'm not sure, she wouldn't elaborate." Pádraig took a noisy sip of cider. "The girl is protective of Margaret though, wouldnae give me a direct answer to any of my questions about how she fared."

"Aye. She seemed hesitant to tell me who her relations were in Lochbuie."

Pádraig made an unsatisfied sound. "I dinnae ken the full story, but even though the girl has living relatives in Donegal she refused to leave Margaret and followed her to Lochbuie. Unusual, that one."

Hector's hand came to his face again. The warmth of Cara's kiss on his mangled cheek lingering. An unusual lass unconcerned with his appearance and grateful for his company. "How have the rest of the clan taken to her?"

Pádraig rolled his eyes. "The way they always take to outsiders. You're the only one they've ever liked. No' sure I blame them after being half-starved to death, being suspicious of foreigners taking work and coin from them."

Hector grunted. "She's hardly a threat."

"Aye, but they dinnae see it that way. The children draw straws to see who must work with her in the morning. Losers get the task. She took quite a slap from one of their mothers yesterday but didnae cry or complain. She just took it like she thought she deserved it."

A feeling of protectiveness knit tight in his chest. "I dinnae want any further opportunities to mistreat her. There must be someone in the clan to show her how it's done. Someone who has credibility with the others who can help her gain their trust?"

Pádraig's forehead wrinkled as he drew solutions to mind. "There is one woman who can help. Rhona. She works in baling, though; it will mean a pay cut for Cara."

"No, it willnae."

"I cannae pay her more than the other balers, and we cannae afford to pay them all a higher wage."

Hector waved his hand. "I'll take care of the difference in her pay, plus a bit extra. She has no husband or male relative to look after her. None of them do. Have you been to the sheepcote since they've arrived? Is there anything they need?" Pádraig looked at him the same way he did on Iona the day God saved his life, and Hector was certain he saw through him.

"I havenae, but Murdoch was out to oversee a patch to the roof a few weeks ago. It's been a long time since I've seen Margaret, but we didnae part well."

"I want you to go there today. Take a mental inventory of anything they need and let me know at once what is needed. I also want you to set aside everything that they will need for the winter from my harvest at the end of the season. Ensure they have what they need and a bit extra."

Pádraig sipped his cider and muttered to himself. "There's something about the lass. Unusual."

Hector agreed but knew he must tread carefully to avoid exposing his feelings further. "You've said."

"I dinnae know the details of her past but there's a heaviness to her. When others heap abuse on her she takes it, and then she apologizes to them. It's confounding. Yet she's no' rattled at the end of the day. Quite the opposite, she seems grateful."

The quality of one who had tasted a deep redemption. "Hope."

"Aye. She's full of hope."

"Then we need to make sure it isn't quenched." Draining his cider, he nodded to Pádraig in thanks.

As Hector made for the door, Pádraig spoke. "Is Léo still arriving today?"

Pádraig could read him better than any man alive, and Hector didn't turn, for fear of what might be deciphered in his expression.

"Late this afternoon. If you will meet me at the gatehouse at sext[1], we can discuss the next few months. Let me know then about the supplies. And Pádraig?"

"Aye?"

"She's no' to know I'm chieftain."

# CHAPTER 7

## LOCHBUIE OIGHREACHD - JUNE 19, 1383

Hector stood at the end of the dock as the galley rowed into the channel in front of Moy. Léo stood at the head of the bìrlinn and stepped out. As they moved toward the keep, Léo bore a look of intense scrutiny. "That's Moy?"

A feral pigeon dipped around the curtain wall and homed in on one of the blocked pigeonholes. The animal attempted to swoop in, collided with the stone, and bounced, landing with a solid thunk at Léo's feet. They stared at the gray-blue bird, its brown eye staring lifelessly off into the heavens.

Hector nodded. "Aye. That's Moy." He switched to French as a courtesy, knowing it had always been Léo's more dominant language. "It needs a bit of repair."

Léo tried to stifle a laugh. "You think any woman will want to live in that? Let alone Elspeth? There's not a chance."

Hector grimaced at the moldering pile. "I dinnae want to live in it."

Léo cracked a smile. "It's a shame. The land is the jewel of the island."

A stone skittered off the keep and landed on Hector's boot. He kicked it away. "Repair to the castle will begin at once. We're scheduled to start this week and expect it will be habitable by October."

Léo's eyes traveled the length of the crumbling keep. "The barmkin looks sound, but the keep needs a lot more than repair. Is it even safe to enter?"

"Yes. It's safe." Mostly. "The barmkin walls were repaired my first year in Lochbuie. The compromised parts of the keep were removed four years ago, and plans drawn up for improvement. I assure you, most of the issues are confined to the top floors only.

Léo stared at the dead pigeon, a look of doubt on his face. "What are the planned improvements?"

"The top floors will be removed, the foundation stones repointed, and three wooden floors will be constructed on top of the stone corbels. The entire structure will be coated with lime and whitewashed to maintain a look of uniformity."

Léo pursed his lips. "October is only four months away."

"Our plan is to obtain extra workers from Duart. They can spare men to help with construction."

Léo's nose crinkled. "It's hideous. Anything is an improvement I suppose."

Feeling as if he were listening to someone insult an ugly sister, Hector frowned. It was one thing if he himself complained about the keep, but quite another when an outsider voiced the same thoughts. "I'll admit it's no' the Louvre, but I'm confident it will be a comfortable home by harvest. Elspeth will have no complaints."

"You don't know Elspeth. Wait just a moment. Where have you decided to place me? Not in there."

"I've arranged for you to stay with Pádraig, my *fear-taic*. It's no' a grand house, but you'll have a private room, and it's clean."[1]

"Pádraig, your uncle? That's a relief."

"I'm surprised you remember."

Léo dropped the familiarity, shrugged, and proceeded down the path, leaving him with a twinge of sadness for their lost friendship. Things were different now.

Continuing the tour of Lochbuie village, the fishery was first, its proximity to Moy offensive as Léo held his handkerchief over his nose muttering oaths in French. The smell did take some getting used to but Hector wasn't sure what the fuss was about. Moving back up the river to the east, the bake house, brewery, inn, and tavern were next. Hector was proud of this stretch of Lochbuie. The inn and tavern were as fine as those you could find in a proper continental district in the north of France.

Léo shook his head. "No market."

His unamused expression deflated Hector in the same way showing up for a banquet with clothes forty years out of fashion might a young lad.

"We travel to Duart or Iona to market," he explained.

Léo remained unimpressed. "Mmm."

The mill and granary were next, and the fields of arable land beyond. Workers moved in steady rows swathing and turning the barley. Hector scanned the workers as they finished their labor but did not see Cara among them. Unexpected warmth filled his heart, and he hoped she'd gone home to begin the Sabbath along with the rest of the balers.

Léo studied the miles of golden fields stretching out at the base of Ben Buie. "Now this shows great promise. To grow a bere barley crop this robust and with such great yield on Mull is an accomplishment." [2]

"It's a new strain from Islay that we've been using the past four years. It can handle the moisture and using the lazybeds has improved our yield as well. This should be our best harvest since I've been laird."

The heavy gold chain around Léo's neck glinted in the setting sunlight, a gold disc with the head of a lion dangling from it. The mark of Charles V. His voice resonated with authority and approval. "Any man can put money into his keep, but a leader knows to take care of his people first."

Hector remembered why they'd been like brothers. Léo may have preferred fine things, good wine, and beautiful surroundings, but at heart, their beliefs were the same.

By the time they made their way back to the gatehouse the sun had almost disappeared under the horizon, but heat lingered in the air. Hector loosened the silver brooch at his shoulder and shed his patched brat as they entered the stuffy office. "Léo, this is Pádraig, my uncle and fear-taic, Tavish my seneschal, Calum, the commander of the Lochbuie guard, and Murdoch, the master of the bowmen."

Léo greeted each man and sat down at the table. "I suppose you all know that I am here to make a thorough investigation of Lochbuie prior to any agreement regarding a betrothal. I must ensure that my sister will have every chance at happiness."

Tavish nodded. "Of course, you must."

Hector looked at his assembled leadership. "I have nothing to hide, and I'm sure that everything will meet Léo's satisfaction. I expect all of you to cooperate with him and give him an honest assessment of where you see the clan moving in the next five, ten, twenty years."

Calum cleared his throat and made a shaky attempt to converse in French. "I heard you are the monkey for King Charles V. I am sure we can come from an agreement that will be to your my liking. I'm having an excellent war battle fellow for the past four years. I am sure that I will contribute by creating breaking wind for the Kingdom of Isles."

Unable to keep his face straight, Léo burst into laughter and Calum looked at him dumbstruck. For months he'd been trying to master French with Hector in his spare time to impress the lasses at Duart.

Hector rolled his eyes. "Calum. Speak in Gaelic. You're making a fool of yourself."

Murdoch looked at Léo who now had tears running down his face. "What did he say?"

Hector rubbed his temples. It was true to form for broken-down Lochbuie, dead pigeons, fish stink, and crude diplomacy. "He's talking about breaking wind for the Kingdom of the Isles."

Calum went furious red against his lightning-colored hair. "No, no... I was saying I wanted peace for the Isles."

Tavish, Murdoch, and Pádraig now doubled over laughing. They sucked their lips between their teeth and tried hard to stifle their chortles.

"I was trying to say I was impressed that he works as a marmouset for King Charles V, and I am sure that we help the marriage negotiations with our expertise."

Léo wiped tears away from his eyes and held up a hand. "I got the root of what you were trying to say. Thank you. For the record, 'paix' means peace, 'péter' means breaking wind."

Pádraig dissolved into a second fit of laughter.

Léo took a deep breath and began again, his eyes still red from laughing so hard. "I will try and spend at least one or two days a week with each of you and will take Sundays for myself to visit Elspeth at Duart. For the first few weeks I'd like to observe how you spend your time."

Tavish recovered their credibility swiftly. "Excellent. I have been able to come up with new record keeping methods and I would value an expert eye and opinion."

Murdoch beamed. "I for one am interested to have you observe our training for a few weeks. Your uncle was Arnoul d'Audrehem."[3]

"Who's he?" Pádraig asked.

"Marshal of France. A general," Calum explained.

Something in Léo's tone made a shift from amused to resentful. "Aye. He was. Though I learned my fighting skills from Hector, not my uncle." All mirth left the room as everyone turned to gape at Hector. His stomach clenched. After the evening at Duart, he was unsure where Léo may take the conversation.

Murdoch scooted forward in his seat. "Based on his limited training with the guard, I ken he's an excellent archer. Better than I. What was the laird like in battle?"

Sweat broke out at Hector's temples and he picked at a divot on the tabletop, knowing he and Léo knew the answer to their question, and wishing they would stop talking. There was nothing about his battle abilities to be proud of. Pádraig met Hector's eyes.

Léo scoffed. "Excellent? No. Not excellent. Exceptional. He's the greatest warrior I've ever seen, perhaps the most skilled to ever come out of Scotland or the Isles."

Hector tried to close the topic of conversation, sick of the speculation that had been following him since the meeting at Findlugan. "That isnae true."

Calum smiled. "You're holding out on us. He refuses to train with anyone in close combat. Why won't you show me everything you know?"

Hector hedged. "You have Léo here. He can show you anything I can do. He's just as good as I am."

Léo's mouth formed a firm line. "No, I'm not. Not even close. It's like he can see what's coming before it happens. I'm quick, but he's..."

The three men turned their heads toward Léo, waiting for him to finish the sentence, waiting for him to confirm the rumors that had been swirling around Hector for years. "Barbaric. As if he has a gift for killing."

Three heads turned back to Hector at the opposite end of the table. Sickness cramped his gut; roaring began in his ears. A feeling of oncoming doom—the certain knowledge that the memories were coming and would not be stopped.

Pádraig alone picked up on the change in his appearance. "Hector?"

He hadn't had a vision during waking hours in more than five years. Sweat drenched his brow. The thunder of hoofbeats thumped through his brain. The slice of swords rent the air.

Breath stole from his lungs. He had to get out of the room. The chair behind him clattered to the floor as he got to his feet. It couldn't be happening again. Not after all this time. Not after giving up drink.

Murdoch's voice mixed in with the thick sounds of battle and contorted into a feral scream for help. "Laird."

Hector got to his feet, burst through the door, and ran.

---

Sprinting through the gate, Hector tore down the night-cloaked road that curved toward Laggan Sands trying to stay ahead of the vision of battle that seemed so real. *Whisky...* his throat burned for the numbing taste of the only liquid that could take away the horrible scenes he would relive. He had to keep moving, had to outrun the horseman that threatened at the edges of his sanity. *God, help me.*

Racing against his darkest memories, chest heaving, the hoofbeats grew louder and he knew visions were about to overtake him. He made it to the shoreline before he tripped and sank to his knees, losing the battle against his mind. The dust rose around him, and he plunged into the coagulated memories of the worst things he'd ever done as if they were happening anew.

Blood trickled down his face from his scalp and into his eyes. Both he and the Englishman had lost their weapons and they grappled; strength drained. He charged forward wrapping his arms around the man's legs knocking him off balance. The soldier staggered backward but maintained his hold on him and tried to gain the upper hand. Reaching between their interlocked bodies Hector managed to get a finger hold on the man's shoulder and forced them apart. The soldier's legs flailed wildly as his big hands came around the man's small throat.

The man squawked in desperation. He tightened his hands around the man's neck until his voice strangled out of him. His arms trembled, but he squeezed until the breath of God left the man's body and he went slack.

A young Léo stood in front of him, horrified and frozen, his eyes fixed on the horizon. Lifting his exhausted head, Hector spied a rider with a sword locked on Léo. As the rider lowered his weapon, Hector sprang to his feet, shoving Léo out of the way.

The icy tip of the sword caught his cheek. At first, he didn't feel anything...his cheek gaped and hung down to his chin, blood filled his mouth, and his teeth chattered with the force of the blow. Pain blasted through his face. He had to get them off the field, had to get Léo to safety. Léo's boyish face full of terror hovered in front of him as he tried to help lift Hector's cheek back into place...

Another memory charged over him. His father stood before him. Shouts of anger spilled from Da's lips. *Murderer. Harbinger of death.* Vexation surged through him as he fisted Da's rough tunic and threw him to the ground. Remorse soon followed as his father grabbed his heart and looked up at him, betrayed. Lachlan shouted and ran to Da's side, but it was too late.

Another memory. He found himself on a small skiff unable to escape. Lachlan shouted, his words unintelligible. As if looking at the scene from a great distance he saw his younger self beating his brother, and horrified, saw Aileen's blond curly head disappear under the water. Innocent, kind, brave Aileen. The pinnacle of his memory's shame and fear.

Memories assailed him from every angle, but he couldn't squeeze his eyes shut. The faces of dozens of men became a blur, streaming like ghosts before his mind, all dead before their time, all dead because of him. He screamed the name of the Lord at the top of his lungs, desperate to find something real. "Jesus—"

Rosemary. His nose filled with the scent of rosemary. Hands touched his cheeks and arms wrapped around his shoulders, anchoring him into the present. He stopped screaming.

Remorse crashed over him as it did on the morning after a battle. Chest heaving in and out, he sobbed with relief like a child. Gentle fingers wiped the tears that flowed from his eyes. The sound of waves filled his ears, and he pressed his forehead to a smooth neck. This was real. He was home on Mull.

"I'm here. I'm here." Irish. The voice that breathed close to his ear sounded Irish.

He took a shuddering breath. "Cara."

Her arms barely reached around his shoulders, but she surrounded him, steadying him in the harbor of her embrace.

Strength left him. "I'm sorry."

Cara locked her arms tighter, shielding him from the fear that had terrorized him only moments before. "Take a moment. You're shaking. I'm here. I won't leave you."

His racing heart began to slow, and he tried to explain his mad behavior. "Visions. I used to get them all the time. I havenae in years. I dinnae ken what brought it on. I..." Guilt overcame him as he remembered his hands around the Englishman's throat, and he was suddenly at the mercy of overwhelming nausea. He tried to get to his feet but could only manage to lean away from her before heaving into the sand.

When he finished, a cold, wet cloth came to the back of his sweaty neck. She placed her hand over his and helped him grip the cloth to his neck.

"Lay back."

Soft hands swept the curls away from his forehead and allowed the breeze to cool his heated skin. He lay still until the beach stopped spinning and the nausea ebbed away. When he opened his eyes, she was still sitting beside him. Arms folded over her knees, head resting on her arms. The heart-stopping waist-length amber waves that had been hidden under her linen head covering floated on the breeze. Her heart-shaped face caught the moonlight giving her a celestial appearance. Stupefied, and unable to think of something intelligent to say, he held out the wet cloth to her.

"Here's your kerchief."

"Hang onto it. You might feel flushed again." She traced a finger in the sand. "Can I ask you about it, or will it make it worse?"

"Go on."

"What is it a vision of?"

He took a deep breath. "My past. A battle I was in. I strangled a man to death. The only man I've ever killed like that." He waited for her to look repulsed, but she remained tranquil waiting for him to continue. "I needed to save a boy's life. The man I killed didnae have a chance. I was larger. I had the advantage. I took my hands and crushed his throat... and..." His voice broke. "Do you ever have regret so great it consumes you?"

"Aye." Their eyes met, and he saw sorrow reflected in their verdant depths.

"That death. It was personal. I felt the life leave his body." A tear leaked out of his eyes, and he cleared his throat. His father would have thought him a weakling. "It starts off as the battle, and then the vision grows. Every terrible thing that I've ever done. A fight with my father. The day my sister drowned. The faces of every life I've taken."

She reached out and intertwined her fingers with his, and he ached, too weak to stop the longing in his heart. "The boy whose life you saved. Do you know what became of him?"

He thought of Léo and the gleaming pendant of Charles V at his throat. "He went on to advise the King of France. He's a good man."

She smiled. "Then that is what you must carry with you. You took a life in battle, but you saved a life too."

Hearing her say it aloud brought light into impenetrable darkness. "Aye."

"You're a gifted warrior?"

Léo's words echoed through his mind. "I dinnae fight anymore. But, aye, I was."

Her thumb traced the rough skin along the back of his index finger. "If God has made you a skilled warrior, don't be ashamed. Sometimes conflict is necessary to protect order, and to overcome those who wish to destroy good. Peace doesn't mean passiveness. Peace requires courage.

You're not a murderer, you're a protector. I've often wished that there was one to protect me."

"Protect you from what?"

A gust of wind tossed her hair and she let go of his hand and gathered it to the side of her slender, pale neck. Freckles danced across her nose and small teeth bit into the full, pink bow of her lips. "From... being small. There's no worse feeling in the world than to be hurt and have no way of defending yourself. To be physically small, and—"

"Insignificant?"

"Aye. God knows what He is doing by giving you the talents you have, it's all for His glory." Something twinkled in her eye. "He knew what He was doing making you as enormous as you are."

He chuckled at the subtle jest. The lass had a good sense of humor. "I suppose He knew what He was doing making you as wee as you are. It makes it easy for you to burrow into a heart." She colored, and he realized he had voiced his thoughts out loud.

Placing her hands over his she bowed her head. He didn't realize what she was doing until she closed her eyes and spoke. "Father, I pray for this soul who is troubled. Send your angelic host to guard him. Chase away the demons that want to remind him of things you have settled long ago. Banish the darkness from his mind. Help him to surrender his past into your hands. Help him to know how best to use his gifts to serve you. Comfort him and lead him in perfect peace. In the name of Father, Son, and Holy Ghost. Amen."

Unable to help himself, he kissed her knuckles. Against his fingers he felt a diagonal patch of scorched flesh. He turned her small hand over in his large one and traced a barbed band of skin. "What happened?"

She withdrew her hand as if she were burned and got to her feet. "Accident with a cauldron—it burst. Got my leg too. I hate it, the scars are so ugly."

Moonlight glowed on her ivory skin and shone off the silken waves of her hair, and for a moment he felt as if he were looking at a forlorn angel, floating high above him, her eyes calling to something in his soul. And then, in only a moment, she pulled a shield over herself, all vulnerability and intimacy between them gone.

She chattered away like a nervous bird. "The laird moved me to a different job, an easier one, and he's raised my pay. I came out here for a quiet moment to say my thanks to the Lord when I saw you come up the shore. I best be getting back home. I don't want Margaret to be worried. Will you be all right?

He got to his feet. "Aye."

She lifted her hand. "The blessing of God on you."

"And on you."

She turned and walked up the beach.

Words he'd needed to hear for thirteen years tumbled through his mind. Beginning to pray for guidance, he sought the One who would light the way in the darkness. For in the moment she began her prayer, his heart was lost.

# Chapter 8

## Lochbuie Oighreachd - June 20, 1383

At noon on the Lord's day, Margaret, Ursula, and Cara sat outside the sheepcote talking to one another and enjoying their Sabbath rest when a horse and cart turned up the lane. Pádraig pinched the corner of his bonnet in greeting.

Margaret shaded the sun from her eyes. "Pádraig is back."

The cart clunked to a stop and Pádraig jumped down, motioning to a man in the back. Cara's breath caught in her throat as the man's honey brown eyes and handsome face lifted into a stunning smile. Pádraig motioned the man toward them.

"Good to see you again," Ursula said. "I'd no' expected you'd be back so soon."

Pádraig cleared his throat. "I've come to bring you provision from Laird MacLean."

Ursula scrunched up her face. "Provision?"

"Aye. He's heard that Margaret and Cara have come to stay with you and tho' you could make use of some furniture and supplies that are no longer needed at Moy now that it's being repaired and decorated."

The three of them stood open-mouthed as the man removed the oilcloth from the cart revealing fine furniture and several barrels of grain. Unable to believe her eyes, Cara gawped at the fine bedsteads, linens, chairs, and a new grain ark to replace Ursula's broken one. Cara's eyes went to the handsome, richly dressed man. "For us? Laird MacLean, I don't know how to thank you."

The man looked at her, confused. "I'm not Laird MacLean."

Pádraig chuckled. "I'm sorry, I should have introduced my honored guest right away. This is Léo MacKinnon."

"Och. MacKinnon," Ursula muttered.

Unsure if he would be a friendly stranger or a dangerous foe, Cara dipped into a curtsy. "My apologies."

His strong tanned hand took hers and kissed it, his warm brown eyes lifting to hers. "*Enchanté.*"[1]

The meaning of the word was lost on her, but the tone of his voice warmed her belly and her toes curled inside their slippers.

"Léo is Elspeth MacKinnon's half-brother, and will be visiting with us for the summer. He is an acquaintance of the laird from their days in France."

Léo kissed Ursula and Margaret's hands as well. "I was going to visit my sister today but decided to stay behind when I saw the goods Pádraig had to bring to you. I thought he could use my help unloading."

At once Ursula overcame her dislike of all MacKinnons and gave a girlish giggle, and Cara stifled an urge to do the same at the purring tone of his voice. Not since she'd met Duncan had the mere appearance of a man made her unable to stop smiling. And Léo was far more handsome.

Margaret was the only one whose wits were still about her. "This is all for us?"

Pádraig nodded. "Aye, Maggie."

The endearment made her go pink alongside Ursula and Cara, and she turned away and went quickly to the front door of the near-empty cottage. "I'll clear a path."

Together, Léo and Pádraig unloaded the furniture into the cottage. Margaret directed them on where to assemble the three beds and put the chairs. When they'd finished, not only was the cottage now clean, but well-furnished and cozy.

A bed so sumptuous it begged to be slept in now filled Cara's side of the cottage. Covered with soft fox fur, it promised a warm night's sleep off the hard stone floor. "I've never had a proper bed."

"We've never had a proper bed," Ursula said, her hands on either side of her face in amazement. "I cannae believe the laird has given us such treasure."

Léo stood silent at the hearth taking in the fine beds and soft chairs the laird had provided, lost in thought.

Cara joined him. "I am quite astonished you would help us, we're total strangers to you."

A wide, toothy smile spread across his face and her stomach did a flip. "I'll admit it was not entirely noble of me. When I saw the fine furnishings the laird had given to you, I was suspicious that perhaps he took an improper interest in a young widow. He is supposed to be marrying my sister, after all."

Filled with genuine amusement at the thought, she laughed, consumed with the absurdity of such an idea. "I'm a nobody from nowhere, Ireland. I've never even seen the laird. Though I admit he seems like a very good man and may make a good match."

He laughed at her jest. "When I saw you, I thought for a moment my suspicions were correct. You're a very beautiful woman."

Her mouth fell open. Léo thought her beautiful? A memory of the foolish lass eager to be hand-fasted to the too-handsome Duncan MacSweeney sobered her. It would take more than looks to persuade her to love again. Unbidden, Hector appeared in her thoughts.

"No. I've never met the man."

Léo rubbed the back of his neck. "Ah, I've insulted you. I only meant, I mean—I didn't mean to insinuate you and the laird—I'm sorry."

She shook her head and raised her hand. "No apology necessary. My husband died only a few months ago, I suppose this talk makes me a bit embarrassed."

Léo brushed a hand over his face. "My apologies again. I know how you feel. My wife, Théa, died two years ago."

"I'm sorry. Truly."

He shrugged. "I would love to tell you that it gets easier to bear. But I'm afraid I still think of her all the time and long to see her."

Unsure how to act, she was certain that he didn't understand how she felt. His wife's death brought him grief; Duncan's death brought her peace. The way forward hadn't been easy, but she didn't miss his temper or long to see him. Memories stole her breath away and she suddenly needed fresh air. "Would you like to sit in the garden with me?"

Léo nodded. "*Absolument.*"[2]

A breath of cool sea air refreshed her as they made their way into the garden erupting with the color of thousands of flowers. Settling beneath the chestnut tree she rested her back against its sturdy trunk. Léo stretched his long body in the tall grass.

"Your words and accent are strange. Are you Manx?"

He chuckled. "I'm from the Isles, the Isle of Skye. My father was Chief of the MacKinnons, a title my brother now holds. My mother was French, and I've lived in France for the past thirteen years."

"Your words are French?"

"Oui. I suppose I am more comfortable in my mother's language than my father's now. She spoke it to me, and I've lived much of my life speaking it."

"It sounds beautiful."

He smiled again and laid back in the warm sunshine, closing his eyes. "Truth be told, my heart has always longed for Skye. I've longed for my brothers to accept me."

Seeking to keep her fingers busy she began to weave a chain out of wild daisies. "I can understand wanting to belong. I've always wanted to fit in with those around me."

"Ah, but then you would miss the fruitfulness of living as an outsider." His hand disappeared inside his shirt, and he produced a gold chain with a disc. He scooted close to her until they were shoulder to shoulder and passed the disc to her. The disc bore the image of a lion, its mane curling away from its head.

Léo's honeyed voice filled her ear. "A gift from a friend on the outside. The lion symbolizing courage, strength, valor, and royalty."

The craftsmanship of the gold was exquisite. It carried the burden of someone distinguished. "You're someone important?"

He smiled. "I suppose I am."

"And yet you long for Skye and your brothers?"

His soft brown eyes melted her with their warmth. "The bonds of brotherhood are something that I've never had. Except with one man—your new laird."

She released the chain and the pendant thumped against his broad chest. "But your brothers have entrusted your sister to you, to see her safely to Mull and to ensure a smooth betrothal."

"Potential betrothal. But aye, they do respect me now." He touched the gold disc. "Because of this."

"They haven't always?"

He laughed. "No. You see my mother was their father's—she was a..." His voice trailed off.

"Their stepmother?"

He chuckled and shook his head.

Knowledge dawned on her and she blushed. "Oh."

He nodded. "Yes. She accompanied my uncle when he met with the Scottish king and met our father at court. Da fell deeply in love with her and brought her to Skye. It was not long until I was born."

His brothers resented him, as her aunt and uncle had resented her once her father had passed away. Yet he had risen above their hatred of him and made something of himself just as she was trying to do now.

"I see."

Léo's eyes met hers, then he dropped his gaze and scooted away from her to a respectable distance. "I tell you these things because it has been a gift. Pádraig tells me that the clan has been slow to accept you."

"Yes. But I haven't given up."

He grinned and raised an eyebrow. "He told me that as well. He calls you unusual, you see their mistreatment of you not as a loss but an opportunity."

"I've asked God to help me, and I know He already has. I don't know that I'm unusual though. The rejection still hurts."

Léo shredded a blade of grass between his fingers. "I know it does."

"Your brothers?"

"Yes. And the laird."

She looked toward the cottage and the generous gift of furniture, the repair of their roof, and the provision of grain to keep hunger at bay. "But he seems such a generous man."

He sighed heavily and got to his feet. "I've said too much. I don't wish to spoil your perception of him before you've even met him."

"You've said as much now. You might as well unburden yourself."

Two lines cut into his right eyebrow and seemed to weigh if she could be trusted. "I've said the laird was the only brother I've ever known and it's true. For years we were inseparable, and then, he lost himself. To drink. To women. I had to watch the most noble person I know become the most reckless person I've ever met. And then, the day that I married Théa he showed up to the chapel drunk. He made a scene and embarrassed her. We argued and he disappeared without making amends. As if those seven years meant nothing."

He ran his hands through the sandy waves of his hair. "A few months ago I received letters from his brother and the king asking for my help. I was told he had changed and made something of himself, and they needed my help and..." He looked away.

"You wanted to help him."

His shoulders rose and fell as he drew in a deep breath. "Oui. I wanted to see for myself if it was true. He seems to have changed, but I still cannot forget the years of trying to take care of him. I want to make him pay for hurting Théa. I want to make him pay for what he put me through. All the taverns I carried him out of. All the fights he started. Trying to clean up his messes after things that he said, lies that he told, the hours of endless worry. So yesterday, I went too far, and I fear I repaid hurt for hurt."

"What did you do?"

"I was cruel to him. I reminded him of how dark he was in those days. I thought I wanted to see him hurt as he hurt me, but he was sick with grief. It was a window into remorse worse than I'd ever imagined."

She went back to her daisy chain. "You want to forgive him. That's why your conscience is burdened."

Léo looked at her aghast and shook his head. "I'm not ready to forgive him. I can't forget the past."

She knew the words he needed to hear but loathed to deliver them. "You must let go of what could have been and accept what is, and not hold it against him. It is something I needed to learn to survive."

He scoffed. "And just how am I supposed to do that when every time I look at him, I can only see his failures and the pain he caused?"

"Is that what the Lord sees when He looks at you?"

Pádraig, Margaret, and Ursula emerged from the cottage, Pádraig laden with jars of Ursula's honey. "I'm one man, you shouldnae give me all this. Even with Léo's help I'll never get through it all."

Ursula picked up Fluffy and put her on her shoulder. Léo squinted at the weasel before turning his face back toward her, astonished. She did not know if her words or the sight of the moth-eaten mink gave him more pause.

"Give it away to your friends then, and to the laird with our thanks," Margaret said. Her eyes traveled between Léo and Cara and seemed to divine that something had happened. "Is everything all right?"

Léo shook the fog away and nodded. "Yes. I've only been getting to know your daughter-in-law. She is, just as Pádraig says, most unusual."

Margaret threaded her arm through Cara's and smiled with great pride. "Lochbuie is starting to see what I've seen for ten years."

He gave a regal bow of his head toward Cara. "Indeed."

# CHAPTER 9

## DUART OIGHREACHD · JULY 29, 1383

T he emotion that Cara stirred in Hector's heart was enough to scare him into a newfound resolve to give a relationship with Elspeth a chance and he began to make the effort to sup there twice a week, lest he fail in his duty. Today was his eighth visit, and the relationship between them showed no signs of improvement.

Since he'd embarrassed Elspeth with his comprehension of her insults, she had exclusively conversed with him in French, testing his understanding and, he suspected, waiting for a mistake.

Tavish placed his eating knife beside his plate and closed his eyes. "These *fleurs frites* when paired with *brochet en doucette* remind me of many pleasant summer evenings." [1]

Elspeth's full lips came together in an inviting pillow of agreement. "Yes, I know exactly what you mean. It has such a light but heady flavor."

It was exactly the sort of tedium that Hector despised. Since his own thoughts on food began and ended at "this tastes good, that tastes bad," he'd invited Tavish along on his last four visits in an attempt to make up for his own lack of gentle upbringing.

Lachlan followed the exchange happening on his left and glowered at him. "Are you hoping that Elspeth will take an interest in Tavish?"

Hector shook his head. He wasn't that fortunate. "Isn't it better to bring someone along to engage her? Tavish is good at chivalric games. They have much in common." Like a love of disgusting French food.

Elspeth leaned back and laughed, placing her hand on Tavish's arm.

Lachlan was clearly mystified. "You spent seven years in France. You learned none of this while there?"

Much of his time in France he'd been lost in his cups or encamped with unwashed men. There was nothing worthy of revisiting. "I learned chevauchée. Do you think she would be interested in burning and pillaging...or?"

Lachlan made a face.

"All right, all right..." He gritted his teeth. "Elspeth?"

The two stopped chatting. She looked at Hector as if he were the most repulsive and unmannered creature in the room. "Oui?"

"Perhaps you could journey down with Lachlan and Mhairi tomorrow? I'll arrange a tour of Lochbuie. I'm sure your brother would like to see you, and I'm eager to show you the progress on Moy."

By eager, he meant obligated, for if it was up to him, he wouldn't waste one minute of time trying to appease an unappeasable woman. Yet, thoughts of loyalty to king and clan safety overrode all misgivings.

She pressed her lips together and pouted, affecting a face no doubt she felt was adorable. "All right," she agreed in Gaelic.

He waited for her to say more, but instead she turned back to Tavish and resumed their deep conversation about his experiences during his studies at Cambridge.

Rolling his eyes, Hector speared another fried squash flower. As he chewed the odd texture of fried blossom and tried to like it, his thoughts wandered once more to Cara and how easy his conversations with her had been. She put him at ease and drew him out of his natural state of seriousness like sunshine behind the clouds. Her words of prayer over him had stayed with him and helped him more than he could explain. There had been no further memories of battle, and he wondered if she was praying for him still. Beyond this, he found himself longing to see her.

Yet he knew that no good could come from pursuing more time

with her. His mission was to create a future with Elspeth. He swallowed the blossom and forced her away from his thoughts.

———

The next day, Elspeth arrived in Lochbuie with Lachlan and Mhairi, dressed like royalty in a heavy brocade gown. Tavish came forward with a large bouquet of white daisies and presented them to her with a bow.

"For you, my lady."

"How beautiful. You seem to know exactly how to make me feel welcome."

Tavish inclined his head toward Hector. "No' from me, from the Laird Hector, of course." They weren't, but he was grateful Tavish had tried to help.

Lachlan pushed him forward. "Get in there."

Grunting, he moved between them and turned Tavish by his shoulders. "How nice of you to greet our visitor. And how unfortunate that you have so much work to complete today."

Tavish looked befuddled for a few moments and then understood his meaning. He was not invited on today's tour. "Yes, Laird. The tithe books need reconciling. It's the end of the month. Léo is observing right after the tour."

Elspeth's face fell. "You won't be able to join me?"

Tavish took her hand and kissed it. "My apologies, my lady."

"Now I am disappointed," Elspeth said as Tavish disappeared inside the gatehouse.

"Well, what do you think?" Hector asked, motioning over the repaired keep. A sense of pride in the structure had begun to grow in him now that he could picture the result, and he hoped she would feel the same. The foundation improvements had been completed, the top two floors removed, and the framework of three new floors had risen from the stone corbels.

"It's wood?"

Hector motioned Léo forward, eager to find some sort of intermediary for what promised to be a wearying day ahead.

Léo tried to placate her. "It looks rough now. But I've studied the building plans and can assure you it will be a fine home, worthy of the chieftain and his lady."

Hector braced. If she thought he could construct an entirely new stone keep with room for guests and grand banquets in under four months, the woman was off with the faeries.

After a long pause, her soft blue eyes left the keep and met his. It was the first trace of warmth he'd found in them since she'd arrived on Mull. "At least it will all be new."

A bit of pressure eased from his shoulders. If she approved of Moy, they may have a chance after all. He stepped forward and offered his arm. "Come, I'll show you the village and then the stone circle for the midday meal."

The feeling of hope grew as he walked with her over what would become their clan territory. As he showed her each site, she greeted their people, then curtsied to him and paid him obeisance. Without uttering a word, she used her femininity and bearing to present him as their chieftain, someone worthy of their admiration.

"You needn't do that at every stop," he whispered into her ear after they left the tavern.

Thick, dark lashes lifted, and she purred into his ear, "Their eagerness to see their chieftain was palpable. As I pay you respect, they realize they should pay you respect."

Lochbuie had been under his chieftainship for four years, but he rarely showed himself as their leader in this way. Instead of drawing attention to himself, his preference was to concentrate on his clan. Yet as he walked through the village, the curious villagers cast glances his way, craning their necks for a better look, and shouting their well-wishes. Commotion began to break in rippling waves over the village as people came out from their crofts to see what was going on. Lachlan gave him a gloating look. Aye, he was beginning to see why the alliance with the MacKinnons and a marriage with Elspeth would be beneficial for his clan. The relief was immense.

As they approached the edge of a barley field, several men and women lined up to greet them. He guided Elspeth up to them and she made sure to find something personal to say to each man and woman.

The laborers were enchanted with her, and the children offered her additional daisies to add to the bouquet in her hand.

Pádraig stepped out from the line and pinched the corner of his bonnet. "Good day."

"Good day," Elspeth responded, offering her hand.

Pádraig raised his bushy gray eyebrows before realizing that he was supposed to kiss her hand. Giving a stilted peck to the back of her hand, he straightened and motioned to the line of people. "Harvest is right on schedule. Our yield will be the greatest our clan has ever reaped."

Elspeth nestled into Hector's side. "Laird MacLean has shown great forethought in using different techniques for cultivation. The other chiefs among the Kingdom of the Isles have taken notice of his great success." She dipped her head to him. "He has no equal. Nor do his people." Murmurs of pride rippled down the line of workers as this regal woman recognized their hard work and success. Elspeth placed her hand on his arm. "They think much of you."

Knowing she was feeding his pride but pleased by her words nonetheless, his chest stuck out a bit in his black leather cuirass.

A line of workers exited the granary and headed down the slope. His breath caught as he spotted the smallest lass among a sea of taller women. Head covered, eyes smiling, she spoke to a beefy woman beside her, a laugh tinkling from her berry lips. *Cara*.

As she approached the crowd, someone motioned the large woman over. "Come. It's the Laird MacLean and his new lady."

A smile lifted the upturned corners of Cara's mouth as she searched for the laird among the crowd, her face full of curiosity. Her eyes traveled the line of people from Duart and found Léo, and she waved—and then she saw Hector.

Every ounce of infatuation he felt for Elspeth leached from his body as he saw Cara's smile widen, then halt. Her eyes narrowed and studied the silver and amethyst thistle brooch at his shoulder, the mark of the chieftain. Before she could meet his eyes, she dipped her chin down to her chest and made herself small, falling in line with the others.

The closer they got, the more his heart swelled with anticipation of seeing her, and guilt knowing how he had misled her.

Cara dipped into a curtsy but did not lift her eyes. "My lady."

Elspeth chuckled. "I am not the lady yet."

Cara made no move to greet him, so Hector spoke the Irish blessing. "God to you, Cara."

Startled, Elspeth looked up at him, and he instantly regretted using her Christian name and the use of her language. Cara gave a slight nod, her slanted green eyes lifting to his before swiftly looking away.

Pressing her pink lips together, Cara swallowed. "God to you... Laird MacLean."

He noticed the expression on Elspeth's face and realized too late that Cara was vulnerable.

"An Èireannach." With one bitter word Elspeth had torn Cara down and relegated her to outsider status.

"Yes, my lady."

Gregor MacFadyen, always eager to instigate a disagreement, chimed in. "That's right, Laird, she isnae one of us. You have an outsider leeching off the clan. Harassed my son Donal at the barley field a few weeks ago." Hurt pricked Cara's eyes for a moment, but something impassive curtained her face.

The large-bosomed woman beside Cara shouted him down. "Stuff it, Gregor! Cara's good people. That was a misunderstanding."

Hector nodded to the woman. "And your name?"

"Name's Rhona, my Laird," she said, putting a meaty arm around Cara's thin shoulders. "And this lass is good people, I can vouch for that." Her endorsement clearly meant something to others in the field and some grumbled their agreement.

Mhairi stepped forward beside Elspeth, her face tight with concern. "Nice to meet you, Cara. What brings you to Mull?"

"Yes," said Elspeth, recovering her manners and not wishing to be outshone. "Please tell us."

Pádraig spoke up beside Léo, lifting his voice over the grumbling crowd. "Cara is widowed but journeyed here from Rathmullan to ensure that her mother-in-law is cared for since she now has no living children." Cara tucked her chin, cheeks blushing.

Mhairi touched Cara's hand. "My condolences."

Cara refused to look up. If only she would meet his gaze. "It's all right, my lady. God has taken care of me."

Léo cleared his throat twice, the two lines above his right eyebrow deepening. "You two know each other?"

Cara looked at Léo and shook her head, opening her mouth to respond but closed it again. There was an intimacy between she and Léo. Jealousy erupted in Hector's heart for moments before he stuffed it away.

Hector's voice came out gruffer than he intended, knowing what Léo and his brother must be thinking. "I've met her in passing twice."

At last, Cara looked to Hector in shock, and his conscience flamed. He'd helped her finish her work and seen her home. She'd kissed his cheek. Then in the throes of a vision she'd comforted him, and they'd prayed together. He was diminishing what had passed between them. Again, she dropped her eyes to her shoes.

Elspeth's face became disapproving. "So, you've been out in the laird's fields gleaning alms out of the hands of the MacLean and MacFadyen widows when you have family in Ireland?"

Hector had underestimated Elspeth. Her charm and influence could work with him as an asset, or if she chose, it threatened to work against him.

Cara shook her head. "Not alms—"

Hector dropped his voice beside Elspeth's ear. "Enough."

Elspeth paid him no heed. "Laird MacLean has been forced to take pity on you and allow you to stay when he has his own widows to care for? Why couldn't you stay with your own clan, Èireannach?"

Rhona stuck a finger in Elspeth's face. "Awa'n bile yer heid. She doesnae mean any harm. There's more than enough for everyone thanks tae the laird."

Gregor picked up a rock and bounced it in his palm. "More than enough for the MacFadyen and MacLean widows. Why should she be allowed tae steal their portion of food and work?"

A chant grew among the field workers. "Go home, Èireannach." The repeated slur affected Cara, and she stumbled back into line.

Léo took Elspeth by the arm and pulled her back from the crowd, a look of contempt in his expression. Lachlan's brow furrowed and he took hold of Mhairi, pushing her behind him, his hand on his sword.

Pádraig shouted over the now unruly crowd. "Enough, back to your duties."

The crowd thrust toward Cara, not heeding Pádraig's command, and Hector put his fingers in his mouth, whistling to try and gain their attention.

Gregor's voice carried over the growing mob. "Why should she be allowed tae take work from our people and disrespect our children? Havenae we sacrificed enough and known famine? Are our women supposed tae starve again for some outsider?"

The crowd shoved past Hector in an uncontrollable stream, moving in and surrounding Cara. Terror formed in her eyes as she was pushed and spit upon.

Hector raised his voice just as Gregor pitched the rock. "STOP—"

The heavy rock clipped Cara on the side of the face and she fell forward, stunned.

Gregor picked up a fist-sized stone, larger than the last. "Get her, lads."

Everything seemed to take on slow movement as Hector homed in, watching her roll to her back, hurt. Her fingers went to her forehead and came away thick with blood. A man delivered a kick to her ribs, another man a fist to her mouth and nose. The crowd swarmed over her.

The hairs on the back of Hector's neck rose. A voice, ancient and brave, called him into battle and spoke two words. *Protect her.*

The berserker, long hidden in the shadows, stepped into the light. Righteous anger roused him from his hibernation and beckoned him forward.

In five quick steps he penetrated the encircling crowd and threw himself on top of her, covering her small body with his own. Her mossy green eyes, hazy with pain, met his own as she coughed on the blood in her mouth and nose.

Rocks bounced off his back and kicks landed against his side and legs, trying to reach her. Steeling himself against the blows, their eyes locked together and he imprinted on everything she was, resolving that nothing would ever harm her again.

A voice screamed over the crowd. "Stop, it's the laird..."

He waited for the blows to subside, then pushed off her and

advanced on her assailants. Senses heightened, the smell of prey scented in his nostrils, his eyes dilated and blood surged into his veins.

The first man tried to scramble away. In one motion Hector's arms fired forward colliding with the man's chest and sending him backward. Drawing his leg back, Hector shot his foot into the top of the man's thigh with a crack, stealing his mobility and forcing him to the ground. Over and over, his foot repaid the man for his kicks to someone so precious, stomping until he was satisfied the man wouldn't get up again.

The second man swung his arm out in a foolish attempt to defend himself. Hector forced away the incoming swing, wrenching the man's arm behind him, locking the elbow and shoving him down by the neck. Hector's fist slammed into the man's face, punishing it with the same heavy blows he'd paid Cara until he flopped against the ground limp.

Panting against his fury, Hector prowled the thinning crowd hunting the object of his rage. Gregor ran for the edge of the clearing looking as if he were about to escape.

Picking up the rock pitched at Cara, Hector launched it into the soft back of Gregor's thigh. His arms flew out, the second rock he'd picked up still clenched in his fist. Screaming, he hit the ground in a heap.

Hector stalked over to him. Gregor shrieked as Hector's large hand closed around his scrawny neck, and he lifted him off the ground.

Hector's voice became a deadly growl. "Drop. The. Rock."

Gregor opened his fist and the rock landed upon the ground with a heavy, sickening thud. A new surge of conferred power stole away any fatigue he might have felt holding Gregor aloft, and he tightened his grip against the beast, determining the most torturous way to tear him apart.

Lachlan ran to his side and tried to pry his hand from Gregor's neck. "Let go, brother."

Not a chance. Gregor had harmed his woman. He'd spilled innocent blood and derived a thrill from frightening her—and now would learn the consequences for his evil. Gregor's hands came around Hector's and he gasped for air, feet straining for the ground six inches below.

Words snarled through Hector's clenched jaw. "You wanted her dead."

Lachlan pulled with all his might against Hector's grip, but it was no use. Something greater than his own strength was racing through his veins, avenging Cara. Gregor's face turned purple.

"Brother, let go—"

"If you have a problem with her presence in my clan, you can fight *me*. But animals like you would rather terrorize and dominate someone half your size." He tightened his fist and shook him. "Murderous coward. How does it feel to be dominated?" Gregor clawed wildly at the hand around his throat.

A small hand touched his steeled bicep. "Mercy, Hector. Let him go."

Rage roaring in his ears, Hector looked into Cara's beseeching face and weakened for but a moment. A dark trickle of blood ran from her head, soaking the plain linen that modestly covered her hair. Her cheek was unnaturally flat, her eye already swollen shut, blood tingeing her lips and nose.

Strength surged through his muscles with fresh potency, and he lifted Gregor up another six inches until the man's eyes were above his own.

He bellowed into his face, spittle hitting Gregor's purple cheeks. "Do you see what you've done to her? And she begs for your mercy when you showed her none."

Lachlan pleaded with him. "Listen to her, brother. You are a better man."

Longing to put down the threat, but yielding to her will, Hector roared and hurled Gregor to the ground, chest heaving with the force of unspent battle rage.

Pacing like an agitated monster he let the bloodlust and vengeance drain from his senses as he always did after battle. When his heart had settled, he returned to her side and cradled her jaw, cleaning the blood from her face with his handkerchief.

She held her cheek and struggled to speak. "I've caused so much trouble for you, Laird. I didn't mean for you to—I'm sorry. For everything."

Tucking her into his side, he guided her back to Gregor and placed his boot on his neck, holding him to the ground. "Dinnae forget that by her hand alone mercy has been given to you this day."

Gregor nodded and Hector kicked him away.

Remorse would not form in his gut; his soul could not turn from hers. He put a knuckle under her chin and lifted her downcast eyes to him. "You are no' to apologize. I will never let anyone harm you again."

Raising his voice, he bound his protection over her. "Clan MacLean of Lochbuie, you are witnesses that Cara is mine to defend. I number her among my household. I bind myself to her as her guardian and protector until the end of my days. If anyone breaches her peace or safety, it is an offense against the chieftain."

He strutted over and plucked Elspeth from Léo's grasp, pulling her on stumbling feet toward Cara. "Apologize to her."

Elspeth nodded with frantic understanding. "I apologize for my rudeness. Perhaps we could take you back to Duart for help?"

Mhairi rushed forward beside Elspeth. "Yes, please, let us make this horrible incident up to you in some small way."

Swallowing hard, Cara inched away from the women and turned to face him. With one hand cradling her cheek, she spoke with great effort. "I appreciate your defense of me and guarantee of safety. I don't wish to cause you any further embarrassment today." She nodded to Mhairi, shouldered her bag, and turned, walking toward the granary.

Léo called to her and jogged to catch up, Pádraig close behind. Mhairi took Elspeth's arm and led her back toward Moy.

Lachlan looked at Hector with disgust. "She called you Hector."

# CHAPTER 10

## LOCHBUIE OIGHREACHD - JULY 30, 1383

C ara stayed behind at the granary baling until evening fell, in
pain but unwilling to let the incident further add to her reputation. Rhona and Léo pleaded with her to receive treatment
for her face, but she refused. Margaret was already against letting her
continue working at the barley fields after her late-night return with the
man who, as it turned out, was Laird of Lochbuie, and she didn't know
how to face her.

After sundown, Pádraig put her in his cart and told her she was
going home. Head throbbing and unable to speak without agonizing
pain, she relented, resigning herself that there would be no mollifying
Margaret once she saw the hideous state of her face.

Pádraig's pony cart ambled up the lane toward the sheepcote, the
bright moon behind them creating a long shadow along the stony path
in front of them like a harbinger of doom. Margaret waited beside a fire,
lines of worry creasing her forehead. At the sound of the rattling
wooden cart, she looked up, and relief washed over her face.

"Cara, thank God. I was about to walk for the village to see if I
could find you."

Cara kept her face angled away toward the shadows as Pádraig helped her down, pain radiating in her abdomen where she'd been kicked.

Margaret rose and tucked her hands into her armpits. "Why are you home so late this time? Did Donal give you more trouble?"

Pádraig removed his bonnet. "I'm afraid there's been an incident."

Skirting around the edge of the fire, Cara moved toward the door. Ursula narrowed her eyes, then took Cara's face in her hands. "What on earth happened to you? Were you kicked by a horse?

Ursula's slender fingers were steady as they touched the bones underneath the swelling that had occurred on her temple, cheek, and eye. Pain burst through Cara's face setting fire to her skin, and she cried out. Margaret hurried over, shrieks emitting from beneath the hands covering her mouth.

Pádraig winced at the horror on Margaret's face. "No' Maggie, stay calm..."

Margaret's hands went to her throat. "You said she would be safe with you, what on earth's happened?"

"Remember Léo, the nice young lad who helped me bring furniture to you?"

"He hit her?"

Pádraig waved his hand. "No, no. Do you remember he's here with his sister to secure a betrothal with the laird?"

Margaret's face screwed up. "Aye. What does that have to do with Cara?" What did it have to do with her? The afternoon still seemed an unreal nightmare to her.

"Well... his sister showed up today and took a dislike to Cara for being foreign, and that caused a wee scuffle with some of the more disagreeable members of the clan."

Words trickled out of Margaret like a leaking dam that threatened to burst. "Wee...scuffle?"

Ursula probed Cara's cheek and pain erupted in throbbing aches through her skull and she cried out again, tears leaking out of her left eye. "It's her cheekbone. I think it must be broken. See how it's gone flat?"

Margaret was wild-eyed. "Pádraig MacLean, start explaining right no' or so help me I'll break *your* cheek."

Pádraig's hands went up. "Easy now, calm down."

Margaret was nose-to-nose with Pádraig, nearly as incensed as Hector had been that afternoon. "Dinnae tell me to be calm. There's nothing makes a woman madder'n being told to be calm. What did Elspeth do? Did she hit her?"

"No, she insulted her. Caused a nasty commotion among some of the villagers."

"Och. The MacKinnons," said Ursula with venom.

Pádraig put a hand on Margaret's shoulder and tried to steady her. "Gregor MacFadyen, Donal's father, started the scuffle. You remember how disagreeable he was."

Ursula nodded. "Och, Gregor. Looking to fight everyone for the smallest slight."

Margaret looked horrified. "He hit her?!"

"No. He threw a rock at her and got a gang of men to attack her."

"A rock...a gang?!"

Ursula touched the scabbed place on Cara's forehead and temple, blood oozing out. "Must have been some rock to break her cheek and open a wound this big on her forehead. Thank the blessed saints it didn't hit her in the skull. It could've killed her." Ursula touched Cara's scalp and fire licked at her hairline, releasing another gush of blood. "Dearie me. This is going to need stitches."

"Ki- kill?? Stitches?" Margaret turned on Pádraig again and started punching him in the arm. "You should have been protecting her!"

Pádraig made no move to stop her "Ow!"

"You said she was safe. You said no one minded her working there."

"Ow, Maggie. Most of them didn't."

"'No one' and 'most of them' are no' the same!"

Margaret took a deep breath, tears filling her eyes, as Ursula guided Cara through the front door of the sheepcote.

Pádraig rubbed his arm. "You should see the marks on Gregor."

Margaret's head snapped around. "Cara, you punched him?"

Cara cradled her cheek and tried to support it as she croaked out the word, "No."

Pádraig touched Margaret's shoulder. "It hurts her to talk, Maggie. Ask me the questions."

Margaret launched herself at him punching him over and over in the arm.

"Ow! I didn't mean for you to attack me again, you wee banshee!"

"You got her into this and now it's painful for her to talk to me!"

Pádraig took her firmly in his pudgy hands and looked into her eyes. "Och. Will you listen? The laird took care of her. Do you hear what I'm saying? He saved her life."

Margaret stilled and her mouth gaped open. "The laird?"

"He moved fast as lightning. Like something else was working through him. Laid himself bodily over her to protect her, put down her attackers in quick succession, and picked Gregor up and nearly choked him to death. If Cara hadn't stepped in, I'm sure the laird would have ended him then and there for what he did." Margaret and Ursula gaped at Cara.

She cradled her cheek. "Yes. The—laird saved me." *The laird.* Margaret and Ursula looked as stunned as she felt.

"Laird MacLean extended his protection over her. From now on, anything the clan does to her, they do to him. He has bound himself as her guardian."

Drawing up her strength, Cara offered further explanation. "He's the man who came to me in the fields and helped me. The man I saw on Laggan Sands. The man I told you about, Margaret."

Margaret's eyes widened. "Is that why he sent us furniture and provisions?"

Pádraig's cheeks went pink. "Aye. The day after he met Cara, he came to me before dawn and charged me to see every one of her needs, and yours, met."

Margaret collapsed into a chair, her hand covering her mouth. After a few moments she shook her head in astonishment and looked at Cara. "You didn't know he was *the laird*?"

She croaked, her tongue swollen where she'd bit into it. "Not an inkling."

Ursula laid her back on the table and began cleansing her wounds. "Hush now—he keeps himself to himself, and people respect that. Doesnae parade around as chieftain."

Pádraig leaned against the hearth. "If the clan didn't respect him before, they do now. I've heard some say Hector was a berserker in battle, but I always assumed they were making a cake out of a crumb. I've known him his whole life, but never seen a hint of it in him…until today."

Cara drew in a breath and supported her cheek with her hand. "I suppose I should have known…"

"Wheesht!" Ursula hissed. "I've gotten the bone stable, but you need to rest it, lass."

Fresh embarrassment washed over her. The kind man who occupied her thoughts and prayers was Laird of Lochbuie. When she followed Rhona to see the laird and his potential bride, she had never expected to see a familiar face. Her heart had given an unexpected flutter before clenching in humiliation. She'd shared secrets, talked of her faith, comforted, and prayed with the ruler of the clan. By the saints, she'd kissed him.

As she took her place in line, Léo's words dawned on her in a second wave of shock. He said the laird had been like a brother to him until he became a drunkard. A womanizing man. Hector said himself that he'd done terrible things. But his faith seemed so genuine. Was he really changed? Or did the omission of his identity speak to a secretive and sinful man?

Beyond all her questions, she was most befuddled by her heart's brokenness as she saw the beautiful woman tucked into his side. He could never be hers, and she, with her foreign blood and humble upbringing, would never be enough to be his. Tears burned at her bruised eye, and she wiped them away.

Ursula put a corrective hand over hers and laid it across her middle. "Stay still. This is the worst part."

Cara took a deep breath as the needle pinched through her ragged scalp, her legs beginning to shake. Margaret rose and clenched her trembling hand.

"It's all right, love. Look at me." A tear ran down her cheek and Margaret lovingly caught it with a finger. "What a day you've had. You didn't deserve any of this. Let us thank God that He has kept you from death, and now He has sent you a guardian. A guardian to finally protect my sweet girl and keep her safe."

Blinking tears away, her flesh came painfully together. Something fierce, but soft, had brimmed in Hector's eyes as he sheltered her body with his own, absorbing the blows meant for her. For the first time, someone had hunted those who'd hurt her, battling the demons surrounding her. In that moment, her heart bound itself to his.

Calum entered through the front door, not bothering to knock. "Evening."

Pádraig got to his feet and tried to push him back through the door. "What are you doing here? Can't you see the young woman is indisposed?"

"The laird sent me." Everyone looked at him as if he had sprouted wings and flown around the room like a faerie.

Pádraig released him. "The laird?"

"Aye. He's on his way here and he wanted to make sure you had fair warning. If you're no' up to seeing him, I can ride back and tell him to come some other time." At once horror and hope spread over Cara.

Ursula paused, her needle poised over Cara's forehead. "The laird is coming here. What an odd evening this is." She looked to Margaret and shook her head. "I'm no' sure it's a good idea. She's no' made much fuss, but she is in tremendous pain."

Margaret wrung her hands. "It's the chieftain of the clan. He gave her his protection and almost choked her attacker to death."

Ursula cut the string from the stitch. "Almost."

"Oh well, then we dinnae have to let him over?"

Ursula sighed. "I suppose he's go' to come."

Margaret helped her sit up and nodded to Calum. "Tell him to come along."

Ursula hurried to get fresh water. "She looks a state. We've go' to work fast."

Pádraig crossed his arms. "I think she looks good, all things considered."

Margaret shut her eyes; her tone strained. "Pádraig, would you kindly wait outside?" He nodded and followed Calum out the door.

Ursula freed Cara's hair from the soiled kerchief and tossed it in the rubbish.

Her heart caught in her throat. Her hair, she shouldn't. "No, I don't—"

Ursula raised her hand. "You are decent, Cara, and you're no' married to Duncan anymore. I'm sorry, but you're no'. You look like you wandered out of Bannockburn with it on. No' wheesht."

Margaret helped her into a fresh chemise and her best leine, the color of a peacock's breast. "I havenae worn this nigh on thirty-two years since I wed Hugh, but it's small enough to fit you." The wool was lightly woven and fit her like a glove. "You'll at least look equal to him in this. If a bit bruised."

Margaret had provided a fig leaf for her shame and restored some of her ruined dignity. Grateful for her love, Cara leaned into her loving touch as she ran a comb through the lengths of her hair and began to plait it.

Ursula dabbed a thin coat of honey and comfrey poultice on the stitches. "Let me tell you about the lad who saved you today. Under the auld laird every member of this wretched clan was starving, and everything we had went straight to the tithe house to keep hold of our land. In secret our spies sent word to the King of the Isles to try and gain his intervention, but no word came for many weeks. Then one day warriors painted black with mud began sneaking through the hills—the man leading them was Hector Reaganach MacLean."

Margaret bent down and secured the long plait with a pink ribbon and Ursula dabbed honey across Cara's battered lips.

"Laird MacLean climbed to the top of Moy castle and waited for the moment when Laird MacFadyen's guard was down. The man was outside eating an apple when Hector shot an arrow."

Her heart sank.

"I know what you're thinking, but he didn't kill the auld laird. The arrow went straight through the apple and pinned it to the ground, and the entire army came out of the fields. They surrounded the auld laird thumping on their shields and chanting the MacLean war cry... 'bas no beatha! Bas no beatha!'"

"Death or life," she murmured.

"OCH—Cara!"

She clamped her mouth shut.

"The auld MacFadyen laird was so frightened all he said was 'I take my leave,' and walked right out of Lochbuie, never to be seen again. Hector had taken over Lochbuie without a drop of blood spilled. That day he gave the credit to God. Right in front of us. He never took credit for himself. He's a good man, Laird MacLean."

Margaret took a seat next to her. "I beg you, daughter—dinnae let pride refuse him. I couldn't bear it if something happened to you."

A knock sounded at the door, and they jumped. Margaret took a deep breath, then rose and opened the door. Hector leaned down into the doorway, one hand on the hilt of his sword. Dressed in his finest attire he looked a ruling chieftain, but the scar on his cheek and hoarfrost eyes attested he was every inch a warrior. Margaret gulped.

"Are you Mistress MacFadyen?"

His voice bore the consonant tone of a military leader and Margaret shrank away to admit him. "Aye. Come in, Laird MacLean."

Hector stooped inside the door unable to stand to his full height under the low ceilings and drying flowers.

Ursula curtsied. "Good evening, Laird."

Hector crouched beside Cara, his eyes traveling over her bruised face, and he held out a wilted bouquet of buttercups. "They werenae so droopy-looking earlier."

Ursula poured water into a cup and took them from him. "They'll perk up by morning."

He rubbed a hand on the back of his neck. "I suppose it's sort of stupid considering you have fields of flowers just outside your door."

"Ah, but no buttercups," Ursula winked. "She cannae talk. Too painful, and the bone needs to be rested."

Hector sat down beside Cara, and the smell of mint overcame the metallic smell of blood that had followed her all day. Studying her face, his eyes bore a look she had never witnessed in Duncan's. They pulled her in as if he were happy to see her. His voice was sweet and low. "You look verra beautiful."

Embarrassed by his words and undivided attention, she looked away and motioned to the side of her face, trying to brush off his compliment.

"The wound is dreadful, aye." A large hand with bruised knuckles gestured to her gown and braid. "But you are lovely."

Margaret sank into the chair opposite them, put a hand over her heart and gave a barely audible, "Oh."

A calloused hand extended toward her face. "May I?"

Heart pounding, she dipped her chin in approval. The back of his finger brushed over her purple cheek then tilted her swollen face toward the fire. His thick, dark brows came together, and his nostrils flared. "I could wring the coward's neck."

"As could I!" Margaret burst.

Hector startled, then nodded in agreement. "I almost did."

"I wish you had."

Fluffy crawled into Ursula's lap and she stroked her weaselly head with two fingers. "I think what my sister means is thank you." Hector's eyes narrowed at the weasel, but he said nothing.

Margaret's hand came over her heart again. "Aye, Laird. There are no words to thank you for taking care of my Cara. She's all I've got."

Hector shifted on the bench, his black cuirass making a flatulent sound. He blushed. "It's the leather."

Pain throbbed in her temple as she smiled at his awkwardness. In quiet moments his manner was so unlike his appearance. There was nothing monstrous or legendary—he was flesh and blood.

"Is it just bruising?"

Ursula shook her head. "No, I'm afraid the cheek's broken, but the bone is stable. I've repositioned the cheekbone so it will no' heal flat if she can stop smiling."

Self-consciousness heated her cheeks, but he winked at her. Tilting her head down he examined the stitches at her scalp. The muscle in his jaw began to tick and he clenched his fist. "I want to assure you that this will never happen again. Under my protection no one may lay a hand on you. I am here to protect you, and to provide anything you need. You're a weaver."

An odd comment to make. Cara nodded.

"You mentioned you left your loom behind when you left Rathmullan?"

He remembered her parting words the night they met and what town she came from. Cara nodded again.

"I sent a courier to Rathmullan weeks ago and have wondered if there would be an appropriate time to give this to you. And I needed to be the one to give it to you." He opened the door and brought in a trunk. Da's trunk. She dropped to the floor dumbfounded, disbelieving what lay at her feet.

Margaret knelt beside her. "By the saints."

Cara's hands traveled over the familiar battered wood and crackled leather, then opened the lid. A lingering smell of pungent mordant tickled her nose. There, disassembled, but as safe and sound as it had always been, was her father's loom. A shaky circle with a clover representing his name emblazoned the smooth wood. Racked with tears that radiated pain through her face she ran her fingers over the wobbly, imperfect mark. It wasn't possible. Hector had done this for her. Why?

"I'm told the woman parted with it quite willingly for a hefty price. Is it right?"

Unable to contain her joy she jumped into his arms, drawing him close and resting her unharmed cheek in his neck. He stiffened before holding her to him, imparting his strength and something indefinably good.

He placed her back down. Cara wiped the tears from her cheek. "I'm sorry," she mumbled.

"Please, for the love of the saints, stop talking." Ursula sniffed through her tears. The room erupted in a round of laughter.

Hector wiped the tracks of Cara's tears with his large thumbs. "I should have given it to you when it arrived weeks ago, but I didnae know how to tell you I was laird. I tho' if you had your loom, you may find a way to make a life for yourself here in Lochbuie that would please everyone. Tell me all the weaving supplies you need, and I will gather them for you on Iona." There was nothing else she needed. He'd restored everything to her.

A small knock tapped against the door and Hector opened it. Ursula scrambled to her feet, dumping Fluffy to the floor, and dropped into a hasty curtsy. Margaret and Cara did the same, for the young blond woman bore the coronet marking her as daughter of the king.

"This is Lady Mhairi, my brother's wife. She insisted on staying behind this evening to see you."

Lady Mhairi stepped forward. "I wanted to see for myself that you

were all right. I am horrified by what happened this afternoon. It is certainly no' the kind of example we want our clan to set. Please promise that you'll visit me on Duart soon. I would be proud to know you."
Cara nodded.

Hector's hand rested on the hilt of his sword again. "We'll leave you in peace now."

Heart swollen with admiration, Cara grasped Hector's hand, trying and failing to convey with one eye the height of her gratitude for what he had given her.

Margaret held her gaze as she turned back toward her beloved loom, and she was certain the woman who knew her best was at that moment guessing the secret hidden away in her heart that she herself dared not acknowledge. The longing for one too high above her. Deep devotion for a man that she'd never dare love.

# CHAPTER 11

## LOCHBUIE OIGHREACHD - AUGUST 5, 1383

Returning to Moy after a week's long spiritual retreat on Iona, Hector felt no sense of peace. The bìrlinn sailed through the choppy waves, clouds threatening downpour. As the shore came into view, he saw Pàdraig leaning against a pole of the galley slip, head resting in his hand. A feeling of foreboding clamped around his gut.

Pàdraig's eyebrows shot up. "By the saints, you look like you've been awake for a week straight."

"I have been." Hector smoothed his thumb and forefinger over his puffy eyes, tossed a rope to a guard on the dock, then stepped out of the bìrlinn. "How is she?"

Pàdraig put his hands together behind his back as he followed him toward Moy. "Getting better. The swelling has gone down, but the bruising looks worse. Ursula says she'll be restored with another week or so of rest."

Climbing the hill toward the barmkin walls, fatigue overcame Hector. Though he'd not seen Cara in the six days that had elapsed since her attack, she'd haunted the corridors of his mind day and night. "I'll go and see her at first light."

"Well, that's why I've met you on the dock, Hec. I've come to tell you there's a planned a supper ceilidh at the village tavern. You're to be the guest of honor. Rhona's planned it."

Desire for the comfort of a bed and dark room overcame him. "Tonight?"

"Aye. Most of the clan will be there. Cara has agreed to come but insisted Gregor and the other two men be invited."

Hackles up, Hector stopped in his tracks. "Why would she do that?"

Pádraig shrugged. "She wants to make peace."

There'd be no getting out of it now. He didn't think Gregor, or the others, would be foolish enough to physically harm her again, but he couldn't allow any further disrespect.

The resolve he managed to find on Iona to entrust Cara's guardianship to Pádraig melted away like frost in the sun. Pádraig could look after her, but only he could keep her safe. His hand rested on the psalter belted to him, certain that God did indeed have a sense of humor.

Pádraig ran a hand over his sagging jowls. "What's the matter? It's no' only that you're tired."

Filling his lungs with a weary breath he looked around for any who might overhear. "It's the entire betrothal. I dinnae want to go through with it seeing how foul Elspeth acted."

"I cannae say I blame you."

He rubbed his tired face in his hands. "I cannae marry someone who would instigate harm on those she dislikes at the expense of my authority and clan peace."

"You should talk to your brother about the match."

"We argued after the attack. Lachlan agrees that Elspeth acted wickedly but feels the greater threat to the clan is the Wolf. And I'm loathed to admit it but he's right."

Pádraig pushed a pebble across the path with the toe of his shoe. "A lifetime is a verra long time to be wed to someone you dinnae respect. Your mother, God rest her soul, wouldnae want you to follow in her footsteps." The memory of his mother's constant sadness married to a man she didn't love remained fresh in his mind, and again Cara intruded into his thoughts.

Hector looked around at the men and women who hurried past, wary looks in their eyes. "There's something else, too."

"What?"

He dropped his voice. "Lachlan heard Cara use my Christian name at the barley fields, and I hers. She put her hand on my arm and stilled my anger."

"Aye, it was the only thing that got through to you."

"He thinks I've slid back into my old ways and had a dalliance with her."

Pádraig huffed. "Maggie would never allow such a thing."

Hector groaned as he watched the miller freeze in his tracks, then hurry the other direction away from him. "My past has tainted Cara. After five years of rebuilding my life with extreme discipline I've undone it in five minutes. Not just with Lachlan, but in front of the whole clan. The man I used to be is still here beneath the surface, and he's as savage as ever."

"Do you regret saving her?"

"No. No' at all. I felt the Lord urge me to protect her. He imbued me with the same battle instincts I had before, but this time it felt different. I wasn't fighting for myself, for coin... I was fighting because I felt devotion to her. Like I was fighting for Him. I cannae shake it."

Pádraig's lips came together in a line, and he shook his head. "I've never seen anything like it before. If God was working through you, it explains why you seemed to have the strength of ten men. But there was something more than that." He dropped his voice to a near whisper. "Do you care for her, Hec?"

He'd been asking himself the same question all week and knew the answer. The outline of the psalter he'd brought back with him from Iona pressed into his side, his soul opposing his reason.

"I suppose I feel protective of her. I dinnae ken much about her. Except that she seems a good woman." An honest answer, but not a full answer.

"Aye. She is. Léo and I have spent every night outside her house for the past week, making sure that there'd be no further incidents from the clan."

Resentment pierced his foggy mood. "Léo?"

"Yes, he's made friends with all three of them. Cara hasnae been able to talk for most of the week, but yesterday they spent much time in conversation. He...what's the matter?"

Hector frowned. "What?"

"You're glowering at me."

"Am no'."

"You are. Scowling daggers at me."

Finding himself in a sudden state of temper, Hector scrubbed his hands over his face and turned toward Moy. "I just need a lie down. I'm tired, that's all."

Stupid betrothal. Stupid Léo. Stupid him for running to Iona instead of facing his fears. Strength draining, he made for his bed.

"Are you coming tonight?"

Hector stopped. He should hand all responsibility for Cara to Léo and Pádraig. He should travel to Duart and finish his courtship with Elspeth. He should marry and be done, feelings be hanged. Yet his soul demanded he take up vigilant watch over Cara.

Pádraig continued to prod. "She wants to see you. Prepared something special for you. I think she'd be crushed if you werenae there."

Exhausted, he relented. "Come and wake me an hour beforehand so I can bathe."

Returning from battling the Wolf, Hector rode back into the gates of Moy. Dismounting, he ran forward, and Cara rushed into his arms. The pink bow of her soft lips came to his own, his hands twined in the silken waves of her conker-colored hair. Between them he felt the roundness of her belly, ripe with his child...

Heart pounding, his eyes shot open. Complete darkness all around him, it took several seconds to realize where he was. Breath heaving, he brought a hand to his chest and swallowed, trying to wet his dry throat.

A knock sounded at his door. "Laird? It's Pádraig. You wanted me to wake you."

He rubbed a heavy hand over his face. "Yes. Thank you. I'm awake."

The same dream had woken him up for the past six nights, and he was beginning to believe he was going mad. It couldn't be a dream from

God; it had to be the product of his own attraction to a pretty, young widow.

Shaking off vestiges of sleep, he made his way to the half-completed first floor and took a cold bath, the frigid water acting as a remedy to his desire to return to his bed and sleep until morning.

Alert as he toweled water from his face, he began to pray for deliverance from the season of torment he found himself in. God knew that the last thing he wanted was to return to the man he used to be, acting selfishly, and letting down everyone he cared about. He'd slipped at the barley field and let himself go berserk, but he'd laid down his sword on the altar. He wasn't a warrior anymore. Was he?

He could do this. He could treat her as... a sister. Guard her as a sister. Aye. That was it. His spirits rose to the highest point in weeks as he pulled on his boots and tightened his baldric around his shoulder. It would salvage the betrothal, save the clan, and Cara, all at the same time.

Elation flooded him as he walked with Pádraig toward the tavern. He knew that if he prayed hard enough, God would deliver him.

As he entered, he gave a cheerful greeting to his clan. "God be with you all."

He couldn't hear the response of the packed tavern.

In the space of one moment his elation singed, the charred cinders floating to the floor. At the back of the tavern Léo stood holding Cara's hand. Covetousness erupted in his chest, and he stormed across the room. Léo had put his hands on his woman, and he too would pay the price.

Cara's face, bruised in yellow and brown, radiated happiness. She dipped into a curtsy. "My laird. How nice to see you."

Léo, still holding Cara's hand, narrowed his eyes. "Is everything all right?"

Breath came in bursts through his nose.

Margaret stepped forward. "Would you like to dance the ceilidh with me, Laird? We've just begun to select partners."[1]

*Ceilidh dancing.* Flute music began and two other couples lined up beside him and Léo.

"I—I dinnae ken the steps."

Margaret took his hand and patted it. "That's all right. It's simple enough. Follow my lead."

The distinctive quavering of an Irish tune persisted, and he had no choice but to follow Margaret's lead. In time with the music, Hector bounced from one foot to another, came toward a smiling Cara, then back again.

With barely contained laughter, Léo looked at his giant, prancing figure and said in French, "You look like a hopping bear."

"Shut up," he responded through a forced smile.

As the music trilled, Margaret pushed him to his left and they changed positions with the couple next to them. Hopping a few more times, they headed back to their original position. Léo, the smug rogue, was light on his feet and outshining him with little effort.

On beat, Cara waved Hector forward and he obeyed. Her wrists crossed and took his hands. Four times she led him in a circle, the copper sunset of her hair swaying behind her. On the fourth turn she released his hands and returned to Léo's side.

Margaret raised her hand to form an archway. He lifted his own arm, the difference in height pulling Margaret off her feet and she slammed against his side. He put her down, his face red. "Sorry...I'm so sorry."

Cara laughed as she passed through their lopsided arch, her hand again in Léo's. The dance repeated over again, the couples having switched sides.

*How long is this dance?* Sweat erupted at his temples and he cursed his size for not allowing him to bow out with grace. He hunkered over and squeezed through the arch of Cara and Léo's raised arms with a laughing Margaret.

The tune grew more furious, and the dancers now picked up their pace. Cara looked at Hector with mischief in her eyes and waved him forward, and again she led him in a circle. The clan crowded around them and began to clap in time with the music and cheer him on.

Emboldened by their appreciation, and wanting to overshadow Léo's natural skill, on the second turn he raised Cara to his side and spun her the last two revolutions before putting her on her feet. The crowd applauded as the music came to an end. He bowed to Cara and Léo.

Margaret touched his shoulder. "Well done, my laird."

"I'm no' as fine a dancer as Léo here. All that time at French court has made him a show-off."

Léo shrugged. "We all have to be gifted at something."

Aye. The memory of Léo's words from a few days earlier caused his smile to fall. *He has a gift for killing.*

Cara released Leo's hand and moved toward a table. Like a moth following light, Hector followed her across the room and stood behind her as she drank deeply from a cup.

"You're a wonderful dancer." The phrase came out in a growling voice, and she startled the same way she had on the night they'd met. For once he wished he might have Léo's gift for social graces instead of his own gift for sinister threats.

She gave a slight quiver and water trickled down her chin. Mopping it with the corner of her sleeve, she recovered herself. "I haven't danced the ceilidh since I was a small girl. I'm surprised I remembered how. I hope I didn't make a fool out of myself."

"No one even noticed you with a doolally giant skipping about."

She snorted into her cup and pinched her nose to stop from choking. He handed her a napkin and she laughed into it. "Ye eejit."

He couldn't stop smiling, so he forced himself to look at the greasy table until he recovered. "How are you feeling?"

She lifted a shoulder to her ear. "Improved. It took some convincing to get Ursula to allow me to come."

"Where is Ursula?"

"Home. She doesn't enjoy crowds or gatherings. How was Iona?"

A memory of the dream, his unrest, and his pleas to God came to mind. He had no peace apart from her the past six days, but here in her presence, he felt stillness. Realizing he'd not answered in several moments he gave a flat answer. "Fine."

She raised her eyebrows and licked her smiling lips. "I have something for you."

From the seat of the chair, she raised two rolled parcels, tied with a ribbon. She handed one to him. He pulled the ribbon, and tartan plaid the same color of the Hebridean sea unfurled in his hands.[2]

"Did you make this?"

"Aye."

The smooth, soft tartan plaid was lightweight yet sturdy in his hands. Subdued but distinctive, with fine threads of crimson and saffron crisscrossing throughout. "It's the finest I've ever had."

Color crept attractively up her cheeks and across her freckled nose. "Tis only a two over two twill. It's common."

He unfastened the brooch at his shoulder and doffed his patched black brat. "Help me don it."

White teeth cut into her healing bottom lip as she draped the plaid over his shoulders and secured it, her eyes studying the amethyst at the center of his chieftain's brooch. She stepped back, something changed in her expression. "As I imagined. Not far from the shade of your eyes."

She'd imagined his eyes? "Thank you for thinking of me, I love it."

Behind him, the door to the tavern banged, and he noticed her tremble. He turned and saw Gregor MacFadyen. Instinctively, his hand found hers behind him.

"It's all right, Laird."

Releasing his hand, she stepped around him and made her way across the tavern. Hector drew himself up to full height and stayed just behind her. Gregor paled, frozen to his spot in front of the door.

Cara extended her hand. Gregor looked astounded but grasped it. She made a deep curtsy and remained crouched in front of Gregor as if she were groveling.

"I thank you for coming. I wish to extend an apology. I am an honored guest; I shouldn't have taken anything from any of your clan, regardless of my intentions. I also apologize for Donal. I said things to him, in frustration with myself, that I shouldn't have. Can you forgive me?" Gregor looked staggered. Why was Cara apologizing to the man who attacked her?

Across the room, Margaret crossed her arms with barely contained rage. Gregor looked around the room at the clan members and swallowed, taking in each scowling face. Léo appeared beside Hector, one hand on his estoc, his eyes dark with fury.

Gregor helped Cara to her feet. "It's I that should be apologizing." He wondered if the man meant it or if he were only trying to save his miserable hide from scorn.

Cara shook her head. "I hope that we can live in peace now. Our laird has obtained my loom from Ireland, and I promise I'll no longer take any work away from the clan."

Gregor looked at Hector and Léo, towering above Cara and glaring at him. "Aye. Peace."

Léo stepped forward. "Where are the other two men?"

"They wouldnae come."

Cara brought forth the other ribbon-wrapped parcel she'd tucked under her arm. "With my compliments for your wife."

Gregor took the parcel, his face wary as though she played a trick. "What is it?"

"Four bandles of Irish linen for a gown."[3]

Gregor's hands touched the fine weave and vivid saffron color. "Why?"

Cara smiled. "'Tis worth a month's wage and is the last of my flax thread. Someone worthy should have it. I prayed about it, and she came to mind."

"I-I... thank you."

She extended an Irish blessing. "May you have goodness."

Stepping alongside Cara, Hector held out his hand. Gregor took it and they shook. Unwilling to let the matter drop completely, he didn't release his grip. "Please send the other two men to Moy tomorrow morning so I may understand why they declined her invitation." Gregor nodded and he dropped his hand, departing swift as a fox through the door.

Rhona wrapped a thick arm around Cara's waist. "You're a strange bird, but a kind one. I'd sooner have given that man a good smack."

"I only want peace. Our Lord says if one demands your cloak give him your tunic also." Rhona, Léo, and Hector looked at each other utterly put to shame by her pure heart.

---

Ceilidh dancing, songs, and storytelling continued for the rest of the evening. Each person present went out of their way to speak to Cara, and a few commissioned cloth from her. After the last course had been finished Léo sat down at the table with Pádraig and him. "I've wanted to talk to you about Elspeth."

Pádraig took his flagon of ale and winked at Margaret. "I'll make myself scarce. There's one I've been wanting to talk to all evening."

Hector chuckled. "I bet you have, you auld bampot. She's half the size of Morág and twice as pretty." Pádraig tossed his napkin in Hector's face and made for Margaret. He chuckled again and turned to Léo. "What did you want to speak about?"

Léo sipped his ale. "I wanted to see if you still wished to continue with the betrothal negotiations. After what she did, I wasn't sure."

Hector watched Cara dancing across the tavern with Murdoch, tossing her head back and laughing. He would never feel for Elspeth what he did for her, yet he hesitated to end negotiations. Lachlan had asked for nothing the entire time they had been brothers—he'd given him a home and support at the lowest time of his life. How could he let him down? If he could deny himself, his family, his clan, and the Isles would be safe.

"Yes. I feel they should continue. It's an important alliance."

Leo's eyes moved over Cara as she spun in Murdoch's arms. "I've talked to Elspeth and admonished her in the strongest terms. What she did was unconscionable. I believe she is contrite. She wishes to come here and apologize to Cara."

He felt a bit of assurance that perhaps he was making the right decision. "She should."

Léo's voice held warning. "But I must ask, in Elspeth's best interests —I know you well and I think you care for Cara. Am I wrong?"

This was the time to say she was like a sister. "I do care. But Cara is..." The word would not come out. "Cara is... as a... sister to me."

A look of relief came over Léo's face. "I'm comforted by that. Not only for the betrothal but because I would like to pay court to her." The lie Hector told turned bitter in his throat. Léo *was* interested in Cara. Envy settled in his gut.

Léo studied him. "You would need to approve of the courtship as her guardian." Léo, another person who had gone out of his way to help him and look past his faults time and time again. Another person he'd let down and hurt. Would his past never remain behind him?

"I leave it to Margaret to approve. I will consent if she does."

"Thank you, Hec." Léo beamed and Hector was filled with grief.

"No trouble."

Hector needed to be alone, and away from the ale and whisky that poured into every glass around him. Away from the happy smile Cara wore for Léo as he took her in his arms to dance. He got to his feet and made for the door.

Outside on the tavern porch, rain came down in sheets and water moved in a rapid stream through the streets forming a muddy morass. His hand touched the psalter belted at his side. *Lord, what have I done?*

Forcing himself to endure, he moved to pull his brat over his head, and found in its place the sturdy light blue plaid. The plaid she made to match his eyes.

# CHAPTER 12

## LOCHBUIE OIGHREACHD - AUGUST 7, 1383

She hadn't meant to take the brat. At the end of the dance with Murdoch, when Cara spied Hector leaving through the tavern door, her heart fell. All evening, he'd engaged in patient conversation with every clan member who'd sought his attention over supper. She found herself too shy to approach him again, despite wanting to spend the evening in his company.

The dark brat discarded on the back of a chair provided her an excuse. She'd made her excuses to Léo, grabbed it, and dashed after Hector hoping she may have the private word of thanks she'd been yearning for.

On the tavern porch she spotted him, trudging through the torrential rain back toward the keep, the new plaid pulled over his head. She called out to him, but her voice was lost in the tumultuous storm, and he did not turn.

Out of necessity, she'd cloaked herself and Margaret in the stiff wool later that evening as Pádraig drove them home to protect them from the driving rain. And now out of longing, in the deserted sheepcote, she pulled it around her shoulders, the heavy weight robing her with a sense of belonging, as if she were wearing his colors.

Running her hands over the coarse brat and its thick seams, she felt him in the dense material and the jagged slash that he'd carefully patched back together with a line of even stitches. Affection filled her breast as she brought it to her nose and breathed him in, leather and mint, sunshine and strength.

A knock sounded at the door, and she jumped up. "One moment."

Bolting across the sheepcote she tossed Hector's brat over her bed and rushed back to the front door.

"Léo." Disappointment filled her, though she could not quite articulate why. "Margaret and Ursula have gone into the village—" Her voice strangled in her throat. Elspeth stood just outside the door, emanating beauty. Cara shrank in her presence, feeling as foreign and inadequate as ever. She dipped into a shallow curtsy. "My lady."

Elspeth stepped forward and lowered her thick lashes. "I've come here today to offer a proper apology to you. I confess, I saw warmth between you and Hector, and I was jealous. I said careless, hurtful things, and I..." her voice broke, and she put her hand over her plump lips. "When the man threw the rock at you, I was terrified. I knew it was all my fault."

Wind whipped Cara's hair and she tucked it behind her ear while Elspeth remained flawless. "Why would you ever be jealous of me, my lady? I'm of no standing to be a threat to you."

Elspeth's eyes dropped to her own. "I-I'm in love with Hector. We're to be married. He remembered you amongst all others there, and... I resented you."

They were in love. The peculiar intimacy Cara shared with Hector ebbed away from her like tide returning to the sea. She was a fool to think of their meetings as anything more than the actions of a kind man. Her deceitful heart latched on to his kindness, so different from Duncan's cruelty. Praying her face did not betray her, she looked toward the sea, wishing she could be alone. "I see."

"Please say that you forgive me."

Jealousy wanted to hold a grudge. Elspeth would enjoy marriage with a man who would never lay a hand on her in anger. Sons would quickly follow their wedding. The thought sobered her. Elspeth was to be Hector's bride for a reason, and she was nobody for a reason. God put each in their place and time with careful intention. Cara met Léo's soft brown eyes, and her own words came back to her memory. She must forgive.

"I thank you for coming here today to make things right. I do forgive you." She meant it. Forgiveness was required as the Lord forgave, whether Elspeth merited it or not.

Elspeth looped her arm through Cara's. "Will you walk with us down to the beach so I can get to know you better?"

Apprehension filled her chest. "We've only an hour before sunset."

Léo headed for the beach. "We must hurry, then."

Following him along the winding path beside the coastline, she wondered if anyone ever bothered to disagree with a pair so good looking. A spot of rejection may do both a bit of good. Still, she found herself going along with them, swept up in their confidence.

Elspeth pulled her down the path. "You must be very close to your mother-in-law to travel so far away. What village are you from in Ireland?"

"Buncrana, originally. Rathmullan after my marriage."

Elspeth appeared uninterested, even though she'd asked the question. "I've never heard of it. What was your husband's name?"

A frustrated sigh stifled in her chest, and she tried to buoy her crushed heart. She didn't feel like revealing herself to one so careless. Yet, in the spirit of peace she cracked open the locks on her heart. "Duncan MacSweeney."

"You loved him a great deal?"

Cara swallowed and picked up her skirt as they stepped onto the shifting sand of the beach, thinking fast about how to answer without seeming like a monster. She'd tried. She forced a noncommittal smile.

"Did he love you?"

*No.* "In the beginning he cared."

The beach was crowded with families seeking relief from the unusual heat that lingered this evening. A refreshing breeze from the sea swept over them. They shed their shoes on the shore and let the icy water pass over their feet, and Cara was careful to keep her skirt lowered over her left calf, not wishing to explain the old wound to Elspeth.

"I'm going in," Léo said dropping his tunic on the beach revealing a tan, chiseled chest. Cara turned away feeling embarrassed.

Elspeth's laughter carried like a songbird over the sea loch. "Are you mad? This water is freezing."

He waved her off and dove into the water, shrieking with shock as the cold hit him.

Cara chuckled despite her gloom. "Eejit. He'll be frozen through in two minutes."

Elspeth cocked her head toward her and lifted one exquisite eyebrow. "Léo likes you. I can tell."

Shock hit her as if she had dived into the freezing water behind Léo. "I think you are mistaken."

Elspeth shook her head. "No. The way he looks at you, not to mention his anger with me." She shielded her eyes against the sinking sun and watched him swim through the surf. "He cares for you."

It couldn't be true. Could it? All week he had found ways to talk with her, or to help her around the house. He'd helped her assemble the loom and watched her meticulously calculate, balance, and hang each string for the plaid and linen. On Wednesday he brought her a clarsach harp after learning from Margaret that she played. He sat with her as she played the next two evenings. Yet, Pádraig had been there. "He's been good company."

Elspeth pulled her down onto the sand beside Léo's discarded tunic. "Tell me, is it too soon after your husband has passed to think about moving on?"

Thoughts of Hector filled her heart. "Yes, it probably is." Warm setting sun caressed her face, and she closed her eyes, pointing her face into the soothing heat.

"Things were not good between you and your husband." The sudden change in conversation back to Duncan was not welcome, but again she pushed down her misgivings. If she were ever to feel more than Duncan's possession, perhaps she should talk about it.

"It became difficult over the years. We were married ten years before he died. The last two were hardest."

Elspeth's giggles caused her to crack an eye open and follow the source of her laughter. Léo floated on his back over the waves, his arms extended over his head as if the freezing cold water was bliss. "That is his

Islander. He has the sensibility and emotion of his French mother, but his love of the water, that is my father."

Léo floated along the shoreline as if he were sleeping, perfectly at peace with the sea.

"It was because you don't have children." All peace fell away as if she had been hit with a second rock. This time, no one came to avenge the blow. Elspeth's eyes pierced her. "The reason your husband did not love you. You could not have children."

She was perceptive. Unbidden tears that even the heavy rock hadn't wrought stung her eyes, and she looked away into the wind. She tried to laugh but instead made a hollow and bitter sound. "He could, but I couldn't."

Elspeth took her hand. "How difficult."

"He was about to leave me for my friend Eve. She was with child."

"His child?"

"Yes."

Elspeth scooted closer to her and wrapped an arm around her shoulders. "Let's not think of it now. It's time for a new beginning."

Her thoughts returned to Hector. Even if he was of no importance and wanted her, she couldn't give him children and he would need heirs —even more so as chieftain. The most fundamental difference between the wife he needed and the wife she would be.

Smarting hurt lingered in her heart for the children she couldn't bear and the husband who hated her for it, and she wiped her tears and took a steadying breath. "You better warn your brother off me."

"Ah, but he already has a son in Calais. His wife died in childbirth. I assure you, your ability to bear children wouldn't matter to him. Can't you see I'm trying to put in a good word for him? I know he cares for you, and he wishes to protect you. Give him a chance."

---

After sunset they returned to the sheepcote. Léo lingered at the door. "In a few days I'm going to take Elspeth to Loch Spelve with a few others from Duart. Would you like to accompany me?" His honey brown eyes melted hers and he took her hand. Her heart squeezed, wishing it was Hector. Why did she feel this way?

The corner of his mouth lifted into a smile. "Please?"

"All right."

"*Bon*. Good. Very good." He lifted her hand and kissed it. "I will be back to see you tomorrow night."

She nodded. "Goodnight."

He bid her goodbye and jogged back down the lane toward Elspeth. Taking a disappointed breath, she pushed the door open and found Margaret and Ursula supping at the table.

Ursula dabbed her mouth with her cloth. "Where've you been?"

"With Elspeth and Léo MacKinnon."

Margaret's mouth made a tight line. "What did she want?"

"She came to apologize and then we got to know each other. Léo has invited me to go to Loch Spelve with them in a few days."

Ursula raised an eyebrow. "And you said?"

"Yes." Cara sat down on her bed and ran her hands over the itchy black wool of Hector's brat. She felt deflated, as if wind had left her sails.

Ursula spread butter over her bread. "What about the laird?"

"What about him?"

"It seemed as though you might have..."

Cara unlaced her shoes. "He's to be married to Elspeth. Elspeth is in love with him. She says that is why she acted the way she did at the barley field. She was jealous. I don't know why."

Margaret gave a weak smile. "I do."

Cara tossed a shoe to the corner, inwardly cursing herself for feeling the way she did. It was wrong to feel this way about a man who was to be married. Margaret was across the room in seconds and caught her hands.

"How do you feel about the laird?"

"How I feel doesn't matter."

"Aye, it does. It's the only thing that matters to me."

Cara felt sick. She wished to unburden herself, but she feared that her feelings betrayed Margaret. "I don't know how I feel. I wouldn't call it love, but I think of him all the time. I don't wish to hurt you, Margaret, but that is the truth."

"Why would that hurt me?"

"Because of Duncan. Because he has only been gone a few months. Because he is your son, and we are family."

Margaret tilted her head and patted her hand. "My dear, I do love Duncan, but Duncan is gone. You're here. I want to see that you are cared for and happy. Especially after all you've endured. I saw something between you and the laird the night he brought you the loom. Deny it all you want, but I believe he cares for you, and you care for him. I had that once, thirty years ago with... someone."

"Hugh?"

Margaret shook her head. "Nay. Pádraig. I was besotted with him."

"Oh, Margaret."

"Aye, tis true. He's rather round-looking now, but Pádraig used to be as handsome as they come. So, you see, I ken what it is to feel such longing."

A dull ache began in her temple, and she didn't know if it was the injury or her mixed-up feelings that bothered her so. "Elspeth loves Hector. I can't do to her what Eve did to me. She acted poorly but I don't think she intended for me to be hurt."

Margaret's jaw tightened. "I still dinnae like her for it, sorry to say."

"There's nothing to be done. I can't give Hector children, and as chieftain he must have sons. Léo seems interested in me, and he already has a son. He's handsome and kind. I should feel something for him."

Margaret gave her a sympathetic look. "Aye. He's asked to court you, and I've given him a conditional agreement."

"What are your conditions?"

"He must respect that you will make your decisions. He must no' force you to do anything you dinnae want. If you say no to something, he must accept it. And, if he wishes to marry you, he must no' move you away forever."

Cara wrapped her arms around her and let Margaret hold her close to her heart. "I could never."

# CHAPTER 13

## DUART OIGHREACHD - AUGUST 15, 1383

P uffy white clouds floated against a clear blue sky over Loch Spelve. There had been many fair days this year, unusual for Mull, but good for the incoming harvest. Hector looked out over the wild water of the inlet and took a thankful pause that was swiftly interrupted by the sound of complaint.

"That is foul."

Teeth gritted, he removed the tail and head from the salmon and tried to keep his voice pleasant. "Would you prefer to eat it with its head on?"

Elspeth made a sound of disgust. "Of course not."

Using great care, he ran the knife up the belly of the salmon and removed the innards and bloodline and tossed them back into the loch.

"Och, that is revolting."

Ignoring her, he put his knife aside, opened the fish, and pulled the backbone out. "How did you think smoked salmon was prepared?"

"I thought you would get cleaned salmon from Duart."

Mhairi laughed. "What's the fun of spending the afternoon on Loch Spelve if it werenae fresh caught?" Elspeth grimaced and sat down on a log.

Lachlan shot him a look and ponassed[1] another salmon. Enjoying fish caught that morning was their idea of fun, but to Elspeth it was somewhere just above having your eyes plucked out.

"There's Léo, thank God." Elspeth got to her feet and hurried over to the approaching pony cart.

Lachlan wiped his hands on a cloth. "I didnae realize Léo was coming. Who's that with him?"

Hector looked up, his heart coming to a crashing halt. "Cara. The lass from the barley fields."

"Isnae she a bit below his station?"

Hector scowled. "What's the matter with her? She's as good as anyone else for Léo."

Lachlan nodded. "That's true, he's illegitimate." What was that supposed to mean? He wasn't sure whether to feel more offended for Cara or Léo. Without noticing his offense, Lachlan walked off toward the pony cart after Elspeth.

With a mighty whack, he removed the next fish head feeling gloomy and irritated. When he gave his consent to allow Léo to court Cara he did not realize that it would be right in front of him.

Mhairi looked from the fish to Hector. "Are you all right?"

Annoyed, he tossed innards over his shoulder and ripped the backbone out. "I'm braw."

"It's true, then? What Lachlan believes?" Backbone dangled from his frozen fist. Mhairi's clear blue eyes skewered him, and she lowered her voice. "No' that you've had a dalliance. But you're taken with her?"

His voice strangled in his throat, and he groaned, knowing Mhairi could see through lies. "Aye."

Léo helped Cara out of the pony cart. A stray lock of her shiny hair caught the wind, and he brushed it tenderly out of her eyes. They spoke to one another, and Cara smiled as he led her toward the fire.

Mhairi looked at Léo's hand at the small of Cara's back and then to Hector's angry expression. "Hec..."

Returning to gutting fish, he took the head off a salmon with a loud whack. "Let's no' talk about it."

Mhairi greeted Cara and kissed her on the cheek. "So nice of you to join us today."

"Thank you."

Cara looked around as if she did not know what to do with herself, then wandered over to him and curtsied. "Greetings, Laird MacLean." He nodded and kept gutting, not looking up. He must conquer this. She rolled up her sleeves. "I love smoked salmon." Without asking, she took Lachlan's knife, removed the head and tail off a fish, then gutted it quicker than he had.

He spluttered. "You dinnae have to—"

In three quick motions she removed the backbone. "Nonsense. I want to help." Her slender fingers worked sticks through the flesh with speed and she laid it aside. Without flinching she scooped the guts into her hands, tossed it into the lake, and picked up the last salmon by the gills.

Elspeth gaped. "How do you stand touching that?"

Cara laughed then cleared her throat, training her face back into seriousness. "'Tis simple—I like eating." Spoken like one who had not known a day of entitlement her whole life.

Hector worked a piece of wood through a filet and lifted his eyes to hers. "Thank you."

Lachlan took the prepared fish, driving them into the base of the fire. "I suppose our women are more used to others doing the labor for them."

He opened his mouth to respond but Léo beat him to it. "Cara won't need to do it much longer."

A becoming shade of berry crept across Cara's cheeks and the freckled bridge of her nose. "That's true, Margaret has always said she can filet more efficiently than I." Léo winked at her.

An overwhelming urge to put his fist through Léo's perfectly straight teeth came over him, and he turned toward the loch to rinse his hands. Stupid Léo. Stupid betrothal. He plunged his hands into the frigid water scrubbing until his skin was red, then got to his feet, colliding with Cara. He caught her arm and righted her.

"Sorry."

"It's all right, I've got to rinse my hands."

She crouched and leaned over the rock and dipped her hands into the quick-moving tide. His hands encircled her narrow waist, preventing her from falling in. Wind whipped her scarlet hair, and it tickled his nose with downy softness. When she finished rubbing water over her hands and forearms, he lifted her to her feet. In his hands, she weighed nothing at all.

Smiling like a daftie, he was drawn into her light. He stood silent while the corners of her shell-pink lips lifted in amusement. She winked one beautiful eye at him, then rolled down her sleeves and walked back to the group. It was then he noticed Elspeth looking at her, and then him, a look of annoyance on her face.

Lachlan rubbed his hands together in excitement. "We've loads of time to kill before the salmon will be ready. Shall we have a few rounds of shooting?"

Elspeth's eyes remained on him, but her voice betrayed no ill-temper. "Yes, let's. What do you say, Cara?"

Cara raised an eyebrow. "I say I will be an observer."

"Have you never practiced shooting? I thought even the lowest classes could shoot."

Cara's upturned mouth pulled down on one side. "I'm afraid I have never had occasion to shoot. My father took care of our hunting, and then my husband."

Léo sat down beside her on the log. "That's all right, I don't have a bow here. I'll keep you company."

A competitive feeling curled around Hector and squeezed. "I've got an extra bow."

Léo looked a bit disappointed. "Oh?"

"Unless you think you cannae handle the draw weight."

What was he saying? He should be stuffing his competitiveness away, not strutting like a red stag in rut.

Léo stood and drew up to his full height, still four inches below him. "I think I can manage."

Aggression and brutishness overcame him. Woe betide any rival who wandered into his path. "Are you sure you're auld enough to handle something so powerful?"

Léo's chin came up. "You can handle it, as decrepit as you are."

Mhairi clapped her hands together and walked between them, giving Hector a sideways look. "Excellent. I've got two bows we can share, ladies."

Ready to engage in the spar and wallowing in his own superiority, he followed Léo and Lachlan to a jutting hill, suitable as a bow butts.[2]

Lachlan lined up his shot with a slender board propped at the center as the makeshift target, drew, and released the arrow. It sank into the board, just missing center. "Look at that. While you two argue about who's best, remember no' to discount the auldest man here."

Léo stepped up next and Hector handed him his lighter weight bow. "Let's hope you have improved since Chiset."

Léo lined up his shot and released. The arrow zipped through the air and landed to the right of Lachlan's, but still missed the center.

Cara applauded. "Well done."

Léo's chest puffed out and he stepped aside. "I saw you hit a man at two-hundred-seventy-five yards at Bergerac; twenty-five yards is nothing to you. Why don't you show us how it's done?"

The running Englishman, the glint of his armor and the arrow sinking into his groin. Aye, he remembered Bergerac. All pride leached from his body. "That was nine years ago."

Elspeth laid her hand over his leather bracer and lifted her eyes to him. "Please show me what you can do." Not soothed, but knowing he should be trying to court her, he relented and walked another one hundred yards away in the clearing. Shedding his shoes, he sank his feet into the gravelly earth and steadied himself. A gust of wind lifted one of his plaits and he waited. After two minutes his plait rested on his shoulder. Now.

*Full draw, angle.* Three fingers relaxed from the corner of his mouth, the string cracking back into place, his left arm bracing the release. The arrow slit through the air, sinking forcefully into the center of the board just as another gust of wind swept over the field.

Lachlan whooped, and Mhairi cheered, but Cara only smiled as she sat down beside Léo in the grass and rested her head on his shoulder. Feeling more foolish than ever, Hector walked back toward the group. Cara was to be a sister to him. Not a mate.

Elspeth approached and pulled him toward her, a warm look in her eyes. He would let her kiss him. This was his future wife. Her voice purred beside his ear, and he tried to enjoy it. "Impressive. I like being courted by a cateran." Her lips lifted toward his wounded cheek, but she flinched and kissed the air beside it.

Feeling repulsive, Hector watched Mhairi and then Elspeth take their shots. Mhairi's shot went just right of the board by a foot, but Elspeth was a markswoman. She took her time, measured the wind, aimed, and her arrow sank beside his own—closer than Lachlan or Léo.

Lachlan patted her on the shoulder. "If you ever tire of being Lady of Lochbuie I will take you into my guard."

Elspeth held out the bow. "Cara, it's your turn."

Cara laughed. "No, thank you. Do carry on."

Elspeth crossed her arms in a mock pout. "Don't make me beg. I'll show you what to do."

A dazzling smile masked a brief look of apprehension. "Oh, all right —but don't be countin' on me to walk clear across the field and sink an arrow."

Elspeth positioned herself beside Cara and fixed her stance, then showed her how to hold the bow in her left hand and nock the arrow with her right. The arrow pivoted away from the string. Cara squirmed. "It feels very awkward." Finding three errors in her stance, he opened his mouth to correct her but shut it again. Léo should be the one to assist.

"Now draw." Arms shaking, Cara drew. "And release." The arrow sputtered off the bow and sank into the earth several yards shy of the target.

Cara handed the bow back to Elspeth. "I knew I'd be rubbish. Thank you for showing me." Léo should come forward and help, but he remained stupidly smiling in the grass.

Hector couldn't stop himself. "Just a second."

Cara stopped and looked at him.

"Let me see if I can help."

Cara shook her head. "I think I'm done."

Ignoring her, he came forward and took the bow from Elspeth. "One more shot and you can be done."

Cara looked to Léo and then back to him. "I don't know."

Mhairi waived her forward. "Hec is the one who taught me. He's a wonderful tutor."

He handed the bow back to Cara and she woodenly accepted it. "Should I move closer to the target?"

"You'll hit it from here. Trust me."

Verdant green eyes pierced his before looking away. He stepped behind her, cleared his throat, put his hands on her shoulders, and lowered his mouth close to her ear so only she could hear him. "First off. What do you feel?"

"Emm..."

"Do you feel the wind?"

The corners of her supple lips twitched. "Aye."

"Wait until the gusts have died down because it will give your arrow drift. Second," he pulled her shoulders back and put his hands on the curve of her hips, "keep your back flat. You're arching your lower back without realizing it. And then," he pulled her hips back toward him and angled them away from the target, "your hips, torso, and chest face forward." He placed one hand on either side of her head and turned it toward the target. "Only your head will look to the left." Releasing her, he stepped back. Good. "Now, nock the arrow like Elspeth showed you."

Hands shaking slightly, she did as he commanded.

He returned to her side and dropped his voice lower. "Dinnae be intimidated. Pretend it's just you before the target." His fingers came around hers and he adjusted her grip on the arrow. "Hold the arrow like this."

Her fingers trembled. "Is this right?"

"Aye, that's right. Now the wind has stopped. When you draw make sure you use your back. That's right. Good. Lift your arm up near your ear and hold."

She didn't move or shake. "Now relax all three fingers."

The arrow shot forth in a straight line and sank a few inches above Elspeth's.

Lachlan clapped his hands. "No' bad for the second time you've shot an arrow. I may have to employ all three of you as archers."

"I think I'll stick with weaving, but thank you, Chief MacLean."

---

Following the afternoon of shooting, they gathered around the fire and tucked into the smoked salmon and delicacies that arrived from Duart, along with a robust ale from the cellars. Hector watched as Léo talked with Cara, hanging on her every word, and laughing at her stories. Dark clouds formed above them, matching the defeat in his chest. His throat ached for a taste of the ale, longing to drink away the pain growing in his heart.

Elspeth settled beside him on the log. "I see that we are equals when it comes to warfare."

Feeling tense, he succumbed to her obvious beauty. Unholy desire filled him for the first time in five years. His eyes traveled over the ale in her cup, the claret color of her lips, and the low neckline of her leine. "The fact that you think we are equal illustrates how little you know about my past."

Her voice was full of morbid interest. "I want to know."

He took the cup from her hands and swirled the familiar brown refreshment. "I can assure you, you dinnae." Thirst for the bitter and satisfying liquid parched his tongue, and he longed for the warm release of drink.

Elspeth's voice purred. "We're the same, you and I." She caught his look and laughed. "Maybe not on the outside, but beneath, we're just alike."

Yeast and grain filled his nostrils as he brought the cup to his nose and inhaled, saliva coating his tongue and his honest thoughts spilling over his lips. "I very much doubt that, woman. Though I'm willing to have a peek."

She leaned forward, her lips not far from his own, begging to be kissed. "We're never cornered. Never afraid. We know what needs to be done and we do it. Imagine what territory we could rule together. You could have all of Mull if you wanted it." The rim of the cup touched his lips.

Movement caught in the corner of his eye. Cara stared at him, her face full of dismay. He lowered the cup and poured it on the ground. "I was always afraid."

Elspeth blinked. "Pardon?"

He dropped the cup into the dirt. "In battle. I was always afraid."

Elspeth followed his eyes and caught sight of Cara staring at him. "Shall we go rinse the fish off us?"

Expression hard, Cara remained fixed to Léo's side. "I don't mind it."

How much had she seen? Remorse filled him.

Elspeth rose and pulled Cara to standing. "Come with me, we'll get Mhairi to go with us."

It was the closest he had ever been to going back on his word to the Lord. Disgusted with himself, he rose and made his way toward Lachlan. "I must go. I have a long ride back to Lochbuie ahead of me."

"All right. Do you want to take some of this salmon with you?"

"No, I just want to get back."

Léo licked his fingers and considered the clouds which had formed overhead. "It looks like it will rain. I ought to get Cara and follow you back."

"No!" The word came out more forcefully than he intended. "I dinnae want to spoil your day. Please, stay." He couldn't bear to ride back with them knowing that Cara had seen him at his lowest moment in five years.

A scream rent the air. Lachlan's face paled recognizing the sound. "Mhairi."

Another scream pierced through the clearing and Lachlan sprinted through the woods, he and Léo close behind. As they burst upon the loch, they saw Mhairi, unharmed, standing on a rock, Elspeth and Cara nowhere to be seen.

Lachlan caught her face in his large palms. "What's happened, are you hale?"

She pointed toward the surf. "Elspeth fell. Cara went into the loch."

Outpacing Léo, Hector bolted toward the rocks and launched himself into the surf, a memory of Aileen's head disappearing under the water driving him on. *Please God, not again.*

The wind drove waves over his head, and he looked around, spotting a flash of white. Swimming toward it, his heart slammed against his chest. Behind him, Léo plunged into the water. Cold seared every muscle in his body as he paddled and kicked against the steady current, drawing him out to sea. The muddy red of hair and pale arms came into view as Cara leaned back, floating Elspeth's limp body out of the surf.

Blood trickled from Elspeth's nose, swollen to twice its normal size. He wrapped an arm around her and took her from Cara. "Are you hale?"

She nodded and tread against the waves crashing over their heads and pulling them out toward the sea. "Take her to shore, I'll be right behind you." He had only a moment to think before Léo swam up and held out a hand for Cara.

Her voice was pleading. "Swim to shore, don't come closer. I can swim it."

Diving under the water, she resurfaced a few moments later closer to shore. Relief filled him. She was a strong swimmer.

Léo wrapped an arm around Elspeth's torso. "I'll paddle with you; it will be easier to get her to shore."

Nodding, he adjusted his grip around her chin and pulled Elspeth behind him. Together, they arrived at the rocks just behind Cara. Lachlan leaned down and wrapped his arms around Elspeth and lifted her from the water. Gripping the slippery rocks, Hector climbed after them.

Léo pulled himself from the loch and tilted Elspeth on her side and cleared her airways, then blew into her mouth. For long, terrible moments he thrummed her chest, whacked her back, and blew.

Mhairi dissolved into tears and buried her face into Lachlan's chest.

Léo shouted at Hector. "Work her arms!"

Hector grabbed hold of her cold, limp arms and began to work them up and down. Again, Léo breathed into her mouth. Finally, she spluttered and coughed up foam.

Mhairi helped her to sit up and pushed hair from her forehead. "Thank God."

It was then that he noticed that Cara was not on shore. Terror seized him and he shouted her name. Everyone on the bank looked around in panic before a small voice answered from the rocks below.

"I'm here, I'm hale."

Looking over the side of the mossy rock he found her, still bobbing in the water, lips turning blue. "Is s-she well?"

"Aye, she's alert. Here, take my hand."

Violently shaking, she motioned him off. "S-send Mhairi over here. I've shed my clothes on the shore." Resting in a heap by the waterside lay her moss green leine and chemise.

"You jumped in?"

She nodded, head trembling. He called to Mhairi, and she was at his side in seconds, chemise and leine in hand.

"Mhairi won't be able to pull you up, but I'll keep my eyes shut and she'll cover you as soon as you're out."

Cara nodded again. He noticed an angry, red swipe at the top of her breast before he forced himself to look away. She was hurt.

Mhairi hollered to Lachlan and Léo to face the tree line. Hector dried his hands in Cara's leine, then leaned his arm down toward her, squeezing his eyes shut. A freezing hand gripped his wrist, and he locked his hand around hers, heaving her onto shore. As light as thistledown, she flew into his arms, shivering. Keeping his eyes squeezed shut, he handed her to Mhairi.

"All right, she's clothed."

Fury and frustration poured out of him, and he gripped Cara by the arms, drawing her up to her toes. "What on earth were you thinking jumping in the water? Why? Why did you do that?"

Terror formed in her eyes, and she covered her face with her arms. Stunned, he set her back on her feet and let go.

Mhairi wrapped her arms around her and rubbed her back, trying to impart warmth while she castigated him. "Elspeth tripped and went right toward her, but Cara stepped out of the way and Elspeth went into the loch. Do you realize she jumped in to save her, you mad bampot? She wasnae going on a wild swim."

"I only meant she should have waited for us and no' jumped in herself."

"If she hadnae, Elspeth would've drowned. Her face collided with a rock, and she went under. Cara shed her leine and dove in after her before I had time to scream."

"I know but I—she could've—" His stomach turned.

Lachlan stood beside him. "He's thinking of Aileen."

Mhairi closed her mouth and said no more.

Léo interrupted, covering Elspeth with his plaid. "We need to get her back to Duart to warm up."

Lachlan nodded. "Yes, everyone come to Duart for the night."

Cara shook her head. "Margaret will be wondering where I am."

Léo rubbed a hand over his soaked hair. "I don't think I should leave Elspeth."

There was but one solution. Hector inclined his head toward his horse. "Take Ghoustie and follow Lachlan's cart back to Duart. I'll drive Cara back to Lochbuie in Pádraig's cart."

Léo blew out a sigh of relief. "Thank you."

Wind picked up and chilled his wet skin and sodden clothing. He motioned to Cara, but she would not look at him. "Let's go."

Eyes on her bare feet, she followed him to the pony cart without speaking, then ignored his offered hand and hoisted herself up.

Pausing beside the driver's seat he wrung the water from the bottom of his tunic. He climbed into the seat beside her and she handed him his old black brat. "You left it at the tavern, and I meant to give it back to you today."

He took it and draped the stiff, dry wool over his shoulders. "Thank you."

The end of the jagged swipe peeked out from the top of her gown. He motioned to it. "It looks like you got a nasty scratch."

Her eyes widened and she pulled her gown up. "No. 'Tis an old wound. From the cauldron accident."

# CHAPTER 14

## LOCHBUIE OIGHREACHD - AUGUST 16, 1383

He wasn't the man she thought he was. The thought darkened Cara's mind as she worked the picking stick, beat down the yarn, and changed foot pedals. The loom's chugging provided a strange sense of needed privacy. Amid the clattering, Margaret could not press her with questions as she had last night when she had burst into the sheepcote damp and distraught.

The two-hour ride back to Laggan had passed in total silence. Hector didn't try to engage her, nor she him. Heartbreak grew and grew with each passing mile, and when the cart finally rolled to a stop in front of the sheepcote, she ran inside, not bothering to bid him goodnight.

Margaret had pressed about her undone state, but Cara assured her she was well but didn't wish to speak. At that, Margaret held her and smoothed her hair until she fell asleep.

The thought of Hector beneath the ash trees, leaning into Elspeth, eyes dark with desire, and taking her cup of ale had broken any hold he had on her heart. She paused and adjusted the weft, squinting back tears that threatened to form. What a fool she'd been.

And then another memory. His face only inches from her own, the anger in his cold blue eyes. He'd been about to hit her. She was sure of it.

Never again. She would die alone before she would cower and lose her self-respect.

A knock sounded at the door and Ursula got up from her chair and answered it. "My laird."

The picking stick slipped from her fingers and dangled from its string. Pretending not to hear, she grasped the stick again and set the loom to clattering. Pull, beat down, change pedals. Pull, beat down, change pedals. Pull, beat down, change pedals. *Please God, send him away.*

Margaret called her name, but she continued to pretend not to hear. Pull, beat down, change pedals. Pull, beat down, change pedals. Margaret called her name again. Not wishing to be rude to her mother-in-law, she stopped, still gripping the loom.

"Yes?"

Margaret gestured toward the door. "The laird is here to see you."

Cara tried to communicate with her eyes that she did not wish to see him. One of Margaret's eyes twitched as she tried to work out the message.

"Cara." The deep rumble of his voice affected her against her will.

"Aye?"

"I've come to see if you would accompany me to Iona."

The island where Duncan had planned to discard her at a nunnery. He couldn't have picked a place she wished to see less. She didn't bother to turn. "No, thank you."

She pulled the picking stick and the shuttle swept across the loom.

Margaret stilled her hands, and Cara looked up into her gray eyes. "I think this can wait until tomorrow. Our *chieftain* wishes to take you for a day of spiritual retreat."

Cara narrowed her eyes and gave an almost imperceptible shake of her head. She would rather eat a toad.

Margaret turned her by the shoulders until she faced him. "Yes, that's a good lass."

Hector's hulking figure stooped between two beams. He held out something to her. "This is for you."

She did not budge. Margaret put a firm hand between her shoulders and shoved her forward. "How nice."

Cara lurched forward and accepted the gift. A small book. She opened the cover and saw sloping handwriting next to a beautifully illuminated page with rigid letters. A stag drank from a stream, gold painted over its antlers; a doe lay beside it and rested her head in the shadow of the stag. Embarrassment washed over her. "I'm sorry, I can't accept it."

She held the book out, and his face fell. "Why?"

Wiping her sweating palm on her apron she tried to quell her humiliation. "I cannot read."

Ursula shuffled her feet and stroked Fluffy's snoring body wrapped around her shoulders. "You could look at the pictures." Her embarrassment grew.

"It's a psalter. I've made it out to you. So, I'm afraid this belongs to you."[1] He put the book firmly in her hand.

She opened the cover and looked at the loops and swirls of his handwriting. "What does it say?"

He came closer and read the inscription in the language of the church. Would that he have written something in Irish, then perhaps she would have understood.

He looked at her expectantly. "It's Latin."

She gritted her teeth. Did he think her stupid? "Yes. I know it's Latin."

Margaret took the book from her hands. "I'll keep it safe for you. Now run along. I'll see you this evening." Again, a hand came between her shoulder blades and pushed her toward the door and out into the garden. Hector followed along and stopped beside her on the path.

Ursula waved and began shutting the door before she could protest. "Have a safe journey." The door banged shut. Irritation crept up her spine and she crossed her arms. Would no one help her?

Hector licked his lips and smiled. "You look lovely."

She looked down at her drab russet-colored work gown. It was shapeless and comfortable but lovely it was not. *Liar.*

Seeing that she was in no more of a mood to talk than the night before, he cleared his throat. "Shall we?"

They set sail from the dock at Laggan toward the mouth of Lochbuie in a small skiff. The tailwind caught the sails and carried them with speed along the Ross of Mull. The fresh sea air worked over her frazzled feelings. A coastal Irishwoman through and through, she inhaled the salt and spray and could not help but thank God for the gift of the sea.

"I like your hair like that." Her eyes came open and her hand went to the disheveled knot and the stick that held it in place. A strand fell out along her cheek, and she tucked it back in.

"I just twist it out of my face when I work. It's no fashion." His eyes crinkled with something, and she felt embarrassed again. "I would've worn something nicer if I knew I was going somewhere today. I feel undone." Another strand of her stubborn hair pulled free from the knot and floated in the wind.

"I like you undone." His eyes grew intense. She realized he meant it. Disarmed, she didn't know what to say. "I didnae drink yesterday. I know you havenae said anything, but I—I want you to know."

She shouldn't believe anything he said. "It's true then? You were a drunk?"

Hardness came over his face. "Aye."

"And had a fondness for women?"

His expression became forbidding. "Aye."

Spray spattered over her cheek, and she wiped it away. What more did she need to know? "What I saw yesterday was a private moment between you and Elspeth. You are to be married; you needn't explain."

Muscled forearms rippled as he steadied the sail against a gust of wind. "You saw a weak moment. I let her beauty affect me. It's no excuse, but I suppose I wanted to feel less alone. And we arenae betrothed."

Alone? Her heart softened ever so much, and she looked in the direction of Ireland, remembering. "I was eighteen when Duncan MacSweeney came to Buncrana. He was the most handsome man I'd ever seen. I allowed him to talk me into meeting him at the edge of my village. I wanted to feel less alone. I wanted to be kissed."

He steadied the boat as it came around the peninsula and into the Sound of Iona. "Did you get your kiss?"

"He hand-fasted himself to me in marriage. I agreed without knowing..." She stopped and cleared her throat, not wishing to relive that day and the terrible memories that began only thirty minutes following their hand-fast. "It doesn't matter. I did get my kiss, though it wasn't what I thought it would be."

Hector secured the sheets. "Where did you learn to swim?"

"My father, Eamon. He loved to swim and sail. Lough Swilly was right outside our door. He'd take me out fishing every Saturday if the weather was fair."

"That explains your skill with a fish blade."

"If it was sunny and warm enough, he'd challenge me to a swimming race. I've been swimming through surf since I could toddle."

He adjusted the sail, slowing them as they approached Iona. "Cara. I'm sorry. For yelling at you, for lifting you up. I was..."

His voice trailed away. Her insides knotted and she wondered whether she could trust him. How many times had Duncan apologized and forgotten his promise never to hurt her again? How long had it been until he made no more promises?

"I couldnae stand the tho' of something happening to you."

"Because you're my guardian?"

Something passed over his expression. "Aye."

For a few moments they stared at each other, and she got the distinct impression it wasn't because he was her guardian. A new chasm of trepidation opened before her. They couldn't feel these things, but she longed to give herself over to it, just for an afternoon. To revel in the warmth in her heart for him and be glad. To pretend he was hers, only for a few hours. Except...she couldn't.

Duncan had taken so many things from her she wasn't sure what she was made of. But she knew what she wasn't made of, and she wasn't a whole woman able to give Hector children. Léo, at least, she could not disappoint with this fact. Even if she didn't feel the same about him, she could learn to. Couldn't she?

The boat glided toward the dock and Hector jumped out, secured it, and helped her onto the shore. His large hand took hers, his thumb brushing over the back of her hand. The small sign of affection filled her heart with a sense of impending doom. They couldn't...but oh how she wanted to.

The isle was vibrant and green like Ireland, and she could not help but feel cheerful despite her resolution not to enjoy the afternoon. A jutting green hill cut across the horizon and rolled to a slope beside the largest stone abbey she had ever seen.

Memories of Buncrana and afternoons with her father filled her heart. "It's beautiful."

He offered her his arm and she took it. "Aye. It's my favorite place in the Isles."

A seal popped its speckled gray head out of the water and looked at them as they walked along the dock before diving back into the beryl sea. Skylark song trilled above them, and black oystercatchers ran along the shoreline and between the rocks in small bands.

Stalls stretched at the end of the long dock and resembled a fair she'd once seen back home. As far as the eye could see, people sold goods along the road to the abbey. Fleeces, leather, nuts, vegetables, furniture, wines, furs, and flax. Cara paused in front of the large white bundles of stalks.

Hector waved the merchant over. "Where is this grown?"

"Grown in Buncrana."

The sound of a voice that sounded like hers made her insides leap. "*Cad as duit?*"[2]

"*Is as Bun Cranncha dom.*"

Light poured through her heart, and she spoke freely in her own dialect. "I am from Buncrana."

The man's face mimicked the lightness of her own, probably because he felt he was about to make a sale. "Who owns you?"

"Eamon O'Ballevan was my father."

"Ah. That's why you'll be needing flax. Eamon did much business with me for his linen."

It had been years since she spoke to anyone who remembered him. "That's right. We're weavers."

The merchant stuck out a beefy hand. "You must be Cara. Name's Cian O'Donnell. I'm a cousin of your Uncle Diarmaid."

At the sound of Diarmaid's name her heart sank. "How nice."

He crossed his arms. "'Tis Eamon I was friends with. Used to talk about ye all the time, how smart ye were and how quick ye could figure his numbers for him."

A hot ball of emotion settled in her throat, and she struggled to swallow it down.

"He always told me ye were as pretty as a primrose, and I see he was not lyin'. No one was ever prouder of a daughter than Eamon was of you."

Tears pricked her eyes. "He was?"

"To be sure. Never wanted a son like other lads. He was proud of his clever lass." The words soothed her like a balm to her battered spirit.

"Shameful what Diarmaid and his wife did. Ye didn't deserve it." Unable to bring words to her burning throat, she nodded and wiped her eyes with her sleeve. She hadn't deserved it.

Hector held out silver to the man. "I'll take six bundles of flax for her."

Cara gaped. "No, Hec—my laird. 'Tis too much. I can pay for half a bundle."

He thrust coin into Cian's hands. "Dinnae listen to her. Six bundles."

Cian took the coin and deposited it in his pouch. "Thank you, very much. Would you like me to bring it to your vessel?"

"Aye. It's a small skiff with the MacLean mark on the side. Could you make sure it's covered? There's an oilcloth."

He nodded and eyed Hector's brooch. "Aye, Laird MacLean. It's been a pleasure. And may I say on behalf of my friend Eamon what a blessed man ye are? You've married the jewel of Ireland. That girl was loved."

She opened her mouth to correct his assumption, but her throat constricted against the pinch of longing for her father's love. Hector looked at her and grinned. "Thank you, Cian."

As they walked along the exit of the market and up the sloping hill toward the abbey, he broke the silence. "He said Diarmaid did something to you. What did he mean?"

Raw emotion broke her will to hide her past away. She wiped tears away from her eyes with her fingers and watched a flock of shelducks land in the sea. "A week after Da died Aunt Maeve and Uncle Diarmaid sold Da's home and all his things. I wasn't allowed to keep anything but the loom—a miracle, that. They kept my inheritance and gave me a room in their leaky barn, and that's where I stayed for six years. It's why when Duncan invited me to meet him at the edge of town, I went. I wanted to belong to someone." A bitter laugh escaped. "What a fool I am."

The crunch of the gravel beneath their shoes and birdsong was the only sound to be heard and she regretted sharing so much.

He paused, his face pinched with incomprehension. "Did Duncan no' love you?"

"My father and Margaret are the only ones who have ever loved me." She kept walking up the hill.

He jogged after her and caught her arm. "That isnae true." He looked at his large hand gripping her arm and let go.

The look in his eyes made her heart skip. "What do you mean?"

Sunlight filtered through the gray clouds and made him squint, then look away. He studied the ground then looked up, the water of his eyes becoming warm. "Cara. I—" He stopped short. "You've said you feel insignificant. Do you ken why I've brought you here?" She shook her head.

"I wanted you to see the place where God saved my soul. I wanted you to feel what I felt that day."

He took a step closer to her, his height towering over her. He raised his hand, and his palm cupped her cheek. "What Cian said fills in some questions I've had. I dinnae ken what you lived through with your family, but I can see you're carrying a burden you were never meant to carry. It appears you married a man in haste, and..." Knees turning to jelly, she wondered if he had divined pieces of how terrible those ten years were. She couldn't bear to see the pity in his eyes. "And it wasnae a love match. Some men are very serious and unaffectionate. Some people dinnae suit."

Relief flooded through her tense muscles. "Aye. He was a serious man." Deadly serious.

"Cara, I dinnae ken much about you. Yet I understand the truth of who God created you to be."

Her fingers clutched his hand resting on her cheek, and she longed to step into his embrace. Instead, she stepped back two paces out of his reach. She tried to speak the words with kindness. "You're right. You don't know. And I'm not yours to know."

His voice became soft. "Aye, but I know what it is to need a burden lifted. Come."

Perched on a hill of lush green, the abbey towered over the Sound. Trepidation clenched her chest, but she followed him up the flagstone stairs and inside the abbey. They dipped their fingers into the font and recognized the savior.

Emptied of visitors, dim and quiet, she followed him to the right of the nave where he knelt on the stone floor. Monks in the adjoining cloister began their plainsong to mark the none[3] hour of liturgy.

"What are they singing?"

He whispered in her ear. "Veni Creator Spiritus." His calloused hand curled around hers. "May I pray for you, as you've done for me?" For the hundredth time that day, emotion bogged in her throat. She nodded. His dulcet voice spoke the Latin words of the Pater Noster, then began his prayer for her.

"O Jesus, Strong Lion, Immortal and Invincible King, I pray for Cara, that she will know that no' for a single moment was she ever unwanted."

His words penetrated deep into the most painful parts of her heart that she tried to keep away from everyone, even the Lord, feeling unworthy of His love. She tried to pull away, but his grip tightened around her hand. "The world has devoured her, but I pray you break every lie that has been spoken over her."

Tears cloaked her cheeks as she remembered every slap from her aunt and uncle, each punishment Duncan had meted out for her failures. Deep sorrow engulfed her, and her shoulders shook. Hector rested her head upon the shield of his chest, guarding her from the world.

"Restore to her the words you speak over her. Words like loved, healed, and forgiven."

His voice wobbled over the word *forgiven* as though he knew well what it meant. She pressed her cheek against his chest and heard his strong heart beating. A feeling of peace and safety surrounded her.

Tears rolled swiftly from her eyes and wet his tunic, carrying years of pain and lies as Hector's prayer and protection penetrated the darkness, inviting the Lord in.

"Take the burden from her shoulders, Lord. Carry her. I ask these things in the name of the Father, Son, and Holy Ghost."

They were silent for several minutes more and her tears stopped, but he held onto her. The unified voices of the monks reverberated through the sanctuary.

His voice rumbled in his chest under her ear. "I have no' heard this song in five years."

"What is it?"

"An invitation for the Holy Ghost to come and guide. The last time I heard it was the last time I was sick with drink. I was a miserable sinner, and I knew it."

She snuggled into his chest. "Why?"

"It's a long story. Left home when I was twenty-one. My father and I had a terrible argument about Aileen, my sister. She drowned on a boat ride to Staffa[4] when I was a child and my father blamed me for her death."

Tightening her arms around his solidness she tried to impart her comfort. "That is why you yelled at me."

His hands came over her shoulders. "Aye. That is why I yelled. I endured years of his drunken tirades against me, telling me I was worth nothing, that I killed her with my recklessness. One night I had enough and shoved him to the ground. I wanted him to hurt the way he had hurt me. I wanted him to stop. I tho' he would apologize, that finally he would be sorry... but he clutched his heart...and died. Right there on the spot. All those dark things he spoke over me had come to pass. I couldnae take it back. I was responsible for Aileen's death, and the death of my own father."

Compassion consumed her. "No, Hector."

"Lachlan and Maw rushed to him, but he was dead as a stone. I turned and ran. Boarded a bìrlinn and sailed that night for Scotland, and then England, and then France. I became a mercenary, fighting one bloody battle and conflict after another, praying I'd be killed. When that didn't happen, I turned to drink. I was running from God. Running from my mistakes. Then one night, after a tavern brawl, utterly blootered, I got on a ship and ended up right here on Iona."

She stifled a chuckle and mimicked his accent. "Blootered?"

"Aye, blootered. I staggered off the ship and ran into Pádraig, and he took me here to confront what I'd been running from. I heard the words of God in this sanctuary and went to Lachlan and begged for his forgiveness and help. A few months later God led me to my clan. Probably the worst choice for laird, but here I am."

"God has chosen the foolish of the world, so that he may confound the wise. And God has chosen the weak of the world, so that he may confound the strong." She smiled and looked up into his ghostly eyes and felt suddenly suspended by the pull between them, surrounded by affection she'd never known before.

"I am confounded by you." The naked statement sent shock through her. His arm tightened around her waist, and his hand tucked a wave of her hair behind her ear.

Heart drumming, she reminded herself of Elspeth, and why it must never be. Placing a hand on the rock of his chest she tried to push away but he held onto her, a heavy look in his eyes. "I cannae get my head around you. My heart is full of you."

Words she longed to hear, and words that made it harder to do the right thing. "Hector, you have Elspeth. She can give you things I can never give you."

He cradled her, his forehead coming to hers, his voice desperate. "The only thing I want is to be near you. I cannae stop this longing in my heart for you, Cara."

Swimming now in the translucent blue of his eyes, her reasons for pushing him away began to wither and she relaxed in his arms. A rough thumb stroked her jaw. The glowing blue of his eyes drew her in, the menacing angles of his face intriguing her, the shadow of a handsome lad so changed by war.

Forgetting good reason, all she could feel was desire to take his darkness away as he took hers away. A powerful hand smoothed up her neck. Angling his face toward hers, he lowered his lips and lingered. His breath feathered against her mouth, their lips a hair's breadth from touching. Her eyes closed.

A clatter sounded to their right and they jumped apart. Léo righted an ewer at the side of the chapel and placed it back on its stand. Her heart pounded. There had been a stone pillar shielding them, but he must have seen something.

Honey brown eyes searched hers and then looked to Hector, the two lines above his right eyebrow deepening. "Margaret said you'd come to Iona. Were you able to pray?"

"Yes. It was healing." She locked eyes with Hector, expecting to find regret in them, but he held her eyes as intensely as he had a moment ago. So much shared yet left unsaid.

Léo cleared his throat. "Shall I bring her home?"

Something shuttered over Hector's face. "Aye. I sail for Duart this afternoon. I have something to discuss with my brother." He looked at her, once more the fearsome laird. "I will have Pádraig deliver your flax to you this week when I've returned."

She had been swimming through waves of something deep and stirring only moments before, and now she was pulled beneath an undertow of what could never be. Hector was not her future.

# CHAPTER 15

## DUART OIGHREACHD - AUGUST 16, 1383

Rain started to pour down as Hector sailed around the Firth of Lorn and continued to come down in sheets until he reached Duart. He tossed ropes to a young guard and shouted his thanks before rushing up the steps into a mercifully warm and dry keep. Auld Malcolm, his father's chamberlain, greeted him at the door with toweling.

"Good day, Laird."

"Good day." He buried his dripping face in the soft linen and blotted water from his beard.

Malcolm winked his rheumy eye. "Treacherous." The man was one of the few men who had the ability to look Hector in the eye. His lanky frame was now bent with age but still reached over six-and-a-half feet. He had the air of a leaning willow shoot, lofty and crooked, as he held out a tremoring hand for the wet toweling.

Hector hung the linen around his neck. "I've go' it. I dinnae want to drip all over Mhairi's floors. I'll never hear the end of it." He kicked off his shoes and wrung his plaid out the door before following Malcolm's bowed figure upstairs, his heart still soaring from his time on Iona. She cared for him. They'd almost kissed.

"The maids laid out dry clothes a short while ago," Malcolm said, noticing his shiver. "I had them taken out of storage and freshly laundered this morning when your brother said you were coming to visit us."

"Thank you. I've go' something to discuss with him."

"Ah." Malcolm was wise enough to keep his questions to himself, but as he led him up to his chamber, he looked over his shoulder and warned, "He's in a temper today."

"I'm afraid that's my fault."

Malcolm unlocked the door to his chamber. The fire was roaring, his clothes carefully laid out, a berry tart and warm milk steaming on the table.

"Thank you," Hector said with sincere warmth.

Malcolm had been a constant figure in the MacLean house since before Hector was born. He had mended his scraped knees and broken up fights between Lachlan and he as children. All the years of his growing up Malcolm had tended to his every need and comfort.

By far Malcolm's most conscientious act of service had been five years ago when he stayed beside him in the locked chamber while his body craved the drink that kept memories at bay. Sweating, overcome with tremors, and imagining the worst horrors witnessed in a dozen battles, Hector succumbed to the process of poison leaving his body. All the while, Malcolm stood faithful guard, tending him through humiliating bodily release. They'd never spoken of those five terrible days and nights, but an unspoken closeness had existed between them ever since.

"It's good to see you well." Malcolm placed a hand on his shoulder and stooped through the door. "The laird is in his solar when you are ready." The door clicked shut.

Hector stripped off his sodden clothes and placed them over the chair positioned in front of the fire. He sipped the milk and took mouthfuls of warm berry tart as he pulled on trews and a fresh tunic. The woolen Duart plaid was wonderfully warm, and he wrapped it around his shoulders.

Taking a steadying breath, he drew up his courage and said a prayer to complete events he had set in motion. He propped his shoes in front of the fire and walked barefoot down the hall to his brother's solar and knocked.

Yesterday as they'd ridden home from Loch Spelve, his resolve crystallized, knowing he could not watch Cara marry Léo and be wed himself to a woman he had not thought of once as he dove into the water. He resolved to figure out a way to protect Cara and his clan, knowing it may mean an act of war.

"Enter." Lachlan sat in a deep velvet chair, staring into the fire, a glass of uisge-beatha in his hand.

Hector pulled the door closed behind him.

Lachlan motioned him over. "I'd offer you some, but..."

Hector raised the cup of milk. "Malcolm's given me better stuff. Milk with nutmeg and cinnamon, just like Maw made."

Lachlan snorted and swallowed the rest of his glass in one gulp. Hector took the leather seat beside his brother and stretched his cold bare feet toward the fire.

They sat in silence for several minutes, the heavy rain pattering against the stained-glass window the only sound in the room. Lachlan was one of the few people in his life who didn't feel the need to fill every silence with mindless chatter. Under normal circumstances he was grateful for it, but today, knowing what his brother had read in the missive he'd sent this morning, it only increased his tension.

After several long minutes of staring into the snapping fire Lachlan looked up. "Will you please explain your letter?"

Inhaling a deep breath, Hector pushed the damp curls off his neck. "Before I say anything, I want to point out that I am here. I do nothing without heeding your will in this."

Lachlan continued to stare into the mesmeric flames. When he did not respond, Hector continued. "It won't work, Lachlan. I've tried with Elspeth, but it's no use. I cannae marry her. She and I will never suit."

Lachlan made a sound of disgust and got to his feet. He strode over to a shelf and removed a decanter. "This isn't about Elspeth; this is about Cara."

"It's about the fact that Elspeth isn't fit to be Lady of Lochbuie. She's prideful, selfish, and vain."

"Isn't fit? The woman speaks three languages. She's spent the last two years running Dun Ringill, before that she ran Duntulm for five years for her first husband. She's beautiful and accomplished."

"Aye—she knows it too, and woe to anyone who threatens her. The woman instigated an uprising simply because she felt Cara was competition."

"I'll no' deny that was... ugly."

His temper rose. "Ugly? If that rock hadn't grazed her cheek, if it had hit her skull, it would have been deadly. No' to mention I nearly lost control of my clan because of her influence."

"I ken," Lachlan snapped. He took a deep swig from the glass.

Steeling himself, Hector prepared to concede defeat to his brother. "You're right though. I suppose it is also to do with Cara."

Lachlan sat down opposite him and visibly braced. "Explain."

"I told you I met her several weeks ago when she first came to Mull. But I didnae tell you that she came upon me on Laggan Sands. I had the memories overtake me again."

Lachlan's voice held a note of alarm. "After five years?"

"I dinnae ken if it had to do with Léo coming back, but the memories of Pontvallain, of Da, of Aileen's death... they came all at once. More intense than I've ever felt before. Cara stayed with me until I recovered and comforted me. She didnae know I was laird —'twas a miracle I didnae frighten her to death, yelling and seeing things."

Lachlan laughed into his glass and then groaned. "Poor lass. You frighten people standing quiet and still."

"No' Cara. She listened to me tell her what I'd done and gave me words of consolation. Then she prayed for me."

Lachlan made the observation everyone made about Cara. "Unusual."

"Aye. Everything about her is unusual. I've had Pádraig looking after her since she's arrived and he—"

Lachlan made a sound of disbelief. "I wondered why you've been so resistant to Elspeth. You've been seeing Cara."

"I'm only resistant to Elspeth because she's repulsive."

"You're the only man in the Isles and Scotland who thinks so, I assure you."

"I dinnae mean her looks; I mean her heart. I am supposed to be courting Elspeth, but Cara is the one who occupies my thoughts. I knew nothing good could come of pursuing Cara. I tried to put her out of my head, but it is no use. I—I've never felt this way about a woman before."

"That's obvious. Just ask Gregor MacFadyen."

Hector put his head in his hands and remembered the ease with which he'd held Gregor aloft. As if a strength not his own had imbued him. Cara was his woman, body and soul he belonged to her, and with his body and soul he would protect and fight for her. "I cannae explain it. It was instinct. When I saw her knocked to the ground, in danger, something inside of me…"

Lachlan nodded. "You were ready to kill for her. I'd do the same thing if it was Mhairi."

"Aye. It was like every ounce of who I used to be took over my body. Every battle instinct was there, except I felt God beside me. Then yesterday when I heard those screams…"

Lachlan rubbed his forehead. "Aye. Reliving Staffa all over again. My only tho' was Mhairi."

"My only tho' was Cara."

Lachlan put his glass down. "Hector, I know you are interested in this lass, but you've only met her a few times."

Indignation bubbled to the surface. "You're one to talk. You kidnapped Mhairi's father, a king no less, two weeks after meeting her and held him hostage until he agreed to let you marry her."

Lachlan's mouth hung open. "Oh, tha's low. 'Twas thirteen years ago, I was a much younger man and hot headed. You're thirty-four. Besides, it all worked out in the end, and I didnae have the Wolf to worry about."

"I know it may be difficult for a time, but I believe I can protect the Isles. Lachlan, I am asking you to go to John and help me. I want your blessing to see more of Cara. I prayed for a woman like her. I must see if she is the answer to that prayer." Lachlan grew still.

Hector interlaced his fingers, afraid to stop talking. "She's been a widow a short time, so I'll need to take things slowly for her. We could wait a year or more to decide if it should go further. Perhaps Léo can help us negotiate an alliance with the MacKinnons without the marriage."

He was desperate that his brother would see it his way. There was no denying his feelings for Cara any longer. He wanted to make his intentions known to her and pay court to her in the way she deserved. He didn't want to offer his protection as guardian, he wanted to protect and care for her as her husband.

"I dinnae think that will work."

His heart sank. "Why?"

"Because Niall will see your refusal to marry Elspeth as an insult. Do you honestly believe Léo would want to help if you take his woman and insult his sister? Things are too contentious."

"Léo may if I talk to him and explain it. Can we at least see what John thinks? I have a plan to assemble a fighting unit..."

"Hector..." Lachlan's voice trailed off in frustration.

He understood without further words being spoken, heart twisting in torment. His brother didn't want to pay his father-in-law the insult of forming a new plan, and he didn't want him to jeopardize the delicate alliance the clan was forming with the MacKinnons. Lachlan wouldn't give his blessing.

Hector knew that as Laird of Lochbuie his decisions were tied to the will of the King of the Isles. If his brother would not help him, his hope of something more with Cara was almost certainly gone. He'd been right. Nothing good would come of more time with her. Only heartache.

Mhairi entered the room carrying a basket of embroidery. "You're here already, Hector."

"Aye, I got here about an hour ago."

She seemed to weigh the sadness in Hector's face and the guilt in Lachlan's. "Is everything all right?"

Lachlan rubbed his smooth face. "Aye, love. Give us a few minutes."

Mhairi nodded and clucked at the uisge-beatha. "No more of this today. Keep him in line, Hec." She leaned down and gave Lachlan a soft kiss. "I love you." She traded her sewing basket for the empty glass and half-full decanter and left the room.

The time had come to retreat. Lachlan called his name before he could make it to the hallway. "Hector. Give Elspeth another chance. Keep trying. It will be much easier to be married to a wife you can tolerate."

# CHAPTER 16

## DUART OIGHREACHD - SEPTEMBER 10, 1383

Cara and Margaret pushed their way through the crowds around the shores of Loch Don. It was the last day of the Harvest Games, and the clans of the Isles had converged on Mull. The atmosphere was thick with merriment and the spirit of competition as everyone anticipated the final archery event.

Four exciting days of events had three clans now tied for first place. The MacLeods easily won sailing, and caused a major upset when they wrested the sheaf toss victory from the MacLeans. With Léo as leader instead of Niall, the MacKinnons had taken a surprise victory in both the stone throw and the dance. And with the combined skill of the Lochbuie and Duart clans, the MacLeans had won the mêlée and hill run.

"*Ma chérie.*"[1] Léo's now familiar greeting for her penetrated through the throng of islanders. Margaret and Cara froze as he hurried through the crowd, not expecting to see him in this part of the grounds.

Cara accepted his kiss to her cheek. "Are you ready for the tournament?"

"Almost." He held up the crios[2] belt she'd woven for him as his token. "Will you secure it?"

"Of course." She took the crios in her hands and looped it around his narrow waist, heart pounding.

Léo kissed her forehead and she shifted uncomfortably, knowing he would be hurt if he knew what she planned. Her hand gripped the small leather book beneath the lummon.[3] Her own token of courage for what she needed to do.

"I'll be looking for you in the stands. Will you be beside Lady Mhairi?"

"Yes. They've arranged special places for Elspeth, Eilidh MacLeod, and me beside the king."

Margaret motioned him toward the bow butts. "You best be running along. You don't want to be late." He kissed Cara's cheeks and rushed off.

Margaret narrowed her eyes. "He is too free with affection."

"It's the competition, he's excited."

"We can discuss it later. Come on, we havenae go' much time."

Margaret clamped her hand and pulled her through the thickest part of the crowd toward the stands that had been erected beside the bow butts. She pointed to a yellowed conical tent amid a sea of others. "Pádraig says he is in the tent just over there. Do you see it by the half dead holly tree?"

She tightened her grip on the precious psalter to steady her racing heart. "Yes."

"I will stand watch outside. If anyone comes close, I will try and engage them for a few moments. Keep an ear out and slip out the back immediately. I believe five minutes is all we can hope for."

It'd been more than three weeks since Cara had seen Hector and they'd almost kissed. She'd returned to the sheepcote in a knot of emotion and lain awake for hours remembering the prayer he'd spoken over her. When the red of the dawn had crept over the sky, she crawled in bed with her mother-in-law, shook her awake, and whispered the truth that had firmly lodged itself in her soul: "I'm in love with Hector."

Margaret silently opened her arms and held her as she whispered her account of what had transpired between them in the chapel. Then after a day in prayer with Margaret asking the Lord's guidance on what to do, he'd provided a way forward through the heartache she knew would come. She must tell him.

Two days later, Pádraig delivered her flax and told them that Hector had decided to stay at Duart to complete the betrothal negotiations with the MacKinnons, entrusting her safekeeping to Léo. He would not be returning home at all before the games, the expected time the betrothal announcement would be made. Three interminable weeks passed, and she'd been left alone with her aching heart without a word of comfort after what he'd confessed.

That was the way of it, then. They both knew they couldn't go forward in their feelings, but her foolish heart wouldn't let him go.

Margaret gave her a resolved nod, her hands clenching in her cloak. "Are you ready?"

Cara trembled, but tightened her hold on the book. "Yes."

They approached the tent and Margaret called inside, "Laird MacLean?"

The tent flap opened. "What are you..." Hector caught sight of Cara beneath the hood of the old lummon.

He moved to the side. "Come in." She entered, and Margaret pulled the flap closed behind them.

Every inch the battle-hardened warrior in his cuirass and chausses[4], her stomach gave an inadvertent flip as she remembered the things he had done and faced.

He crossed his giant arms over the shelf of his chest, his face impassive. "Is there something you need?"

The coolness of his voice stung. There was a new reserve in his manner, and she knew that he was returning a silent no to the question her presence posed in his life.

Wavering, her hands began to shake, doubting the task the Lord had led her here to complete. She pushed doubt away. She could do this. "Yes. I do need something."

She placed the small book at his feet and unwrapped the lummon from around her body. The peacock wool gown Margaret gave her clung about her in a way that made her feel self-conscious and she hoped she did not look as ridiculous as she felt. Her hands carefully removed the pins that held a gossamer veil in place, and she unwound her loose plait.

He uncrossed his arms, his dark eyebrows lifting, the coolness melting away. "What's this?"

Exhaling a shaking breath, she knelt at his feet. She smoothed her hair then took his rough hands in her own. "An uncovered head is required for a pledge of fealty."

"Cara..." The surprise in his tone made her bow her head, and she wondered how she would get through it. She kept her eyes fixed on the psalter for fear she'd lose her courage.

"I am Cara O'Ballevan, the only daughter of Eamon O'Ballevan, a distant descendent of the Chiefs of Uí Briúin of Connacht, a gentlewoman of no standing. I become your faithful servant from this day forward, Hector Reaganach MacLean of Clan MacLean, of life and limb, and of earthly fealty, and unto you shall be true and faithful, and bear to you my faith for all that you may require of me, saving the faith that I owe to our sovereign Almighty God. This is my solemn vow."

"Cara..."

"I've come here to pledge my fealty to you as a widow, renouncing all others and my homeland. Please accept me into your clan." She drew in a breath to finish what she had come to say, the words spilling out in a rush. "And if that should please you, accept me as one who has loved you from first I saw you. You do I love, as I've never loved before. You alone suffice me for all things. Y-you are locked within my heart and forever there will you rest."

He was silent for long moments. She heard him breathe out roughly through his nostrils. His words would break her heart, as they must break her heart. For even if he were free to love her, she could not give him the heirs he would need as chieftain. Hearing them spoken aloud would cut the lasting tethers of hope tendering him to her. She must let him go.

"May you be blessed by the Lord, Cara, truly. Your kindness in this act, and your words and prayers, have meant more to me than I can explain. You need no' fear or want for anything. You have protection within my clan as long as you live. I esteem your fealty as laird, but what is between us, what you feel for me, and what I feel for you, cannae be. Léo is a younger and better man than I. You have given him your favor for the games?"[5]

The tenderest places of her heart reverberated with a blow that wounded worse than any rock. She nodded and swallowed back tears. Rising, she touched the folds of the soft woolen tartan that rested upon his shoulder. She tried to impart humor she didn't feel. "I have given him my favor, but I fear my loyalty belongs to another as I watch the games."

He looked at the plaid gathered regally about his noble shoulders. "'Tis too fine for a man like me."

She shook her head. "You're equal to it. A high king like Brian Boru." She was losing the battle he waged on her emotions, but she lifted her face into a smile. "My prayers go with you in every strand. Thank you. For everything. I break your guardianship of me. I cannot bear it."

"Cara. I cannae do that."

Tears blurred her vision and clogged her throat. "As you say, what is between us cannot be. I no longer wish to have a guardian. I have Léo. I beg you, Hector, please, let me be."

His eyes flickered and then dropped. "Please remember me when you are happily married to him and surrounded by your children and grandchildren." She cleaved in two. If only he knew. There would be no children or grandchildren.

Margaret's voice lifted from outside the tent. "Léo. There you are... again."

Léo answered Margaret, and Cara made for the back of the tent, wrapping the lummon around her in haste and snatching up her veil. Hector motioned her toward the back flap and held a crack open.

It would be the last time they were alone together. She fixed him to her memory, and then, as she had when they met, lifted to her toes and pressed a kiss to his scarred cheek. "I will love you always."

When she cleared the tents, she broke into a run until she reached the stands surrounding the bow butts. Dipping around the corner of the risers she collided with Pádraig's chest. "Cara."

He caught his arms around her as she crumpled. "Tha's all right, lass. Tha's all right."

# CHAPTER 17

## DUART OIGHREACHD - SEPTEMBER 10, 1383

The tent flap opened just as Cara slipped away. Hurt and disbelief clouded Léo's face. "Why was Cara in here?" Groping for an excuse that would save her and coming up empty, Hector could only stand silent.

Recognition dawned in Léo's expression, and he knelt and picked up the psalter left behind on the floor. He opened the cover, reading and comprehending the inscription Cara could not understand.

Léo blanched, his face full of disbelief. "I wasn't imagining what I saw on Iona. You kissed her."

He wanted to give a full denial of what he felt and what he now was sure she felt for him. Instead, he could only offer a meek excusal. "I've no' kissed her."

Rage colored each word of rapid French as he waved the book in the air. "Don't begin with lies again. You've been engaging in a dalliance with her."

"I have no'."

Léo flung the book across the room, got to his feet and advanced on him. "You make me sick."

Fury fired through his veins, but he kept rein on his anger. The

154

words that Cara had just affirmed came to his lips. "It is no' a dalliance. We—I love..."

Léo shook his head. "Dispense with the excuses. Love is what I had with Théa. You're in lust, as you always were."

Frustration collided with jealousy and his words oozed out like hot pitch over his defenses—resentment for Léo's freedom scorching his good sense. "Cara and I both know it cannae be. I will marry Elspeth. We finalize the betrothal at dusk, as agreed. Cara is yours. You're free to marry her, free to make your own choice of wife."

Léo's face was clouded with rage. "Mine? Well, thank you for letting me have her. You're a plague upon your family, and a plague upon this friendship. If my family's fortunes did not ride upon this betrothal, I would break it now."

Sick at his stomach, Hector knew their friendship was over for good. He turned away, overwhelmed by the last ten minutes, and needing to be alone. Léo stalked him, not allowing him to escape the anger he had coming. "I know what I saw on Iona. The way she looked at you. She's almost as accomplished a liar as you are."

Whatever sorrow he felt only seconds before for what he'd done to Léo converted into high dudgeon. Anger roared in him, and he stepped forward, towering his height over Léo. "I warn you. You may say what you like, believe what you like about me, but that is the last insult you will pay her. She's given you no cause to set her aside."

Léo squared with him. "You think I'm afraid of you? I wouldn't marry her now. Not after this. She'll die alone, and that will be your fault. Live with it." Anger radiated from his face. "You both make me sick. Using a holy place for your meeting spot. I have to say, it's low, even for you. It's a miracle she isn't pregnant yet."

The fires of wrath licked up his insides. "I warned you."

Léo charged forward and swung, and Hector dodged the upward thrust of his arm then dipped backward to avoid his other fist. Again and again, Léo loosed blows and he deflected them with his forearms. Léo's left hand slammed into his temple, fighting like the experienced combatant he was. Hector righted and pushed him backward.

Setting his jaw, Léo charged again, and they locked arms, pushing and pulling, trying to unsteady the other. In a rush of fury, Hector stepped forward with his right foot and pivoted at his hip, his arm coming over Léo's head and neck. Extending his leg, he pulled Léo forward, tripping him and dumping him to the ground.

Léo's chest heaved. "You're the same as you always were."

He crouched, remorse warring with agitation. "I may be the same man, but at least I learn from my mistakes." His hand fisted around Léo's collar. "Dinnae defile her name again. You think you're too good for her? Why? Because she was vulnerable enough to care for someone who did nothing more than assist her when she needed help? I've never touched her, but I'll no' deny I love her. She's too good for either of us, but you're the victor here. Make your peace with her and dinnae dare think of hurting her."

With a jerk, he let go of Léo's collar and stalked away.

# CHAPTER 18

## DUART OIGHREACHD - SEPTEMBER 10, 1383

Pipes droned over the field and the drums began to thump, announcing the arrival of the clan champions at the bow butts. Cara's stomach dropped as if she'd crested a wave. The crowd cheered as Iain MacLeod and Léo strode across the field. Eilidh MacLeod, Iain's twin sister, gripped her arm and pointed. "There they are."

Cara rose alongside Eilidh as their champions took their positions and waved to them. Léo's hands tightened the crios belt, as Iain held Eilidh's scarf aloft and tucked it into his cuirass.

"I'll be happy when this is over," Eilidh muttered through the clenched teeth of her fixed smile. "I hate bein' the center of attention. Unlike..." Eilidh motioned her head as Elspeth rose, her back straight as a rod, a twinkling simper on her face as she waved to the crowd.

The piper changed tunes and Hector strode onto the field, the crowd of spectators exploding into frenzied shouts. After his performance in the previous day's mêlée his reputation as a berserker had reached mythic heights and he was favored to win the day's event.

Eilidh rolled her eyes at Hector's late entrance. "Reckon they planned that?"

Elspeth blew a kiss to Hector as he secured her ribbon to the bicep of his shooting arm. The spectators cheered their approval. An image of Elspeth and Hector on their wedding day formed in Cara's mind and she was beset with nausea. "I may vomit."

Eilidh sympathized. "As will I."

John of the Isles walked onto the field, escorting his daughter. Mhairi wore a practiced expression of serene pride as they walked in time with the drum.

They climbed the steps, and John gave her hand to Lachlan. The soon-to-be sisters-in-law kissed one another in greeting, and Mhairi waved to Eilidh and Cara before taking her seat.

John remained standing and addressed the crowd. "Champions! You may take two practice ends before your first scoring end. You will shoot one arrow at each of the eight marked targets, increasing in difficulty from one hundred to three hundred yards. The highest collective score wins. As winner of the mêlée, clan MacLean will be shooting last, clan MacLeod shoots first. As a reminder, the winner of this competition wins the games for their clan and he and his lady will be crowned as sovereign and consort for the feast."

Cara whispered to Eilidh. "What does being a consort entail precisely?"

Eilidh leaned over, her voice low. "You are crowned with a chaplet of heather and take the place of honor above all ladies present. Everyone must pay you obeisance for the rest of the evening. The sovereign gets boasting rights, and the honor of carving the goose at the bonfire feast. Oh, and you must lead an entertainment to officially close the games."

The thought made her want to sneak out the back of the stands. "With the sovereign?"

"No. By yourself."

Cara was horrified. "I hope I don't have to do it."

Eilidh inclined her head once more toward Elspeth. "Well let's hope one of us gets it so we dinnae have to spend the rest of the day bowing and scraping to Lady Snooty."

"She's not so bad." Even as she said the words, doubt washed over Cara as she remembered the way Elspeth tripped toward her at Loch Spelve. As if she had intentionally tried to harm her.

Eilidh scoffed and whispered, "I haird she instigated a fight at the barley reaping in Lochbuie and nearly go' yer head smashed in. Is that true?"

"Aye," Cara admitted. "Though she apologized for everything. She's been friendly with me since...since Léo and I..."

Eilidh's tone went warm. "He's a braw man. Those eyes. Och and his purring accent. I love a Frenchman; they could describe gong removal and make it sound pleasant."[1]

Within four rounds of the tournament, it became evident that Léo and Hector were in a league of their own. Iain MacLeod hit each target but was slightly afield of center each round. A strong and promising young warrior, but inexperienced still.

Léo proved to be magnificent. Each round, he took his two practice shots, then turned to look at her in the stands and wink before sinking his arrow in the center of the target. By the fourth shot, the crowd began to cheer each time he turned and winked in deference to her. Yet there was something a bit like a performance to his manner, and she wondered again if he had seen her leaving Hector's tent.

Hector stayed fixated on Léo's shots and did not look back to Elspeth or play off the crowd's emotion. He studied his opponents with obsessive calculation. When his turn arrived each round, he would arc two practice shots at the top and bottom of the target before ciphering his shot incrementally closer to center than Léo.

Eilidh clicked her tongue. "I guess that's the MacLeods out. Let's just be glad no one had tae sit through my flute playing at close of games."

Elspeth leaned over. "Léo has been shooting since he could walk. How wonderful for you that he has chosen you as his lady." There was a note of something false in her voice.

Cara tried to be kind. "Aye, but Hector is in the lead. I'm sure he will clinch it."

The entire games rested on the final round, Léo and Hector equally matched. The three-hundred-yard target was impossibly far away. Eilidh gripped her hand. Leo drew and released two practice shots that fell short of the target.

Eilidh muttered under her breath. "Come oan. Come oan."

Léo recalculated, drew, and angled higher before releasing, forgetting to look back at her before the shot. The arrow appeared to hover, and for a moment she lost it as it silhouetted against the gloomy clouds that blanketed the sky. Then she spotted it. Diving through the sky it hit the center. He whirled and raised his hands above his head in victory. Cara got to her feet beside Eilidh and applauded him. He pointed to her and winked, the crowd roaring its approval.

The Lochbuie MacLeans began to clap their hands, drowning out the support for Léo, chanting their war cry.

Hector stripped off Elspeth's favor, his leather cuirass, wiped his brow, then kicked off his shoes.

Elspeth gasped in embarrassment. "What on earth is he doing?"

Lachlan sat forward in his chair, arms perched on his knees, his fingers steepled before him. "Settling himself. Our father showed us when we were children."

Cara imagined him wiggling his toes down into the soft earth and taking a steadying breath. He nocked an arrow, aligned his body, then lifted to full draw. The first arrow flew through the sky with power before landing at the top of the target. The MacLeans screamed in excitement, but Hector betrayed no emotion. He pulled one of the long plaits that controlled his unruly dark curls to the back of his head and wiped his hand against his chausses. Again, he nocked, drew, and released. The arrow landed at the bottom center of the target. All the MacLeans were jumping up and down, howling with pride. Cara's heart pounded. *Lord, please let him do this. Help him, Lord.*

Hector nocked, drew, and stopped. Casting his eyes to heaven, he withdrew. Then, with intent, he turned in her direction and locked his gaze with her eyes. The crowd already almost out of control, went mad, believing he was acknowledging Elspeth.

Eilidh twisted a lock of red-blond hair around her fingers, her mouth falling open. "He's looking right at... you...no' Elspeth."

The screaming did not abate. Cara kept her eyes on his and gave a slight nod of her head. Hector turned back. She saw his back muscles employ, chest and stomach engage as he leaned into full draw. He angled high and released.

The arrow sailed beyond the target, landing in the cow pasture far behind. The MacKinnons rushed onto the field and hoisted Léo onto their shoulders.

Cara rose to her feet, searching for Hector among the throngs flooding the field. He had thrown the competition. She was certain. Why had he done it?

Eilidh embraced her. "You've won."

Elspeth looked dumbfounded. "I don't understand."

Mhairi jumped to her feet and embraced Cara. "You've won. Join Léo."

Cara looked to her right and left, looking for the only person who could make sense of what she had witnessed. "Where's Margaret?"

Mhairi pointed to her small figure threading through the crowd. "Here she comes."

Margaret wrapped her arms around her and lowered her mouth to her ear. "He wanted you to win." Cara wrapped her hand around hers needing to anchor herself in Margaret's love as her heart squeezed in loss.

The crowd parted and Hector stood at the edge of the field, his eyes locked on her. Mhairi looked to Hector, and then to Cara, and seemed to understand.

Margaret urged them forward. "Go, love. You must go to Léo."

Mhairi wrapped her arm around her shoulders and guided her through the crowd, away from Hector, and toward Léo. Léo scooped her into his arms, and she rearranged her face into a look of delight.

John of the Isles came forward with two chaplets of heather. He raised the first chaplet of heather and the crowd grew quiet.

"Léonid MacKinnon, you have elevated Clan MacKinnon as victors of the Harvest Games. I name you sovereign of the games." He placed the heather crown upon his head. "Well done and congratulations."

Mhairi divested her of the old lummon and pushed her forward toward John. The din quieted down as she stepped forward.

"Cara O'Ballevan, chosen lady of Léonid MacKinnon, I name you consort of the games." The king placed the heather chaplet upon her head.

"May all pay you veneration." He knelt, and one by one, each member of the mighty clans of the Kingdom of the Isles bowed before her.

Hector held her eye for a moment, then took a knee and bowed his head. Emotion caught in her throat; he'd wanted her to have this moment. Her heart broke. She would rather have him.

# CHAPTER 19

## DUART OIGHREACHD - SEPTEMBER 10, 1383

A raucous celebration echoed across the shores of Loch Don. The leaders of the Council of the Isles unwound from their reserved dignity and passed the horn around their number, toasting and boasting. As demanded by tradition, a sip was taken, then the horn passed to the next member. The game had gotten out of hand three rounds ago, each toast maker now downing an entire horn of mead after trying to top the last boast. Hector sat among the steaming pack of chieftains sipping a warm cider and thanking God his drinking days were over.

Iain MacLeod got to his feet and swayed. Eilidh held onto his arm to steady him. "Than' —thank you. I ken wha' yer thinking. Iain MacLeod doesnae have an-any boasts to his name."

An enthusiastic round of "aye" circled around the group.

"Bah ye see, since ma good mate Hector over here doesnae partake of mead..."

Boos and oaths rippled around the group and Hector chuckled.

"I tho' I would steal some of his boastin'ns so they no' go to waste."

The pack of drunk Isles chiefs burst into squawks of laughter. Iain wobbled around and drew himself up to his full height. Pulling his shoulders back and pushing his thin beard forward, he turned, effecting a stern expression. His brow furrowed; his mouth drew tight. He dropped his voice several octaves to mimic Hector's sonorous voice and spoke from one side of his mouth. "I am Hector the Stern."

Lachlan burst into hysterical tipsy laughter beside Hector.

Iain squinted one eye and bulged the other, one eyebrow perfectly arched. "You laugh at me, brother?"

"Tha's you lad," Donald MacFie shouted across the darkened clearing.

Iain pointed a finger at Lachlan and put a fist to his hip. "I may be the second born son but am the size of all yer sons, Mhairi, and you, put tae-gether." His voice dropped to a threatening rasp. "No' shut yer gob."

Mhairi wiped away tears, gasping for breath. "That is your growl exactly."

Hector found Cara in the crowd, seated in the place of honor beside Léo. Her face was amused, but she did not join in the laughter with the others.

Iain fixed his hand on his belt and glowered raising a flexed bicep. "I go' legs for arms, and a keep tha's fallen doon aroouund me ears."

Lachlan laughed so hard no sound came out.

"Aye. You remember Moy. The tower I climbed using my bar' hands. Go' tae the top and shot an arrow at auld Laird MacFadyen and skewered his apple to the groound. I canny understand it. Wenty the shooty match taeday...me arrow missed an hit a coo." Roars of laughter shook the loch.

Iain motioned to Elspeth with the horn, and mead sloshed out of the top. "Perhaps ma wee hen is bah luck."

Elspeth fumed, silent beside him. Her mood had been cast iron since they left the bow butts that afternoon, the sour look of a spoiled child fixed on her face. Eilidh caught her murderous look and wrested the mead from Iain's hands. Groans of disappointment rose as she guided Iain back to his seat, followed by loud applause for his impression.

Iain plopped back down on the bench with a loud thud, then hiccuped and fell backward. Hector caught him by the shoulder and righted him.

Iain belched and looked at him with blootered appreciation. "Thanks, aul-auld man." He belched again. Not a good sign as Hector could remember. "I dinnae understand. It's like you wanted tae lose tae-day. Wha' happenened?"

Elspeth snorted in disgust.

"I tho' I heard something," Hector said.

"What?"

"God."

He had been about to release his final arrow when he'd heard the voice speak boldly. *Protect her.* And he'd known. He'd made the most howling mistake.

He'd turned, and found Cara with little effort, his soul searching for hers. Beside her, Elspeth looked exultant, ready to be crowned his consort. Ready to lord over everyone in attendance. There was only one consort he wanted.

Iain burst into another fit of laughter. Then steadied himself realizing Hector was serious. "I fergo' yer a holy man now. Canny drink or do annaethin' f-fun." Iain's face suddenly went green, and he ran to the loch and vomited.

Hector called after him, "A sound argument. What fun I have missed."

Eilidh shook her head. "He'll be back in a moment. I'm sorry, Laird MacLean."

"No bother."

Eilidh joined her brother by the loch and patted his back while he recovered.

Elspeth crossed her arms. "I cannot stand them. They speak as though they were raised in a barmkin yard."

Hector rolled his eyes. "Iain was jesting. You arenae bad luck."

She looked away and returned to pouting. Hector sipped his cider, unaffected by the tricks that no doubt worked on her brothers and suitors.

A cheer rose from the crowd as Mhairi came forward to continue the evening's entertainment. "I would like to thank you all for coming to the Harvest Games here on Mull. I extend my warmest congratulations to Clan MacKinnon for their fine performance this week and to all the competitors and winners of the individual events." Applause and whoops sounded around the fire. "Before we close the games, I would like to introduce you to our consort for this evening, Cara O'Ballevan."

Cara came forward, the crowd cheering and bowing to her as consort. Firelight caught the gloss of her hair, the shape of her figure, and the shimmer of her lips as she smiled. Hector was hit with a powerful blast of attraction, and by the sound of the manly whistles that followed her, so was every other male present. He frowned, feeling unsettled by their enthusiasm.

"I thank you for your warm welcome. 'Tis an honor to be chosen for this privilege by dear Léo. I hope that tonight I do my homeland proud, and his as well." Hector's heart cramped.

Drunken whoops sounded from the MacKinnons. "You've done us proud."

She smiled. "Ah, perhaps that's enough mead."

Laughter echoed back to her. She held the audience in the palm of her small hand. "I do thank you for your support, Clan MacKinnon. I'd now like to invite up the pride of Clan MacFie, winner of the piping competition, Andrew MacFie." The small contingent of the MacFie clan hooted and cheered as the handsome, red-haired Andrew made his way forward.

"Andrew has kindly offered his accompaniment on flute." Andrew winked at her. Hector's frown deepened.

"Do you think I can't see the way you are looking at her?" Elspeth hissed into his ear. "Do you think I didn't see you look at her before you lost the competition?"

God help him, theirs would be a miserable marriage. Already annoyed, he swallowed his temper and lowered his voice. "We can discuss it after she's finished."

Léo turned and shushed them. "Do you mind?"

Elspeth rolled her eyes. "Oh, let's not be rude to the Èireannach."

Cara introduced their song. "We'd like to perform in the sean-nós style for you tonight."[1] A delighted murmur rippled through the clan. "I invite you to close your eyes in the Irish way and see the story of the song."

The audience obeyed and all closed their eyes except for Hector and

Margaret. They met eyes across the crowd. Margaret smiled at him and put a hand over her heart.

Andrew began the feral grounding notes for her song. Remembering the joyful lullaby the night they met, he was unprepared for the tormented wildness of the lament. The otherworldly emotion in her voice netted him, pulled him under her tide. He was lost in her.

Her lilting gave way to lyric. A lad met a girl at the bend of a green and desolate forest. The lad fell in love with the girl's good heart, and desired to marry her. Enchanted by her, he followed her to a foreign land, but her family would not allow the match. Begging her ardently to be with him, he pledged every inch of his heart to her, but in the end, her family forced her to reject her only love.

Every man and woman leaned forward, eyes closed, carried away by the purity and power in her voice.

Her voice wavered as she began the final verse. The man could do nothing but lament, for he loved only the girl from the wood. He returned to her, begging for her hand, pledging to love only her. But her mother thwarted their love, and forced him to tie her wedding rope, hand-fasting her to another.

Cara repeated the last lament, eyes closed, heart surrendered, her voice lilting in love toward heaven and in agony breaking toward earth. Goosebumps broke out over his arms and scalp as her voice trilled wildly, feeling the pain in her heart, the pain he'd caused her.

His chest burned with the raw emotion in her voice as the final note faded away, and he was filled with bitter regret.

John got to his feet and began the applause. Mhairi and Eilidh wiped tears from their eyes, moved by her voice and the story she wove around them like linen. The gathering erupted in whistles and applause, her words of thanks lost in the thunder. She waved to the crowd, then motioned the other musicians forward. A slow reel began, and the crowd snapped out of their trance.

The king stopped in front of the Duart and Lochbuie leaders and tipped his bonnet to Cara. "May I join your party?"

She smiled. "Yes, please, sit with us."

John settled on the bench next to her. "Your voice has a purity like a clear water burn. I haven't heard a voice so emotive since my mother was alive. Who gave you instruction?"

"My mother. I learned sean-nós from her when I was a child. My father often harmonized with her. I feel as though I've been singing my whole life long. Of course, now I don't have many occasions to sing, except with Margaret."

"Who is Margaret?"

Cara gestured across the celebration where Margaret sat talking with Pádraig. "My mother-in-law, just there."

Mhairi touched her father's arm. "Margaret is from the MacFadyens of Lochbuie, and Cara has made her home with her. Margaret moved back to Mull shortly after the death of her son, Cara's husband."

John took Cara's hand and kissed it. "How fortunate for you that you have so many people to love and instruct you, especially now that you've lost your husband."

Elspeth erupted in laughter beside Hector.

John's eyebrows pulled together, and his eyes crinkled. "What is it?"

Alarm drenched Cara's expression.

"The girl doesn't have any people who love her. Other than Margaret, that is. If only you knew her history. She's been an outcast her whole life." Lachlan and Mhairi looked at Elspeth aghast.

John looked between Cara and Elspeth, confused. "I beg your pardon?"

Elspeth's expression went innocent, and she held up her hands. "She told me herself."

Hector grabbed Elspeth's elbow, not caring who heard his words. "That's enough. Stop talking at once."

Elspeth jerked her arm out of his hand. "She forsook her family in Ireland to come to the Isles for a woman who isn't even a relation. I couldn't understand why, considering what her husband did to her."

Cara looked ashamed and humiliated. "Elspeth, please."

John's expression hardened.

Elspeth's ugliness hidden beneath a shallow pool of beauty was now on full display. "Remind me, Cara, how long were you married?"

Cara's eyes closed. "Ten years."

"No children in ten years. How odd."

Cara seemed to grow smaller before Hector's eyes. Then, the horrible truth dawned on him, the reason why Cara said she was a burden to her husband, why there was not love between them. The truth that Elspeth was about to betray.

"But the problem was not with your husband, was it? He had a dalliance with your acquaintance...what was the name?"

Two tears slipped from Cara's closed eyes. "Eve."

"How much did Eve's son look like your husband? Identical, weren't they?"

Eilidh gasped.

"Unloved. Unwanted. She's bold though, I'll give her that. Having her own dalliance with a laird at this very gathering, and from what I understand it has been going on for a long time. I finally understand why she had to leave Ireland. She has no morality."

Léo had gotten to his feet. His mouth opened and closed, and he looked at Elspeth appalled.

Tears cascaded from Cara's eyes as she looked to Léo and shook her head. "It is a lie. I didn't... I would never..."

An uneasy silence came over the clans. The music halted as spectators looked over to listen to Elspeth's sordid tale. Margaret stood at the edge of the loch, her hands balled into fists. Unable to sit among the chiefs, unable to protect the daughter of her heart.

Lachlan raised his voice. "This is ridiculous. I'm inclined to believe by the look on her face that Cara would never do such a thing."

Elspeth shrugged. "Believe what you like. Léo saw it himself today when she came out of Chieftain MacLean's tent. We all know Hector's reputation. She would make the perfect leman. No consequences."

Mhairi gasped, her face in total shock. "Elspeth."

Elspeth struck. "Who could take you now, Cara? No one."

Anger pounded through Hector's heart, and he rose, filled with holy fire. *Protect her.* His voice came out darker and more foreboding than even Iain could mimic. "Enough."

Lachlan, Léo, and John's eyes followed him as he threaded through the crowd, and he stared at them in defiance—knowing where his highest allegiance lay. He crouched before Cara. Tilting her chin, he lifted her wounded eyes toward his.

Her voice was choked with tears. "Send me back to Ireland."

Hector placed his hands on her cheeks and wiped her tears away with his thumbs. He rested his scarred cheek upon hers and lowered his voice so only she could hear. "I'm no' sending you anywhere. Your place is here beside me in my clan, as my wife. Let me become your husband."

Cara looked into his eyes with teary astonishment. "But I cannot give you heirs."

His forehead touched hers. "I dinnae want heirs. I want you."

Cara's hand gripped his, and she nodded in agreement.

He would marry his Cara. Regardless of the threat of war. Regardless of an ability to have children. Whatever lay before them would pass first through the hands of the Father, and he was certain God would be faithful.

Hector stood and removed the resplendent plaid she had woven and prayed her love into. He spread the wings of the garment over her shoulders.

He raised his voice so all could hear and bound her with his fealty. "You are witnesses that I pledge this day that Cara O'Ballevan shall be my wife. Unto her am I betrothed, and bear to her faith for all that she may require of me, saving the faith that I owe to our sovereign Almighty God. This is my solemn vow."

Elspeth shrieked and crashed through the wood heading in the direction of Duart, her face a furious shade of purple. Léo shook his head, his eyes full of betrayal, then followed close behind.

Sheltered now in the safety of his garment marking her as his bride, he pulled Cara to standing beside him and entwined his hand with hers.

John stepped forward and gripped Hector's hand. "We are sworn as witnesses to your betrothal. You've made your choice. I ask that you come to Ardtornish as soon as you are able. As the alliance is now out of the question, we have much we need to settle." John dropped his voice. "This may mean your future as chieftain."

Hector nodded. "I understand."

# CHAPTER 20

## DUART OIGHREACHD - SEPTEMBER 13, 1383

Light had not yet begun to penetrate the dark sky when the door to the chamber opened. Cara opened one eye and observed a slight figure place a basin on the table, then stoke the embers in the hearth. The girl tucked a dark curl back inside her bonnet and laid a new brick of peat on the fire.

"Good morning," Cara croaked.

The maid looked over her shoulder and gave a brief nod of acknowledgment but remained focused on her task, blowing into the embers until the smoking brick of peat caught light. "Good morning, mistress."

Cara buried her face in the softness of the pillow and wondered how she would ever be able to pull herself out of the warm bed.

"I'll send Bethia up to you and be back with some food to break your fast." The girl curtsied. It was a new and odd feeling to have someone curtsy to her.

"What's your name?"

"Aoife." An Irish name, but the girl's voice was burred with Scottish.

"Thank you, Aoife."

The door clicked shut. Stretching against the deep mattress, Cara yawned, shaking the last vestiges of sleep away. Despite the predawn hour, she'd never felt so rested. The smell of leather and mint clung to the pillow, and she breathed deep, inhaling Hector into her senses. Peculiar as it was to be plunged into his world, she could get used to the feeling that he was near. Though, at that moment he was back at Moy seeing to the completion of improvements to the keep before the wedding.

Sleep threatened to blanket her once more, and she sat up and hung her head limply. Mhairi was counting on her to arrive to chapel on time, and she couldn't make a poor impression.

Half-awake she swung her legs over the side of the bed and rose, forgetting the small footstool she'd used to hoist herself into the hulking bed the previous night, and falling three feet onto her backside.

"Grand."

Alert now, she sat for a moment, the great differences in their height a reminder of the stark differences between her world and his.

Trying to quell paralyzing thoughts, she committed to memory to ask that steps be constructed for their marital bed at Moy and staggered to the table. Upending the jug into the basin, she splashed cold water onto her cheeks. Soap, beautifully pressed into a smooth, ivory cake, sat on top of fine linen. Cara felt the tightly woven, yet porous, linen and lifted the cake to her nose and inhaled sage. Everyday luxury here at Duart, but another stark contrast to the dark tallow soap at home.

Shedding her chemise, she washed, skin prickling against the cool harvest air. Having finished her ablutions, she opened the trunk positioned at the foot of the bed where she'd stored her four leines and a few undergarments, removing a fresh chemise and one of Hector's woolen tunics. The tunic hung past her arms by a dozen inches, but she was grateful for the warmth it provided her skin and the strength it imbued to her heart.

A knock sounded, and Aoife returned carrying a tray, followed by an older woman dressed in striking blue, her head covered by a wimple.

The older woman curtsied, her pale wrinkled cheeks lifting into a placid smile. "I am Bethia, Lady Mhairi's maidservant. My lady has instructed that I supervise Aoife as she sees to your needs here at Duart. Aoife has served as maid to many guests here at Moy and was maid to Elspeth MacKinnon."

Guilt cramped her stomach as she remembered Léo escorting a livid Elspeth off MacLean land two nights previous, the hurt in his eyes, and the barely disguised judgment in the eyes of every Council member, including Hector's brother.

A fresh memory of Elspeth's face pinched with anger assailed her and she swallowed. "How reassuring." Aoife's face smothered a grin, clearly picking up on her tone.

"Elspeth had a few complaints about her work, so if anything displeases you, summon me at once. Lady Mhairi has asked that if she meets with your approval, she goes with you to Moy permanently."

She wondered if this was a welcome move for the girl. "I'm sure Aoife will do quite well."

Bethia's face betrayed no agreement or disagreement with her statement. "We shall see. The tailor will be here this afternoon to take your measurements, along with a selection of fabrics for your new wardrobe. He will also see to the creation of your mantle for the wedding."

Cara shifted to one foot beneath Bethia's penetrating stare and tried to decide how to give a polite declination. "Thank you, Bethia. I don't think that will be necessary. I have a trunk of clothing coming to me from Lochbuie. Everything I have need of is in there."

Bethia crossed her arms, fortifying herself. "Nonsense. You must have clothes becoming a lady of your station, no' a common weaver."

The old maidservant had the look of a hardened ox, as if she had never heard anything so ridiculous. A hot feeling of embarrassment slit through her gut and perspiration needled her armpits, Hector's tunic suddenly feeling too warm. Taking a deep breath, she came out with the truth. "What I mean to say, Bethia, is that I have no tocher. No means of paying for a wardrobe."

Aoife shot her a sympathetic look over Bethia's shoulder.

Bethia's tone once again revealed no hint of opinion or judgment. "Laird Hector MacLean has paid for the creation of your wardrobe— leines, chemises, shoes, headwear, wedding mantle—everything."

As he had for the past two days, and since the moment they met, Hector met every need. What would she bring to the marriage except trouble?

Bethia curtsied and motioned Aoife into action as she rattled off orders. "Aoife will dress you and get you ready for the day. Lady Mhairi will be expecting you in the chapel when you are finished for Lauds."

As the door clicked shut, Cara felt homesick for Margaret and Ursula and their simple morning routine of porridge and chores.

Aoife pushed a lock of dark ash-colored hair over her shoulder and arranged food on the table. "Dinnae let auld Bethia intimidate you. She's been maidservant for almost thirty years. Come from Ardtornish, the MacDonald house where Lady Mhairi were raised. She could command the MacLean guard."

Cara took her seat at the table and Aoife uncovered a few small dishes, and she was comforted to find a simple meal of porridge, apples, and milk. "I supposed you wouldnae want anything fussy since you're an Irish lass like my mam."

The warmth in Aoife's tone was a welcome balm of comfort after two days of drifting without Hector at Duart. "To be sure."

Aoife chose a simple yellow leine from the trunk. "This will work for the first part of the day. After the tailor is finished with you, I'll dress you for dinner. I've heard talk downstairs that Laird Hector MacLean is coming for supper tonight. Is there a color his lairdship is partial to?"

Cara's mood made a sudden rise as if she'd gone from hopeless winter to flowering spring. It would be the first time since they'd seen each other since he'd betrothed himself to her. There was so much left unsaid, so many unanswered questions multiplying by the hour.

"Black, I think."

"Oh dear," Aoife said looking at the limited selection of two other leines and a few chemises. Her lack of gowns suitable for the endless meals and activities at Duart meant she had already cycled through her three choices of green, the peacock blue, and yellow. The only other option was her beloved shapeless brown work dress which was not even considered.

Aoife studied her limited options and decided. "Emm...I think this green. It will match your eyes. Plus, it's the color of young love."

Cara paused with her spoon halfway to her mouth. "I trust you know much more about these things than I do. Though I'm not sure we are young, nor that he would call it love."

Aoife unwound the plait at the nape of Cara's neck and pulled a comb through it. "I hope you'll no' think me impertinent, but I was at the bonfire feast. I saw what the Laird Hector did. I saw how he claimed you as his own. If that isnae love, I'm no' sure what is."

It had been the most humiliating moment of her life, and yet the moment that had changed everything. Did he love her, or did he choose her out of pity? She longed to see him and have a few moments alone with him.

"Do you love him?" The boldness of Aoife's question surprised her. But she was young, and the tone in her voice was curious, not impertinent.

Cara sipped from the cup of warm milk and contemplated the night they met beneath the bright moon, the night on the beach, Iona, the arrow that sailed past the target and into the cow pasture. "Aye. I love him very much."

Aoife wet the comb and sectioned her hair before plaiting it over her ear. "I suppose you dinnae need to be in love to be wed though."

"True enough." Most marriages were based on respect, or convenience, not love. Doubt began to niggle her stomach.

"If you are marrying the love of your heart, that is a good foundation. Laird MacLean will come to love you in time if he doesnae already."

A wave of foreboding set her adrift. Duncan had never grown to love her, nor she him.

———

It was half past four in the afternoon before she had another quiet moment. She listened intently as Mhairi went over the financial books with her. The five financial expense accounts were kept in separate ledgers so that all income was appropriately reconciled, just as her former clan had kept ledgers. Familiar with the system, she found her mind wandering and her weary body longing for a lie down.

The first book recorded gifts to the poor. Mhairi recounted the amounts paid to petitioners this morning and Cara recorded each sum carefully in the ledger. When she finished, she worked the arithmetic in her head and balanced the account.

Mhairi blinked, astonished. "You completed that without additional figuring."

Cara stifled a yawn. They had been going from one activity to the next without stopping all day. "I did—in my head. My father taught me to figure. Much of weaving is planning and calculating. The smallest part is the execution."

"Remarkable."

Mhairi resumed the lesson. The second book contained monies for operation of the household and lands, and rents paid to the chief. The third book contained monies paid to the guardsmen, officers, clerks, and clan leaders. The fourth account book was for her patronages including artists, musicians, and craftsmen. The fifth and final account was her personal treasury for the family's expenses and needs.

"Do you understand, or have I overwhelmed you?"

Cara looked at the sums neatly recorded at the bottom of the page and checked the arithmetic. "No, the numbers you have here at the bottom are the ones I came to."

"You did the figures for this entire page in your head?"

She second-guessed herself. "Aye. Am I wrong?"

Mhairi laughed. "No, no' at all. This page would have taken me several minutes to check and I would've needed additional pages to work out the sums."

Cara licked her lips, Mhairi's expression beginning to make her nervous. Her mind had always easily digested figures, but when she'd assisted Duncan with clan ledgers, speed was also a necessity to avoid punishment. Unsure how to explain the ability, she shrugged. "I suppose I have a mind for numbers."

"What an asset you will be at Moy. If you take over the accounts, Tavish can focus solely on clan matters with Hector."

Joy flooded her and she let out a sigh of deep relief. It was a much-needed boost after an entire day spent feeling out of her depth. They began the morning at chapel, then proceeded to meet with petitioners in need of alms, then came the large midday meal with clan leadership and officers.

When that concluded, they retired to Mhairi's solar for embroidery and needlework with the wives of clan leadership. Which sounded like a respite, but upon arriving, Cara learned it was really a political meeting. The carefully constructed clan hierarchy depended upon Mhairi's stewardship of relationships with these women.

Once that had concluded, Mhairi visited the sick and delivered packages with food and medicine. They returned to Duart at the none hour, and still had vespers[1] and supper ahead of them.

Cara rubbed the wrinkle between her brows. "I don't know how you have the stamina to accomplish all that you do. It seems there aren't enough hours in the day."

Mhairi straightened the papers on the large oak desk. "Remember I've been working at it since childhood. It didnae happen overnight."

Unsure if this fact should cheer or depress her, Cara worried her fingers along the account book. "I don't want to let him down. He's put faith in me. I'd hate to dash it."

Mhairi squeezed her arm. "Dinnae think about all that now. You've only been betrothed two days."

"But the banns will be completed in three weeks' time. I have less than a month to learn everything there is to know about being a lady."

"What you've shown me today gives me great hope. You have a gift with our people, a natural warmth. You're also a marvel at numbers, which is the hardest part of my day. And if it gives you any comfort, Moy's household is far, far smaller than ours."

Trying to loosen the plaits tightly wound at her throbbing temples, she worked a finger along her scalp. "An upset husband is hard to soothe. I don't want to send him into a temper."

Mhairi looked confused. "I dinnae think Hector will be impatient with you. It will take time to learn your role. He understands that—he's still learning to be laird. He wasn't raised for it either."

"Aye, but he is much smarter than I. I can't read or speak French. I don't know anything about the world outside of Ireland and this island. I'm bound to frustrate him with my stupidity."

Mhairi gave her a quizzical look. "You're far from stupid."

Duncan's words formed a whirlpool around her. Fear flowed from the heights of her pain, tumbling through the unknown. Weightless, she dropped over the precipice of her own lack, drowning in ten years of harsh words and angry slaps. What was she doing here? She would never be enough.

Mhairi's eyebrow twitched as she studied her. "Cara, if the source of your feelings is from Elspeth, I wish to assure you that I dinnae agree. If I knew what she was about I would have recommended to my father and Lachlan to have her removed from Mull at once."

"You can't control what she says or does."

"Aye. But that day at the barley fields—and then at Spelve. I should have tried to intervene sooner. Only the marriage treaty was so critical."

The whirlpool swirled faster, and her heart pounded. The feeling of foreboding that had followed her all day returned with new strength. "Why?"

A look of concern crossed Mhairi's face, and Cara could tell she waged a silent debate on whether to disclose the full story. Finally, she relented.

"There's a powerful noble in the Scottish court with great wealth, land, and a terrible reputation that Léo's brothers have been friendly with. My father asked that Hector form a marriage alliance with the MacKinnons to protect Mull and the Isles from further claims to land."

"What claim has he got on the Isles?"

"The nobleman has recently come into land on Skye, thanks to his marriage."

Skye was the seat of Clan MacKinnon. Cara began to understand. "If Hector married Elspeth, it would have given the MacKinnons pecuniary and familial reasons not to cooperate with this nobleman."

Mhairi tapped her quill on the blotter. Concern crossed her face and Cara knew she wondered if she said too much.

"Who is this nobleman?"

Mhairi relented. "Alexander Stewart, son of the king, Earl of Buchan. They call him the Wolf of Badenoch."

Cara was horrorstruck as her mind translated the words. "The son of the king. King of Scotland?"

Mhairi nodded. "For fifteen years he has been growing in political power and influence. He is called the Wolf because of his use of his caterans to pillage, kill, and plunder the people under his jurisdiction to increase his holdings or to punish those who have gotten in his way."

Cara felt nauseated. "And the marriage to Elspeth was the key to controlling the MacKinnons and keeping them from giving entrance to the Wolf."

Mhairi cast her eyes downward. "Aye. That is the problem, and that is why Lachlan was so set on the match between Elspeth and Hector."

"Hector knew of the Wolf's reputation?"

"Aye. The Wolf tried to recruit him to lead his caterans while Hector was in Ireland six years ago. Hector may have struggled with many things then, but he had no interest in killing innocent peasants and persuading noblemen to sign over their holdings using violence."

Feeling defeated, Cara looked over the account books in front of her. "What good is it to have a mind for numbers when everyone may lose so much because of me?"

Mhairi placed an encouraging hand on hers. "But my father supports your match now. No' all hope is lost. It will take time to figure out a way forward. Perhaps through Léo. I told you these things no' to crush you, but so you understand. Hector will need your support in every way possible, and that includes your mind for numbers. If you can manage the books for Tavish, Tavish can manage the clan disputes for Hector, and Hector can focus on helping my father and the council."

With Duncan her only shortcoming had been her own lack of ability. With Hector she could add the threat of war. How would he ever love her? "I cannot let him do this, Mhairi."

"It's too late, Cara. It's done. He's taken you to himself as his intended wife, and he's made up his mind."

Hot tears escaped over her cheeks, and she swiped them away. Another husband to resent her. She'd prayed that she would never feel this way again, and yet here she was.

Mhairi looked at her with suspicion. "What are these tears? This isn't about what Elspeth thinks or the Wolf."

Fear clawed at her heart. The whirlpool sucked her under. Dear Lord, she could not live in a resentful marriage again. Breath shuddered through her lungs, and she looked up at Mhairi, drowning and unable to speak.

Mhairi's brow creased. "What Elspeth said about your husband, and the baby, that part was true, wasn't it?"

She nodded. Mhairi pulled a handkerchief from her pocket and handed it to her.

"There's something else though. Was he cruel to you?"

Overcome with shame she wiped away the tears from her heated cheeks. "Aye. It was my fault though."

Mhairi clucked her tongue and took Cara's hand. "Husbands must love their wives and no' be bitter or harsh. Did he strike you?"

Unable to bear the pity she knew she would find in Mhairi's eyes, she remained silent.

"Cara, look at me."

Mhairi's own eyes glistened with tears but held no pity. Her voice wobbled. "Did he strike you?"

"Every day." Like a flood, the entire story came gushing out. From the day she met Duncan until the day he was laid in the burial ground. Every cross word, every barren month of failure, each punishment he tortured her with, the reasons she calculated and learned quickly. Mhairi's arms came around her and pulled her close, her lips mumbling apologies for past wrongs that they both knew could never be erased. "Please don't say anything to anyone, Mhairi."

Mhairi pulled away but kept her hand firmly around Cara's. "Of course I won't, but you must tell Hector."

The thought of Hector knowing filled her with dread. She was already a pathetic creature, now twice in need of his rescue. The thought of him knowing how feeble and pitiful she had always been was out of the question. She couldn't be that shell of a woman anymore, she was someone else now. "There is no need to tell anyone. What good would it do? He cannot fix it now."

"No, but he should know because..." For moments, Mhairi searched for an explanation, her hands spread wide apart. "He should know so that he will know. So that he may pray for you, listen to you, care for you. He should know so that he will fill you with the truth. For instance, Cara, you arenae stupid, and I worry that that is only one of many lies you believe about yourself."

Cara shook her head. "I don't want to burden Hector with such things."

Mhairi gave her a disapproving look, rubbed her forehead, and sighed. "You have much to learn about Hector. Perhaps you need to build your trust before you can let him into the deepest hurts within your heart. But may I tell you something?"

Cara nodded.

"Lachlan and Hector are worlds apart. Lachlan is a good man, inherently principled, full of self-control, wisdom, and scrupulous." She brought her hand to her heart. "I love him for it. Yet, he does have a hard time seeing past himself and his own reasoning at times. Hector, on the other hand..." Her voice trailed off and she searched once again for words. "Hector has learned much the hard way. He's been a fallen man, he's been hurt and done hurting, he is a warrior, and he is a casualty."

Cara remembered that day on the beach, the broken and haunted man she held in the sand.

"He has the most compassionate heart. He is considerate and forbearing, and he is a safeguard for the darkest pain in you. You may trust him with your suffering because he too has suffered."

Blotting tears from her cheeks Cara took a deep breath, trying to find words to explain. "I know, but I don't want—I don't want him to see the woman I used to be. I'm sorry, Mhairi. He can never know."

Pain seared her heart, a longing to be whole. It was the one thing Hector could never provide for her, the one peril he could not rescue her from. The damage was already done.

# CHAPTER 21

## DUART OIGHREACHD · SEPTEMBER 13, 1383

Hector followed the MacLean clan leaders up the steps to Duart for evening supper stifling a yawn. He skirted the other guests once inside and found his way to the private corridor just outside the great hall where Lachlan and Mhairi were already waiting with the boys.

Young Hector lit up. "Uncle Hector, you're back."

"Aye, just for the evening, and then back to Moy." He grew wearier as he remembered the two-hour journey home at the end of the meal and hoped Tavish had managed to wrest time away from the accounts to see his chamber in order.

Lachlan took in his haggard appearance. "What's happened? You look pure done in."

"I've been up all night and day helping assemble furniture, hang tapestries, put down hides. I dinnae ken how we will be ready in three weeks; they're still plastering the great hall and the corridors. The artist comes tomorrow. I reckon I'll have him start in Cara's chamber."

"Why isn't Tavish seeing to that?" Mhairi asked.

"He is balancing the books, it's almost the end of the month again."

Mhairi said nothing, but her mouth made a hard line. Had he

gotten more sleep he may have queried her assessment of the situation, but he was too knackered.

He gave her a beseeching look. "I dinnae have a woman's touch, Mhairi. Please dinnae make me beg."

Mhairi smiled. "Would you like me to come down later this week and help you get things arranged for her?"

"Aye."

"All right. I'll see if I can get away on Thursday."

Somerled, the youngest of the five boys, grabbed onto one of his hands and began swinging back and forth. "I met yer bride, Uncle Hector."

"Aye? And what do you think of her?"

"She's verra bonny. She has pretty red hair like Young Hector."

Young Hector grimaced. "My hair is no' pretty."

"Nay. It's ugly, ye frog," said Young John.

Young Lachlan and Neil, the twins, started a shoving match, always eager to fight. Soon, all five boys had descended into mêlée. Somerled tripped and smacked his mouth on the stone floor, promptly descending into wails. Mhairi scooped him up while Lachlan encouraged the fracas.

"John, you cannae stand Young Hector up straight when you do a headlock, make sure you keep his body bent."

Hector's head throbbed, and his temper rose. In the space of five seconds, he picked up each twin by the collars of their tunics, swept the feet out from under John, and pinned Young Hector to the wall with one of his legs.

"Will you all please shut yer gobs and be still?"

A tinkle of laughter sounded behind him, and he turned, a twin still in each hand.

Neil, legs dangling, lifted his bonnet. "Evenin', Auntie."

Cara struggled to train her twitching mouth. "Good evening, Neil."

Putting both children back on solid ground, Hector bowed to her, feeling sheepish. She curtsied back. There was something different about her hair, and his heart affected him. "You look…"

Somerled lifted his head from Mhairi's shoulder and withdrew his thumb from his mouth. "Bonny."

Cara laughed and ran her hand over the five-year old's feathery blond hair.

Remembering that he was allowed to feel the things he was feeling for her, Hector agreed. "Aye, bonny."

The piper began to play, and Lachlan and Mhairi lined up, their boys in twos and threes behind.

Hector gave Cara his arm and pulled her into his side.

"I look like your child," she said looking up at him. "How tall *are* you?"

He chuckled, his darkened mood lifting now that they were together. "Six feet, nine inches. How tall are you?"

"Five feet. That reminds me, can you have a small set of stairs constructed for my side of our bed? I fell right onto my...em... getting up half asleep this morning."

A warm feeling besieged him with a relentlessness he had not felt in many years. He could not believe his ears. "You're no' wanting your own chamber?"

Cara lowered her voice, her tone brittle. "Why would I want my own chamber?"

He kept his eyes fixed and blank, navigating his conscience away from the temptation to think of them sharing a chamber. The effect was that his voice came out strangled and wooden. "I tho' I would sleep in the third-floor chamber."

Hurt registered over her face. "Oh."

Knowing he should be assuaging her fears, but still so astonished he couldn't speak, he was besieged by manly pride as they followed Lachlan and Mhairi into the great hall.

It was the first time they had appeared together in front of their clan betrothed. Cara held her head high, and his chest filled with adoration as she smiled to those she recognized and acknowledged them. His clumsiness hadn't extinguished her kind spirit or had any effect on her treatment of others, and he felt acute relief he wasn't betrothed to Elspeth.

A servant approached with wine as they took their seats. Cara leaned forward. "Could I have water instead, please?"

"You dinnae want claret, mistress? It's one of the laird's finest."

"No, thank you. You'll have to excuse me; I don't mean to offend. Gilbert served me at the midday meal, I thought he would be here again. What's your name?"

"Ingram, miss."

"Thank you, Ingram. Could I please have water if it isn't any trouble?" Ingram nodded and left to retrieve a pitcher.

Her relaxed manner with the servants spoke to the humble nature of her upbringing, but he rather liked it. "You dinnae want claret?"

She gave a reserved smile. "No. I've never liked wine, or ale, or whisky, or any of it. I'd rather have water."

"It's strange to feel you ken someone's substance, but not the basic things about them like what they like to drink, or eat, and what they dinnae."

"I don't like organ meat," she said without missing a beat.

"Och. What are ye talkin' about? That's the best part."

She stuck her tongue out and scrunched up her nose. "Liver especially. That aftertaste."

"Quit yer haverin', ye dinnae ken what's good. Liver makes you grow big and braw. Eyeballs as well."

Sensual green eyes flitted over him. "Ah...you ate nothing but liver and eyeballs as a child."

"Aye, and you ate only porridge. Stunted your growth."

Their banter was drawing looks from leadership, and Cara shushed him between stifled peals of laughter.

Ingram returned and filled both their cups with water. Hector took a deep breath and hoped he could explain his feelings to her about the chamber without causing further hurt. "Cara. I didnae mean to hurt you suggesting I keep my own chamber. It has nothing to do with being displeased with you."

She sipped her water, traces of hurt reappearing in her eyes. She didn't believe him.

He shifted. "I only meant I wanted to give you time. You've been through a great deal this year. I dinnae ken very much about you."

She studied the filigree at the base of her cup and lowered her voice. "You know many things. And you don't wish to share my bed."

He slid his rough hand into her velvet palm. Warmth snaked down his back. "I assure you, I do. Verra much."

For a bare moment he almost forgot himself and their audience and kissed her. Maintaining his self-control, he released her hand and reminded himself that such feelings and thoughts would be allowable in only three weeks' time but did not honor her now. It was best not to touch her and invite temptation until they were wed.

His voice came out rough. "I want to understand everything about you. I want to be encompassed by your thoughts. I want to learn who you are. And I want you to learn me."

A ripple of something passed over her features and she gave a wary smile. "Everything?"

"Aye."

There was a sadness in her voice when she spoke. "That could take a long time."

He felt suddenly sobered. "I've been waiting a verra long time. I'm no' the man I used to be. I never tho' God would give me a wife. I want to honor the treasure he's given to me."

She kneaded her temples and chuckled. "I'm in trouble. Keep saying such wonderful things and I'll be the one pining away."

He smothered another urge to kiss her and instead tucked into the smoked salmon that Ingram brought forth, grateful for the distraction.

"Hector, I know about the Wolf."

Inhaling a piece of salmon, he choked and hacked, causing the table in front of theirs to look at him with annoyance. He sipped on water and tried to clear his throat. "Aye?"

She pushed a currant dumpling around her plate, worry creasing her brow. "It isn't too late to call this off. To go to the MacKinnons..."

He dropped his eating knife, clouds reforming on the horizon of his mood. "Has Lachlan said something?"

"No," she said lowering her voice and looking around. She put a hand to his arm. "Nothing. He's been most kind. But I—I feel so guilty. You've taken such a risk. I don't have a tocher of land and money from my family to offer. You're bearing the expense of the household goods, my wardrobe... I bring nothing."

He picked up his knife and speared salmon together with the currant dumpling. "Mhairi's tailor came today, then?"

She blinked. "Yes."

"I instructed him to bring the finest materials for you to consider. Were they to your liking?"

Cara's gaze dropped to her trencher. "Aye, everything was fine. Too fine."

"And his plans for your wedding garments, did they please you?"

"Yes. Very much. Hector, I only want to be sure you don't make a mistake. I don't want you to resent me. I cannot give you an heir."

He rested his arm over the back of her chair and brought his mouth close to her ear. Goosebumps formed along her neck among her freckles.

"Dinnae rob me of my blessing. You are my gift. Wherever God leads us, or whatever he calls us to, his provision is already there. It might be just enough, not an abundance. But it is all that we need."

Unable to resist, he kissed her on the cheek.

# CHAPTER 22

## LOCHBUIE OIGHREACHD - OCTOBER 8, 1383

An almighty roar rose from the clan as Hector rode to St. Columba's chapel from Moy castle. Well-wishers shouted their blessings and waved handkerchiefs as he passed by with Lachlan and his nephews.

"May the hills lie low, Laird!"

"May ye be healthy all yer days!"

His nephews threw gold coins to the children, and they scrambled to pick them up.

Lachlan pulled his palfrey alongside Ghoustie. Although he'd not raised any objections to the marriage, a distance had grown between them that had never existed before. They continued polite conversation and pleasantries, but there were dark circles under Lachlan's eyes. Taciturnity and worry etched in his face. The unspoken disagreement weighed on Hector's mind.

"You still dinnae approve of her, do you?"

Lachlan rolled his eyes and waved to the clan lining either side of the road. "Do you wish to get into this now?"

"I dinnae wish to enter into this without my brother behind me."

Lachlan shifted in his saddle and cast his eyes over the swoops of bunting festooning cottages and crofts and the clan members cheering and waving. "They're behind you."

"Aye. They're behind *me*. But she will need the support of all of us. They're still wary of outsiders here. Elspeth's insults and lies didnae help matters, either. She needs your support."

Lachlan slowed his palfrey. "It's no' that I dinnae like her. On the contrary, I think she's risen to the task you've put in front of her quite well. Mhairi says she's bright."

"But?"

A group of gray-haired women waved their handkerchiefs at them. "God bless you, Laird MacLean and Laird MacLean!"

They waved back and put smiles upon their faces, but in his stomach, remorse began to form.

Lachlan sighed. "I am worried, Hector. With your betrothal to Elspeth all this heartache could've been avoided. If you'd left Cara alone, I believe she would have found her way. Now we've made the MacKinnons more resentful, the Wolf is breathing down our necks, and you're seating Cara as your lady when there've already been attempts made on her life from your clan."

The words that had gone unspoken between them now in the open, he almost wished he had not asked.

Lachlan cleared his throat. "I've received a missive from Léo that he plans to return to Mull next week."

"Will he be staying at Duart?"

"Aye. He has quite personal reasons for returning, and I do feel it is my duty as your brother to warn you that they are to do with Cara."

"Cara?"

As they approached St. Columba's chapel, Lachlan picked up the pace. "We can talk about it later. The most important part of his stay is that he's agreed to continue to help us with the Wolf."

Regret for hurting Léo and relief that he was still willing to help grew side by side like weed and flower. Even though he'd done nothing to deserve it, Hector wished that Léo would be standing with him in the chapel along with Lachlan.

They stopped their horses just outside the stone gate of the church yard and dismounted, handing their reins to the groom. Hector put a hand on Lachlan's arm and stopped him. "I've never had any wish to harm you or your family, brother. I regret that I've let you down, and the worry I've caused you."

The clear blue of Lachlan's eyes that matched his own, their mother's eyes, met his for the first time in three weeks. "You never intend to harm, but you do. When will it change?"

The honesty of Lachlan's words stung him, and he knew he had cause to speak them. Yet a sense of war settled over him. God had made his path clear. The hairs on the back of his neck stood on end. *Protect her.*

Hector spoke his resolution. "Concerning God, and what he has put before me, it willnae change. My words remain—she needs your support."

Lachlan looked away, and the gulf that had formed between them in the past three weeks reopened. "I'm here as your brother, and in that you have my support. But no' as chief of this clan." He turned and gathered his boys to him then made his way up the rocky steps that cut into the hillside and led toward the church.

Time lost meaning for a few moments, and he felt the same sense of leaving home he had thirteen years earlier. Only this time, he was certain Lachlan was in the wrong and he was in the right.

A persistent voice tore through his consciousness and caused him to look around. Among the trees, thickly decorated with ribbons, he spotted a stony-faced Rhona. Four small children clung to her, but her focus was on him alone as she wagged a finger at him, one eye narrowed. "Laird! You be good to our Cara now!"

One side of his mouth hoisted at her marching orders, and he called back to her, "God to you, Rhona. I swear to you I'll be taking care of your Cara."

She cupped her hand around her gap-toothed mouth, raising her voice. "Aye, you better!"

Strengthened by Rhona's mandate, Hector strode up the stony steps and into the churchyard as the church bells began to ring the tierce hour. It was time.

The arched door opened, and Father Timothy stepped out and

squinted against the bright sunlight, so unusual this time of the year. "You couldnae have asked for more beautiful weather."

A far away sound of pipes began to increase in volume and cheers rose from the edge of the village. Hector felt his stomach drop and for a sickening moment he thought he might pass out. Edginess like he had never felt in battle rattled his bones. He was about to be a married man. And not to any woman, not to Elspeth, but to the bright love of his heart.

Father Timothy opened his book. "That must be your bride." A trickle of sweat ran down Hector's temple and landed on the opened book, and he wiped his brow with the back of his shaking hand. "Sorry."

Somerled looked up at Hector. "You look a pure mess."

Young John crossed his arms. "Aye. You look like you are ready to boak."

Young Lachlan tugged on the corner of Hector's plaid until he turned around and held out a sprig of mint. "Chew on this."

"Will that calm me nerves?"

Young Lachlan shrugged. "No, but it will make your breath fresher for the kiss." All five boys erupted into hoots of laughter. Thinking it not a bad suggestion, he took the mint from Young Lachlan's hand and chewed.

Young Hector put a hand to Hector's shoulder and handed him his handkerchief. "Were you like this before battle?"

Wiping the sweat from the back of his neck with Young Hector's handkerchief he hoped he would not lose his stomach. "Nay. Never." Neil, John, and Somerled snickered.

The sounds of the one-hundred-and-twenty MacLean massed pipes and drums shook the ground. His heart pounded, and he quickly spat out the chewed mint. The pipers entered the churchyard and the MacLean guard assembled along the road. The crowds parted, and his heart leapt.

When he'd prayed to God for his wife, he never could've imagined how the blessing would overflow his cup. Surrounded by her chosen kin, angelic in gold, white doves embroidered along her sleeves and neckline, white silk veiling her face, she seemed to have just stepped out of the Kingdom of Heaven. Paralyzed with wonder he drank her in. Sunbeams of joy radiated from her face as their eyes met.

Mhairi greeted Hector with a kiss then took Lachlan's arm and whispered something in his ear. Hector prayed it was a word of support.

The bagpipes silenced, and Hector extended a shaking hand toward his bride. Margaret and Pádraig placed Cara's small hand into his. It was cold, and it too was shaking. He lifted it to his mouth and blew warmth onto her pale fingers, then put his cheek to hers and whispered the words he had longed to speak for months in her native tongue. "You are the most beautiful thing I've ever laid eyes on. I love you, my darlin'."

Surprise traveled across her face. "Me?"

He chuckled and kissed her cool fingers. "Aye, you."

She responded in assured Scottish. "I love you, Hector."

Father Timothy cleared his throat, then began the sacrament. "Chieftain Hector Reaganach MacLean has come here to wed Cara O'Ballevan. The banns have been read thrice. If anyone knows any just cause why these two should no' be wed, let him speak now."

Hector unwound the pouch of gold from his baldric and placed it on Father Timothy's book and then the tiny gold ring.

"Hector Reaganach MacLean, wilt thou take Cara O'Ballevan, here present, for thy lawful wife, according to the rite of the holy church?"

He looked into Cara's eyes, confident in the love they had spoken over their marriage. "I will."

"Cara O'Ballevan, wilt thou take Hector Reaganach MacLean, here present, for thy lawful husband, according to the rite of the holy church?"

She smiled. "I will."

"I join you together in marriage, in the name of the Father, and of the Son, and of the Holy Ghost. Amen."

A deep feeling of rightness overtook his soul. Cara was now his wife. He squeezed her hand, and she squeezed back.

Father Timothy made the sign of the cross over the ring and began the blessing, sprinkled holy water over it, and handed it to Hector.

Hector held out Cara's hand sliding the ring partway over her thumb. *"In nomine Patris,"* he moved the ring partway over her index finger, "*et Filii*," he moved the ring over her middle finger, "*et Spiritus Sancti*," he moved the ring over her fourth finger and slid it on. "Amen."

Father Timothy turned and walked into the chapel and began to sing a psalm of blessing. Guiding his wife inside, Hector could not take his eyes from her. They stepped up at the doorway to the altar and Father Timothy turned to pray over them in Latin.

Once the prayer concluded, Hector led Cara before the holy altar and they knelt prostrate, the care cloth Margaret lovingly embroidered to match Cara's mantle handed to their witnesses. Margaret, Lachlan, Ursula, and Mhairi each held a corner of the cloth and lowered it over them until it touched their heads. It was the holiest moment of their wedding ceremony, as God blessed Cara to him as wife.

Father Timothy now prayed in Gaelic for her to be joined to him, his partner, endowed by blessing, and invoked God's defense and protection over her. Cara kept her eyes tightly shut and murmured her agreement with the words of his prayer and blessing.

"Let her be fruitful in offspring; be approved and innocent..."

A tremble passed over her. No, he would not let her feel as if she were not enough. Hector interlaced his fingers with hers, bringing them under his arm and to his chest and kissed them.

"May they both see their children's children to the third and fourth generation, and may they reach the old age they desire. Through the same Jesus Christ, thy Son, our Lord, who with thee in the unity of the Holy Ghost liveth and reigneth God."

The care cloth lifted off them and Father Timothy bade them to stand. He held up his hands and said the Pater Noster. Having finished the final blessing, he kissed Hector on each cheek, the sign of peace. The moment had come; it was his turn to impart the sign of peace to his wife. His heart pounded. She was his to love, his to kiss, and his to protect for the rest of their lives. His heart burst with joy but also trepidation.

Carefully, he lifted her veil and placed each of his hands on her small, faerie face and completed the soft kiss he had longed to give to her on Iona. A soft gasp breathed in through her mouth, the cushion of her lips curved to his own, imparting her own love to him. They pulled apart and smiled at each other.

The pipers began the MacLean victory song as they stepped outside the church. The clan broke into earsplitting cheering and hooting. The MacLean guard unsheathed their swords and beat on their shields in time with the drums.

Spurred on by the sounds of triumph, Hector turned to his wife and fitted his mouth to hers again, savoring her softness, because he could. When they broke apart, he swept her into his arms and the berserker living within him let out a wild cry of victory.

# CHAPTER 23

## LOCHBUIE OIGHREACHD - OCTOBER 8, 1383

Darkness cloaked Lochbuie and the brilliant light of a full moon illuminated the contours of Hector's face as Cara sidled up next to him in the barmkin yard where the wedding feast had been laid for the clan to enjoy. Only one more wedding ceremony lay before them, and it was the one she'd been anticipating for three weeks with dread and curiosity.

His eyes warmed as she tucked into his side, his arm naturally falling around her shoulders.

"Father Timothy is ready to go home. I am going inside to prepare for the em…"

A smile came to Hector's eyes, then spread to his lips, half-revealing two rows of even teeth. "Oh?"

She gave him a playful smack on the arm, and he pretended to be wounded. "Cheeky beggar."

Mhairi took her hand with a wink. "We'll see you in a few minutes."

As they made for the keep, raucous hoots and shouts began among Hector's guard. "Nearly time to become a man. Come, lads, let's get him ready."

A bawdy song lifted over their merry number and carried through the walls even after Mhairi and Cara entered Moy. Never having been inside the keep before, Cara was awed by the clean and modern furnishings mixed with the older stonework. "'Tis too fine for a weaver."

Mhairi guided her up another flight of stairs. "Och. You should have seen this place a few months ago. Lachlan wouldn't let me inside for fear something would fall on me. The wooden structure was a good decision. It's warmer than Duart in here."

They exited on the second floor and turned right down a long corridor. Aoife waited with a candle before the second door and dipped into a curtsy. "Good evening, Lady MacLean." Cara looked at Mhairi before realizing this was her new title.

Aoife snickered then fished in her pocket for a key, opening the heavy wooden door.

Cara's eyes grew wide. The massive chamber was nicer than the one she had stayed in at Duart. Smooth hides softened her steps on the wooden floors, candles bathed the room in sultry light. A massive bed laden with furs and blankets dominated the room, and curtains cloaked it in privacy. The walls were painted a lovely shade of ivory with motifs of thistles and clover. She turned toward the hearth and her heart stopped. Above it, was an intricate mural of the annunciation.

Gabriel appeared before Mary, his golden wings pointed aloft, sheltering the Blessed Mother. Beside Mary's haloed head, a dove kissed her temple and her arms folded in front of her cradling her fertile womb.

Trepidation spread from Cara's prickling scalp, down her spine, and into her legs. "How lovely."

Aoife began the work of readying Cara for bed, dutifully ignoring the torches of alarm firing through her as she unpinned the veil.

Mhairi followed Cara's eyes. "I suggested that he paint over it, but he wanted you to see it first before calling the artist back."

Trying to banish the feelings of inadequacy that threatened to ruin the happiest day of her life thus far, she forced a smile to her face.

Mhairi helped Aoife remove Cara's gown. "It is a beautiful painting. Perhaps something to inspire your prayers?"

Cara swallowed and looked at the holy dove of Spirit that imparted a miracle to the young woman. If only she too could receive such a miracle. Perhaps it was something to hope for. Or something to haunt her.

She forced words to her dry throat. "It's too exquisite to paint over." Yet she turned, unable to look at it anymore.

In silence, Mhairi and Aoife undressed her and laid away the wedding finery. The diaphanous linen of her wedding chemise went over her head and Cara blushed. "I don't know if I have the courage to wear such a thing. I'm used to my thick woolens by this time of the year."

Aoife winked at her. "We'll make sure you are covered to your neck with blankets."

After plaiting her hair and securing it with a satin ribbon, they turned back the covers and helped her up her requested bed stairs into the thick, soft feather tick. At the end of the hall, the noise of raucous laughter grew in volume.

Aoife tucked the blankets tightly around Cara and kissed her on the cheek. "Blessings upon your marriage, my lady."

Mhairi kissed her other cheek. "Blessings upon your marriage."

Her heart thundered in her ears, and then thundered again. It took her a moment to realize the sound was a heavy knock. She tightened her grip on the blankets, praying this time would be different than last.

From the corridor, shouts began, and Hector was pushed into the room wearing only a long tunic. His tightly plaited hair had been unwound and a riot of curls made him seem larger and more intimidating than she had ever seen him.

Lachlan entered the room, followed by an unruffled Father Timothy, who shut the door on the loud chorus of the next bawdy song. He nodded his greeting and averted his eyes to the Blessed Mother.

Aoife turned back the covers, and for the first time Hector looked at Cara. Something passed over his face before he cast his eyes to the floor and bowed to her.

The drumming of her heart was so loud she wondered if he could hear it from across the room as Lachlan put a hand on his shoulder and guided him to the bed. The bed dipped violently to the left as he sat down on the mattress, and she clung to the blankets for dear life, praying they would not slip below her chin and reveal her. When Hector had stretched his legs to the end of the tremendous bed and been tucked in and blessed by his brother, Father Timothy began his final ceremony, sprinkling the bed with holy water. He held his hands up.

"Let us pray. Bless, O Lord, this marriage bed and those in it, that they live in your love and multiply and grow old together. Amen."

Mhairi bade them goodnight and followed Aoife and Father Timothy out of the chamber, pulling Lachlan along with her. Before the door closed, crazed, and she suspected drunken, shouts emanated from the hallway. "Be gentle with him, Cara!"

Hector scrambled up, launching her in the air, and bolted it behind them. He hesitated at the door, his hand frozen on the latch, his head bowed. He wouldn't turn and look at her. "Should I go?"

Never had Duncan ever taken into consideration whether she wanted him, but Hector relinquished all rights he had to take her. Her heart longed to have a private moment with her new husband, a moment of quiet that they'd not enjoyed all day, and her apprehension began to dissolve.

"You've only just got here."

"Aye, but if you would like the room for yourself, I can sleep in the chamber upstairs."

"Could you stay for a little while?"

He turned but did not raise his eyes to hers.

"What's the matter?"

"You're so beautiful, and I fear I may no' be able to control my thoughts seeing you in my—our bed."

Stilling her wild heart, she removed one hand from its blanketed fortress, patting the bed next to her. "You don't have to control your thoughts. 'Tis not a sin to think them for your wife."

Hector bit his lip, eyes blinking hard, and returned to the bed, keeping a wide valley between them.

Amazed that he didn't take even the smallest liberty, she shifted to her side. When he still didn't come closer, she snuggled nearer to him, keeping a tight rein on the velvet coverlet. For the first time since Iona, she rested her head upon his chest. She could hear the pounding of his heart and her head lifted as he took a shuddering breath. At last, a heavy arm curled around her shoulders.

She imitated Iain MacLeod's thick brogue. "Auld Leg Arms."

No doubt remembering Iain's drunken impression, he burst into laughter at her jest.

She listened to his chest. "Your heart is beating as fast as a hare."

"Aye, and my mouth is dry as sand."

Removing a bare arm from the heat of the blankets she curled it around his middle, getting used to his closeness. Closing her eyes, she ran her hand cautiously along the bands of unyielding muscles and imagined the many battles and fights that had honed him from boy into man. "Your stomach is like stone."

Hector snorted.

Feeling bold, she smoothed a hand over his hard chest. "You needn't be afraid of me, Hector."

He snorted again and she jangled against him. "I'm no' afraid of you, wee wife. I'm afraid of me."

Genuine laughter bubbled over from her and she brought her face close to his and smoothed her hand over his cheek.

He raised his hand, hesitated, then picked up her long plait, fingering the cords as they interweaved each other. "Your hair is like liquid fire."

Touching the smooth loops of the plait, his eyes held such reverence a weight freed itself from her shoulders. He didn't ravage her with violence—he would never harm her.

As if he read her memories, he queried her. "What was your first husband like?"

A log snapped in the fire.

"Duncan?" She paused, not wanting to bring that time into the holiness of the moment between them. The day had been more than she'd ever dreamed. So different from the quick handfast at the edge of Buncrana, with no witnesses, no prayers, no blessings. Different because this time, she married a man who loved her.

Hoping to avoid giving him any suspicions as she had with Mhairi, she tried to answer. "He was certainly not as tall as you. Ruddy, handsome, and strong." She groped through her knowledge of Duncan trying to think of any positive qualities. "He—he was a good provider."

Hector stilled. "I'm no' ashamed to admit I'm jealous of him. He understood everything about you."

Her fingers traveled across his chest and touched the warm, bare skin at his neck. If only Hector knew that he understood her better than Duncan ever did. In truth, Duncan understood nothing about her—except how to torment her.

Hector pulled the ribbon off the end of the plait. Again, she watched amazed as he touched her hair with admiration, not lust. Nothing seemed to quench his hopeless fascination with her. The safety that she always felt with him multiplied in his arms, and she longed for him to stay.

"Have you loved many women?"

His hand stopped moving against the red of her hair. "I dinnae wish to lie to you. I know Léo still remembers and resents it."

"Go on."

"Love wasnae something I was seeking. But I was a lonely man."

Leaning back into his arm she looked up to his face, finding regret, and perhaps pain. "There have been many others?"

Hector closed his eyes. "Aye."

"Go on."

"I hope you believe me...I've lived chaste since God changed me."

Tightening her arm around his middle, she nestled her head to his chest. How could she be angry with a man so gentle and concerned to do right by God and their marriage? "How've you managed?"

Hector exhaled sharply as if he'd well and truly suffered. "A lot of prayer."

Laughter overtook her and shook the bed. "You poor man."

It was Hector's turn to look amazed. "My past doesnae matter to you then? You're no' upset?"

Laughter abated and she considered his words. "It matters. I don't like it, but I better understand why you want this to be different, and how careful we must be to honor it. No, I'm not upset over things you've been long forgiven for."

Hector unwound her plait with his fingers, threading them through the waves. Her hand slipped inside the neck of his tunic and rested upon his heart. Her body grew heavier, and sleep beckoned her. They lay in silence for long minutes. If he was going to return to his own chamber he should do it now, but the thought of being away from him brought her no comfort.

"Hector?"

"Hmm?"

"Did you mean it? That you love me?"

A heavy arm tightened around her, and he kissed the top of her head. "Aye. I love you, Cara."

A peace that passed all understanding settled upon her and forced her heavy eyelids to close. She was loved. "I love you, Hector."

"Cara?"

"Hmm?"

"May I stay with you tonight? Only tae hold ye?"

"Course ye can, daft man."

Cara crouched before the fire and put another brick of peat in the open hearth, blowing the flame to life. Satisfied that it had caught, she rose and found herself in the familiar stone walls of her cottage in Rathmullan. She walked the rush-covered floors and made sure everything for dinner was laid out in precise order.

The door latch lifted and sweat broke out along her back. He was home late, never a good sign. The door flung open and there before her stood Duncan, moldering, his head hanging at an unnatural angle.

Words came to his lips, but she couldn't understand them. She gestured to the table, and he stalked forward trailing dirt behind him. He looked with disapproving eyes over the meal, the table, and over her. Then, he lunged.

Face twisting into a sickened grimace, he tackled her to the ground and pinned her. His fist recoiled again and again. Her nails dug into the earthen floor as she tried to pull herself out of his grasp, but she couldn't get away. Panic raced through her as his hand went into the embers of the hearth and removed the wax press, the high ridges of three boars glowing orange. She screamed and kicked, but his hand came around her leg and she couldn't get away.

Yelling with all her might, she cried out, but her voice was weak. "Hector."

Where was Hector? She needed Hector. The press descended through the air.

Taking a deeper breath, she filled her lungs and screamed the name of her protector. "God, please—*Hector!*"

Shaking began in the cottage and Duncan dissolved.

"Cara. Wake up. Wake up, love."

Eyes opening, heart pounding, she looked into the face of the one she needed most, the forbidding angles of his face gathered in concern. "What is it, love?"

Breath coming in bursts, she launched herself around his neck, needing his protection. Strong arms lifted her, then came around her and held her tight. Realization and humiliation crashed over her, followed by sobs of terror. The panic wouldn't dislodge from her chest.

"I'm here. I'm here, love."

She buried her face in his neck and pulled his arms tighter around herself, needing to shut out the dream and the horror of returning to the worst day of her life.

He kissed her shoulder and rocked her back and forth. "It was only a dream, love."

Her dry tongue fused to the roof of her mouth and wouldn't allow her to speak the words she needed to. It hadn't been only a dream.

"Nothing can harm you, lass, I'm—"

The loud pealing of church bells reverberated the timber walls around her, and she struggled to make sense of what was happening. The latch of the door began to shake up and down and in the blink of an eye she had been deposited beneath the bed.

"Dinnae come out until I tell you it's safe."

She struggled to slow her heaving breast. Hector held a finger over his lips then retrieved his sword before opening the door and bursting into the hall. The sounds of a struggle met her ears, then voices.

"Tavish. By the saints, I almost ran you through. You didnae knock."

"I'm sorry, my laird. I've come to warn you. We're under attack."

# CHAPTER 24

## LOCHBUIE OIGHREACHD - OCTOBER 9, 1383

Hooves pounded against loamy earth as the MacLean guard
started to gain ground. Primordial forest canopied a narrow
shelf trail that suspended above black upheaving rocks and
the swirling dark water of Loch Buie below. As the woodland trail gave
way to open fields, Ghoustie picked up speed, charging after the last
contingent of caterans that had nearly destroyed the village to the far
west of Hector's territory.

Flames leapt from the tops of cottages and warmed Hector's face
with intense heat. He spotted movement on the edge of the hedgerow,
barely distinguishable in the fire's dancing light, and he steered Ghoustie
toward the six remaining caterans trying to escape on stolen palfreys.

Raising his quarterstaff, Hector indicated the direction to the guard
behind him. One cateran straggled behind, stuck with a sorrel-colored
palfrey of unremarkable pace. He gave Ghoustie a confident squeeze
with his legs asking him to finish the chase. The destrier exploded in a
burst of speed, closing the gap on the stolen palfrey. The cateran looked
over his shoulder, whipping the sorrel horse mercilessly, but she
couldn't contend with the stallion's dispatch.

"Good lad, Ghoustie. Go."

Couching the quarterstaff beneath his arm Hector braced for

impact. With a sharp snap, the staff connected with rider, shattering into pieces as the man tumbled forward, arms outstretched. Hector circled his horse, the rest of the guard thundering past. The man must be taken alive. The stunned cateran lay sprawled on the ground where he landed. Hector slowed Ghoustie and dismounted.

Dressed in black and covered in dark mud, the man wobbled to his feet, gasping, and readying for a fight.

Hector rolled his eyes at his obviously disoriented opponent. "I wouldnae try it if I were you. Surrender now and I'll no' harm you."

Listing from side to side, the man doddered forward and hooked an arm over Hector's neck. Muscle memory engaged. In a flash of frenetic movement, Hector pivoted under the man's arm, dodged his right fist, and dipped to avoid his left.

The man swung again. Hector caught the man's arm in the grip of his left hand and swung the outside of his right fist like a hammer against the cateran's temple. Momentarily stunning his opponent, Hector delivered his fist to the man's opposite temple before folding him forward to the ground and pinning him.

"Stop struggling. I told you I'll no' hurt you if you cooperate."

Something dawned in the man's face. He swore at Hector and kicked his legs like a feral horse, trying to reach his right boot. Hector descended on him, landing a walloping blow to the man's face.

Body limp beneath his legs, Hector stopped, realizing the man was unconscious. "It's your own fault. You wouldnae listen."

He found the concealed dagger in the man's boot and gave a bitter chuckle at his incompetence, then secured it in his own boot and retrieved a length of rope from his saddle.

One by one the MacLean guard took down their targets and rounded the stolen palfreys.

He called out to Calum, "Is it a total loss?"

Calum's white-blond Viking features glowed orange in the inferno, and he nodded, a look of disgust in his eyes. "Aye, Laird."

The rest of the MacLean guard poured into the destroyed village of Glenbyre. The smell of burning turf lingered in the air. A mixture of pride at the guard's response to their first threat on Lochbuie, and disgust at the amount of damage twenty raiders had wrought in only a few hours, gave Hector a heaviness of heart.

The sorrel mare paced behind Ghoustie in circles, lost and agitated. Her eyes were wide, and her nostrils flared. Ghoustie perked his ears, perceptive of the mare's distress. Hector gave a low whistle and Ghoustie came to him. The mare whinnied and called to Ghoustie, then followed the animal's peaceful manner toward Hector. Ghoustie lowered his head, smelling her neck and mane, and offering his to her.

Dropping his voice to his lowest timbre, he extended his hand. "Aye, you're all right, lass. You're safe." He scratched under her ginger forelock and handed her reins to Calum.

"Take her to the pasture. I'll get our cateran friend up and follow with Ghoustie."

Ghoustie nickered, his eyes following the mare as she was led away. He went forward a few paces.

"Stand."

Ghoustie stopped and looked back at him, then nickered again, lovesick. "Ah poor lad. We'll be along after her in a moment."

He pulled the cateran up over his shoulders and ambled toward Ghoustie, the man groaning with each step he took, beginning to regain consciousness. "I told you no' to put up a fight and look what happened."

The man groaned again.

"What clan are you from?"

The man became silent. He understood what Hector was saying.

"Campbell?"

The man groaned. Hector took Ghoustie's reins and began the walk toward the pasture.

"Irvine?"

The man groaned as he stepped over a swale.

"Stewart?"

The man stopped groaning, and guilt made Hector's stomach drop. In less than a day since his marriage, Alexander Stewart struck right at the heart of his clan. The timing could not be a coincidence. The MacKinnons were almost certainly involved.

Beside the pasture he dropped the man unceremoniously into the brush. Three guards stepped forward to take stock of the last surviving cateran, vengeful looks on their faces.

"Get a wagon and take him to the bottle dungeon on Morvern. I dinnae want him near my wife."

"Aye, Laird."

Hector put a hand on the nearest man's shoulder. "It's imperative he arrives on Morvern alive. Do you understand me?"

The man exhaled in frustration but nodded. "Aye."

Ghoustie stomped at the gate to the pasture. Hector opened the gate, and the Iberian ran right past every fine-boned palfrey mare and toward the small, pretty sorrel.

Calum's eyes narrowed. "He's never shown interest in any other horse before. How odd."

Hector thought of Cara's dream and the way she'd cried out for him, and tried to hold onto the faith that he'd done the right thing. "Aye. He's protecting her."

Pádraig strode over, a worried look on his face. "That's all the cottages in Glenbyre. Plus, several on the west end of Lochbuie village. The cattle have been driven off into the woodland. It'll take days to get them back, if we can at all."

Heart sinking, Hector spied six blackened figures in the tall grass beside the cottage and pointed to them. "Dead?"

Pádraig nodded. "Aye. Parents and four children. Every other family managed to get out."

Nausea beset him as he imagined their final moments, and he hoped they had died sleeping and not burned alive. "What family lived here?"

"Brian and Rhona Rankin. Their children—Eilis, Peter, Wallace, and Holly."

His chest constricted. "Rhona?"

"Aye. The kind woman who threw the celebration you attended at the tavern. She stuck up for Cara at the barley field..."

A lump formed in his throat and his vision blurred. "Aye, Cara was a favorite of hers. I saw her outside the church yesterday before Cara arrived. She told me to be sure to take care of her. Their children played —played barley break with us in the evening."

Pádraig looked away, pinching his lips between his teeth, eyes watering.

Hector summoned five young guards over and pointed to the blackened figures. "Collect and cover the family. Bring them to St. Columba's and see that they are prepared for a proper Christian burial. See if there are families who would be willing to take anyone displaced. If there are others who need shelter, bring them to the inn. I will cover the cost of their rooms until new housing can be established."

The guards nodded.

He watched the stiff, charred bodies being loaded into a wagon, the cateran being led away, and the great plumes of thick, acrid smoke, and for the first time he wondered if he had made the right decision.

# CHAPTER 25

## LOCHBUIE OIGHREACHD - OCTOBER 10, 1383

It was lauds, two days after their wedding, and Hector still had not returned to Moy. Heartache gripped Cara's chest as she recited the dawn prayer. "Lord, open my lips and my mouth will proclaim your praise."

The morning prayers to hail the dawning of a new day did nothing to assuage the feeling of sorrow growing in her heart. She bowed her head and whispered her prayer, searching for the one to make sense of it all. "O God, come to our aid, O Lord, make haste to help us."

Hector had issued strict orders that she was not to leave the confines of Moy and no one was to enter or leave until he returned. For two days she'd been adrift at Moy, unable to gather Margaret and Ursula to herself, but assured by the guard that they were safe and tending the families who'd lost their homes to the fires the caterans had set. They'd lost everything. Because of her.

A knock sounded at the door of the solar.

"Enter."

Tavish stepped into the solar and ran a hand over his smooth jaw. "Aoife relayed your query. Still no word from the laird, my lady."

Cara turned back toward the window, watching the black smoke appearing over Moy's walls, soul-crushing guilt weighing on her.

Tavish leaned a muscled arm on the window frame, his spring green eyes soft with concern. "You seem troubled this morning."

Cara palmed the book of psalms, wishing she could read the words to still her mind, and tried not to feel inadequate. "I am."

He took her hand in his and led her toward two burgundy-colored chairs. "Come."

Taking the seat beside him, she fingered the spine of the psalter and traced the pebbled grain of the leather.

"What is it, my lady?"

Unbidden tears stung her eyes, and she cursed her emotions, wishing she could wear the mask she could so easily don in front of Duncan. As the months passed and she drifted farther away from that time, the more difficult it grew to deny herself.

"It's all because of me."

A feeling of helplessness overwhelmed her that she seemed always at the mercy of her own weaknesses. "I'm not qualified to be his wife, to be the lady of the clan. I'll never belong now."

Tavish rested his elbows on the arms of the chair and threaded his fingers together, his handsome face open and full of concern. "Do you regret your marriage?"

The question hung in the air. "I—I don't know. I love Hector, I want to be his wife, but I don't think I can do this. I wish that he was just a weaver."

He chuckled. "Ah, but he's no', is he?"

"No." The tiny word held great weight. Hector was chieftain. For better or worse, God had chosen him for this path, and somehow, she found herself his wife.

Tavish raised his eyebrows. "He wasn't born to this role. Yet, he has transformed a dysfunctional, impoverished clan into a unified province. Taken just on his past and qualifications, I'm no' sure anyone would choose him to lead this clan."

A smile warmed her face. "Aye, I suppose you're right."

He tapped a knuckle off her chin. "I'm no' sure you need to think of being his lady as a matter of qualification. You only need to do your best each day. Embrace the the things you can do, and what sets you apart."

She puzzled. What did set her apart?

"I have a mind for numbers. Mhairi suggested I take over the clan accounts from you, that way you would be able to assist Hector with other matters."

An awkward pause stretched between them. Tavish cleared his throat. "I'm not sure that would be an effective strategy at the moment. The clan needs tangible relief now."

Embarrassed for suggesting such a foolish thing she could feel herself growing red.

He laughed at her expression. "Let me help you. You've learned the name of each man and woman in our household in under two days. Your recall for details is quite remarkable. And you have an advantage over some high-born lady."

She couldn't imagine what advantage a lass from Buncrana might have over someone like Mhairi. "What's that?"

"You've come from nothing and lived what each one of these people have—despite what they may tell you, you're one of them. Distribute alms for our clan with some of our staff. I'm sure the clan would respect your efforts to help them."

Such an endeavor would require her to leave Moy and disobey Hector's orders. Never had she ever dared disobey Duncan, to do so would have meant punishment. "I don't know, Tavish. Hector gave the guard orders. They won't open the gates without him here."

"As Lady of Lochbuie, you're in command of the household and the guards in Hector's absence. You'd be helping him. These are things he will need to do when he returns. By taking this responsibility from him, he is free to focus on defense of our territory."

It *would* be something she could do to help him instead of burdening him, and their clan.

Tavish lifted a shoulder. "The guards will open the gates and take you into the village if you invoke your title."

Invoke her title? She could never do such a thing. Could she? Or if she stayed shut up in the castle, would they think her once again the outsider?

Misty morning fog crept across the barmkin as she exited the keep, in full knowledge that she was disobeying her husband's orders. A needle of guilt laced through her heart. Hector wanted her to stay shut up in Moy safe and sound until he returned, but she could no longer hide away from her clan.

Murdoch's look of disapproval was obvious as she left the keep, his dark eyes piercing her from the far end of the barmkin yard, his arms crossed over his chest.

Her heart pounded as she approached him, her chin high and shoulders back. "Murdoch."

He bowed to her, his eyes raking over her work attire. "My lady. Is there something I may do for you?"

She swallowed. "Yes. Please arrange an escort. I'm going into the village."

Murdoch looked at the six tall warriors on either side of him and they shook their heads. "I'm sorry, my lady, you're to stay within *the keep* until the laird's return."

It was the resistance she'd expected and the answer she knew she'd receive. "Aye, I understand that. But the threat of further attack was lifted last night, wasn't it?" She hated the uncertainty in her voice and tried to affect her best look of high-born authority.

Murdoch made a sound of annoyance and blinked. "Aye, but our laird has no' returned."

"Our clan has been hurt badly by these attacks. I must go to them."

He took an intimidating stance over her. "Our laird has no' returned."

Knees knocking, she tried to sound confident. "I don't wish to report this to my husband. As Lady of Lochbuie I am well aware that in his absence, it isn't you who is in charge of this guard or this household, but I."

His shoulders dropped and he looked toward the sky and swore aloud, then called the guard to attention. "Lady MacLean, give us your order."

"Open the gates to Moy, and escort us to the village where we'll be distributing alms to those families who need it. Then send a contingent to Laggan Sands to retrieve my loom and begin assembling it on the third floor. I will return this afternoon to assist. My mother-in-law can direct you on how to take it apart and put it back together. Do you understand?"

Murdoch's nostrils flared with agitated breath, and he responded through gritted teeth. "Aye, my lady."

She nodded, trying to look resolved and in charge.

Murdoch shouted the orders and the barmkin gate began to lift. For the first time in her life, men listened to her command and heeded it because of her own authority. A pang of guilt, not power, resonated through her heart, but she closed her eyes and prayed for strength. *Hector isn't like Duncan. Help me not to be afraid.*

Together they walked from Moy castle up the long lane toward Lochbuie village. Smoke smoldered from the edges of the pastures in the distance, and villagers crowded together in groups along the road. When they reached the edge of the village, she paused before the tithe barn.

Trickles of people made their way across the fields, their faces dirty with soot. Their expressions broken.

She issued her orders to Murdoch. "I'd like stations to be set up. Food carts over by the trees, and grain at the tithe doors. Household items like soaps and candles beside those trees. Can you write?"

Murdoch nodded. "Aye—a little."

"I can't write words but can do numbers. I would like you to record the type and lengths of cloth these families need, and I'll prepare it for them."

Murdoch cocked his head to the side and looked at her askance. "Lady MacLean, dinnae you think you should wait for the laird before—"

She cut him off before he could diminish her before her staff and villagers. Drawing up to her full five feet she verbalized her displeasure in the kindest of tones, as she'd seen Mhairi do. "I don't believe it's your place to question, but I take it into consideration. My husband is quite busy now, and it is our job to support Laird MacLean by doing things we can. There's no need to add burdens to his shoulders when we may sort this out."

Murdoch's face smoothed but something doubtful remained in his eyes. "As you wish, my lady."

Rolling up her sleeves, she took a place beside the cook and assisted in making porridge and oak bannocks[1]. One by one, the affected villagers made their way through the line and a light hubbub of fellowship grew among their number.

A round woman in a vibrant yellow leine took the place beside her and began to help with the food preparation, incorporating eggs with the soaked oats. "Do you remember me? I'm Sheena MacFadyen, Donal's mother."

The woman gave her a soft look of apology, and Cara did not mention the incident with Donal. She passed her a large bowl. "Aye, of course. Thank you for the help."

Sheena sifted flour into the bowl and helped her turn the mixture. "It's strange to see you here. I dinnae believe we would have seen Elspeth MacKinnon elbow deep in batter."

Cara stifled an urge to laugh at the image she conjured and scooped batter from the bowl into the hot greased pan, hoping Sheena wouldn't belittle her. "I know more about being a wife than a lady. I can cook, and I can keep house. I didn't know how else I might be of assistance."

Sheena began a new batch of bannocks without needing instruction from the cook. "Aye, I understand what you mean. I feel so helpless, at least this we can do. My family hasnae lost anything, but I am grieved to see these poor souls who have. I'm glad you've tho' of a way to contribute. We were wrong about you...my lady."

Cara felt acute relief, but said nothing, not wanting to embarrass Sheena.

They worked in silence making hot mealie bannocks and placing them on extended trenchers. One by one, more villagers showed up with carts, laden with spare goods and food stuffs. The fishery passed out smoked salmon, farmers distributed goat milk, and women assembled, distributing extra clothing to villagers in need.

A few who'd ganged up on her in the barley field made a point to remove their bonnets and bow to her as she handed out trenchers of food, blessing her for the meal. The suspension in hostilities filled her with praise. Thank God, Tavish had been right.

By midday a fine misting rain had begun to fall. Consigning herself that she would be getting wet, she pulled her hood over her head and continued to see to the distribution of goods. At the none hour she was on the point of beginning her tenth batch of bannocks when rumbling could be heard at the edge of town. The villagers crowded together behind the guard as they all recognized the sound. Hoofbeats.

The trees at the edge of the fields rustled, and the MacLean guard surged through them, Hector at the front upon Ghoustie's silver back. His plaid streamed away from his shoulders, the black spirals of his hair thrown back as he charged across the fields. Feeling awed, she realized that she was again witnessing the fighter he was. A warrior king, magnificent and frightening—and hers.

The squad of guards halted in front of the tithe barn, a wagon rolling to a stop behind. Cara rushed forward on shaking legs, longing to leap into her husband's arms, the horror of the last two days abating now that he had returned.

Hector dismounted and strode right toward her, and she stopped dead, suddenly overcome with timidity. An indiscernible look was contorting the malevolent angles of his face. She began to back away, tripping over the edge of her skirt as one massive hand circled her bicep and drew her up to his spectral eyes. Panic ruptured over her senses and her breath shriveled away.

"Why have you disobeyed my orders?"

Words refused to form on her tongue, her mind went blank, and her knees buckled. He lowered his tone, but his voice growled, saturated with anger. "One of the MacFadyen guard rode to us this morning with a missive informing me you'd ordered my guard into Lochbuie as commander. What are you thinking?"

*Run*, her instincts commanded. *Run back to Moy. Run home. Get away.* Trembling chattered her chin, and she pulled her arm backward, needing to be free. He tightened his grip.

"You offer no explanation for this?"

Murdoch came to her side. "I believe she was trying to help."

Abruptly, Hector released her arm and she tumbled backward into the mud. Hector rounded on Murdoch, his face inches from him. Murdoch didn't betray any sign of backing down. Her heart hammered in her chest. What had she done?

"Why did you let her out of the gate?"

Murdoch's face grew hard. "She threatened to report me to you if I didn't. She invoked her power as Lady of Lochbuie."

Words stammered from her mouth. "Th-that isn't what I—I-I-I'm sorry M-murdoch..."

Hector towered over her, and she almost screamed as he reached toward her. Her arms locked between them, and she held him away with all her might. His face twisted into confusion before picking her up from the ground and placing her back on her feet as if she weighed nothing. A strange bearing floated in the cold pools of his eyes, and it took her a moment to name the expression. Hurt.

Involuntary shaking consumed her body as she ignored its need to run from harm. She struggled to find her voice.

Pity saturated Murdoch's expression and he looked at her as though she were a wounded animal, crying and struggling to get away. "Our clan saw her example and it's grown to what you see here. Everyone has shared what they can spare, and maybe even more than that."

Head trembling, she brought her eyes to Hector's. "O-our c-clan needed me."

Hector looked to his people, and then to her. "Thank you all for your generosity. It is with great regret I announce that there has been loss of life in Glenbyre."

A murmur rippled across the clan and men removed their bonnets.

Hector inclined his chin toward the wagon. "Please offer your prayers for the Rankin family. Brian...Rhona, Eilis, Peter, Wallace, and Holly."

Cara's eyes traveled to the cart where six bodies were covered with coarse linen, the smallest only a tiny bump beside other small bumps. Someone in the crowd cried out in horror. She must have wobbled, for Hector's strong and steady arm held her upright.

"Please dinnae disperse, stay if you have need. It's good to be together now. My wife has done well in organizing this, a testament to her pure heart. If you'll excuse us, we will join you again tomorrow morning."

Tears did not form in her eyes, no emotion resounded through her chest. Her body went numb. The shaking subsided. All thought exited her mind, and she could only watch the scene unfold as if from a great distance away. The following hours blurred behind her as the numb shock remained. She felt herself lifted onto Ghoustie's back and led back to Moy. She remembered Margaret's soft voice and smooth hands.

"It's happened once before, the day... It doesnae matter. So long ago it was. She's only tired out."

Cara remembered being led up the stairs by Aoife and sitting beside the fire, staring into the dancing orange embers that glowed in the hearth. She remembered sitting there for hours. And yet, no thought penetrated the quiet depths of her mind.

At compline[2], the door to their chamber opened. Hector knelt before her and took her cold hand in his, kissing her fingers and blowing warmth into them. "Cara, please forgive me for my anger."

Hurt pinched her heart and penetrated her numb mind. He'd frightened her and admonished her in public. When he grabbed her arm, she was sure a blow would be next, and then it didn't come.

Lines formed in his forehead. "I'm sorry."

Something urged her to speak her mind. "I wasn't trying to cause harm. I know you issued orders to your guard, but how could I stay here? I felt terrible being locked away from my kindred for two days. And then Tavish said..."

"Aye, lass. I know what he told you. When I give an order, especially one involving your safety, it must be followed. You have power as Lady of Lochbuie, but a leader knows how to wield those powers with wisdom. If I'd been incapacitated or killed, then you had every right. But until that happens, those guard are mine to command."

Had she abused power? Hurt and confusion burdened her. Hector's face seemed disappointed and frustrated. Remembering how Duncan needed soothing after she'd done wrong, she knew with a sick, sinking feeling that Hector was waiting for her to make it right. Mind recalling everything Duncan had taught her, she tried to disconnect from her mind and what was to come. She leaned forward and brought her mouth toward his.

"I'm ready to make it up to you. Let me please you the way I know how." Hector's eyes went wide at her tone, and she hated herself as she said the practiced words.

Moving her hand through his hair she delivered the passionate, seductive kiss of invitation she knew he'd want.

Rocking forward on his knees, he captured her face within his hands returning her kiss and pulling her into his lap. The smell of peppermint and woodsmoke flooded her senses, and his hands were temperate and considerate as he held her close.

He murmured her name. "Cara, my lass. My darlin'..."

Tenderness surrounded her as he stroked her neck and kissed her face, and she grew unsure that this was for him, or if he was giving himself to her. He kept pushing back and giving her affection, not taking the passion she offered. A small piece of her heart wavered. Was she ready for this? She pressed harder.

He broke her fervent kiss. "Slow down. I'm no' going anywhere."

Desperate to prove her remorse and avoid punishment, she urged him faster, her kisses growing more heated and zealous, her hands bold. His hands discarded her veil and entangled in her hair. Self-hatred and longing battled within her.

"Wait, wait..." His forehead rested on hers and his breathing was shallow.

Need for intimacy and affection overwhelmed her, but she became afraid the longer he waited. "Please don't stop. I don't want to think."

He emitted a guttural growl and swallowed as though his insides scorched him as he eased her hands off him. "Cara, wait. You *must* think. There is still hurt in your eyes."

Touching her lips to his again she ignored his query, needing to lose herself in his affection, trying to reignite the spark into flame, not wanting to feel the hurt she carried. She needed him. His lips responded but once again he caught her hands with his own and eased her off him in one abstinent motion.

"Why are you pushing yourself to do this in an act of apology?" The army of his love waited at her gates, besieging her defenses, and she longed to surrender. But if he knew the reasons why, he would realize how unfit she was for wife; he would see what Duncan saw.

Trying for nonchalant, her voice instead came out as a bitter challenge. "After five years of chaste living I know you have needs."

Even as she spoke the words of deflection, she knew they trampled on his offering to God with temptation and disrespected the man he was. As soon as they were spoken, regret formed in her heart.

He hung his head and got up. "I cannae do this. I've done it this way before, and I dinnae want you this way. This is no' a contrivance to appease me that you are fine when you are no'. I want to be the one you trust. Body and soul—I want all of you, Cara."

Shame and disgust hit her like a physical blow, and she needed his goodness. "Contrivance? I wasn't...I thought you needed...Hector, please. Don't leave."

"There's something you're no' telling me, you're still hurt. What is it? What have I done? Do you no' see why I was angry? Do you no' see what a risk you took?"

Helplessness weighed down her arms and legs as he gathered clothes from his trunk. She stepped forward, wanting to let him in but not wanting to relive those days, that used and broken woman.

"Hector I—when..." The story, the beatings, the torture, what came after, her feelings of inadequacy that continued to haunt her even now... the explanation would not form. How could she ever tell him how base and hated she was?

He stepped forward, his hand took hers. "Yes?"

"It's nothing you've done. I'm fine."

Disappointment flattened his mouth. "You're no' fine. I'll stay upstairs. I cannae trust myself to lay chaste beside you." He leaned forward giving her a brotherly kiss, his whiskered cheek scratching her own. "Goodnight, love."

After the door clicked shut, she turned back to their empty solar. Alone. No Hector to fill her arms. No Margaret to take the sting away and build her up. Mary looked down at her from above the hearth as the Holy Ghost kissed her temple. She made it to the middle of the room before she fell, years of abuse and shame bringing her to her knees.

"God, please help me. I don't want to be broken anymore."

# CHAPTER 26

## LOCHBUIE OIGHREACHD - OCTOBER 24, 1383

Hector sat stonily in the cramped gatehouse with Calum and Murdoch, agitated, tingling with frustration and another year older. His flesh longed to put a fist through someone's face, but his spirit kept him frozen in his hard wooden chair.

"Last night, all four guards dead. The cateran prisoner has escaped."

Calum's words enhanced the gloom of the afternoon. A biblical rain had descended on Lochbuie three days prior and had not abated for even an hour. Hector was glad for it, for it would be much harder to deal with the murkiness of his mood in dazzling sunlight.

It'd been two weeks since he had the object of his deepest desire in his arms, willing to give herself to him fully. Two weeks since he'd kissed his wife. Two weeks since the tug in his soul had forced him to turn her down. Two weeks since he'd kept his infernal word.

Murdoch cleared his throat. "We've notified the families and retrieved the bodies. I'm afraid the Duart holdings on Morvern were also attacked. Cattle reived, but the homes left intact this time. Léo returned to Duart last week and brought word that the cateran we captured wasnae one of the MacKinnons. All their guard are present and accounted for."

Hector rubbed his hands over his face and through his hair. "If we take him at his word."

It was the latest in a series of attacks that hadn't abated in the two cursed weeks since his marriage. The attacks were so well coordinated and difficult to detect that he suspected the Wolf, but Léo's ill treatment of Cara—the way he'd gone to Elspeth with what he saw at the games, his failure to defend her against the accusations, and his unexplainable return to Duart lit his suspicion that he may be trying to gain favor with his brothers.

"Any other communication?"

Calum smoothed his ink-darkened hand over the map of Mull. "Chief MacLean wishes to know if you will be at the Duart assembly this week. The council chiefs who've experienced attacks and wish to compare evidence ahead of the meeting on Findlugan? Your opinion and experience are valued. As well as Léo's."

Tavish crossed his arms. "I dinnae see why Léo's opinion is worth more than Hector's. The man causes trouble. Trouble to his family, and trouble here."

Hector shifted in his seat, his cuirass squeaking against the wood. "What do you mean, here? Cara?"

"That. His return. The problem of the rapidly draining MacKinnon treasury on Staffa. His willingness to keep working with a man who stole his woman—no offense—to resolve a problem that shouldn't matter to him at all since he lives in France. He mentioned several times while he was here how much he resented the man you used to be."

Calum scratched his flax-colored beard looking hesitant. "I have the same suspicions."

Murdoch nodded. "I do as well."

Hector frowned and took a piece of vellum, inked his quill, and scratched a short missive, telling his brother to expect Cara and him as soon as it was safe to sail. He dripped wax and sealed it, then secured it in a leather correspondence pouch and handed it to the courier.

"I want every galley but one in the waters surrounding our territory at all times. No man is exempted from duty. As soon as it is safe to enter the waters, do so."

Calum and Murdoch nodded. "Aye, Laird."

Hector rose. "May I tell Cara you three will attend tonight's supper given in my honor? With the weather, Lachlan and his family won't attend, but I want to be sure it looks full since it's her first banquet."

A wide smile broke over Calum's face. "Aye. I'm also told your young maid Aoife will be there?"

Murdoch frowned and gave him a shove. "Keep your mind on your work."

Hector grinned. Calum had ferreted out of Murdoch that he fancied the pretty dark-haired Aoife and had not let up in his teasing in a week.

"I'll see you three this evening."

After a mad dash through the downpour, he swung the door open to the keep and almost collided with his wife.

"Cara."

"Hector."

They stared at each other in awkward silence for a few moments before she turned and pulled the rope for the well that cut into the stone of the ground floor.

"Here, let me." With speed he hauled the bucket upward, emptied it into her pail, and hefted it.

She extended her hand. "I can take it."

"Nonsense, I can carry it for you. Where's it going?"

"Up to our—my chamber." Awkward silence refilled the room and extinguished the fresh air. Not knowing what more to say, he began to climb the stairs and Cara followed him.

*Say something eejit.* "Calum, Tavish, and Murdoch assure me they will be in attendance at tonight's supper."

Her voice was small behind him. "I'll need to let Flora know where to seat them."

Bloated tension grew as they passed the great hall and continued to climb toward their—her chamber. He longed to toss the bucket over his shoulder and carry her into their room, but she remained a closed fortress, impregnable with lingering offense against him. No weapon in his arsenal had yet worked to breach her defenses.

Instead of demonstrating his commitment to honor their marriage, his absence from their bed had only made things worse. Perhaps he should've tried to reconcile with her using love, but in the moment it'd felt shallow.

The memory of bold kisses and her hands against him caused him to fumble. Water sloshed over the top of the bucket and onto the floor. A servant ran forward with a cloth and mopped the puddle around his feet. "I'm sorry, my laird, I wanted to retrieve the water for our lady, but she insisted."

He investigated the man's plump face and tried to remember his name. "Thank you—em..."

Cara stepped forward. "Cameron."

Hector hefted the bucket once more, annoyed that in the space of two weeks Cara had shifted the allegiance of his staff handily to her own side. He'd caught their sidelong glances when he emerged from his separate chamber each morning. He admonished himself for his feelings, knowing she'd not spoken a word against him, but her ability to recall names, faces, and the inanest details of the personal lives of twenty servants had outshone his own aloof manner and forbidding appearance.

He came to a stop outside her door, and she hesitated before opening it for him. She remained at the door as he brought the bucket into the room and placed it upon the table. The comforting smell of rosemary, the same smell as her hair and the smooth skin of her neck filled him with longing. All he wanted was an opening, any small sign that she forgave him for his anger, and he'd make her his own.

He paused for a moment before the hearth half hoping she would enter the room with him, but instead she waited for him to exit.

As he stooped through the door, she caught his wrist. He looked at her tiny hand on his leather bracer and then into her heart-shaped face, something passing over the freckle of her nose and across her lips. Hope formed in his chest.

She released him and added a boulder to the top of the walls fortressed around her. "I'll see you tonight."

Why would she not forgive him?

"I'll see you tonight."

More irritable than he'd been that afternoon, Hector descended the stairs before the banquet sour and tired, wanting nothing more than to go to bed. The sound of a raised voice rang through his throbbing head. Below, Tavish unloaded wrath on an unknown recipient.

"Dinnae be ridiculous. What on earth do you know about accounts?" He couldn't hear the responses of the person he admonished, but Tavish's tone continued to rise. "I'm telling you it's inadvisable."

Intrigued, Hector paused, listening for the voice of the other party to the argument.

"I appreciate your concern, but as Lady of Lochbuie, I'm afraid I must insist that I see your books."

His stomach dropped. Once again, she invoked her title to obtain something she had no business interfering in. Disappointment flooded him. It was the kind of thing he might have expected from Elspeth, not Cara. He descended a few stairs, skirting along the wall to hear better.

"You're illiterate, no' trained in figures. If you make a mistake, it could be detrimental to the entire clan."

"This is not a request, Tavish. I'm lady of the house, you're the seneschal. As lady I must insist—"

Frustrated and fed up, Hector placed a hand on Cara's shoulder. "Choose your next words verra carefully."

Cara looked up in shock.

"My laird." Tavish stepped back and he seemed to consider how much of their conversation Hector had overheard.

A crinkle appeared between Cara's eyebrows as she looked at his hand on her shoulder. It was the first time he'd touched her in days, and he removed his obviously unwelcome touch.

"What's going on?" Hector's voice came out strangled as he tried to ignore how alluring she looked in the berry-colored gown clinging to her, and his mood continued to darken.

Tavish lifted a hand. "Has my accounting displeased you, my laird?"

Trying to remain calm, Hector kept his answer to a one-syllable response. "No."

Cara brought her hands to her temples. "I only wish to see to my duties as head of this household and complete the accounts. I don't mean to suggest there is any deficiency in your work."

Tavish opened his mouth, and Hector raised his hands to stop their arguing, trying not to widen the gulf between himself and his wife. "Enough. Cara, love, I appreciate that you are trying to help, but Tavish is seneschal, and well within his role to keep the accounts."

Cara pinched the bridge of her nose as if the two of them were wearing her patience thin. "Aye, I'm aware Tavish is the seneschal, a point which he's reminded me of many times. Now, let me inform you that Duncan was seneschal to the chief of the MacSweeney clan. My husband may have been a great many things, but I assure you he was devoted to his role."

Hector's chest cramped with jealousy as she referred to her first husband, a sound of fealty in her voice. They may have been ill-suited, but she clearly still cared for the man. His temper crept higher.

She crossed her arms and continued. "As memory serves me, it was not Duncan running the chief's household, the accounts, and the servants, but it was he who assisted the lady of the house, helping her as she needed and tending to the overflow of clan matters from the chief."

He clenched his jaw. "Cara, we can discuss this later?" She shook her head and his temper spiked again. "What is it?"

"You've made your mind up again, and that's that. My thoughts don't matter."

*Again?* She danced a perilous reel across the boundary of his anger. Was any of this his choosing? She was the one holding a grudge. Was he supposed to allow someone well-meaning but inexperienced and, aye, illiterate, to run the accounts?

"Tavish was educated at Cambridge. I have no cause to remove him from those duties."

"Even if you need to shift your attention from the rebuilding to protecting your holdings? Could Tavish not assist Pádraig and the rest of the clan so that you may be unburdened? I assure you I can handle our accounts as well as he can. I have a mind for numbers and I used to help—"

He held his hands aloft once more. "Cara, I warn you. This subject is now closed."

A piper, stinking of whisky, wandered into the hall and hiccuped. "S'is where I'm supposed to be?" The sweaty-faced man hoisted a decaying set of pipes and wobbled back and forth.

Hector stared at the obviously drunken stranger. "Who in the name of Somerled are you?"[1]

"Ar—Art—Artair MacAvoy. Your p-piper."

He looked at Cara utterly puzzled. "You've hired an outside piper? The MacLeans have sixty pipers at Duart."

A furious blush rose over her cheeks as she looked at Tavish and himself. "Artair, you may go to the hall, we will enter upon your tune."

Tavish pursed his lips, a look of disapproval on his face as Artair listed into the great hall.

A great whine drowned out all thought and stabbed into Hector's throbbing brain and he clamped his hands over his ears. "Oh, for the love of the saints."

Cara took her place beside him, her eyes fixed ahead, chin raised. Tavish nodded to them both and made for the hall.

"It was...who recommended..." Her voice was drowned out by the worst bagpiping he'd ever heard. He offered Cara his arm and she jerked her arm through it, evidence of her own anger growing. The voices of the guards and clan leaders died in the piercing cacophony of pipe squeals and he strained to hear their greetings as he led his wife toward the dais.

As he sat down, pipes finally abated, he noticed Cara remained rigid, eyes fixed on Margaret's sympathetic face.

Able to finally hear himself think, he took in the hall decorated with ribbon and candlelight and knew her efforts had been long in the planning. Servants came forth in two straight lines bearing the first course.

"I thank you for the work you've put in for my birthday."

She lifted her water to her lips. "You're welcome."

No warmth imbued her words. He settled back in his chair and wished for the first time in weeks for the sweet release of uisge-beatha. A servant came forward and placed a tray of fruits and cheeses and an egg cup in front of each of them.

He lifted a spoon. "Duck eggs. My favorite. How did you know?"

Cara breathed a heavy sigh. "Mhairi."

Now certain he'd deepened her grudge, he lifted his spoon and gave the egg a whack. Yolk streaked across his plaid.

Consternation tightened across her features. "What on earth?" She lifted her spoon and gently tapped her egg, removing the top and finding it raw.

He motioned Cameron over. "These eggs are raw."

Sounds of confusion rippled across the hall, and it became apparent that not one, but all the eggs served were raw.

Cara blanched. "Make haste and take them away before more of our guests have an unfortunate accident like our laird."

Cameron nodded and waved the other servants around the hall.

It was the first proper clan supper hosted at Moy, and so far, they'd quarreled, been piped in by a drunken man playing what sounded like a bag of squalling cats, and been served raw eggs. A sideways glance proved that she was on the brink of tears.

He lifted her fingers to his mouth and kissed them. "No' to worry, love. It's your first time holding a supper. You're bound to be inexperienced."

She snatched her hand away from him and replaced it in her lap. Confused, he tried to meet her eyes, but she refused to look at him. "What did I say?"

Her face threatened tears and she responded in tight Irish. "Away with ye, Hector. I don't feel like talkin'."

The woman was off her head. "I'm trying to smooth things over."

When they'd sat in stony silence for nearly an hour with no sign of the next course arriving, Margaret approached them. She motioned to the table of the MacLean guard who were growing rowdier by the minute. "Cara, will the meal be served soon?"

Cara swallowed and dropped her tone. "I don't understand. I checked on the progress of it all day, nothing went unnoticed. It looked perfect this afternoon."

Margaret inclined her head. "I'm afraid those lot are deep in their cups, dear. They should have something soon before they're out of hand."

At that moment, Bruce and Gilroy MacLean began arguing about the outcome of the sheaf toss at this year's games, their voices carrying throughout the hall, causing guests to turn and look in their direction.

Cara put her hands to her cheeks. She motioned for Cameron, and he came forward. "Where is the meal? I don't understand. It looked almost finished when I checked this afternoon."

Cameron fiddled with the edge of his tunic. "I'm afraid there is a problem with the liver."

Cara's face went red. "What kind of a problem?"

"They're burned, my lady."

"The whole lot?"

Cameron nodded and Cara buried her face in her hands. "There's nothing we can do now, Cameron. Tell Cook to send it up."

Margaret patted Cara on the shoulder. "There, there dear. It'll be all right. Liver is hard to get right even on the best of days."

"That's what I was trying to tell her. She's no' learned how to give a proper dinner yet."

Judging by the look on Margaret's face, he knew that he'd just made the situation much worse. Margaret gave a slight shake of the head, indicating to him to stop trying to make things better. Cara skewered him with a fierce look. Margaret kissed her daughter-in-law on the cheek and made her way back to her seat.

A terrible smell akin to burning gong began to grow in putrid strength.

Cara held her hand over her mouth and nose. "Oh no."

Platters of smoldering liver were served to each guest, the terrible rancid stench taking over the air and making guests gag. Hector poked the hardened liver with his eating knife and attempted to saw through the crispy outer crust. The liver moved back and forth on his trencher and emitted a puff of noxious smoke. He placed his knife down and watched as the guests looked to one another and back at him, wondering what to do.

Tavish approached. "Shall I have Cook bring up the wines and an assortment of pastries? Perhaps some smoked salmon and bannocks?"

Relieved that at least one level head was thinking far enough ahead to salvage the dinner, he nodded with appreciation. "Yes. Please take care of this at once."

Cara's eyes were now fixed upon her lap. She didn't look up as Murdoch wandered forward, a flute tucked under his arm. "Did you still wish to give Laird MacLean his birthday song?" She shook her head.

His heart began to crumble for his wife, adrift in humiliation. "Song?"

Murdoch nodded. "We've been practicing a few of your favorite tunes."

He touched her knee. "I'd enjoy some music. Please, love?"

When she raised her head, two tears escaped down her red cheeks. "I'm sorry."

She made her way toward the door just as Gilroy MacLean launched himself on Bruce, colliding over the table and rolling around on the floor. Men encircled them and began egging them on, encouraging the wild punching and kicking.

By the time he managed to separate the brawl and edible food had at last appeared at each place, Cara was nowhere to be seen.

He made his way over to his mother-in-law and knelt beside her, trying to keep his voice low. "Have you seen her?"

Margaret gave him a sympathetic look and pointed toward the stairs. "She went that way. Ursula and I tried to follow her, but she wished to be alone."

He kissed her cheek, grateful that she, at least, did not bear him a grudge. "Thank you."

Taking the steps two at a time he reached the door to her chamber and found it locked. He put his ear to the door and heard Aoife's voice consoling her, and muffled sobs. He knocked. Their voices murmured together before the door cracked open.

Aoife gave him a pitiful smile. "Lady MacLean isnae feeling well, my laird."

Behind her he heard the distinctive sounds of gasping tears and a sniffing nose. "Please, Aoife, let me in. I need to see my wife."

Aoife bit her lip and looked in the direction of the bed. "I'm afraid she's indisposed my laird."

He put his hand to the door. "Please, Aoife."

From within the bedroom, he heard Cara's agonized voice. "I'll see you in the morning, Hector. Go away."

He nodded. There was nothing more to say. He stepped away as the door clicked shut, further away from breaching her defenses than he'd ever been before.

# CHAPTER 27

## LOCHBUIE OIGHREACHD - OCTOBER 25, 1383

While Hector was out the following morning seeing to the repair of some of the cottages, Cara lingered in the corridor. In the pouch hanging from her belt, her finger traced the iron key. Her eyes followed the stairs as they curled upward toward the third and fourth floors, where Tavish kept his study. The halls were silent, the sound of her breath the only disturbance in the keep.

Heart pounding, knees shaking, her legs climbed the first flight of stairs. On the third floor, Hector's door stood solid and shut, and she paused for a moment on the landing in front of his chamber, longing to feel near to him and his strength. Then his words of the previous night came rushing back. He thought her incapable of doing what she knew in her heart she could do. He wouldn't listen to her. He didn't give her the chance to explain.

Strengthened, she continued up the long curving staircase, climbing higher toward the top floor of the keep. Late harvest wind bit through the arrow lancets and sent chills up her spine. It was Tavish who had urged her to go into Lochbuie against Hector's orders. Tavish who had recommended the piper to her. Tavish who'd helped her execute last night's banquet. Tavish who'd been resistant to every effort she'd made to take over the household.

Assurance strengthened her heart. *You're not incapable. I've given you talents. I've made you perceptive.*

The top floor was deserted. She listened down the staircase for sounds of footfalls but heard none. Making as little sound as she dared, she tried the first door and found a chamber with a simple bed and table. Closing the door behind her, she moved to the second door. It opened to an empty room with a wide window, late morning sun casting a yellow glow across the wooden floor. Crossing the hallway, she tried the next door. It opened to another empty chamber. Palms sweating, she tried the final door. The door did not budge. She knelt and peered through the small latch.

A narrow sliver of sight revealed a desk piled with books and papers. She produced the iron passkey she'd taken as Hector snored away in his bed and fitted it in the lock. It clicked.

The inside of the chamber was more ornate than she'd expected. A large bed stood near the window, and stuffy objects decorated every surface of the room. A large tapestry of gold and silver adorned one wall, and she noticed the soldiers stitched upon it adorned with the MacFadyen plaid. She touched one warrior. It must be near as old as Moy itself.

Remembering her task, she moved toward the oak desk. Figures were scrawled on every surface, and she lifted a few papers, replacing them back in the same position. The drawer in the desk opened easily and revealed a large green account book.

Pulling out the deep velvet chair, she settled before the hefty volume and opened the wax-stained cover. Running her finger over the numbers she calculated the first row of figures, then followed it to the next page, then flipped back to the front.

Something wasn't right, but she couldn't read the marks beside the matching group of sums taken from one account and added to another. She flipped forward a few more pages and noticed another group of numbers. At the top of the column, she recognized a word that Mhairi had recorded in her own logbook. *Tithes.*

Tallying the numbers, she came to the balance then flipped back to the first page, studying the looping script of each letter, mentally matching them to words she knew and began to understand what the column was. *Credits.*

These were sums paid by the clan to the laird, but not every sum was recorded in the total balance of household monies in the front pages of the book. She checked the Tithes column against the total balance at the front, realizing in only a few minutes what was wrong with the accounts.

Tavish was underreporting rents, making it appear as though a smaller amount had been received. The same process was repeated in the tithe account. Recorded tithes to the church from household monies were a fraction of what was truly owed. Tavish was stealing from Hector and stealing from the church.

Footsteps sounded in the stairwell below. Moving fast, she replaced the account book in the drawer, closed the door behind her, and dashed across the hall to the empty chamber. Licking her dry lips, she put her back to the door, her chest heaving in and out.

The footsteps stopped on her floor. Taking care to produce as little sound as possible, she sank to her knees before the latch and inclined her eye to the opening. Tavish felt in his robes and produced a key. He fitted it into the lock and paused. Her heart stilled. She'd forgotten to lock the door.

Tavish held the small iron key and studied it, spinning it in his fingers. He placed a hand on the door and opened it, dropping his leather satchel. Papers skittered across the floor, spilling everywhere. He swore and collected the papers, disappeared for a moment, then reappeared with another stack of paper. Cara braced her hands on the door and balanced, angling her head to see what he was doing.

Flipping through the papers, he accumulated a small pile, then stoked the fire and fed it to the embers. He took another pile and a flash of words grouped tightly across the page made it obvious to her eyes what they were. Letters. Light illuminated his face as the pages went up in frenzied color. He stood and jammed at the embers with the poker, then turned and looked directly at her.

Cara held still, knowing if she moved, he may notice the change of light pattern at the latch. Panting, she waited for him to break his line of sight. At long last he rose and shut the door. She sank to her hands and knees. What was the man doing?

She flattened her ear to the door. No sound came from the corridor. A small squeak escaped as she lifted the latch, but his door did not open. Taking a steadying breath, she pulled the door toward her.

Ruffling paper sounded from the study. She sucked in a breath and stepped into the corridor. The door was large and heavy, but new and still fitted soundlessly in its frame. Saying silent prayers of thanks, she hurried down the staircase to the third floor.

The door to Hector's chamber popped open just as she stepped onto the landing. She jumped out of her skin, her heart screaming with fright.

"Cara?"

A wave of faintness overtook her and she doubled over. "Y-You frightened me."

"I was coming to see if Cameron knew where you were. You look terrified."

She shook her head and gave an uneasy laugh. "Just startled."

"I wanted to speak with you, please come in."

He stepped aside and admitted her to the chamber. A tub filled with steaming water remained before the hearth and the smell of peppermint soap hung thick in the air. Feeling her cheeks flame, her eyes raked over his bare chest, back, and arms as he closed the door to the small chamber. She rubbed a trembling hand over her forehead, trying to quiet her racing mind and attempting to look natural.

Damp raven curls spilled over his shoulders and powerful chest. Her stomach gave an almighty flip. Any imagined thought she may have had about his body as they kissed a few days earlier fell far short of the reality before her. He brought toweling to his hair and squeezed water from it.

"About last night, Cara, I'm sorry. I was in a temper and no' feeling quite myself. I'd like to discuss it with you. The attack, dinner, the accounts, everything. We need to get used to talking things over with each other."

She averted her eyes and retreated to the corner beside the fire, wishing the floor would swallow her whole. "I'm fine."

Her mind whirred with shock from what she'd just discovered, and painful shyness brought on by his half-naked body.

"Cara, look at me. What is it?" He put his hands to his narrow waist, cinched by his sword belt, his stomach muscles and chest rippling.

She took a deep breath, her cheeks burning from red to purple. "Could you please put your tunic on?"

He followed her gaze, dropping his eyes to his bare chest and stomach, his eyebrows shooting up. A smile of pure male pride dominated his features. The wide smile curved as far north as his mangled cheek would allow and he stalked toward her.

She clamped her hands over her eyes. Silence. "Stop smiling, ye eejit."

"I'm no' smiling."

Parting her fingers, she peeked and found him flexing every muscle in his body, the biggest smile she had ever seen upon his face.

She squeezed her fingers shut. "Ye daft man."

Rumbling with laughter he tried to explain himself. "I cannae help it, Cara. You please me." Footsteps padded around the room. "I've put my tunic on."

She parted her fingers and two strong arms descended over her, capturing her into his solid wall of tunic-covered chest.

"I've longed to hold you again every day I've been up here." He clutched her to him and rested his forehead upon hers. Damp curls fell onto her collarbone. "Tell me, Cara."

Inhaling peppermint and feeling delirious, she wasn't sure she understood what he was asking. "Tell you what?"

His eyes peered into hers before he brushed her hair to the side, dropping kisses along her neck. Her heart swelled. "Tell me how to scale your walls and I'll do it with my bare hands."

His army once more encamped around her and she opened her mouth, longing to let him into her confidence. They must trust each other, and trust was impossible to build without the truth. The stolen key heavy in her pouch, she wanted to tell him everything—but how? "I don't know how to tell you."

His adept lips moved over hers, his hands tucking beneath her ears. He shared the warmth of his mouth with her, the sweetness of his lips, her tender gasp of breath. He deepened the kiss with skilled adoration. Her mind went blank, her knees went weak, she put a hand against the wall to keep herself from falling. Dear faeries, did the man know how to kiss, and she never, ever wanted him to stop.

A knock sounded at the door.

"My lady?"

He touched his forehead back to hers and whispered, "Do you want to know why luck isnae real?"

"Why?" she whispered back.

"Because it's never on my side."

His eyes flitted over the neckline of her leine, and he tilted her chin up to kiss her.

The knock sounded again. "My lady?"

Hector growled. "See?"

Her voice squeaked. "Coming, Aoife."

He ran his hands down the sides of her body, and she squeaked again. He chuckled, then released her. Legs wobbly, she made her way to the door and opened it.

"I'm sorry, my lady. I couldn't find you below and tho' I may find you here. The galley is ready to take us to Duart."

Hector wrapped the plaid over his shoulders. "I think the time away at Duart will do us well." He gave her a meaningful look.

He disappeared down the hall and she gulped. She'd been almost ready to let him into her heart, but would he believe her when she told him that the man he trusted most was a thief?

# CHAPTER 28

## DUART OIGHREACHD - OCTOBER 25, 1383

Mhairi took one look at Cara's forlorn expression and her eyes grew wide. Hector shot her a look trying to communicate that he had no idea what the matter was. Although Cara had briefly let down her defenses in his chamber, she'd been quiet on the journey to Duart, unusually so.

Slack jawed, Mhairi attempted to recover her senses. "Cara, I—that is—how are you?"

"I'm well." There was a heaviness in her tone that had grown day by day since they'd wed, and Hector felt himself on the edge of surrender, beginning to recognize the signs of defeat. The lass seemed utterly out of place and unhappy.

Mhairi bit her lip and kept trying. "How is Moy? Are you finding your way?"

Cara gave a weak smile. "I've found my way."

Lachlan strode down the stairs. "Ah, Hector, Cara, you've arrived."

Mhairi eyed Cara, and Hector knew she was parsing out the change in her. "Shall we retire to the solar before the evening meal? I'd love to catch up."

Cara made no move to follow her. "I'd rather fancy a lie down. The boat ride made me a bit ill. Can you tell me where my chamber is?"

Hector stiffened. In the many trips he'd made to Duart and Ardtornish over the past few weeks, he neglected to mention that they were keeping separate quarters. When asked, he simply responded that Cara was well. Which she was.

Mhairi's eyes traveled between them. "It's the same chamber. Hector's solar."

Hector hurried to save Cara the embarrassment of an explanation. "Take the chamber, Cara. I'll send Aoife when it's time to get ready for the meal." She nodded, her hand going to her head as she disappeared up the stairs. Was that all it was? She was ill?

Lachlan looked like he'd been hit with a club. "You're no' sharing a chamber?"

Mhairi held up a hand. "Not in the corridor. Come."

Once in the safety of the solar Mhairi unloaded on Hector. "What did you do?"

Hector leaned on the mantel and looked into the fire. "She's been this way for weeks, but she's acting most peculiar today."

Mhairi crossed her arms and tossed him an accusing look. "Weeks? Hector, again I ask, what did you do? She was flourishing the entire time she was with me."

He shrugged. "I didnae do anything."

Lachlan snorted and settled into his favorite chair. "That means you did."

Mhairi nodded her head, suspicions affirmed. "Something happened then."

Hector eased into the sturdy chair beside the fire and warmed his feet. "It started the night after the attack on Lochbuie. A rider came to me in Glenbyre with a missive from Tavish advising she was outside the walls disobeying orders. I was angry she'd put herself at risk and when I got back, I took her in hand and admonished her. She's been a different person ever since that day."

Mhairi looked at him with alarm in her eyes. "You didnae."

"Aye. I was on the wrong side of it being angry like I was, but she retreated into herself, and I couldnae pull her back out again. I apologized, and she said she was fine."

Lachlan rolled his eyes. "They're never fine when they say they're fine."

"She tried to fix it with intimacy, but I couldn't bring myself to..."

Mhairi covered her mouth with her hand, the look of alarm growing in her eyes.

Lachlan's eyebrows raised. "It's been weeks since the attack—she ought to be thawing by now. Are you sure that's all?"

Hector winced. "Last night she held her first banquet, and it went about as bad as you might expect no' having put together one of these things before. Food burned, a piper from the depths of hades, raw eggs, the guards started brawling. Worse though, I found her trying to order Tavish to hand over the accounts, in the same way she commanded the guard to take her outside the keep. Tavish refused. We quarreled."

Mhairi pursed her lips and shook her head as if she'd been affirmed in her belief he'd done something moronic.

"Why did Tavish refuse?" Lachlan asked.

"Because she's uneducated and...illiterate."

Mhairi scoffed. "Listen to your pity. Is that how you speak to her? She's no' uneducated."

Hector sighed. He had no wish to fight a battle with the sisterhood. Shouldn't he be able to state an obvious fact without being harpooned?

Mhairi put a hand on her hip. "I see the look on your face, Lachlan. She isn't uneducated. Her father taught her, and she's got quite a mind for figuring. I told you this while she was here."

Lachlan rolled his eyes. "That's no' *quite* the same as Tavish's education."

Relief burst over him. Finally, someone saw his side. "Thank you."

Mhairi crossed her arms. "I didnae have Tavish's education, yet I'm qualified enough to keep our accounts. I'm also able to keep mine in better order than Tavish from what I gather. Our household is four times as large, and it takes me half the effort."

"That's different," Lachlan protested. "You were raised at Ardtornish. Had the finest tutors and training available. You can read and write and do arithmetic. You mean to tell me Cara can read and write? A weaver's daughter?"

Mhairi rolled her eyes. "She cannae read or write letters, but she can do numbers. That is a form of literacy."

A twinge of disquiet formed at Hector's gut. "She can?"

"You didnae know that? Why do you think her fabrics are so remarkable? She must calculate where each string should go, her materials, even advanced arithmetic to make sure everything is balanced. She performed all the accounting here at Duart for three weeks and did it perfectly, in half the time I can. She can calculate in her mind enormous sums and is astonishing with fractions. I cannae tell you the number of days I've wished she was here to help me since she's gone to Moy."

A sinking feeling unsettled him. He'd judged her and widened the gulf between them, no wonder she was acting so despondent.

Lachlan looked confused. "How does she know what each line says? She cannae read the name of the expense."

"I'll admit, I had to tell her what each line said—household, clothing, credit—but she made her own mark near each and understood what it meant to her. By the end, she could recognize the shapes of certain letters and understood without me having to tell her what it said. Hector, she's so clever she could probably learn to read with little instruction, or on her own, for that matter. Did you even ask her why she wanted to take on the accounts, or what she could do?"

He felt ashamed. "I tried to broach it with her today."

"Did you test her to see how she could figure a page of numbers?"

"Nay."

"Her first husband was a seneschal for the MacSweeneys. Did she tell you she would check his arithmetic?"

"She mentioned that he was the seneschal last night but didnae mention she helped him on their accounts." Or perhaps she'd been about to, and he hadn't given her the chance before closing the discussion.

Mhairi threw up her hands in exasperation. "You've been married to her for weeks and you didnae know he was a seneschal for one of the largest clans in Donegal?"

He assumed Duncan was a tenant and that they seemed to have a distant relationship owing to Cara's barren womb. That was all. "Nay."

Mhairi collapsed into the leather chair beside him and put her hands to her face. "What else? Has Tavish allowed her to run her staffing, meal planning, entertainment?"

"She tried last night, but as I say, it was a disaster. I let Tavish take over dinner last night, and was intending to let him continue when we return. She seemed submerged under the responsibility."

"You let her try one event and now you're taking it all away from her?"

"When you put it like that it sounds cruel. I wasnae cruel."

"She planned every menu, meal, entertainment, and staffing schedule for three weeks straight while she was here. Our staff and clan are quadruple the size. Och—I've never seen someone male or female with such an aptitude for things. She watches it a few times and understands how it works. We didnae have one issue while she was here. Things that took me a lifetime to learn took her weeks. I had every confidence you had chosen the correct bride. I told Lachlan so."

"Aye. She did," Lachlan admitted.

Mhairi balanced her head on her hand. "So, she had one off evening. She's just gotten married. There'd just been a raid."

Hector's senses sharpened. Cara did have an aptitude for detail. Something didn't make sense, but he couldn't identify where it had gone wrong.

Lachlan shifted in his seat. "This is precisely why I didnae agree with your choice of bride, Hector. She's unable to cope and the attacks on the island have increased."

Temper flaming, he rolled his eyes. "A helpful observation."

Mhairi shook her head. "Or you both have misread the entire situation from beginning to end. She must feel you dinnae want her."

"I *do* want her." Voice raising, he simmered, fed up with being berated for acting with only half the information. Information Cara could have given him at any time.

Mhairi pounced. "Your actions say otherwise. If you wanted her, you would've facilitated her success, you would've sided with her and given her a chance. How's she been filling her days?"

"Weaving. She meets with the staff for prayer in the morning and then weaves from sunup until sundown. She's filling requests from the households affected by the raids. On Fridays she goes to Margaret's and stays until the end of Sabbath."

Mhairi made a face. "Why no' have Margaret come to Moy?"

"Margaret could come to Moy...she just hasnae."

Mhairi pushed back into her chair, brow furrowed. "She doesnae feel comfortable having her family to her own home. Probably because you've discouraged her from giving anything of herself to her household. And separate chambers? Hector, I—there's no easy way to ask this..." A glint of something indefinable sparked in her eye.

"What is it?"

"Have you... on your wedding night? Or was trying to fix her mistake with intimacy the only time?"

"That was the only time we almost... I wanted to get to know her better and see that she was ready and comfortable with me."

Lachlan sat straight up. "If you havenae consummated the marriage, it can still be undone. We can set Cara up with a good sum of money and her own estate. Maybe on Jura or Morvern."

Hector growled with anger. "Out of the question. If you wish me to stay here and help with the council, you'll no' voice that suggestion again or we're done."

Mhairi fell apart, her face crumpling and tears springing to her eyes. They both stared at her dumbstruck. "Hector, you've crushed her. You dinnae ken, do you? She hasnae told you."

Bells of warning rang through his mind. "What?"

Mhairi choked on a sob. "If she h-hasn't told you, Hector, that is no' my story to tell."

Sickness and dread filled him. He knew Mhairi wasn't one easily overcome with emotion. "Mhairi, please, I am begging you. I cannae lose her. Tell me what I've done, so I may repair it."

She wiped tears from her eyes and took a breath, her voice strangled. "You cannae repair this, Hec."

Struggling to keep fear and anger out of his voice he crouched before her. "Tell me. You're scaring me."

Finally, she relented. "I will give you the pieces, but she must give the details. You know about Duncan's leman and their baby?"

Lachlan smoothed a hand over his mustache. "Aye, I think the entire kingdom knows about that."

"Did she tell you anything else about him?"

Hector thought back to their wedding night, Cara's small body pressed against his. Her shiny plait in his hands. "She said he was a good provider."

Mhairi shook her head. "That's all? Did she tell you about Hugh, Margaret's husband?"

"Pádraig mentioned Hugh married Margaret on pass through Mull. Mhairi, please?"

She wiped a fresh batch of tears from her eyes. "Margaret married an evil man. Wasnae afraid to beat the senses out of her or his child." She choked and snorted, and his heart dropped, sickened at the direction the conversation was heading.

"Duncan grew up to be just like Hugh, but far, far worse. Beat the senses out of Cara every day—he was a violent, bloodthirsty man. If she got in his way, she was hit. If she didn't check through his accounts fast enough, she was hit. He put a mark of ownership on her so she would know to whom she belonged. Each month she didnae get pregnant he found a new way to torture her, to punish her for her shortcomings— things she couldnae help. The kind of man that given enough time would have killed her for simply being herself."

Mhairi blew her nose and continued. "I suppose that's why God gave her the ability to learn quickly—to save her from being beaten. When cornered she makes herself small. I saw it the afternoon at the loch, and at the barley field. She apologizes for everything because for ten years everything was her fault. Then when he'd finish torturing her, he'd make her make it up to him with—"

Behind him Lachlan swore and passed a hand over his face.

Stricken, Hector got to his feet, everything in their relationship taking on new shape. The fear in her eyes the night they met when he touched her calf. The cauldron accident that caused scars. The way she'd cowered after he'd been angry at the loch. Their wedding night and the nightmare she'd had, screaming for him as if she were being murdered. The raw terror in her eyes when he returned to Lochbuie and took her in his hands, and how she'd tried to hold him at bay. The petrified stupor she'd remained in for hours, unable to speak or comprehend what anyone said to her. The bold demeanor so unlike herself that night. Nausea beset him. *I'm ready to make it up to you. Let me please you the way I know how.*

He was disgusted with himself as he recalled last night's argument, the defeat, the betrayal in her eyes, and then the wall constructed quicker than he could comprehend when he refused to take her side. Cara wasn't mad at him, she was afraid of him. Afraid to trust.

Heartbroken, he paced and prowled, longing to avenge her wounds and fix her hurt. He wanted to dig up Duncan MacSweeney and kill him all over again. But Mhairi was right, this he couldn't protect her from, this he could not fix. He fled the room, full of battle rage that had nowhere to spend itself.

# CHAPTER 29

## DUART OIGHREACHD - OCTOBER 26, 1383

Aknock sounded at Cara's door at dawn's first light. She rose, groggy from a fitful sleep, and cracked the door open. Hector stood in the corridor, a look of concern swimming in his ocean blue eyes.

"I've Aoife with me. I need you to get dressed and come with me."

She rubbed the vestiges of sleep from her eyes. "Is everything all right?"

His eyes went soft. "Yes, love. I've something to show you." He took her hand and kissed it. "I'll meet you downstairs in twenty minutes."

Sluggish, she followed Aoife back into the room and puzzled as the maid laid out her shapeless work dress and lummon.

Cara splashed water on her cheeks and looked at the outfit with a raised eyebrow. "Where is he taking me?"

"Somewhere outdoors, my lady."

With no further information to be gleaned, Aoife dressed her with speed and gave her a small bowl of porridge before she was hurried down the corridor and into the front hall. Hector waited for her with a woolen bonnet in his hands.

"Where are we off to?"

He fitted the warm woolen bonnet over her head. "A secret spot from when I was a young lad."

Intrigued, she followed him to the barmkin and was astonished to see Ghoustie waiting beside a sorrel mare.

She smiled and scratched him on the withers. "When did you get here?"

"Late last night." Hector made a clicking sound. "Come, lass." The red sorrel mare raised her head and trotted over to him. "This is Clover. She's no' particularly tall or fashionable, but she is clever and biddable."

Clover lowered her head and nuzzled her nose against Cara's neck, breathing deeply. "She's a beauty."

"Do you like her?"

She chuckled as the mare nuzzled closer to her neck and rested her head upon her shoulder. "Aye, what a charming lass."

Hector smiled. "She's for you...well, and for Ghoustie. He fell in love with her weeks ago and hasn't stopped pining and nickering for her since."

She smoothed her hand over the mare's white nose. "I've never had my own horse." She looked at Hector, a glow of warmth extinguishing the feeling of dread that had settled in her stomach yesterday afternoon. "I don't know how to thank you."

He lifted her hand and kissed it. "No thanks necessary. Shall we be off?" He knelt and his large hands came around her calf boosting her into the saddle as he had the night they met and her heart squeezed at the memory.

Setting an easy pace, they rode across the brown, frost-covered moors that surrounded the castle. Hector perched in the saddle and circled her with a broad grin on his face as Clover trotted at a slow and steady pace. For the first time in weeks, she felt the same lightness they'd shared on Iona, and she laughed at his playfulness, wondering again that such a man could be her own. They rode toward Craignure and up the sloping banks of a hill into a pine thicket. A large slab of stone jutted from the ground, forming a wide table of rock. Hector slowed Ghoustie and dismounted, then helped Cara down.

"Is this what you wanted to show me?"

Hector smiled. "I know it isnae impressive, but this is where

Lachlan and I had some of our best adventures." He motioned to the table rocks. "This is Dùn MacLean."[1] He looked at her with expectation and then shrugged. "Lachlan was twelve and no' terribly creative when he named it."

She laughed. "This was your fort?"

He led her up the moss-covered rock and lifted her onto the top, then jumped up beside her. "It was our hideaway. From Da."

Her heart pinched, understanding in a way she wished she didn't. "I didn't realize you needed to hide from your Da."

They sat down on the edge of the rock and he intertwined their fingers. "Aye. No' every day, but some days he'd be so grief-stricken and deep in his cups he'd lash out. It didnae matter who was nearby, they'd be on the receiving end of a punch. It helped me hone my battle instincts. I got good at dodging them."

Cara snuggled down into her lummon against the early morning cold and her own memories.

"It's how I got this scar beside my right eye. He pushed me and I went right into the corner of a table. Lachlan and I would come here for a few hours, or maybe for the night. However long it took Da to dry out. "

She studied the tiny scar beside his eye, chest tightening. "Your Da did that?"

He nodded. "Aye. He didnae mean to. At least, that's what I told myself then."

He smoothed his palm over hers, turning it upright in his hand. His finger traced the seared white welt that spread across it. "I am wondering about this scar on your hand. How did you get it?"

She swallowed. "I told you, the cauldron."

He kissed her palm and replaced it in her lap. He reached out his hands toward the lummon and hesitated, then unfastened it. Rough fingers smoothed across her neck and her collarbone before pulling the neck of her leine down two inches, tracing the red swipe at the top of her breast. "And this?"

"A seashell scraped me on a visit to Fanad Head." It was not a lie but an omission of who had wielded that shell.

"It wasnae the cauldron?" Understanding lived in his eyes.

246

Tears formed as she realized he'd caught her in a lie, her stomach dropping, her fears realized.

He secured the lummon around her, then took her left ankle in his hand. Heart pounding, she fought the urge to jerk her leg away. She'd worried for weeks over how she would keep the mark hidden.

Pushing her skirts up, his hands eased along her hose and pulled the ribbon above her knee. Tears overflowed her eyes, and she shook her head back and forth. "Please don't."

His phantom blue eyes flickered as he rolled her woolen hose down. He lifted her leg across his lap, massaging the ankle and feeling for the raised mark seared in a crooked mass across her left calf. His eyes were horror-struck as he traced the image of three boars. The mark of Clan MacSweeney.

"And this?"

Her voice became a whisper. "Duncan."

She looked away and pulled her hose up. His fingers turned her face toward his. "What happened, love?"

The loyalty Duncan had drilled into her refused to dislodge. "He wanted to change. He swore he would change. I prayed so hard—" Tears clogged her throat. "I prayed so hard that he would change."

Hector took her marred palm. "Did he?"

"If I could have given him a son he may have. But it was my own fault. My own failing."

His voice was full of tenderness. "Och. Love. That is no' a failing."

She pulled her palm away. "What is it then? You heard Father Timothy at our wedding. My role as wife is to bear children. Yet I cannot."

His clear eyes looked over the pines and lifted to the sky watching hen harriers swirl and swoop. "It is a reason for you to depend all the more on God. And if the result is that you have come to faith because of it, it is the greatest blessing upon your life."

Once again, Hector's words reframed the greatest pain upon her heart, fitting broken pieces back together and helping her function once more.

He continued. "The Lord will allow what will bear good fruit in your life, even if it causes you to hurt for a time. Duncan was so busy blaming you that he missed the promise in your pain."

Taking a deep breath, she drew her left leg up and rolled her hose down, angling her leg across her lap and touching the three hideous boars with their tongues outstretched. "He was home late that day."

Drops of her tears wet the ugly white mass on her leg. Hector's strong hand covered the brand, imparting comfort to deep pain. "I was always afraid when he was home late. It meant he'd had a hard day and would be in a foul mood. Our cottage was spotless, as he liked. Food prepared, as he liked. Table set, as he liked. I put on my blue gown, the one he favored so much, in hopes that the promise of love later would soften his mood. Instead, he came through the door and became convinced I'd dressed up for Tom Boyle who lived across the way. I swore to him—"

Her voice broke and he wiped the tears from her cheeks.

"I swore to him I'd never even spoken with Tom Boyle beyond *good morning*, but he didn't believe a word I said. He put the seal press he used on documents in the embers of the hearth. I knew what he was about and tried to run, but he caught me by the hair and tackled me to the ground.

"I was powerless. Nothing I did could free me. I dug my fingers into the floor and pulled myself away, but he sat across my knees and pushed the seal press into the back of my leg. I screamed so loud Margaret came running from next door and scared him off me."

She pulled her hose up and retied the ribbon, afraid to look at him, desperate to remain the woman he fell in love with. "Does it change me in your eyes?"

He brushed away tears that formed in his eyes. "It changes nothing. *Nothing*, do you hear me? Except that I love you even more for what you have overcome. I am in awe of you, my strong, bonny lass."

His arms crashed around her and held her tight, and she wrapped her arms around him, safe in the lock of his embrace, steadied by his solace and love.

"Can I tell you the other reason I've brought you here?"

A harrier swooped down into the tree line and emerged with something in its claws.

She sniffed as he released her. "The excellent birdwatching?"

He chuckled. "No. To teach you how to fight."

The thought was so absurd she burst out laughing. "And who am I to fight?"

"Me."

She almost doubled over. "You are nearly two feet taller than I. What can I do to you?"

He got to his feet and extended his hand to her. "I'll show you."

They moved to the soft grass in the middle of the thicket and he had her remove her lummon and hat standing with her back to his front. His mouth moved beside her ear. "The most important lesson that you need to learn is to observe your surroundings." A chill ran down her spine, his deep voice rumbling through her consciousness. "If you're alone, you must be aware of everything in front of and behind you. Listen for movement and stick to well-traveled paths. Even then, never let your guard down."

He placed a hand on her shoulder. "The second lesson is that an attacker will move with speed and violence, when you're most vulnerable. By the time you understand what's happening it will be too late."

Remembering the speed with which Duncan's mood could change, she nodded.

Hector cleared his throat. "I hate that you understand what I am teaching you without me having to explain."

She lifted a shoulder. "Go on."

"If you're traveling in a group, it's important to maintain your space. Keep your distance from those around you. If they get closer, you take steps away."

She nodded. "If Duncan could catch the string of my apron or my hair I was done for."

"How did you avoid him?"

She thought back. "I would try to keep furniture between us, and away from anything he may be able to throw."

"Good." The tone of his voice was bitter, but he kept talking. "Only do what you need to get free and run. You're a small woman, it isnae sensible to believe you can overpower a man."

249

She'd never been able to free herself from Duncan no matter how hard she tried.

"Do you think you are ready to learn a few strategies to get yourself free?"

She tried to calm her racing heart. "Are you going to hurt me?"

"Absolutely no'. If it becomes too much, say stop and I will stop that instant. That night, how did he grab you, from in front or behind?"

"Behind. He grabbed me here." She motioned to the crown of her head.

Hector's brawny hand fisted in the hair at the crown of her head, but he made no movement. "Like this?"

Her breath quickened. "Yes. He jerked me backwards so fast I didn't know what was happening."

"I'm going to pull back slowly. I want you to wrap your hands around mine and widen your stance like so." He released her head and demonstrated a wide-legged crouched position. "Stay on your feet, and dinnae lose your balance." She mimicked his stance. "Good. Now let's try it slowly."

He moved behind her once more, his hand fisted in her hair, and began to pull back. "Grab. Stance." She did as he instructed and managed to stabilize and stay on her feet.

"Do you feel how it makes it harder for me to move you around when you're in this position?" He moved her head in his fist, but it wasn't as easy for him as when he began. She maintained a sliver of control as he pulled her backward.

"Yes. But if you used your full strength I would be on the ground in seconds."

He released her again. "Let's no' focus on that for the moment. You may be overpowered, but let's walk through this first. Dinnae give up. Fight to get away, no' to win."

He resumed the position and she got into the stance. "This time, stay tight in my space and crash backward into my body. Ready?"

"Yes."

He grabbed her hair and pulled her backward and she completed each move he taught her. "Good. Elbows in. Crash into me as hard as you can. Harder. Right, move backward." Hector shifted and struggled to continue to move her around. "Beautiful. Now stop."

Her heart was pounding from the effort, but a beam of self-confidence began to glow. He released her. "How did that feel?"

"I stayed on my feet."

He smiled but maintained a solemn tone. "Yes, you did—but once someone has hold of your hair, the chances of you getting free arenae good. You can try to land blows and he may release you."

Doubt filled her. Every man she'd ever known was bigger and stronger than she was. "Punches?"

"Elbows. Let me show you."

They repeated the exercise. He grabbed her, she wrapped her hands around his, tucked her body and widened her stance, then crashed backward into him. He stopped.

"Yes. Now..." he tapped her right elbow, "bring this back as hard as you can and try to jab me."

She maintained her stance. "I don't want to hurt you."

"Nonsense. You're fighting for your life. Jab as hard as you can. Go." She jabbed backward and connected with his middle. His voice raised into command, urging her forward. "Keep going, Cara, harder! Stomp, anything you can." Elbow connected with gut, and he gave a small grunt then stopped. "Very good. Now from this position, try and spin inward so that you're facing me."

She did as he showed her and twisted by her hair dangling in his grasp, making it difficult for him to maintain his hold and he released. "Excellent. As soon as it breaks, run. Dinnae look back, run as fast as you can."

They ran through the move a few more times before he stopped her. "Are you ready to try this at greater strength?"

Tingles ran through her muscles. "I don't know. If I'm caught off guard, how will I remember it all?"

"Practice. I will practice with you as much as you wish. You can train your body to remember and train your mind to stay calm. That day in the village after the raids, your mind panicked and froze. Remember, you're always in control of your mind, it is where you must live, even if you're knocked to the ground. No man can enter your mind, and no man can take it from you."

She blew out an affected breath and tried to remain calm but fought a wave of silly tears and became angry with herself. Hector crouched and brushed a lock of tangled hair from her face. "What are you feeling?"

"I don't know. I'm angry with myself. Why did this happen to me?"

He kissed her cheek and held her face in his palms. "It happened because Duncan MacSweeney was an evil coward. Praise God for keeping you safe and getting you to Mull. We're going to go through it one more time and I want you to channel every angry feeling you have into the beast who's doing this, no' yourself. None of what happened is your fault. None of what is happening is your fault. I want you to fight like fury. You can do this, Cara. Fight for yourself."

Closing her eyes she imagined every slap, every kick, every belittling thing Duncan had ever said or done to her. Anger formed in her gut, and she channeled it to her muscles. When her head jerked back with force, she was ready. Gripping Hector's massive hand she centered her body and widened her legs, then moved backward in a swift crash, letting loose blow after blow with her elbows and legs. She heard him grunt as she connected, stomping her feet, and kicking into him. When she spun away, he lost his grip, and she sprinted as fast as she could toward the wood.

Behind her a war cry rent the air. She stopped dead.

Hector yelled with pride. "How about that? Dinnae pick a fight with Lady MacLean."

Triumph swelled in her chest. For once, she'd not been overpowered. Love overwhelmed her and she ran back to him, throwing herself into his arms. "Did I do it well?"

He squeezed her and put his hand to the back of her head, kissing the place where he grasped her. "I've never been prouder of any warrior."

# CHAPTER 30

## DUART OIGHREACHD - OCTOBER 26, 1383

Supper had begun by the time Cara and Hector returned to Duart. As they parted to bathe and dress for the evening, Hector tingled with the heady mix of fresh air and laughter. As much as Duncan had wanted to squash and destroy the very essence of who Cara was, Hector wanted nothing more than to protect and nurture it.

Nothing, he was certain, could've prepared him for the stark image of the boars pressed deep into her fragile flesh. Anguished, he stared at the brand as his mind's eye recreated the physical and mental torment she must have felt in that moment, and every day for ten years of marriage to a thorough monster.

Unable to bear the thought of her helpless at the hands of another man, he resolved to show her that she could defend herself. He hadn't gone easy on her as he'd shown her each method of escape, but she'd borne it well, and then become confident. He'd never met a person with a better ability for recall. What he showed her only a few times she remembered and executed as if she had been escaping all her life. And maybe she had.

Today was a turning point. The portcullis around her heart had at last lifted and she'd ushered him in to her most secret and trusted places. The honor she paid him affected him and he took care with his appearance before supper, wanting to be worthy of the treasure she was. Treasure plunged into fires of evil, but rather than being destroyed she had emerged refined, purified, and more valuable.

Having finished washing and dressing in his finest attire, he raised a hand mirror to his face and found his dragon-like reflection staring back at him. He frowned and tried to affect a look of courtship that Léo had often used on women, but only managed to appear deranged. Shrugging, he headed downstairs, anticipation knotting his stomach like a lad. He knocked on her door and waited.

Sumptuous midnight blue velvet embraced the swells and ebbs of her figure as she stepped into the corridor. A silk veil covered the thick waves of hair pinned behind her shoulders. Heart skipping, he bowed, then kissed her hand. "My lady."

"You look very braw." Overcome with the urge to impress her as if they were a pair of courting eagles, he puffed his chest out and pulled his arms upward to flex his muscles at her in a ritual display. The blush that swept across her freckled cheeks filled him with manly pride.

"Cheeky lad."

"Would you like me to pick you up over my head and press you? Bend a bar of iron?" He offered her his arm, bicep flexed.

She took it and lifted on her toes, kissing his scar. "No need for displays of strength. I know there is no match for you."

The sober remark went straight to his heart and a tight thread pulled rigid between them as he guided her downstairs. All day he wished to kiss and hold her, but he'd kept a distance. Now, in the quiet dark of the keep, he longed to secret her away. A small entresol between the floors provided an opportunity and he pulled her into its curtained enclave.

A grin lifted the corners of her berry-pink lips and she whispered, "What are we doing?"

Slivers of moonlight trickled through lancet windows causing her ivory skin to glow. He brushed the smooth plane of her jaw. "So bonny."

The grin ebbed away, and her lips parted. He touched the silken pad of her lip and tucked his hand under her ear, pulling her close but not yet kissing her. Her breath tickled his lips, and he felt fully at her mercy. "Tell me what you want, and it's yours. I'll give you anything."

"I want your strength."

Folding his arms around her he formed a refuge, and she rested her cheek upon his chest. "Do you promise to keep me safe?"

"I promise. My body is yours, to protect and guard you all the days of my life. Nothing will ever harm you again."

A small hand reached beneath the soft folds of plaid at his shoulder and ran down the muscles of his arm, resting on the bare skin of his forearm, clinging to its substance. She looked up into his eyes. "With you beside me I feel untouchable."

Unable to help himself any longer he pulled her into his kiss. Their lips met, eager and deep. After a few moments she pulled away, remembering the duty and purpose they had in coming below stairs. "Hector, they're waiting for us."

"I cannae help it, Cara. You've gone straight to my head like whisky. I've been wanting to kiss you all day. I'm craving you."

Thirsty, his mouth found hers again. Fitting his hands around her small waist, his thumbs moved along the delicate arch of her ribs. Her hands found his and moved them back to her waist, keeping them fixed and not allowing them to travel north or south. He smiled, knowing she'd guessed their hoped for destination and she chuckled against his lips.

A throat cleared just outside the entresol, and they broke apart, grinning at each other as if they were seventeen and had sneaked away from their parents.

"It's probably a servant," she whispered.

"In that case I dinnae have to stop kissing you," he whispered back.

In a flash, his arms circled around her and held her close, not allowing her to escape. He was just leaning down to continue when the throat cleared again.

Snickering, she put two hands upon his chest. "They're waiting for us."

Cursing, he flipped back the curtain covering the door and found himself face to face with Léo.

Léo leaned against the wall, arms crossed, expression annoyed. "Laird and Lady MacLean. What were you doing in there?"

Cara blushed a furious shade of scarlet, and Hector cleared his throat, pulling her toward the great hall, Léo trailing behind.

Inside the hall, leaders from the Council of the Isles sat around a large table, heads down. At a table beside the hearth, their wives sat together laughing and chatting. The mood at each table couldn't have been more disparate.

Lachlan looked up, expression intense. "Nice of you to decide to join us. Cara, Mhairi and the other wives are over there." His tone was sharp, and by the look on her face, she picked up on it.

Sobered, Hector turned to his wife and kissed her cheek. "I'll rejoin you at the end of the evening."

The confidence that had built in her all day wilted, and she walked toward the table of women wide-eyed and visibly smaller.

Sliding into the chair beside Léo, he dropped his voice low. "What've I missed?"

"You mean before your brother sent me looking for the pair of you? They're discussing the raid—last night. Sixteen members of the MacQuarries killed. Men, women, children. No livestock this time, just people."

The MacQuarries were one of the oldest, and one of the smallest, clans of the Isles. Their leader, Dunslaff, had yielded chieftainship to Lachlan five years earlier, because they'd come to depend on the MacLeans for protection. The loss of sixteen men, women, and children was a heavy blow to the tiny clan.

Dunslaff rubbed the back of his neck, his face creased with worry. "We arenae sure how they got through the patrols of bìrlinns, but the tracks were there this morning at first light. Cowards trapped them in their homes and set fire to the roofs."

Remorse pinched Hector's chest as he remembered the charred body of good-hearted Rhona as it was loaded into the wagon. These people were not the object of the Wolf's interest, but he'd used them effectively to achieve power just as he had been doing in the highlands for years.

Dunslaff continued. "A few families managed to escape, but more than twenty homes were lost. Someone must have disclosed information about where our stores were. They found the granary and set fire to it despite it being kept in a secret location. We've no provision for the winter months."

The bulging granary on Lochbuie came to Hector's thoughts. "We'll send you our surplus from this growing season. We reaped almost double our normal harvest. It would provide for your numbers for at least six months."

Lachlan nodded his head in approval. "Aye, Duart can spare two months. Is there anyone else who can cover the difference?"

Brodie MacNeil erupted with incredulity. "It seems to me that Hector ought to provide for the entire loss out of his stores."

Léo swirled the wine in his goblet. "He's offered his entire surplus. What more would you have him give? He has his own clan to feed."

Brodie leaned forward and bopped a meaty fist on the table. "His entire store of grain. The MacFadyens have already survived three famines and know how to survive on less. Why should the rest of us have to deprive our people when it's his failure to secure an alliance with your wretched brother that's gotten us into this mess?"

Hector was nearing his limit of shouldering the blame for the Wolf's interest in the Isles. "Had I secured an alliance with the MacKinnons, there was no guarantee that the Wolf wouldnae have attacked, it only guaranteed us more fighting numbers."

Brodie leaned forward, teeth bared. "The attacks began once you married. If you'd been as committed to the council as you'd been to your Irish harlot, none of us would be in danger."

The anger simmering in him boiled over at the sound of the foul term and he fisted MacNeil's tunic yanking his paunchy figure across the table, dishes and trenchers clattering into each other and across the stone floor.

Music came to an abrupt halt as every member of the assembled leaders got to their feet. Brodie's cloudy eyes were wide, but he continued headlong into his rebuke. "Do you see? The man is led by his basest instincts like an animal. He has no self-control."

Hector spoke through gritted teeth. "Withdraw your words against my wife."

Lachlan slammed his fist on the table causing the jumble of flagons and trenchers to jump. "Let him go, Hector. He's right."

Stunned by the betrayal, Hector's head snapped to his brother.

Lachlan's nostrils flared and his cheeks grew red. "You heard me. This is my home; you will honor it. Let him go."

If only this pusillanimous worm knew how chaste his relationship with Cara had been. If only he knew the lifetime of insults his wife had endured and the care with which she deserved to be treated. The echo of the vile term rang through the rafters of his patience.

"I will personally cover four months of grain from my stores in France." All heads jerked back to the opposite end of the table where Léo calmly savored his claret. "That will take the MacQuarries well into the next harvest. Now let Brodie go."

Hector looked into Brodie's cloudy eyes. "Dinnae ever speak of my wife again." He let go and the man flopped onto the table, landing in a trencher full of gravy-soaked venison.

Brodie peeled himself off the trencher and got back into his seat. One by one the councilors followed suit, sitting down around the table looking unsettled.

A gush of venomous disgust obliterated any fealty Hector felt for his brother as he sank back into his chair. Lachlan glared at him, and he glared back. Had there not been fifteen men between them they might have come to blows for the first time since that fateful day near Staffa. Since the day Aileen died, they'd made an unspoken pact not to fight. They were always on the same side.

The memory of that day intruded on Hector's thoughts, and he forced himself to look away. Familiar guilt began to blanket him, the guilt that had driven him to nearly drink himself to death and told him he could never change.

From across the room Cara gave him a sympathetic look, and he winked at her, causing a small smile to form at her lips.

No, this wasn't the same. He wouldn't carry the guilt for the Wolf's attacks as he had for Aileen's death. He was certain he'd done the right thing in marrying Cara, and pretending any ill-conceived marriage alliance with Elspeth would have spared them the Wolf was folly.

Firm in his conviction, he got to his feet, ready to propose the plan that he had wanted to bring to Lachlan months earlier when he had sought his support and been rejected. The plan that he had proposed to King John just after the Harvest Games. The plan that God had seeded in His heart on Iona as he stared at the radiant moon. This time he wouldn't yield to anyone's will but His.

"Alexander Stewart would be attacking now with or without a marriage alliance. He has no fealty to anyone but himself. I offer my support by means of grain, men to fight, and expertise, but I'll no' shoulder the wickedness this man has wrought. I say we fight for our king as Brodie first suggested."

Iain MacLeod drummed his fist upon the table in support of Hector's words and was joined by the MacKenzies, MacKays, MacQuarries, and a shocked Brodie MacNeil.

Lachlan held up his hands. "If you really believe that then you'll have no qualms volunteering as war chief to the king."

As war chief he would be required to pick up his sword which he had laid down at the altar. Hector's preference was to remain out of conflict, and Lachlan was defying him to do it. But he'd already done it.

Hector squared his shoulders. "Sometimes conflict is necessary to protect order, and to overcome those who wish to destroy good. Peace doesnae mean passiveness. Peace requires courage. Aye. I offered my services as war chief to King John the night before I married. With the council's consent we are ready to wage war."

Drumming began once more on the table as the leaders signaled their endorsement of his leadership.

"These attacks are increasing and will continue until answered. With the council's consent, I would like eight to ten of the most elite warriors representative of the council clans to come to Lochbuie and train with me. With a team of warriors, I believe we can conduct offensive raids and cripple the Wolf before he reaches the Isles. These men must have correct motives. I dinnae want seekers of revenge, glory, or fame. I want men who wish to protect our islands and our people, and who fight for the good God has established in this world."

Lachlan held up his hands. "Fine. We will convene our first war council with the king at Findlugan the first of November."

Less than a week until he returned to war. Until he must leave Cara. He turned, not wanting to waste one more second of his time left with her.

Lachlan got in his way, aggression oozing out of every pore. "What were you thinking? You're plunging us into a war, Hector. What about my family? Did you no' think about what this would cost me? You'll never change. You wash the outside of the cup, but the inside remains filthy."

Sheltering with his brother had saved Hector and provided him a place to recover for five years, and for that he would always be grateful. But it was time to leave the shallows of faith and swim into deeper waters.

"You've that backward, brother. What you see on the outside may be the same man, but everything in my heart has changed. I refuse to be chained to a past I've been forgiven for. Da couldnae understand, and it seems you dinnae either."

Lachlan looked staggered. "How dare you compare me to him."

"My allegiance is to my own family, to Cara. You sat there and let Brodie belittle her today after everything you heard Mhairi tell us, and then endorsed his remarks in front of the council. I'll no' forget that. You've made your choice. I've made mine. Cara and I leave at first light."

Hector stepped around him and strode over to the party of women. "I'm sorry to interrupt, ladies. May I borrow my wife?" Ever perceptive, Cara's face cloaked with concern.

Eilidh MacLeod put a hand to her heart. "Newly married."

Plastering what he hoped was a convincing smile on his face, he nodded. "Yes. Exactly."

At the opposite end of the hall, Lachlan unloaded on Mhairi who watched them leave, an expression of fear on her face.

Cara tightened her grip on his arm. "Is everything all right?"

Aoife collided with them as he hurried Cara around the corner. "I'm sorry, my laird."

"It's all right, Aoife. Please be sure to pack Lady MacLean's trunk tonight. We are leaving for Moy at dawn."

She nodded. "Aye, my laird. I'll see to it right away."

He muttered his thanks and pulled Cara up the three flights of stairs toward his chamber.

Cara gripped his hand. "What's going on? You're worrying me."

"I need to speak to you in private."

In the solitude of his room, auld Malcolm was putting away his cleaned clothes. He eyed Cara and bowed. "I'll be going."

Hector held up a hand to stop him. "Before you go, is my trunk ready for a return journey?"

"No, my laird, but I could see to it straight away."

Hector shook his head. "I'll send someone from Moy later this week to collect my things. I'll be taking everything."

Malcolm raised a grayed eyebrow. "Everything? Even the things you store here year-round?"

"Yes. Everything. I've my own home, there's no need to keep anything here anymore." Something sparked in Malcolm's eyes, but he bowed and excused himself from the room without another word.

As soon as the door shut, Cara spoke. "Please tell me what's happened. I saw you grab Laird MacNeil and heard your raised voice with Lachlan."

"MacNeil said something very ill-advised, and Lachlan agreed with him."

She paled. "To do with me?"

"Yes."

She sank into the chair before the fire and put a hand to her head. "I bring you nothing but trouble."

"Nonsense. You havenae wrought anything upon the Isles that wasnae already in motion."

"But your things. Your brother. I don't wish to come between you."

He tilted her chin toward him and touched her cheek. "We are one, Cara. It's time to move forward."

Her hand covered her stomach and she visibly braced. "Is that what you brought me here to tell me?"

Hector shook his head. "The council has decided to fight back against the Wolf."

"War?"

"Aye."

Disbelief washed over her features. "You'll be going back into battle?"

He nodded. "I've volunteered as war chief."

She perched on the edge of the chair. "What does that mean?"

261

"It means I'll need to travel to Findlugan in six days. I'll oversee the command of our war party and forces in the Hebrides." He hesitated. "It means I'll need to travel between the Isles and maintain the King's defenses with only brief periods at home."

Sadness formed in her eyes. "You're leaving? We'll be apart?"

"Aye. I want Margaret to move into Moy, and Ursula if she wishes, so you're no' alone. And I dinnae want you to go anywhere without a guard with you. You'll have Tavish and Pádraig to help you run things while I'm away."

"Tavish?"

"I know you dinnae get on, but tomorrow I'll have a word with him. You'll be given the accounts and anything you request. I'm leaving you in command of Moy."

She got to her feet and paced the room. "Hector, I..." Her voice wavered. "I want you at home."

He took her hand and squeezed, trying to impart strength. "To protect you, and the people of our nation, someone needs to organize our forces and defend us. I'm the man best equipped to do that. You've helped me see that this ability for warfare is God-given. I've a responsibility, Cara."

She paused, studying his expression. "We only have six days left together?"

He nodded. "Aye, love."

Releasing his hand, she walked past him and bolted the door. Mind groping, he watched in disbelief as she turned with longing in her eyes and removed her veil. Heart slamming into his chest, he diverted his eyes to the ceiling.

Her voice was small. "You don't have to look away."

Marshaling his courage, his stomach clenching in knots, he looked down as her leine puddled at her feet.

His eyes traveled slowly down the fiery cascades of her hair, inviting green eyes, the joyful tilt at the corners of her lips, the freckles that scattered across her nose and cheeks. All of it wrapped around his heart and crushed him. But the diaphanous white silk chemise embroidered with dainty clover, beautifully adorning his bride, knocked the breath out of him. Need struck him like a physical blow.

Shyness betrayed her in her shaking hands. This was his Cara.

"'Tis my wedding chemise. I've never worn anything so...but earlier I thought we might stay together...so I..." She looked down and gestured, cheeks pinking, voice uncertain. "Do ye like it?"

Eyes wide, he nodded like a daftie, unable to voice his thoughts out loud.

The power she held over him unwound every tether of restraint and he was mesmerized as she rose on tiptoes, pulling him down, wrapping her arms around his neck and fitting her mouth to his, giving him a kiss not of quick passion, but of profound love.

Control dangled by a flimsy thread, and he dared not touch her for fear that he might break her, or his promise to honor their marriage. He took a step back.

His voice strangled out. "I must know, Cara. Are you ready? I'll no' be displeased if you arenae. I'll wait forever for you if I must."

Her palms smoothed against the bands of his stomach pushing his tunic up, sending gooseflesh across his skin as she struggled with it, giggling as she hopped, pulling it over his head.

Her hands came to his cheeks and she looked deep into his eyes, a bright smile illuminating her face. "I'm ready. You've seen into my soul and know all that's there. I love you, Hector."

The remaining thread of his control snapped, and he swept her into his arms, rushing her to his bed, whispering precisely what he thought of her chemise and his never-ending love into her ears.

# CHAPTER 31

## LOCHBUIE OIGHREACHD - NOVEMBER 22, 1383

Rain battered Lochbuie for twenty-seven days straight. Cara squinted against the moisture and fog as she dashed inside the barmkin walls toward the keep and Murdoch jogged back to the gatehouse.

Sparkles danced in her vision as she climbed the stairs to the second floor, and she slowed to catch her breath.

Margaret took the basket from her hands. "You're soaked to the skin."

Cara pulled her lummon, heavy with rain, away from her trembling body. "I ran all the way from Laggan Sands through the driving rain with Murdoch. Ursula sent her love, and three pots of honey, and a tincture for your cold."

Margaret held a handkerchief to her congested nose. "Thank you, love. Although if you keep traipsing about in the rain, you'll be needing it more than I. You look a bit peaky."

Cara handed the wet lummon to Aoife. "I'm hale, just a bit tired."

"Oh, before I forget, this arrived while you were out." Margaret fished in her apron and produced a vellum letter, an axe among branches visible in the heavy wax seal. It was Hector's mark. Joy lit through her chest, and she tore open the missive, staring at the loops and flourishes.

Helpless to read it, she refolded it, tucked it within her sleeve, and took the lummon back from Aoife.

"You're no' going back out in this, are you love?" Margaret protested.

She secured the soaking lummon around her. "I must know what he says. I'll be back soon. I'm going to Pádraig's."

Aoife held her arm. "At least let me summon the groom to bring Clover around."

Cara shook her off and headed back down the stairs. "No, thank you. I'll be halfway to his house by the time she's saddled."

Without looking over her shoulder, she dashed back down the stairs and out across the barmkin, waving off an annoyed looking Murdoch, and trotting up the southern road toward the fear-taic's house. Her thighs burned as she jogged the sloping road and navigated the boggy ground. Water seeped inside her shoes, but she continued to hurry along, needing to hear Hector's voice in the words on the page.

Pádraig held the mossy door open as she neared, looking surprised. "I thought that was you, my lady. What brings you here in this weather?"

She hurried inside, and flipped her hood back, water droplets creating a wide pattern on the immaculate wooden floor. Digging in her damp sleeve she produced the vellum missive. "This. It's his mark."

Pádraig took the message and pulled out a chair beside the fire. "Have a seat."

Noticing the fatigue in her muscles, she eased back into the chair and fought an urge to lay her head against the oak table. Pádraig ladled cider into a cup and placed it in her hand. "You could've sent for me, and I'd come to you, you ken?"

The cider filled her shivering body with warmth and settled her swimming head. "It would've taken too long. It was quicker to jog here."

He chuckled, took the chair across from hers, unfolded the pages, and began to read.

"'My darling Cara. I pray that this letter finds you well and safe. Murdoch wrote that you've been doing well in your command of Moy and taking care of our clan. And I'm surprised, but relieved, to hear that you've allowed Tavish to continue running the accounts.'"

Cara winced. She hadn't allowed anything. The man had flat out refused to hand them over despite Hector's orders, and she'd been too scared to argue with him.

"'I'm very proud that you've come to a compromise with him. But that's your nature—you're a peacekeeper and a treasure. The council on Findlugan concluded and I've been in the north. We've engaged with the Wolf a few times, but I'm well. I'll need to stay away until December but hope that I'll be able to spend Advent with you.'"

Heaviness returned to her breast, and she felt a sudden urge to ask Pádraig to read slower, not wanting his presence to fade away. "'I think of you every minute, and of the week we shared before I left.'"

Against her will, her cheeks flamed. For six days they'd scarcely left their solar except to eat. For six days she'd known what it was to be a true wife. He'd been gentle, taking his time to give her all the love and affection she'd never known. Her heart ached and she closed her eyes, longing to feel him close to her.

"'I long to see you again and pray for you every hour of the day. Please be cautious and take care of yourself. With all the love in my heart, Hector.'"

Pádraig handed her the missive, and she touched the single word at the bottom of the page. His name. She'd not realized she was crying until he pressed a handkerchief into her palm.

"Are you hale, my lady?"

"Yes. I don't know what's the matter with me."

He gave her a pitying look. "You miss him?"

She wiped her nose with the handkerchief. "More than I've ever missed anyone."

Pádraig sipped his cider. "Never had any children of my own. No one has been more a son to me than Hector. I'm consoling myself with the knowledge there've been no attacks in the Isles for two weeks."

She swallowed her tears and took a breath. "You knew him when he was a child?"

"Aye. Held him the day he was born." He shook his head. "An enormous baby."

Barking with laughter, she wiped the remnants of her tears away, the cider and conversation soothing her aching heart.

"His poor mother almost died giving birth to him. Ah, but his father was proud. Hector always had qualities Lachlan never did. I suppose that's why Lachlan grew to resent him."

She couldn't believe her ears. "Lachlan? You're jesting."

"I'm no'. Hector was bigger, stronger. Better with a sword. He's clever and decisive. Some of it came from the freedom of being the second son and the middle child, but some of it was God-given. At least that's what I've come to believe. Lachlan was a fine son, too, but he resented the attention Hector got and the pressure his father put on him to be more like him."

She ran her fingers along the folds in the letter. "Hector's also mentioned a sister, Aileen."

Pádraig nodded. "Aye. Aileen was the youngest, their only girl. She had her da wrapped around her finger. Sweet girl, blond like Lachlan, riotous curls like Hector and his da, and those same blue eyes all the children inherited from their mother. She loved spending time with her brothers, I suppose that was why she snuck onto their boat the day they sailed to Staffa. Lachlan started a fight with Hector over it, and as usual, Hector finished it. But somewhere in the middle of their fighting, Aileen fell into the water."

Pádraig's eyes grew misty. "Poor lass. Hector and Lachlan dove in after her, but she must have sunk like a stone. They never found her, or a body. They had to return home without her."

Pádraig steadied himself and a picture of a distraught young Hector seared her heart. "His father was never the same after that. Took to drink like our father. And..." Pádraig's voice strangled, and he took a gulp from his cup, gritting his teeth and hardening his face. "Grew to hate Hector. It didnae matter that Lachlan started the fight, that Aileen was leaning over the bow, that Hector was only eight years old, or that his father allowed such young boys to take a skiff all the way to Staffa."

Her heart broke and she wished she could befriend the little boy who would become her husband. "Is that why Hector fought with his father and left home?"

"It led to it. His da would call him worthless, a murderer, and other

267

foul things no' fit for your ears. When those things are spoken over you for years, it takes a toll. One day his da was on top of him, calling him names and daring him to do something about it. He pushed him, and Hector snapped. He was no little boy then but a fully grown man, twenty-one years old. He shoved his father away from him and his da landed right on his back in the mud. Died of shock in the blink of an eye. And Hector? He ran. We didnae see him again for eight years. 'Til I saw him on Iona."

She warmed her hands against the stone cup, fitting the pieces of Hector's past together. "The day he found God."

Pádraig shook his head. "The day God found him. Hector wasnae looking for anything but more drink. Smelled it on him. Drink, sickness...fear. I couldnae believe what he'd become. Bigger and stronger than any man I'd ever seen, his handsome face scarred, his eyes haunted from years of war. He was hearing things and seeing things. Full of guilt, believing he'd become like his father. Yet, as I held him, I felt it. He wasn't like him. His heart was still soft. He was a lost man, no' a bitter man."

Pádraig's eyes grew misty again and he sniffed. "What's the matter with me? I'm as soft as my auld granny."

She put down her cup and squeezed his hands. He squeezed hers back and continued his story. "He went into that abbey a tormented man and emerged a quiet man. No' to say he hasnae struggled since that day. He has. But God examines the heart. And Hector has a good heart. He lets God work in it. That's why he's nothing like his father. And that's why he's set apart from his brother."

Cara nodded. "It's what I love most about him. My first husband didn't believe in God."

Pádraig grunted, the small sound conveying his great resentment and understanding. "Maggie's told me about that."

An idea came to mind, and Cara fished the small book Hector had given her from the pouch tied to her crios. "Can you tell me what this says?"

His eyebrows shot up. "What, the whole thing?"

She rolled her eyes. "No. What he's written in the front."

Pádraig opened the volume and looked at the inscription. "I'm sorry.

This is Latin. I can read the letters, but the meaning is lost on me. How odd. Why did he write an inscription in Latin?"

He placed the small book back in her hands and she looked at the words, frustrated. "I don't know."

"Why no' ask him what it means?"

She placed the volume back inside the pouch. "I did and he read it aloud. I believe he already thinks I'm an ignorant twit. I was too afraid to admit I don't understand Latin."

Pádraig scrunched up his face and rolled his eyes. "Nonsense."

Her voice came out high and agitated and she lifted the letter. "Well, he seems relieved about Tavish keeping the accounts."

Pádraig pulled a face. "Well..."

"I believe Tavish ruined that first supper at Moy, and when I looked at the accounts..." She stopped herself, aware that she had just invited Pádraig into her knowledge of the theft.

Suspicion creased his face. "What's this about the accounts?"

Biting her lip, she wished to call the words back, certain he wouldn't believe her. "I have some skill with numbers."

"Aye. Margaret's told me. Of course, why shouldn't you take over the accounts? Doesnae Hector agree?"

"Not at first. We disagreed and he sided with Tavish. But he did have a change of heart."

His eyes narrowed on the letter. "Did you entrust the accounts to Tavish after Hector left, as he says in the letter?"

Feeling herself in a tight corner, she tried to find a way out that didn't require a lie. "Not exactly."

Concern cloaked his features. "What do you mean no' exactly? Hector has entrusted the running of Moy and the clan to you in his absence. He was explicit in his instructions to Tavish and me that we support your directives, not the other way around."

The uneasy feeling in her stomach returned and she shifted in her seat. "I've asked for the ledgers, and he refuses or ignores me. I'm too afraid to challenge him."

Pádraig rose from his seat. "I'm going back to Moy with you and we are going to straighten this out right now."

She got to her feet, wringing her hands, and tried to decide what to do to fix the situation. If Pádraig interfered and made Tavish resent her, if she was wrong about the numbers, she would look foolish in front of everyone. "That's not necessary, Pádraig. I'm sure I can handle it." And she must handle it.

"You said you *looked* at the accounts though."

Back against the wall, she tried to determine what to do. "I did...find them in his study and took a quick glance. And I thought I saw some...anomalies."

Pádraig frowned. "I havenae the mind for numbers. But Léo does. Perhaps we should write to Duart and see if he'd come down for a few days to assist."

*Léo.* They hadn't had a proper talk since her marriage, and she was certain she'd hurt him. "I don't know why he would come to help me."

"That's why he returned to Duart. Out of concern for you. Lachlan told me. At any rate, he's already looked at the clan books and will be able to assist you with what you're looking at. It might soothe Tavish's ruffled feathers coming from him instead of you."

Shame filled her, for the way she'd treated Léo. Yet, she needed his help. "All right. Can you write to him for me?"

"I'll do it right now."

# CHAPTER 32

## LOCHBUIE OIGHREACHD - NOVEMBER 29, 1383

The welcome sight of Moy rose out of the thick, creeping fog like a bastion of peace. Hector breathed a sigh of deep relief. In a matter of minutes his wife would be in his arms. He hadn't planned to return for another month, but having established a brief disruption in the Wolf's raids, he found himself needing to be around the ordinary everyday of home. He'd once been able to live in a constant state of war, but found he no longer had the stomach for it.

Excitement built, and he jumped upon the rickety wooden dock, jogging its length past dozens of his clan all needing his attention. By the time he reached Moy, he was in full sprint, his need for Cara outweighing the litany of questions and complaints from the crowd of people hurrying behind him.

Cameron looked up from the shelves of the buttery and got to his feet as he crashed into the ground floor of the keep, closing the door on the crowd following him.

"My laird. We werenae expecting you back until the end of Advent."

"I'm only here for a few days. Where's my wife?"

Something flickered over the man's face. "She's taken ill, my laird. Been in your solar a week and hasnae even come out for meals—"

Without bothering to wait for the rest of the explanation, Hector raced up the stairs, fear pounding in his chest. By the time he reached the third floor, he was imagining the worst.

Crashing into the solar he found Cara sitting in a chair, pale, resting her head upon her hand. Léo held her right hand and crouched in front of her, a look of affection lifting his lips into a smile.

Outraged jealousy overwhelmed any concern he'd just felt. "What's going on in here?"

Cara sat straight up in the chair at the sound of his voice. He expected to see a look of shame upon her face, but all he found was shock. She got to her feet and wobbled. Léo caught her around the waist.

Anger seethed through him. "What's going on here?"

"Hector." Her voice was nasal and congested. Dashing over to him, she flung herself into his arms and buried her face in his chest. "Thank God you're safe. Thank God."

Léo folded his hands behind his back, and scrutiny tightened his features. "She's taken with Margaret's cold, but it's been much worse for her."

A familiar smell of rosemary clung to her hair and for a moment he allowed himself to close his eyes and feel her embrace, the longing in his heart abated. When she let go, the joy in her face seemed masked behind something else, and she looked at Léo.

Hector crossed his arms, wondering what he'd interrupted. "What are you doing here, Léo?"

"She sent for me. I've been here for a few days trying to convince Tavish to let me have another look at your account books."

Temper rising at Cara, and frustration with finding another man in his solar when all he longed to do was have her all to himself, his words came out clipped. "I tho' you werenae getting involved with the accounts."

She looked at her shoes. "There's something I haven't told you, Hector."

Léo stepped beside her and took her elbow. Hot with jealousy, Hector struggled to comprehend the intimacy in the gesture.

"What?" The single word came out in a harsh bark, and she jumped.

"I took your key and went into Tavish's solar a few weeks ago and had a look at the account books. From what I could figure, it looked as though he'd been underreporting the tithes and manrent and taking large sums of coin."

His mind boggled. It wasn't the pronouncement he was expecting. "You took my key?"

Color drained from her features, and she placed the back of her fingers to her mouth, thunking down in her chair. She rested her forehead in her hand and tugged at the bottom of Léo's tunic. "Send for Aoife. Tell her it's happening again."

Léo nodded and rushed from the room.

Confusion, fear, anger, envy, and protectiveness mingled together, and he stood paralyzed, unsure what to do. He stepped toward her, wanting to comfort her, but hesitated, annoyed that the homecoming he'd envisioned wasn't coming to fruition.

Her voice sounded from inside her palms. "I'm sorry I took your key."

"You could've asked for it. Or asked me to look at Tavish's books."

"It was the morning after that awful dinner. I thought you'd dismiss me. And then when my fears were confirmed, we left for Duart, and I didn't know how to tell you. I'm sorry."

Anger began to override empathy. "So, you sent for Léo as soon as I left and had no problem telling him?"

She lifted her face from her hands, traces of her own annoyance in her voice. "It wasn't as soon as you left. I tried to get Tavish to turn over the accounts for weeks, but he refused or ignored me. Then I got your letter, and I talked to Pádraig, and Pádraig sent for Léo."

Hurt sliced through his chest. Was she still that afraid of him? "Pádraig knows about this?"

She blinked. "Yes, but—"

"And Margaret?"

"Yes. But Hec—"

His voice rose with his temper. "Everyone knows about this supposed theft but the chieftain of this clan, your husband?"

Aoife knocked upon the door. Hurrying by him with a look of reproach, she slipped a cup into Cara's hand. "Here, my lady, drink this."

Cara took the cup with shaking hands and sipped.

Concern resurfaced in Hector's heart. "What's that?"

Aoife gave him a look. If it could kill, he would be dead and buried. "Ginger root extract from Ursula. She's been peely-wally for over a week no'."

Cara lowered the cup and attempted to blow her blocked nose into her handkerchief. "Thank you, Aoife. It's working already."

Léo leaned against the open doorway, arms crossed, his expression concerned. "Is there anything else you need?"

"No. Thank you, Léo."

Boiling now, Hector tossed his fur over a chair, then unfastened the keys from his belt and nodded to Léo. "Come on."

Color now returning to her face, Cara straightened. "Where are you going?"

"Up to Tavish's study to see the books."

Cara got to her feet and handed the cup to Aoife.

"You stay here," he ordered, pushing toward the stairs. Léo followed behind.

He heard Cara's voice as he reached the fourth floor and slid the key into the lock. "Hector, wait—"

The lock clicked and he pushed into the room. Tavish looked up at him wide-eyed from his desk. "My laird. Léo."

A clammy hand pulled at Hector's arm, and he turned, frustrated. "I told you to stay in the solar."

Cara dropped his arm and recoiled as though she'd been hit. His conscience gave the barest of pinches.

Tavish cleared his throat. "Is there something I can do for you?"

"Produce the account books. Now."

Cara slid between Léo and himself, her voice desperate. "Hector, I should've told you, I'm sorry."

Tavish placed a large account book on the table.

Cara approached the book and touched the green cover and quirked an eyebrow. "This isn't it."

Tavish's voice evidenced frustration. "This is the only account book the clan has, I assure you."

Hector stepped forward and flipped open the cover, his eyes

running the length of the columns. Cara stepped forward and studied the page.

"Cara, step aside. Léo?"

Once more, she looked at him as though he'd bodily shoved her away, and she stepped back to make room for Léo. It'd be a hard lesson to learn, but she must learn to come to him first in these matters.

Léo took a piece of paper and inked a quill, recording numbers and beginning to add them.

Cara tapped the page. "It's 298,683. Flip forward to tithes."

Léo looked up at her. "You added these seven figures in your head?"

Looking straight into Hector's eyes with disdain, she nodded. "Yes. Flip forward to tithes."

Léo made room for her at the desk and flipped forward, his finger running down the column recording months of tithes.

"Column 1—314,370, less tithes of 15,687. It balances," Cara said with disbelief.

Astonishment washed over Hector. A mind for numbers fell far short of what he'd just witnessed. She'd added nearly sixty entries and balanced it against the household account in under two minutes.

Tavish folded his arms across his chest. "Are you satisfied?"

"No." Insistent, she pushed the book away. "This isn't the same book."

Hector breathed a warning. "Cara..."

Tavish got to his feet, his good looks mutating into something ugly. "I won't stand here and be insulted. Just what are you implying?"

She rounded on him, all vestiges of illness fading away. "You're a thief. The book I saw had a small wax stain on the front."

"Preposterous!"

Cara turned back to Hector and gestured around. "Let's search his room."

Fed up, Hector strode into the hall and called for the guard. Stomping back, he advanced on her. "If you're wrong about this, you will issue a full apology."

From the desk, Léo lifted the quill. "It balances. She's right."

Cara lifted her chin. "I'm not wrong. Not about this."

Five members of the MacLean guard entered the room and began tearing the room apart, looking in every corner, drawer, nook, and cranny. Still, no additional book could be found.

Tavish leaned against the wall, arms folded across his chest, simmering. As the minutes ticked by, Cara wrung her hands. Aoife patted her shoulder and whispered into her ear.

At the conclusion of an hour's-long search, Tavish's room was completely upended. Feathers wafted across the floor, papers lay in piles, books scattered about.

Embarrassed that he'd allowed her to take them on a wild chase, Hector pulled Cara forward. "Apologize to Tavish for poking in his room while he wasnae here, and for your error in calculation."

Her hands twisted into knots in front of her, her eyes filling with tears. "I didn't make an error."

"Everyone can make an error, especially adding in your head when you cannae see your work."

Her voice was pleading. "I didn't."

Tavish's was outraged. "Is this how I'm to be treated by Lady MacLean? Like a criminal? She comes up with a baseless accusation, and I have my room torn apart just to put me in my place?"

She'd clearly made an assumption about Tavish because the two did not get along, and she investigated the accounts with her mind already made up. However well-intentioned, she was in error. Now she'd learn the hard way why she should bring matters to him first. "Cara. This is the last time I shall say it. Apologize to Tavish."

Cara looked over to the desk for help. "Léo?"

Losing his temper, Hector rushed forward and slammed the book shut in front of Léo. "Tell her this is the same book that was here when you were working at Moy this summer."

Léo's brown eyes softened toward her. "It is. Cara, this is what I warned you of days ago, but—"

"You're on a fool's errand, wife. Apologize to Tavish, now." Hector's anger was growing by the second as she refused to yield.

She backed toward the door, her head shaking back and forth. She switched to Irish. "You're just like Duncan."

Her arrow found its mark. "How can you compare me to him?"

"Because this is something he'd do, he'd belittle me and call me stupid. He wouldn't listen to me. That's why I didn't tell you."

He looked at Aoife. "Fetch Margaret. Maybe she can talk sense into her."

Something in Cara's eyes and voice broke. "I'm right here. I'm not stupid. I know what I saw. I don't need anyone to talk sense into me. That isn't the same book."

Aoife's eyes bounced between them. "Mistress Margaret is at Laggan Sands for the day with her sister."

Cara retreated out into the hall and down the stairs.

Head swimming with anger, he followed her. "Where are you going?"

"Back to Laggan Sands. Home to Margaret and Ursula. Maybe back to Ireland. I don't belong here. Nobody wants me here. *You* don't want me here. You're reacting exactly as I feared you would the morning I discovered it. You think I don't trust you—but it's you who doesn't trust me."

His heart pounded with discomfort. "That isnae true. Stop. Listen!" He grabbed her arm, and she lifted it, rotating at the waist and pulling her elbow straight back from his grasp, just as he'd shown her.

Sudden understanding of what he'd done to her crashed over him. He'd proved her fears to be correct and broken her fragile trust.

Her eyes burned with fury and strength. "Get your hands off me. I'm no man's property anymore. Don't you dare follow me or send anyone after me. I'll take care of myself."

# CHAPTER 33

## LOCHBUIE OIGHREACHD - NOVEMBER 22, 1383

Rain pattered as Cara reached the sheepcote. Her fury had given her the strength she needed to walk to Laggan, but as she climbed the hill and knocked on the door, the cold she'd been fighting all week sapped her of energy. She lifted a shaking hand and rapped on the door again.

When it opened, she flung herself into Margaret's arms, the tears she'd staved off spilling over.

"Cara, whatever is the matter?"

"It's over, Margaret. It's over." Sobs choked her voice away as Margaret held her tight.

"What's over?"

Trembling, she couldn't bring herself to say the words.

Ursula touched a hand to her shoulder. "Och, lass. What happened?"

Pushing her wet face away from Margaret's shoulder she brought a shaking hand to her swimming head. "My marriage. We—I—"

Margaret wrapped an arm around her shoulders, guiding her beside the hearth to the chair. "Collect yourself, love. We can talk about it in a few minutes."

Fluffy wound herself up Ursula's apron and curled around her neck. "Let me fix you something to eat."

The thought of weasel-tainted food made her stomach roil, but she nodded glumly and wiped her cheeks with the back of her hands. After a few minutes, with a cup of cider beside her, she unburdened herself to Margaret.

"Hector didn't believe me about the accounts."

"He's home?"

She nodded. "Aye."

"For how long?"

Her heart clamped. "I didn't get a chance to ask him. He was in such a mood when he got home, we didn't discuss it before we argued."

Ursula set a pan on the fire. "What's this about accounts? You're so good with figures."

"I discovered a few weeks ago that there was something wrong with Tavish's accounting. But today Hector looked at the accounts and it all added up. Except, I don't think it was the same book. I think it's a false account book."

Ursula rolled her eyes. "Och. Tavish."

Margaret scrunched her nose. "What's the matter with Tavish?"

"I cannae stand the man. Neither can anyone else in the MacFadyen clan. I've never understood why he's been allowed to continue to run things up there at Moy. Except that he does know how auld Laird MacFadyen kept things. More reason in my opinion he shouldn't be kept as seneschal. He was starving us to death for his father five years ago."

Margaret looked confused. "His father?"

"Aye. He was tànaiste[1]. Laird MacFadyen is his father."

Margaret and Cara stared at Ursula, shocked. Margaret recovered first. "How was he allowed to stay in charge of things at Moy? How is that possible?"

"I suppose Laird MacLean wanted to try and keep peace. You notice he has a mix of MacFadyens and MacLeans in leadership roles. Tavish can be as slippery as a sand eel. Looks handsome, speaks a charming word or two, and he can convince anyone what he wants is what they want. Seems as though our Cara werenae fooled by it."

Cara lifted her cup to her lips, astounded by this new information. The sweet and tangy smell of cooked apples filled her senses and cramped her stomach, and saliva flooded her mouth. She put the cup down, heart pounding. "Oh saints."

Margaret touched her arm. "What's the matter, love?"

"I'm—I'm going to be—"

Ursula thrust a basin in her lap just as she doubled over and retched, emptying ginger extract and cider, but not much else. Her stomach cramped again, desperate to empty itself of what it thought was ailing it. She heaved, but nothing more came up. Sparkles flooded her vision and cold permeated her body. Putting the basin on the floor she got to her knees and lay down on the rushes and hard stone, struggling to stay alert against faintness.

Margaret came to her side, holding her shaking body steady. "Are you ill?"

"I have your cold." Cara put a hand to her forehead, her stomach still for the first time all day.

Ursula crouched beside her, touched her pelvis, then withdrew her hand. "Do you mind, love?"

Cara closed her eyes to still her dizziness. "No."

Ursula's hands came to her pelvis and pushed, then gently squeezed her breasts. Pain shot through her, and she jumped.

"Did that hurt?"

"Yes."

Margaret and Ursula looked at each other.

Ursula's eyes raked over her. "Any other signs from this cold? Sore throat? Cough? Achy in your joints?"

Cara shook her head. "No. Just a blocked nose."

"Are you dizzy? Feeling tired?"

"Aye. Very tired, and I've been terribly faint all week, I haven't been able to bring myself to eat much the last few days."

Ursula's mouth twitched and she stroked Fluffy's dark brown fur. "Because you're nauseated?"

"Yes."

"And when was your last menstrual flux?"

The question took her off guard, and she thought back. "Four days after the wedding." Margaret's hands covered her mouth. Ursula winked at her.

"Nothing since then?"

Foggy disbelief shot through her. Her menstrual flux had come as reliable as night and day for ten long years but hadn't come mid-month, yet with Hector gone she hadn't noticed. "No. It's—I'm...late. It should've come mid-month."

Margaret's eyes shone and she grasped her hand. "My dear."

Ursula touched a hand to her pelvis and beamed. "I think you're with child."

Cara touched her hand to her low belly. It was no bigger than it'd ever been, but it was firm.

God in heaven, was it true? After years of hoping and praying, only to be smashed upon the rocks of disappointment month after month, she could scarcely believe it.

Tears sparkled over Margaret's cheeks and Ursula embraced her. "You're going to be a granny."

Margaret gave a wet chuckle, then embraced Cara and helped her up. "You must take care of yourself, love. Let's get you off the floor, you can rest on the bed."

On shaking legs, she was guided to her old bed. Ursula removed a tart from the fire and swirled honey over it. "I know you dinnae have a mind to eat but take small bites of the fruit in the middle. A little bit of sweetness sometimes helps your stomach settle in this condition if you've no' eaten. You need to make sure you eat regular, even if you cannae tolerate the tho'. It keeps the retching at bay."

Cara took tiny bites of berry. As her stomach began to feel warm and full, disbelief took hold. "I cannot be pregnant. It isn't possible. I cannot get pregnant."

Ursula stroked Fluffy's patchy back and settled down on a stool. "I cannae explain it, but I know the signs. Sickness like this is a good sign your baby is strong."

Her baby? The word boggled her mind. "Baby."

Margaret hopped up and down. "Ooo lass. Baby. You're a mother."

"Mother?"

Margaret continued hopping, joy radiating out of her as she lifted her arms. "You're a mother. Oh...I'm a grandmother. Hector is a father."

*Hector.* Cara got to her feet. Only moments ago, she'd been sure her marriage was over. Sure they couldn't be right for one another. Sure that this disagreement couldn't be overcome. But now... all she wanted to do was see him. Her hand brushed over her womb where somewhere inside their child lived. His child. Part of the man she loved beyond her love for all others. "I must tell him."

Margaret pulled at her apron. "Let me see you back, lass."

Cara held up her hand as she exited. "No need. I'll see you tomorrow morning like planned. I want to tell him myself—have a private moment."

Dark purple clouds were the only indication the sun was about to set in the gloomy twilight. Disbelief, joy, and regret for her words to Hector weighed her legs down. Never had the two-mile walk seemed longer as she hurried along.

Navigating the thick fog, she slowed as the road curved around the outcropping of rock. It was getting thicker by the minute, so she followed the edge of the wood to help her find her way.

Joy warmed her confused heart. It was a miracle. God had heard her prayers, but not allowed her to conceive a child with Duncan. In his perfect faithfulness and plan, he'd made her wait until the perfect time. With a man who truly loved her and would never harm her or their baby. She stopped and lifted her face to the misty heavens. "Thank You, God."

It was the last thing she remembered before the world went black.

# CHAPTER 34

## LOCHBUIE OIGHREACHD - NOVEMBER 30, 1383

When Hector woke, it took his mind several minutes to understand where he was. Instead of a tent, he was inside. Instead of feeling cold, he was covered in a light sweat beside a dying fire. He was at Moy. Peace settled over his chest, and he leaned his head against the leather chair, his eyes shutting once more.

"Laird."

Margaret's voice penetrated through the haze of sleep and fatigue, and he lifted an eye. Events reconstructed themselves with swift awareness. Cara. The fight. What time was it? Margaret's voice spoke, but he couldn't comprehend what she was saying.

"What did you say?"

"I said congratulations. Aren't you thrilled?"

He rubbed his hands over his face and tried to wake up, looking around the great hall as servants scurried around with preparations for a meal. He'd fallen asleep waiting for Cara to return, his chair positioned toward the stairs to catch her as soon as she came in.

"Thrilled?"

"Aye. About the baby?"

The word clanked around the emptiness of his brain and fell out. "Baby?"

Margaret chuckled, her face wide with happiness. "Yes, Papa, your baby."

Pain pinched in his lower back, and he looked around, trying to get a sense of the time of day in the windowless hall. "What time is it?"

Margaret cocked her head to one side. "It's well past terce[1]."

All remnants of sleep dissolved as he got to his feet and climbed the stairs. He'd slept through the night and let the sun go down upon his anger. He needed to find her and apologize.

He swung open the door to their solar. "Cara?"

Bed coverings were undisturbed, and the room was empty. He repeated her name over and over as he searched the large room and the adjoining chapel.

Margaret stepped into their private solar and looked around, her voice full of concern. "Isnae she here?"

Hector walked back into the corridor and climbed the stairs to her work room, listening for the distinctive clamoring of her loom. The corridor was silent, and he wrenched the door open. "Cara, love?"

From the silent loom, threads of blue, red, and gold hung still. Panic began to rise in his chest, and he turned toward Margaret. "I tho' she was going to Laggan to see you. That's what she said when she left."

Margaret's face was consumed with fear. "She did. She was with us. But then we had the news—she didn't come home at all and speak with you?"

Heart thundering now, it took all his restraint not to yell. "No. I waited in the chair and fell asleep. I tho' she might've slipped in without saying hello to me since we were—are—quarreling."

Dismay spread over Margaret's face and she shook her head urgently. "No. She wouldnae have done that. Never."

"I think she might've. I hurt her badly."

Margaret gripped his arms, beginning to shake. "No. I'm telling you. She left us on her way to see you, to tell you—to tell you..."

Something about the horrified look in her eyes, the mother's fear that lived in them, frightened him worse than anything he'd ever witnessed in battle. "What?"

"About the baby. Ursula determined she was pregnant while she was with us yesterday. As soon as she recovered, she headed straight here to tell you. That was just before sunset."

Disbelief, joy, and trepidation filled him. "But she cannae..."

Margaret shook her head. "Ursula is certain. She's carrying your baby. We tho' it a miracle."

Nausea cramped his stomach as he pushed past her and ran down the stairs, stopping in their solar for his cuirass and sword. As he belted them in place, he began to whisper prayers.

Margaret appeared in the doorway. "She never made it here?"

"No."

He crashed down the stairs and out into the barmkin, screaming for Murdoch and Calum. They rushed forward.

"Where's Léo?"

They looked at each other and then Hector. "He left yesterday after Lady MacLean."

Hector screamed the command to assemble, and guards spilled out of the gatehouse and into the barmkin yard.

Margaret burst through the door of the keep and into the yard, tears streaking her cheeks.

"Margaret, go to the chapel and have Father Timothy ring the bell for assembly. I want every person of this clan searching for her." Margaret nodded and ran through the opened gate toward the church.

Hector turned to his guard. "My wife—" His voice faltered and he choked. "My wife didnae make it home from Laggan Sands last night. And I've only learned she is with child." His child. "She may be sick, or incapacitated, or worse. The Wolf was last seen off the coast of Rùm, but he is a stealthy attacker. Be on your guard."

# CHAPTER 35

## LOCHBUIE OIGHREACHD - DECEMBER 2, 1383

Three days. Cara had been missing for over three days. Desperation filled his chest as Hector dragged his tired body into St. Columba's chapel. In the darkened sanctuary, air spiced with incense, he walked on heavy feet toward the cross at the center of the chancel. Light glowed from dozens of candles, all lit in prayer for the safe return of his beloved.

Only two months prior they had knelt here and been blessed as husband and wife. He folded his long legs beneath him, bowed and touched his face to the floor. Words of prayer would not form on his lips. Grieving his broken promise to never let harm come to her again, he wept. "Dear God, where is she?"

Every inch of his territory had been searched. Every corner of the forest, lochs, and hills. Glenbyre, Carsaig, the Ross of Mull. He'd sailed around the coast looking for signs of intruders and found none. Messengers were sent to Duart, Iona, the Isles, and the search had expanded into the northern territories, but no signs of her were found.

The vision of Aileen's small, blond head disappearing into the waves haunted him. The look on his father's face as they returned without her. His father's fists pummeling him as he admitted he'd thrown the first punch. And here he was, twenty-seven years later, his actions leading to the disappearance of the woman he couldn't live without, and their child. Sobs racked his body.

A hand came to his shoulder. "Son."

Pádraig eased him off the floor, and Hector wrapped his arms around his small, round uncle in his fruitless search for comfort. "What've I done?"

Pádraig's arms tightened around him. "It was a fight. She chose to leave without protection."

"Aye, and I chose to let her go thinking she would be back. As dangerous as it is."

"Dinnae blame yourself. We will find her. We will."

Wiping his nose on his sleeve, Hector looked up at the shining cross, illuminated with her candlelight. He folded his hands once more. "Dear God, please send me a sign. Tell me which way she's gone so I may bring her home."

Pádraig prayed with him for several minutes, and when they'd begged God for everything they could think of, they sat in silence.

"Why did I force her into doing what I wanted her to do? She was right. I was like her first husband. I came home angry. I should've sent everyone away and talked it through. She tho' I would react badly, and instead of proving her wrong, I proved her right."

Pádraig sniffed. "Aye. You should've done that bit better and no' let your temper get the better of you. But who would have tho' Léo could do it?"

Léo hadn't been seen in two days. He hadn't returned to Duart or reappeared anywhere on Mull. Hector let out a frustrated growl. The image of Léo holding his wife's hand, fetching her medicine, imparting comfort with his eyes assailed him. "I didnae trust that worm and his reasons for being there. Lachlan said he came back to Duart for reasons to do with Cara, and I assumed it meant he still cared for her. He told Lachlan he was concerned for her safety."

Pádraig smoothed a hand over his white beard. "Aye. I believed he did. She reminds him of his wife, he told me so."

"Then where've they both gone?" His voice thundered off the walls and he winced. "You dinnae suppose she went with him of her own free will?"

Pádraig shook his head. "No' at all. She was beside herself without you. As she told you, it was my idea to send for Léo. Lad, she's the mother of your child, she would've never left you for him."

Hector wiped the wetness from his aching face, remembering his fight with Léo at the games. "He said he was disgusted with me, he said she would die alone, and it would be my fault."

Pádraig nodded. "I know."

Heavy silence grew between them, and he prayed again for her return and for the protection of the Almighty over their baby.

The door at the side of the church opened and Tavish rushed in. "Tracks have been found at Knockvologan. The guard are waiting for you there."

Hector sprang to his feet.

# Chapter 36

## Isle of Scarba - December 2, 1383

Shivering started again and Cara shifted her body toward the dying fire, wrists protesting the chain. With but a few feet of clearance, she could only extend her numb toes toward the pitiful flame.

The leader would be back soon. Through the sliver of sight at the bottom of her blindfold she could make out a man's legs as he came to check on her once a day. She'd tried to engage him in conversation, but he didn't speak a word. It was the leader who'd held her to the bottom of the boat as they'd sailed to Scarba, head throbbing and fading in and out of blackness. The leader who'd carried her up a shelf trail to a sea cave overgrown and forgotten high in cliff. The leader who'd chained her to a boulder, alone and isolated.

In between the leader's visits, a cycle of three different-sized men checked on her every few hours. Never speaking or responding to her requests for food, only staying long enough to put eyes on her and toss her a skin of water. From the crack of the blindfold, she could only see that one man was quite large, and the other two were not much bigger than Duncan.

Stomach roiling, she curved onto her side and tried to ease the nausea that beset her. Ursula said it was a sign that her baby was strong,

289

and she took comfort that her tiny link to Hector still grew within her. She hadn't eaten anything since leaving the sheepcote, and she prayed that God would somehow strengthen her child and provide nourishment for them both soon.

Footsteps grew at the mouth of the cave then pounded toward her. Her heartbeat increased and she tried to steady her breath. She was in control of her mind. As long as she stayed calm, she was in control. She tried to make out every sound, listening for evidence as to the identity of the leader.

The footsteps sounded different this time. Running.

Struggling to her knees she tried to face the source of threat as Hector taught her. The footsteps came to a halt and legs crashed into her side.

"Cara, thank God." She cowered away. "Cara?" The blindfold lifted and she found herself face to face with Léo.

Disbelief stole her breath away and she tried to make sense of seeing him in the cave after so many hours in solitude. The russet color of his trews matched the legs of the leader. She jumped backward, her hands yanking against the restraints, wondering why he'd taken her to this place.

"Please don't hurt me, Léo. Tell me what you want."

His eyebrows knit together, and he blinked. "I would never hurt you."

Her breath came in bursts. "Please don't leave me here. I only want to go home, please."

"What are you talking about? You think I put you here?" He grabbed the chain binding her and followed it toward the rock, then yanked against the bolts, muttering in French.

She stared at his muscled legs, the same height and build as the leader's, and she wondered if he was playing a trick, pretending in order to gain her trust. "Your legs, they're just like his legs."

His face screwed up. "What are you talking about?"

Her voice wobbled, feeling confused and wanting to trust that he was here to help her. "Hector told me if I was ever attacked or set upon to remember all the details I could about my attacker and surroundings."

He continued to try and yank the chain from the rock. "There's four of them. The three thugs have kept me down on the beach in the elements since we arrived—"

The loud rattling of the chain as she shivered against the cold interrupted his efforts to pull her free. He unfastened the leather at his shoulder and removed his plaid, wrapping it around her. His warmth flooded her shivering body, and she snuggled in the coarse, thick plaid, hating herself for allowing him to comfort her.

"I could see through the crack of the blindfold. I know it's you who's brought me here. Pádraig told me you came back to Mull because of me. You told Pádraig you were concerned for me, but you wanted to take me, didn't you?"

Léo recoiled. "No. I swear it. I was concerned about you because my—"

He stopped talking and he held up a hand. Footsteps sounded at the mouth of the cave, and she tried to make sense of what she was seeing. Barely illuminated in firelight, a figure inched along the cave wall, light bouncing off the silver of Léo's estoc. Her eyes went to Léo's empty baldric.

Léo positioned himself between her and the man—the leader.

"There's no use trying to hide. I see you there beside her."

In the weak firelight, Tavish stepped forward until the end of the long, pointing estoc nicked Léo. A trickle of blood traveled down his thick neck and onto his chest.

"How did you escape your restraints?"

The two lines above Léo's right eyebrow deepened. "Does it matter?"

Tavish pushed forward and widened the hole, a sick look of pleasure upon his face.

Léo gasped and moved backward. "All right, all right. I worked the ropes over the rocks at the edge of the beach until they unraveled." He held out his wrists which were red and raw.

Tavish flicked the end of the long estoc in an upward motion, creating a slice in the neck of Léo's tunic. "Get up."

Cara couldn't believe her eyes despite having her suspicions confirmed. "Tavish."

Tavish's hard green eyes snapped to hers, and he laughed, mimicking the fright in her voice. "Yes, Tavish. You should've stayed out of it. It doesnae matter though; we've plans for you. I said rise, *Frangach*."[1]

Léo got to his feet.

"Turn and walk forward." Léo cast a final look over his shoulder at her, his expression angry, then did as instructed and walked toward the mouth of the cave.

At the center of Tavish's web, fear gripped her heart as she thought of laying in the dark cave alone without Léo, waiting an unknown fate. "Wait. Please let him stay here. There's no need to take him back down to the beach. The three of us can stay together."

Tavish stopped at the mouth of the cave. Upward gusts of wind carried up the side of the rocky cliff and lifted a lock of Léo's sandy hair. "I'm no' taking him back to the beach."

"You're not?"

Without warning, the estoc lowered, and Tavish's foot launched in the center of Léo's back, sending him sprawling forward, out of the cave, and onto the rocks below.

# CHAPTER 37

## KNOCKVOLOGAN, MULL - DECEMBER 3, 1383

I n the pre-dawn light of the moon, Hector jumped into the icy
waters of the bay and pulled the small skiff onto the sandy beach
of the tidal island. Seeing no traces of his guard, he wondered if
he'd somehow confused the message Tavish gave him. Hand on sword,
he looked around. Surrounded on three sides by water, he advanced
inward searching the ground for signs of disturbance. Finding tracks, he
followed them as they made their way through dunes and moved toward
high rocky cliffs. He was readying to scale upward when something
heavy crashed down upon his head.

Stunned, he staggered and blocked an incoming blow. Three men
advanced on him, swords drawn, and he struggled through his confusion to unsheathe his own. A sword slashed through the air, and he
parried, then thrust upward catching a man in the chest, his vision
fading in and out. Driving forward, he ended the threat, the man falling
at his feet.

Stars gathered in his eyes as the other two men joined the fight. He
withdrew his sword from the first man and had just enough time to
parry, pushing the second man's blade away from his own. The third
man cut his sword straight up, and Hector caught the powerful thrust,
his sword skittering along the man's blade.

The second man's blade caught him by the flat. The force thrummed into his side knocking him off balance. He struggled to stay on his feet, his vision swimming with stars and fading in and out of darkness.

Head screaming with pain and haze, he gave a heavy blink as he briefly lost all sense of the ground, his feet faltering, his body swaying.

He must stay conscious. *Cara, please. God help me.*

A strength beyond Hector's own lifted his arms and swept the sword over his head, plunging it into the second man's chest. The sword stuck and would not be freed, falling away from him as the second man fell dead. Vision failing, Hector staggered and fell onto his back into the rocks behind him.

Dazed, side aching, he struggled to keep his vision focused as the third man clambered on top of him. Knees pinned his arms to the ground; two hands came around his throat and squeezed. He was a big man, almost as big as himself, and Hector couldn't shift his weight. Breath squeaked out of his crushed throat. He was about to die.

Hector's eyes rolled back and to the stars peeking through the gray clouds in the night sky. Final thoughts raced through his mind in short bursts as his throat constricted needing air. *God please, protect Cara. Help our child to grow strong. Save my wife.*

The hands around his throat went slack, and air rushed into his lungs. The man collapsed on top of him with a heavy thunk, dead as a stone. The weight of the heavy body was dragged off him.

"Are you alive?"

Hector turned onto his side and coughed. His head was throbbing, his vision spotty, but he was alive. "Aye. Barely."

The sound of waves lapping at the beach mingled with the smell of death, and he almost vomited, his senses overcome. He shoved himself into a seated position and touched the back of his head. His fingers came away bloody.

"You took a mighty blow to the head."

He looked up and squinted in the darkness toward the man who'd saved him, recognizing the French. "Léo?"

Léo plunged Hector's sword into the sand and sat beside him, chest heaving. "Oui. Just like old times."

"Where've you come from? Where've you been? Where's Cara?"

Léo pulled a skin of water from around his neck and drank deeply. He gulped for air and rested his arm across his leg. "I've come from the bìrlinn over there," he said pointing to the beach. "I've been on Scarba where I've been held prisoner the past three days. And that is where your wife was until about two hours ago."

Hope filled his chest. "Cara is alive?"

"Alive and well—all things considered."

Relief flooded him and tears pricked his eyes. "Who has her?"

"Tavish."

It made no sense.

"I just left Tavish."

Léo swigged from the skin of water. "That's who's been keeping us tied up the last few days." He gestured around them. "These three thugs have been doing his dirty work. He's been coming in the evenings to ensure we were still secured. Tavish was putting things in motion to take us to Lochindorb, Cara in exchange for your surrender, me in exchange for my treasury in Paris—pointless since I am the only one who can access it."

Léo took another deep drink from the skin of water. "They knocked me out as I waited for Cara outside Ursula's sheepcote. I followed her there hoping to bring her back to Moy so we could convince you to keep looking for the missing account book. From what I gather, they knocked her out on her walk back to Moy after she received the news that..."

Hector took the offered skin of water from him. "I know she's pregnant. Margaret told me."

Léo raised his eyebrows. "Congratulations, by the way. I overheard as I was waiting. Margaret was shouting it from the rafters. Don't remember much after that. Fitting that what knocked Cara and I out only stunned you momentarily."

Rubbing his hands over his face and through his hair Hector wanted to scream. "I'm scared to death."

Léo put his arm around him. "Remember what you told me before Chiset? Everyone is scared before a battle. The ones who aren't are lunatics. This is worse. If it was Théa or Gabriel, I would feel scared to death. God will protect her, Hec."

The feeling of his friend's arm around his shoulders, the lad who'd lived through a dozen battles by his side, imparted a comfort to his soul he'd not felt in days. Somehow, with Léo next to him, he began to feel confidence that the enemy he faced would be conquered.

Hector wiped emotion and stars from his eyes, his vision beginning to return to normal. "How'd you know to come here?"

Léo motioned to the three dead men. "They left earlier this afternoon and I heard them mention Knockvologan. Not one left behind to watch me. I figured you must be next to be nabbed or killed if all three of them went and left me unattended. They were keeping Cara high above me in a wall cave. I climbed up to try and free her, but she was chained to a rock, bolted in tight. Then Tavish found us."

"Why didn't you overpower him? You have three inches on him."

Léo rolled his eyes. "He has my estoc." He gestured to the dried blood on his neck. "Bold in using it, too."

Hector got to his feet but was unable to move forward without wobbling, his balance still affected. He sat back down. "How'd you get away?"

Léo ran hands through his hair and pulled an agitated face. "I didn't get away. Cur's son marched me to the wall of the cave, kicked me square in the back, right over the cliff. I guess my gold wasn't worth the trouble." He lifted his wet tunic and showed him a purpling bruise on his back. "I missed the rocks and landed *derrière*[1] first in a freezing cold, but thankfully deep, tidal pool. I saw him march Cara down to the beach. A bìrlinn picked them up."

Hector growled in frustration with himself for not seizing Tavish the moment Cara went missing. "Cara must have been a threat to him from the minute we wed. She was right, the lady of the clan always assumes responsibility for the household. Do you think he's working with your brothers?"

Léo helped him to his feet and put a solid arm around him to steady his wobbling steps.

"That's why I came back. When Elspeth and I arrived back at Skye, no one seemed upset that a marriage alliance that was supposed to restore the clan wealth had failed. Nor did anyone seem concerned that Elspeth was just passed over for a common Irishwoman of no noble blood or standing. Niall gets murderous if his porridge isn't made correctly, so that didn't make sense. Not even Elspeth continued to act upset after we left. Make no mistake, she hates Cara, but she didn't seem to mind losing you much—no offense. Considering how much wealth you were about to share with her, it was odd."

Hector nodded in agreement. It was no secret that the MacKinnon treasury on Staffa had been dwindling for years. The rumors were that they were near empty when negotiations began.

Léo helped him step over a low stone wall. "I thought perhaps they were about to abduct Cara and imprison her in an attempt to raise ransom from you in retaliation for your mistreatment of Elspeth. You know how Niall and Fingon love locking people away to raise funds when needed."

Hector remembered the Chieftain of Mishnish. "Mowbray MacKinnon has been trapped in their prison for years."

Léo scoffed. "Oui. I suppose I was only half-wrong about that. It was Tavish, not my brothers. But I can't shake the feeling they're involved somehow; the timing is too suspect. After the raids on the MacQuarries, I remembered Tavish knew the location of their granary since their manrent and tithes came through Lochbuie this season on Lachlan's request. Lachlan confirmed that was Tavish's idea. I wanted to talk to you about it, but I wasn't sure how to broach the subject after our last exchange at the games."

"I would have listened to you. It's...we've been through too much."

"Oui, but when I saw how you handled Brodie and Lachlan at Duart, you seemed to be a bit sensitive about Cara. And given that I care —had cared for her, I didn't think you'd trust me. I suppose I wasn't wrong about that either, given your anger with me a few days ago. I've been trying to get through to Lachlan for weeks. He's more hardheaded than you are. It's annoying."

Guilt flooded through him. Léo had never given him cause to doubt his motives, and he'd assumed the worst of his intentions toward Cara.

Léo cleared his throat twice. "I guess this means I won't be returning to the French court anytime soon."

Hector stopped. "What do you mean?"

"I'm your first volunteer to help you take down the Wolf. Not just to get your wife back. If anybody else volunteers, you'll need a second-in-command."

Assisting with the Wolf would require Léo to move back to the Hebrides, to leave his court position.

"Aye, I do. You'll need to be close by. Perhaps at Moy?"

Léo smiled. "Perhaps. As long as there are no dead pigeons."

Hector held onto his friend and took a cleansing breath, thanking God that the mistakes of the past six years had finally been overcome.

They leaned on each other and made their way toward the broken down bìrlinn at the end of the beach. Hector looked at it with doubt. "Where'd you get this thing?"

"It's the only boat the monks at the monastery on Scarba would let me borrow. I had a rough time sailing it by myself with no one at the oar. But I managed." Léo helped him into the rotting bow and shoved the boat forward into the water before jumping in the back. "Sheets or oars?"

"Sheets. And Léo?"

Léo tossed him the sheets. "Oui?"

Affection clogged his chest. Despite everything Hector had ever put him through, Léo was always there for him. "Thank you."

Léo shrugged it off. "It's what brothers do."

---

They arrived back at Moy as the sun came up. It took a few hours of searching before Léo discovered the false panel in the desk and a green ledger with a small wax stain, just as Cara had said. It looked identical except for the stain, and the additions of dozens of notes beside debts where Tavish kept track of his personal expenses.

Disbelief made his stomach plummet as he worked the figures in the large green ledger. "Cara was right, he's underreporting the rents in the household account."

Léo flipped the pages, his fingers wandering across three different sheets of vellum. "Read this."

"Father McElduff—15 gold. He's paying a priest?"

Léo pointed to the entry above. "Ring—25 silver."

They looked at each other in disbelief and spoke at the same time. "He married?"

Léo looked at the recorded date. "Around the time I returned to Duart. Father McElduff, I recognize that name. He works at Kyleakin chapel on Skye."

"The week after we married, Tavish went to Iona for pilgrimage for a few days. Do you think he married your sister?"

A rapid string of enraged French spurted from Léo. "What in heaven is she thinking?"

*Imagine what territory we could rule together... You could have all of Mull if you wanted it.* Elspeth's insistence that they were the same, her interest in his past. "She's thinking she wants to rule Mull for the MacKinnons and kick the MacLeans out. It would be the largest land holding in the Isles if undivided."

Hector eyed Tavish's slanting hand. "N.M.—850. Recorded October seventh. The day before our wedding. N.M., Niall MacKinnon?"

The entry appeared a few more times coinciding with times that the MacKays, the MacLeods, and MacQuarries had been attacked.

Léo's eyes narrowed. "Elspeth's bride price. Paid out in increments. He pays Niall? Niall uses his influence to inform the Wolf where to attack? Tavish forces your surrender for the chieftainship?"

Hector's stomach sank. "Aye. What do you suppose is in it for the Wolf, though?"

Léo eyed him. "An island to launch from, central to the rest of the Hebrides? A military leader who could be devastating to the king if he could force your loyalty to him using Cara?"

Calum and Murdoch burst into the room. "The tithe barn is empty, Laird, just as you tho'. No sign of Tavish anywhere."

A situation that was preventable in every way. Sickened and full of self-contempt, Hector took two steps backward before putting his fist through the shutters. Filled with rage, he ripped the tapestry off the wall, flipped the desk over, and screamed in anguish.

"Brother." Lachlan appeared in the doorway. "I got your missive."

"This is all my fault. Just like Aileen."

Lachlan crossed the room and pulled him into a tight embrace. "This isnae your fault. Aileen wasnae your fault. None of this is. I'm here with your volunteers. It's time to fight."

Iain MacLeod, Angus MacKay, and David MacKenzie entered Tavish's solar, each giving Hector a pat on the shoulder, their faces grim.

Iain's laddish face bore a look of gallantry. "We haird yer words at the Duart meetin' and we've come to volunteer to help ye fight. There's oonly three of us, a fraction of what ye requested, but when we haird about Cara goin' missing, we had to help ye."

Hector opened his mouth and Iain held up his hands. "Ah ken. I'm only twenty—but I'm chief of the MacLeods, and I've brought my fastest bìrlinn to help ye get wherever ye need to go as quick as ye can. And I'm no' so terrible with a spear if needed."

David MacKenzie came forward and clasped his hand. "I may no' be an Islander, but Clan Chattan[2] has been terrorized by the Wolf for far too long. I want to help you take him down. I know the Monadh Liath[3] mountains better than any man alive. I can get you to Lochindorb."

Lochindorb, the Wolf's Lair. A massive keep set in the middle of a freshwater loch, once the fortress of the powerful Comyns. Imagining wee Cara at the mercy of yet another brutal man, and no way to reach her, he almost howled in pain.

Hector shook his head. "That place is a former prison and one of the most impenetrable strongholds in Scotland. Our guards combined couldnae force a surrender."

Angus picked up the battle-scarred sword from the floor and hefted its weight in his hand. "But you dinnae need the Wolf to surrender. No' yet. You just need to get inside. We can get you there and help you get home without detection. I ken what signs to look for to follow your wife, and how they'll track you when you escape with her. For an army it would be impossible...but for the Lord of armies, who bends the bow and breaks the spear, who scorches shields with fire, he will cause kingdoms to bow at his feet."

Calum nodded. "Aye. We only need to be swift and fearless. And there's four volunteers, no' three."

Murdoch hefted his bow. "Five. Let's get her."

300

Léo put a hand on Hector's shoulder. "Six. I'm going in there with you. Together our odds are better. If one of us goes down, the other can get her to safety."

Sunlight penetrated through the hole his fist made in the shutters and bounced off the silvery blade.

Angus held the sword out to Hector. "Will you lead us?"

# CHAPTER 38

## LOCHINDORB CASTLE - DECEMBER 16, 1383

Water bubbled in Cara's ears as she emerged from the depths of the steaming bath. She wiped her face against her hands, thankful that, for the first time in two-and-a-half weeks, she'd been given the opportunity to bathe. Banishing the purpose of making herself clean from her thoughts, she stared into the depths of the roaring fire.

"He's requested you wear this tonight." Euphemia held up a scarlet gown, low cut in the neckline, and fitted through the waist. Cara gripped the side of the tub and balanced her chin on her fingers. "I don't know if that will fit."

Euphemia gave her a quizzical look. "Dinnae fash. You're so thin."

Aye. She was thinner in places from lack of regular meals in the last few weeks, but thicker in her breasts and low belly. Euphemia held the small gown up to her fuller figure and sighed. "I'd love to wear it. No' for him though."

Cara recognized the haunted look in Euphemia's eyes and knew how she must be suffering. Yet Euphemia seemed to cling to joy even in the midst of what must be tremendous pain.

The cloying smell of rosewater seized her from nowhere, filling her mouth with saliva. She got to her feet and trudged across the fine hides, sloshing water everywhere. Naked, she bent over a chamber pot and vomited the rich meat she had eaten a few hours earlier when they arrived at Lochindorb. Shivering from her wet skin and sudden faintness she curled into a ball beside the pot and tried to distract her stomach with thoughts of Hector as she had the past few weeks.

One by one she recalled each of his physical traits. His impossibly tall frame. The way his long, dark spirals of hair fell over his chest and down his back like Samson. The clear burns of his eyes that froze over with glacial blue. The soothing rumble of his voice. The protection their child would feel in his arms. Distracted, her stomach began to calm.

A blanket covered her, and Euphemia rubbed her back. "Are you with child?"

Cara nodded, swallowing back excess saliva. A wish for her stomach to settle mixed with comfort that her tiny baby was still alive and strong, despite two-and-a-half weeks of arduous journey over the Monadh Liath. Elspeth and Tavish had tied her in the back of a pony cart, chained to an aging and overweight cateran that smelled of body odor and rotting vegetables. She'd retched over and over as they crossed the snowy peaks of the mountains, choked by the stink of a man who hadn't bathed since Robert the Bruce was alive.

Their destination was far in the forbidden hills, the Wolf's favorite keep, Lochindorb. The castle stood in stark isolation in the middle of a stinking loch, the bleak moors surrounding it warning off any visitors— and any rescuers. She'd yet to meet the Wolf of Badenoch, but she'd been locked in a high-tower room with his loathed, but good-natured, wife Euphemia of Ross.

She pulled the blanket tight around her as Euphemia knelt and combed the tangles out of her hair, trying to hang on to her stomach.

"Is your husband really Hector MacLean?"

"Yes."

Euphemia shivered with a frisson of excitement. "I saw him seven years ago when my father visited Calais. Legendary warrior in France, he is. Big and braw, too."

Annoyance pulled at her as the comb snagged on a knot. "Yes."

"I danced with him. He was an awkward partner, but a merry man."

Realizing she may be talking with one of her husband's old conquests, Cara sat up and tried to regain some of her dignity.

Euphemia must have sensed her discomfort. "Dinnae fash. Hector wasn't much interested in any lasses that night. He was more interested in the wine."

Becoming increasingly uncomfortable, she stilled Euphemia's hands. "Thank you, I can finish."

After combing out her hair, Euphemia helped Cara into the scarlet gown. As she thought, it was too tight in the bust and low belly.

Euphemia rested her cheek in her palm. "I know."

Sorting through Cara's dirty clothes, Euphemia located her woven crios and looped it around her waist. The colors of red, green, and yellow picked up against the vibrant scarlet gown and cloaked where the fabric tightened around her distending lower belly.

As Euphemia gathered up her discarded clothes, the small psalter fell to the floor from its pouch. She picked it up and flipped the cover open. "Oh, how lovely, a psalter."

Cara stopped, her heart beating. "Can you read what it says?"

"I'm a little rusty on my Latin, but aye." She put a hand to her heart and read the Latin aloud then laughed. "Those rumors about the two of you are true. He did throw off Elspeth MacKinnon because he fell in love with you. How very humorous. Elspeth always was full of herself."

Cara stepped closer and licked her lips, not caring if she looked ignorant in front of Euphemia. "Can you read it again in Gaelic?"

"'Beloved—Put me as a seal upon thy heart, as a seal upon thy arm, for love is strong as death, jealousy as hard as hell, the lamps thereof are fire and flames. Yours faithfully, Hector.'"

*Love.* He'd loved her in mid-August when they'd gone to Iona. Before she realized that she loved him. When he'd been courting Elspeth. When Léo had been courting her. Why had he secreted his love for her in a book that she couldn't read?

"It's from Canticum Canticorum." Then noticing the blank look Cara was sure was on her face, Euphemia added, "Song of Songs. The poems of Solomon for his wives." Euphemia flipped through the pages of the psalter. "Have you noticed the psalms he's chosen for this volume? He must have commissioned it."

"I'm unable to read. Is it Latin as well?"

Euphemia shook her head and grinned. "No, it's in Irish."

Touched that he'd thought to commission a book of scripture in her native tongue, her heart longed to understand the letters on the pages. "Can you read it to me?"

Euphemia held out the book and placed her finger above each word of the psalm, showing her the words. "'As the deer covets flowing streams of water, so my soul covets you, O God.'" Euphemia ran her finger over the image. The antlered stag cast its protective shadow over the doe as it drank from the streams of life.

Euphemia turned to the next psalm. "'My heart is steadfast, O God. My heart is steadfast. I will sing and play your praises.'" A red-haired angel sang in the heavens and a man from the earth looked at her.

She turned the page again. "'I love you, Lord, You are my strength. You are my rock, my fortress, and my savior.'" A warrior scaled the walls of a castle, toward the red-haired angel waiting upon a high tower. Euphemia smiled and flipped through the remaining pages. "They're all psalms about love and devotion."

The Lord was her rock and fortress. In the years she'd been crushed by Duncan, the Lord had given her Margaret's love to sustain her. When Duncan had been ready to discard her, the Lord had delivered her from his hand. When she'd been nearly killed at the barley field, the Lord had sent Hector to protect her. Now, Euphemia was able to translate the psalter when she needed to hear from him most. The Lord would not abandon her, no matter what lay ahead.

Cara steadied herself in the Lord's presence. "My husband knows the scriptures well."

Euphemia bit her lip, her eyes puzzling. "Aye, I can see that. But also, I think he is expressing his love and devotion to you as a gift from God." She wrinkled two pages between her fingers. "These two pages are stuck together. Look at this, the curly-haired warrior holding his bow above his head and shouting with joy in front of the red-haired angel. You're the angel, the reason he's rejoicing."

Cara shook her head thinking Euphemia was reading too much into the psalter. "I don't think so, 'tis just a picture."

Euphemia pointed to the words snaking around the page in

Hector's sloping hand. "The pages were stuck on the ink." Her finger traced the single line that looped around the margin. "It's in Irish. No' the holy language of the church this time. *'Beloved, let us love each other, because love is from God. The one who loves is born of God and he knows God.'"*

Euphemia folded the small volume shut and handed it back to her. "The entire book is filled with passages expressing the godly love he has for you."

Cara tucked her hand beneath the crios, touching the tiny part of him she carried with her. She was a fool to compare him to Duncan. Hector was not a perfect man, but he was a repentant man. They would find their way through, with the Lord, and with their love. If only she could get away. Grief filled her chest and she wished she could feel his embrace. Where was he now?

Euphemia clasped her hand. "He will come for you."

---

The banqueting hall at Lochindorb resembled a cathedral more than a place for meals. Its white walls arched two stories above and colorful banners hung from the ceiling. In the middle of the room a long table was laden with meats, cheeses, and fruits. It should've been filled with clan leaders, but was empty except for a tall, blond man at the head of the table. Tavish and Elspeth sat to his right, their hands joined together.

The guard marched Cara and Euphemia forward, poleaxes and swords in hand. Euphemia took the seat beside her husband and motioned for Cara to sit beside her.

"Ah aye. Lady MacLean." The Wolf's voice sounded more English than Scottish, and his countenance was unremarkable, but he was well formed of body, like a warrior. He made a close examination of Cara and she squirmed.

Fixing his gimlet eyes on her bust stuffed into the too-small gown, he smiled. "Yes indeed," the man said with great approval. "I can see now why Hector cast off Elspeth for you."

Sickened, she fixed her eyes to the floor. She knew his kind. Duncan was his kind. Summoning the submissive mouse she used to be, she curtsied to him. "May I sit, Your Grace?"

He made a pleased sound. "Why, of course."

Stepping around the chair, she sat, her right hand on the firm little bubble low in her belly. With her left she palmed the pouch hanging from her crios that carried the psalter. *Lord, please help me to get through this. Send Hector.*

Elspeth sneered at her, and rammed her eating knife into a thick piece of beef. "What a pathetic act."

Tavish took her hand. "No' everyone is as spirited as you."

Cara remained silent and took the plate laden with food that Euphemia offered. *Keep your mind calm.*

Lifting her eyes with discretion she examined the entrances and exits. There were only two, and guards stood at both. Her eyes returned to her plate, and she scooped berry preserves with her knife. While not as good as Ursula's, the sweet berry flavor agreed with her stomach, and she felt herself relax. *Nourish your baby. Don't think about what's next.*

The Wolf eyed her. "I suppose you know who I am, Lady MacLean?"

Dabbing her mouth with a cloth, she considered her words with caution and swallowed. "You're Alexander Stewart, Prince of Scotland. Son of the King. Earl of Buchan. Lord of Badenoch." Careful to use his whole title, she lifted her lashes and kept her face neutral.

He smiled, pleased with her. "Did your husband tell you about me? I enjoy how that sounds coming off your tongue."

She bit into a piece of beef, chewing slowly to settle her stomach and to give herself time to think of an appropriate answer. "Only that you've come into some territory on Skye thanks to your marriage to Euphemia, and about when the wedding was. Things that would interest a woman."

Elspeth barked with laughter. "She lies. Hector told her all about your exploits in the north."

Cara kept silent and took another bite of beef, keeping her mind on eating. Duncan never liked her to give an unsolicited opinion, and she guessed the Wolf wouldn't like Elspeth's opinion either.

As expected, he took a sharp tone with her. "Tell me Elspeth, are you ever silent? A man cannot hear himself think with you jabbering away."

Tavish's jaw tightened.

Foolish woman. Mentally, Cara moved a pawn across the board, ready to play the game she'd played every night for ten years with Duncan.

The Wolf broke his bread and spread butter across it. "How long have you been married?"

"Two months, Your Grace."

"Barely any time at all."

Cara advanced her bishop. "Long enough to know how to take care of my husband."

His face became intrigued, and he turned to Euphemia. "You would do well to study how well she knows her place."

The Wolf sipped his wine and winked at Cara over his cup. Careful not to show her distaste, she smiled with her eyes and moved her first knight forward. One way or another, he would reveal his plan to her.

"Did your husband mention that I tried to recruit him six years ago to help me in my conquests of Moray and Aberdeen, but he refused?"

Knight forward. "No, he didn't." It was true enough. Mhairi had been the one to reveal those details.

"It seems he had objections to the way I treated the church lands and my tenants. Why do you think he'd feel that way?"

Advance bishop. "I'm not sure, Your Grace. I've been treated most well, and thank you most sincerely for your provision since I've been here."

Elspeth made a sound across the table, but Cara didn't look up. The crucial moment had come.

"Hector has indeed found himself a prize."

*Castle.* "Thank you, Your Grace. Perhaps you could visit us at Moy. I'm certain I could persuade my husband to reconsider your offer."

His handsome features contorted into a sick grin. "I'm afraid that isn't possible."

Biting into her buttered bread she tried to look empty-headed. He was about to reveal the plan.

"Your husband has offered himself for you in negotiation. He'll be here in two weeks' time to surrender."

Feeling the blood drain from her face, she curled her fingers around her belly and did her best to appear unbothered. "Negotiation?"

Tavish smirked. "The MacFadyen chieftainship will be restored."

*Keep your mind calm.* "Your father is returning to Lochbuie?"

Elspeth continued to stab her eating knife into the beef. "No, twit. Tavish killed him over four years ago when he surrendered his birthright to that worthless drunkard. The chieftainship rightfully belongs to Tavish, and to me. Along with my tocher, including all the lands from Glengorm to Killiechronan."

*Tocher.* It wasn't just Elspeth then, it was the MacKinnons too. "That doesn't mean much to an Èireannach."

Elspeth raised an eyebrow and sipped her wine. "It means we'll be in possession of all the lands on Mull except for Duart. Now that Hector has trained the MacFadyen guard, it shouldn't be hard to oust Lachlan. If nothing else, we can pick off his wild children one by one until he surrenders."

Food turned to ash in Cara's mouth, but she managed to hold on to her composure. "If Hector surrenders, then I may leave with him?"

The Wolf chuckled, then laughed, then became hysterical. Beneath the table, Euphemia took her hand.

"You're an innocent. Hector will be given two choices. Join with our forces and lead them against John MacDonald—or death. Either way, you'll not be returning to Mull. Or Ireland."

His eyes raked over her body. "You'll be taken to my estate at Glen Lyon if you've done enough to please me. If not, death is always an option." For the first time all evening she was in danger of vomiting. "Tonight, I think I shall see for myself how pleasing you can be."

# CHAPTER 39

## LOCHINDORB CASTLE - DECEMBER 16, 1383

Crouching low in long-dead grass on the shores of Lochindorb, Hector stalked his prey. Pebbles from the shore dug into his bare feet as he waited for the signal, his body covered in black-tinted seal grease. A fleeting, misty cloud of breath curled from his nose as he lay in wait—a beithir ready to slip into the sluggish waters of the loch and devour the Wolf.

The low hooting of a short-eared owl began to his left, then echoed closer, and closer still. Calum had spotted the guard leave his post.

Silent and steady, Hector slipped into the loch, the bite of the cold waters tempting him to cry out. Keeping his mouth shut tightly, sucking frigid air through his nose, he stifled his reflex to gasp, wading forward until only his toes touched rock.

Holding the leather strap of the tar-coated basket with his teeth, he pushed forward off the slimy bottom and scooped his hands away from his chest, catching water and propelling forward with speed, careful not to splash or make a sound.

As he approached the middle of the loch the wind picked up and the water became choppy, making swimming more difficult, but disguising his wake. From the south tower of Lochindorb, a guard emerged, rounding the parapet. Hector adjusted the strap between his teeth so that he had a few feet of clearance, then dove beneath the black waves.

Shock hit him afresh as his head went into the freezing depths, the peaty taste of loch water flooding his mouth. Pain radiated in burning waves from his arms and legs. He must train his mind. Focusing only on swimming and not the cold, he began to pray.

After a short swim he collided gently with the rocky edge of the small island, then surfaced and looked up. A guard would need to look over the wall and risk a fall to spot him. Thanking God, he pulled himself out of the water one part at a time to avoid noise. Head, shoulders. Right arm, left arm. He pulled his lower body out without making a splash.

Placing the basket on the narrow shoreline he worked with speed to restore heat to his shivering body, wiping the grease from his hands with the small bit of toweling, squeezing water from his plaits, then donning his chausses, tunic, cuirass, belt, and shoes. He secured his sword upon his back, axes to his belt, and a dagger in his teeth.

He crouched over the side of the rocks and sank the basket into the water. The report of the bubbles as it was sucked under was louder than he had anticipated, and he slipped into the shadows. He heard no movement above.

Cold, tingly, but relieved to have made it this far, he took a steadying breath and finished his prayer. Survival of this night would require Father, Son, and Holy Ghost.

The curtain wall rose steep in front of him. Blowing heat into his numb fingers, he tried to restore sensation. Once feeling had returned to his toes, he removed his shoes again and secured them to his belt. Fingertips sliding over the wall he found that the two-hundred-year-old keep was solid, but eroded enough to provide holds in the cracks between the stone.

Squaring his hips, he found a toehold with his left foot and pushed himself up. Finding no more than a pinch of room in the stone at the lowest level, he braced his fingertips and reached, thanking God as he navigated upward that his body was as long as it was. Though his height had made him a target in battle, here on the wall he advanced to the midsection of the keep with speed.

His eyes traveled to a window set high in the wall to his right. If he could make his way over to it, he may find a way into the castle without having to go over the curtain wall blind. Using counter pressure to his advantage, he pushed into a foothold and navigated to the side. Arms burning, he settled into a fingerhold and swung to the window.

Blessedly, the castle did not have glass windows as Duart did, and he pushed on the wooden shutters. They held fast. He listened for sounds of breathing, talking, or movement and was met with silence. Sweat pricked at his palms as he climbed up and over the window, bracing his body over the opening, and tested the shutter again with his foot. It gave a little but remained secure.

Bracing his arms, he lowered his lower body with control and repositioned, resting his feet on the wide sill. If he could pop the shutters open, he could drop into the room. He kicked again with more force and the clasp gave, shutters clattering open. Wasting no further time, he swung into the `room.

Something hard came down on his shoulder and he braced into a fighting stance, removing the dagger from his teeth, whirling toward the unseen assailant. Hector's arms came around the man and clutched his head. A high-pitched yelp escaped, and he brought his hand around a small mouth.

"Shh..." he whispered. "Dinnae scream and I'll no' hurt you." As his eyes focused in the firelight, he realized that he held a plump woman in his hands. Her breath came out in quick gasps above his palm, and her heart hammered beneath his left arm, pinning her to his body. A broken chamber pot was still suspended in midair from her outstretched hand.

He whispered into her ear. "I'm looking for my wife. If you tell me where she is, I'll be on my way and no' frighten you anymore."

To his surprise her body relaxed in his arms and her heart rate slowed. A knock sounded on the door. "Countess Ross, we heard a sound. Is everything all right in there?" She tapped his arm.

"Dinnae scream," he repeated, removing his hand.

"Y-yes. Everything is fine. I tripped in the darkness and kicked the chamber pot. I'm well."

Footsteps wandered away from the door and he relaxed, letting her go. "You're Euphemia of Ross."

She took a shuddering breath and put her hand to her heart. "Aye. We've met before but I dinnae believe you remember me."

He could recall a banquet in Calais, and Euphemia at the edges of the crowd, back against the wall, face hopeful that some lad would ask her to dance. As the night wore on, she'd grown more and more deflated, and so he'd asked her for the honor of a rondet.[1]

"Aye. Calais. You're a wonderful dancer." It was not a lie. She'd been a better dancer than even his wee wife, and a good conversationalist. Intelligent, kind, and fluent in six languages. She was the prize of the entire gathering but discounted for surface-deep reasons.

Euphemia's face lit up. "Yes. We danced the night away."

Hector smiled and said a silent prayer of thanks. Of all the rooms he might have climbed into, he'd been led to Rahab. "Please. My wife. Where is she?"

The good humor in Euphemia's face trickled away. "They've just taken her to my husband's chamber no' five minutes ago."

Staggered, he gripped the back of a chair, strength sapping from his muscles. He'd missed her. Euphemia wrung her hands and shifted from foot to foot. "They'll bring her back here when he's—"

Before she could finish the sentence, he was at the door, trying the latch.

"He keeps me under lock and key, you won't be able to get to her."

Frustration caused his temper to rise, anguish filling his chest. "I cannae let him do that to her." He yanked at the door and pulled with all his might.

Euphemia pleaded with him. "She'll be back, Laird. If you wait for her to return, I'll hide you and you can escape together." Her face stilled. "Unless...the chamber he uses is two floors higher than mine, at the corner of the tower." She hurried to the window and stuck her head out, then pulled herself back inside. "If you can navigate to it from the outside, you'll be able to enter. There are no shutters on his chamber. It's on the uppermost floor, only accessible by the parapet. Or the window."

A cold rush of December air stung his damp face as he looked down the wall and made out a window some distance away. He pulled himself out, bracing his legs on the sill. Euphemia looked up at him, watching him as he hung off the wall.

"God bless you, Laird."

He looked into her round face, sorrow pinching his chest that the charming girl from Calais had inherited such a fate. Squinting in the darkness, she waved her hand and pointed below.

On the shore, Léo donned his tunic. Reassurance filled Hector's chest as he climbed along the wall toward the western tower. The window grew closer, and he swung higher, ready to take down his prey.

# Chapter 40

The click of the lock sealing her inside the room made Cara jump. Shaking with fright, she felt her way through the darkness until her hands found a candle on the table in front of her. Lifting it she made her way to the faint orange glow of the embers in the hearth and stuck the candle inside until it caught, wax dripping down its length and scorching her hand.

Trembling, she seated it back into the flat pewter holder. The minuscule beam of light had the same effect on her as a night light from her father. The unknown darkness was now known, and a bit less frightening. She looked around the freezing room that was barren except for a heavy table and the largest bed she'd ever seen.

Calling Hector's words to mind, she squeezed her eyes shut ...*you're always in control of your mind...it's where you must live...no man can take it from you.*

The barrenness of the room was unnerving. There was not an object she could use to fight back against him, no curtains to hide behind. Perhaps that was the point.

The handle of the door moved, and keys jangled. There was nothing to be done, no plan that could be formed, no escape. She must live within her mind until it was over and get herself, and her baby, out safely. *God, give me strength to endure.*

The door opened and the Wolf removed his keys. Eyes eager with desire, he closed the door and tossed the keys upon the table. A pinprick of confidence penetrated her heart. If he fell asleep or was incapacitated, she could use those keys.

"Would you like to play a game?"

The single candle provided little light as he circled the darkness of the room, watching her from the shadows. Her heart picked up speed as he appeared beside her, his blond mustache curling over his bared teeth, then he disappeared back in the shadows. She turned, trying to determine where he was, knowing she was being hunted, and trying not to be afraid. Like Duncan, he thrived on fear and was empowered by it. *Live within your mind. Don't freeze.*

Out of the darkness her head ripped backwards. Instinct kicked in and she gripped his hand, centered her body, and widened her legs, then shoved herself backward, jamming her elbows into his body. He roared in pain and tightened his grip, nearly pulling her to the floor. She widened her legs again, and spun, trapping his fingers and crushing them with all her might. He howled and let go, and she broke away, aiming to get to the table and the keys on top. She almost made it when he caught the long skirt of the gown and pulled her to the floor.

Desperation took hold. His muscled leg pinned the skirt to the floor while he took position over her. With her feet, she held onto his hips, locking him in place. A torrent of blows started on each side of her body, and connected with her face, and she curled forward to protect her baby. Her mind paralyzed—the memories of Duncan, the pain, the fear—it was happening again, she couldn't stop it. Gaining ground, he yanked her skirt up.

A feral scream escaped her lips as his cold hand felt its way up her leg and she snapped back into an attack. No one was going to do this to her or her child. No one. Never again. *God, make me a warrior.*

Unable to muscle him off, she locked her legs around him, then used her shaking thighs to propel herself upward just as she'd practiced with Hector, over and over again. Her heel found his hip again and she wedged herself against him, pushing him away with all her might to save herself and her child. She slid out from under his body.

Scrambling forward, he clenched her leg, and the brand of possession seared onto her calf. Battle rage scorched her senses, and she screamed, this time with the mighty protective fury of motherhood as she pulled her right leg back, kicking him over and over, as hard as she could directly between the eyes.

He slumped forward, limp.

Muscles buzzing, she rolled him off her legs just as a huge, black-cloaked figure crashed through the opened window. She scrambled away toward the corner of the room.

"Cara?" The deep, resonant voice that had frightened her the first night they met now filled her with comfort, alleviating the deep fear in her heart.

"I'm here."

Getting to her feet, she stumbled and fell. He was at her side in an instant, lifting her into his arms. His massive arms tightened around her juddering body and held her as a flood of tears spilled from her.

Hector pulled her face into his hands and looked into her eyes, speaking in a rush. "I'm sorry. You were right, love. We found Tavish's book. You were right." He kissed her lips and her cheeks leaving a sticky trail. "My bonny, bright lass."

A thick smell of roasting fat clung to him, and he was gluey in dark grease. Yet, it didn't matter. She kissed his viscous cheeks and spoke the words she'd longed to for weeks. "I'm sorry, I'm sorry. You're nothing like Duncan. Nothing. I love you, *mo mhuirnín*[1]. I love you so much."

Placing her on her feet he slid down her body, his arm curving around her bottom as he cradled her womb beside his cheek, then kissed it. "Hello, wee bairn. This is your Da. You're safe. You're both safe."

She laughed through her tears and mimicked the comforting sound of his brogue. "Ya ken?"

He got to his feet and took her face in his palms. "Aye. My wondrous lass, I ken."

Another figure pulled itself into the room and collided with the floor. Hector got up and helped him to his feet. "She's safe."

Joy filled her. "Léo? You're alive."

317

Léo pulled her into a tight embrace. "I heard the screams. I was terrified."

Hector's eyes went to the floor, noticing the collapsed figure of the Wolf sprawled in front of the dying fire. "Is he dead?"

She clung to his arm, not wanting to be parted from him. "Unconscious, I think. He had me on the floor. I kicked him between the eyes again and again until he went down."

Hector's expression was furious, and he growled, pulling her close. "Thank God. You did it, love. I knew you could."

She pulled away and picked up the heavy set of keys from the table. "We need to get out of here. Is there a boat?"

Hector and Léo looked at each other with concern and then out the window they had just entered. "We'll have to swim it."

Cara looked at the window, her mind boggling as she realized they must have climbed the wall to reach her. "How will we get down?"

Hector looked at the size of the window. "I won't be able to get through it with her on my back, nor she on yours."

She placed the keys in his hands. "There is a water gate on the eastern side of the castle, and there are boats there. You can access the stairs from the parapet, they go straight down to the gate. It's how we arrived, and how they took me up here."

Hector and Léo donned their shoes swiftly and adjusted their weapons. Léo pulled her behind him, and they moved toward the door. At the last moment Hector hovered over the Wolf and drew his sword.

Léo held up a hand. "Don't."

Hector's teeth were gritted. "He tried to defile my wife."

"I know. And he deserves death. But he's the king's son. If you kill him like this, you'll invite death on everyone in the Hebrides. Let's get out of here. Vengeance belongs to the Lord."

Hector clenched the pommel of his sword in both hands, raising it above his head. Cara grabbed Léo's arm in fear. Plunging it down in a swift motion, the blade nearly connected with the Wolf's chest but stopped only fractions of an inch from its mark.

A growl strangled in Hector's throat, and he passed a hand over his face, sheathing his sword. "Let's go."

Opening the door, she pointed toward the end of the corridor and whispered two words. "Parapet. Stairs."

Hector nodded and the three of them hurried down the passageway. Cara placed her hand on his shoulder as he unlocked the door to the parapet. "Guards."

He nodded and eased the door open. No one lingered in the corner lookout. Hector pointed and they raced forward. They'd almost reached the southern tower when a warning bell pealed through the night.

Panic seized her senses as the door behind them banged open. "His Grace has been attacked!"

Guards flooded around the parapet from the eastern corner and traveled south.

Léo turned and pushed her back toward the western tower. "Back the way we came."

Sprinting in a swift retreat, they approached the western tower and now found two guards rushing forward with swords drawn. Hector drew his axes stalking toward them and Léo pulled her out of the way.

In the bright moonlight, Cara watched with reverent fright as the berserker was fully released in unrestrained ferocity. Eyes glowing, senses honed, Hector deflected the first man's swing with one axe and swung hard with the other, clipping him across the bicep. The man howled in pain and cut upward with his sword.

The second guard surged toward Hector and Léo gave a war cry, charging toward him planting his boot in his chest and hurtling him backward, the man's sword flying across the stone walk. Léo stormed forward again, locking his arms around the man, and pulling him up the side of the parapet wall and dropping him over the side.

Hector swung again and again, and the first guard jumped back, the blade missing his other bicep by inches. The guard sliced his sword through the air. Wielding deadly strength with one axe, and other-worldly precision with the other, Hector maneuvered the sword away with two swift strikes. Using the momentum, he spun and brought the axe down with lethal force, penetrating through the man's bascinet.

Horrified, she could only stagger along as Léo lifted her over the body and pulled her around the gate behind Hector's charge, toward the northern tower. Breath heaving, stars sparked her vision and she stumbled. Léo lifted her to his side as if she weighed nothing and continued to run. Stealing a glance behind them, dozens of guards advanced but were no match for Hector and Léo's long strides.

As they began to round the north tower toward the east and the stairs beyond, a door beside her swung open. Before she had time to comprehend what was happening an arm came around her, squeezing the breath from her throat and lifting her off her feet.

Tavish squeezed tighter. "Drop your weapons, MacLean, or she dies."

Without hesitating, Cara tucked her chin and flailed her fist backward into his groin. He grunted and crumpled forward, and Hector advanced, plucking her out of his grasp and throwing her into Léo.

Tavish staggered to his feet, raising his sword just in time to avoid Hector's axe.

As Hector attacked, Léo took her hand, pulling her around the fight and toward the stairs. The clatter of sword on axe caused her to look backward, but Léo pulled her forward. "I've got to get you out of here. He'll follow if he can."

She stopped. "No. I'm not leaving without him."

He tightened his grip and pulled her toward the stairs, but she wrenched her hand away, running back toward the fight.

Léo screamed her name, but she didn't stop. Tavish parried again and again, better with a sword than Cara expected. She'd almost reached him when she was shoved aside. Léo brought his sword up and deflected the slice that headed right for Hector's neck.

Hector and Léo moved together as if they were one living, breathing monster, performing motions of a war dance that carried the intimacy of seven years of battle and brotherhood. Engaged on two sides, Tavish parried Léo's strikes and jumped away from the deadly cut of the axe. Hector hooked his axe over Tavish's sword and yanked it away and Leo's fist connected with Tavish's jaw.

A blow landed in the middle of Cara back, and she hurtled forward between the notched openings in the parapet walls. The unseen force shoved her forward and upended her legs. Her palms scraped against the jagged stone, and she clawed for a finger hold. "HECTOR—"

Her toe caught on the corner of the wall just before she went over. She flailed, finding a hysterical Elspeth shoving her backward.

Over Elspeth's shoulder, Hector dropped his axes and drew his sword, plunging it without hesitation into Tavish's chest.

Elspeth gave a feral cry and pushed against Cara with unrelenting force. Feet skittering along the wall Cara plunged toward the edge. "Hector!"

Tavish fell to his knees and Hector kicked him over, barreling toward her just as her toe lost its grip and she tumbled backward. A massive hand gripped her ankle and held on, pulling her back toward safety. Elspeth clambered over the parapet and bit into his arm.

He yelped in pain but did not lose his grasp on her ankle. Léo came to his aid, struggling with his sister, pulling her off Hector. Kicking, punching, crazed with grief, Elspeth scrambled forward one inch too far. Her hand sailed over the edge of the wall, carrying the rest of her body with it, and she fell with a sickening clap onto the rocks below.

Léo grabbed Cara's other leg, and together, they hoisted her back onto the wall. The guards flooded through the gate, and she had only a moment to think before Hector and Léo yanked her toward the stairs.

Around and around they traveled, one story, two, three, four, five. A boat floated at the edge of the stairs that created the water gate. Hector jumped into it and Léo handed her off just as the guards crashed through the doorway. Léo ran forward, shoving the boat away from the stairs and into the water with all his might, then raised his sword and rushed into the crowd of men.

"Léo!" Her useless cry echoed against the stone walls as she watched him go down.

Hector pulled on the oars and at slow speeds the tiny rowboat cut through the water. An arrow sliced through the air and sank into the wood of the boat.

His deep voice brooked no argument. "Get down against the side!"

Trembling, Cara spied another boat launch after them before ducking down into the bottom. Rowing like a man possessed, Hector drove the small boat the short distance to land, as arrows continued to sink into the flimsy vessel. At the shore, he jumped into the water and pulled it onto the pebbly beach.

Murdoch ran out into the waist-high water and began loosing arrows at the boat behind them. One by one, he picked off each man in the boat. In the distance, three more boats rowed for shore.

Calum ran toward her. "My lady."

With one quick motion he hefted her into his arms like a sack of grain and began to sprint. She had no time to think or protest. Behind them, Hector raced after them, followed by Murdoch. Even with the extra weight, Calum shot through the woods until there was a gap of dozens of yards.

"Don't leave him, please Calum!"

Calum tightened his grip on her legs. "He'll reach us... dinnae worry...my lady.... Orders are...for me to... get you to safety."

They blasted into a clearing where Lachlan, Iain MacLeod, and another man waited.

Calum panted and bundled her into Lachlan's arms. "Léo didn't make it... she can ride Fantôme... back."

Without flinching or reacting to the news, Lachlan hefted her onto a massive black stallion and Lachlan and Calum mounted their horses.

Hector and Murdoch ran into the clearing and mounted. "Go!"

Hector took her reins and urged Ghoustie into a run. Terrified, she held on for dear life as the muscled black stallion matched each of Ghoustie's strides, and they broke away from the others. In the distance, two companies of soldiers ran into the clearing and began lobbing arrows, but they were too far out of reach.

Angus MacKay appeared from nowhere on a speckled horse and pointed to an obscure freshwater burn that traveled north. Hector guided the horses into the water and they rode for ten minutes up the waterway before exiting and heading west and into the mountains.

After an hour of climbing, they stopped to rest their horses before the mouth of a cave. Hector dismounted and helped her down, his arms crushing around her.

The unfamiliar man approached. "We can only rest for an hour and then we need to be off again." Hector nodded, his face drawn.

Lachlan pulled her under his arm. "I'm so thankful you are safe, sister." She returned his embrace, her spirits crushing, tears at her eyes.

Hector's clear eyes were wet, and he squeezed the bridge of his nose.

Lachlan put a hand to Hector's shoulder. "He's gone?"

Hector nodded. "Aye. He pushed us into the water as hard as he could, then ran back and..."

Cara buried her face in his chest, remembering the sight of Léo going down—the look of agony on his face. He'd given his life for theirs.

"...and he was gone."

# Chapter 41

## MacKenzie Oighreachd- December 22, 1383

It took four days to travel down Loch Ness to Loch Lochy, and finally to the River Lochy, where the keep of Clan Chattan stood and High Chief David MacKenzie, her unknown rescuer, had given them respite in safety. They slept for two days more, fatigue from the journey and the pain of losing Léo weighing heavily on their minds.

On the sixth day they woke, and Hector loved her well, both of them craving the connection to each other that they had missed for too many long weeks. After, as she lay in his arms, his hand traveled down her middle and stroked her belly.

He kissed her ear. "I can feel where the wee one is." His hand moved over the slight, round bump. "I cannae believe it. I'm a father."

She mimicked the sound of his brogue. "I canny believe it, either. 'Tis a miracle." Her hand covered his and they lay there, cradling their child.

A brazen smile lit up his face and his brogue thickened until he almost sounded like Iain MacLeod and began to boast. "Hoo much of a man am I? Got ye prignant on the first try." Laughter overtook her and she swatted his leg.

He smirked. "Ow. I'm jus' statin' facts, ye wee hen."

They lay in silence and his thumb traced around the bump. "Do you think it's strong? You've suffered so much the past few weeks."

Right on schedule, a wave of uneasy sickness passed over her. "Aye. I need to get up and eat. It's a ravenous little thing."

He smiled against her neck and kissed her again. "Tha's my good lass. Growing a big, strong MacLean."

"Between my height and yours I think we may expect one normal-sized child."

Her eyes fell on the small psalter on the bedside table. She reached over him and picked up the book. "Why did you give this to me? I can't read it."

He pushed up on his elbow and traced the contours of her face and the freckles across her cheeks. "I commissioned it on Iona the week I went away for spiritual retreat. I couldnae get you off my mind. The Lord kept me awake, night after night. Every time I closed my eyes you were there. You were my wife. You were carrying my child."

He took the psalter from her hands and opened it to the inscription. "I didnae know how to conquer my flesh. I prayed for God to help me feel something more for Elspeth, but my heart felt only for you.

"When this was completed, I sat beneath the same kind of bright pink moon that hung in the sky the night we met, and my head was filled with you. I gazed at the radiance of the moon, and I knew." His sea-glass-colored eyes looked into hers and he kissed her. "I knew I loved you and I'd never love another." He touched the page. "I could hear the monks in the chancel chanting this verse."

She touched the inscription. "That's why it is in Latin?"

"Aye. For weeks I wanted to give it to you. I was still warring with myself between protecting the clan and protecting you. I began to think I was being selfish in my pursuit, but the Lord kept lighting the way just as he told me he would. Lighting the way to you. That radiant moon hung in the sky. First the night we met, then on the beach, the night I saved you on the barley field, then on Iona, and on the night we married, and finally the night I swam Lochindorb and scaled the walls to find you."

He turned the pages. "When you told me you couldnae read, I wanted you to ask me to teach you. I wanted to see your face as you read for yourself how much you're loved by me, and by God. I wanted you to know that you were chosen before the world began, no' to be my wife, but to be his child. I wanted you to see your significance."

She pulled him down and kissed him and touched his battle-scarred face. "Euphemia read it to me, just as I needed it most. I knew that God would save me. That you would come for me. I only needed to hold on."

"Aye, love. I will always come for you." He took her hand and placed it in the middle of his firm chest. "Your brand has been seared on my heart since the first time I saw you there, singin' in that field. You own my body, my heart, my very soul."

Emotion moved her and she traced the jagged edge of his scarred cheek. She needed protection, and he became her fortress. With him, she belonged. With God, who had delivered her from the pits of hell, she belonged. She wanted to know more.

"Hector?"

"Yes, love?"

"Will you teach me how to read?"

# Epilogue

Ascream rent the air as Hector sprinted up the steps toward his solar. Lachlan called to him from the bottom of the stairs. "That's a good sign, the bairn isnae here yet."

A bead of sweat trickled down Hector's face as he crashed past Cameron, knocking him onto his bottom. "It doesnae sound good!"

Fear gripped his heart as he rounded the stairwell, knowing how his own birth had nearly killed his mother, and Cara was much smaller than she was.

He collided with the locked door and pounded. "Let me in! For the love of the saints, let me in!" The latch sounded and he knocked Aoife backward as he rushed to Cara's side.

Face covered in sweat, red hair falling in ringlets around her damp forehead, she panted hard. "Hector."

Face contorting in pain she yelled again. Margaret and Mhairi took each of her legs and he put a supporting arm behind her. When the pain had passed, she collapsed back against him, sweating and spent, resting her head into his neck.

Whimpering, she groped for his hand, and he found hers, holding it tight. "I thought you were on Islay."

In awe of what she was enduring, he tried not to feel terrified as he looked into her mossy green eyes. "I was, but Lachlan came for me."

Agony streaked across her face, her body went rigid, and she rocked forward, crushing his hand and releasing a ferocious cry.

For the first time since he was ten years old his voice came out high and scared. "Is this normal?"

Ursula braced her hand upon Cara's knee. "Aye. Your baby is crowning. You're almost there, love, bear down." They adjusted Cara higher in the birthing chair and she gave an almighty yell that shook the walls around them. And then, she went slack.

Hector could only watch in great admiration as she groaned and extended her head back in relief. The strong cry of his bairn echoed softly around the room as Ursula rubbed it clean. Little arms shot straight out, and ten tiny fingers reached to the sky.

Ursula's voice was full of excitement. "It's a boy! A muckle boy! God bless you, lass, he's huge. Look at these long legs. There's the heir to Chief MacLean of Lochbuie!"

Overcome with emotion, Hector laughed and cried at the same time. He braced his arms around his exhausted wife as tears streamed down her face. Ursula placed the precious, naked baby upon her chest and covered them with a blanket.

Tears fell down his cheeks. "Muckle? He's so small."

A shock of red fuzz curled over his boy's slightly pointy head, and he quieted, nuzzling into Cara's breast.

Extending a trembling hand, he covered his son's little back with the span of his palm. The baby's soft cries slowed, and he lifted one disapproving red eyebrow and opened his eye. A bright, aqua blue eye inspected him, and he whimpered.

Affection for his strong lass lodged in his chest, and he leaned over, kissing her in gratitude, in wonder, and amazement of what she had delivered into the world. "You've done it, lass. You've done it all. We have a son."

Cara lifted the baby and placed a kiss on his cheek before lowering him with shaking arms back to her chest.

Hector could see fatigue overcoming her as she wrapped trembling arms around their son. "Ursula, can I move them to our bed?"

Ursula finished cleaning up and nodded. "Aye, Da. Go right ahead."

Da. He was a da. Heart bursting with love, he placed his arms around his wife and son, and carried them over to the high bed, laying them among the pillows. Aoife tucked the covers tightly around them.

Mhairi pulled him into an embrace, and he wrapped his arms around her, his heart a throbbing mess.

She squeezed him tight. "I'll be going home to get some rest, but I'll be back in a few days with the boys so they can meet their new cousin."

He kissed her cheek. "Thank you, Mhairi. For everything. If you hadnae gotten word to me, I would've missed it."

Concern and disappointment mingled in her expression. "How long can you stay this time?"

"Only a few weeks."

Cara called for him sleepily among the pillows. "Hector?"

Mhairi kissed his cheek and took her leave. "Glad to have you home for the time being."

He knelt beside his wife. "What is it, love?"

"Do you want to hold your son?"

"I dinnae ken if tha's a good idea. He's so little. I may break him."

She blinked away her fatigue and chuckled. "No, you won't. He wants his da."

More nervous than he was the first time he walked into battle, he took the small bundle from her arms. A wee cry rent the air, and he instinctively pulled his son close to his chest and began to rock, kissing his baby cheeks. "Wheesht wee Beithir."

Cara made a sound of disapproval. "I've already told you, I'm not calling my baby a monster name."

Hector smiled and winked at her. "But it's my war name." Since their midnight escape from Lochindorb, and his team beginning to frustrate the Wolf's plans, his reputation, and the sobriquet, had grown infamous, a Hebridean answer to the Wolf himself.

Adjusting the baby in his arms, his sweet lad began to quiet. A tiny fist wrapped around the tip of his finger and the whole of his heart. He had his mother's upturned nose and angled eyes, and Hector's long arms and legs. A perfect mix of them both. He kissed him again. "Our fighter."

Hector climbed into the bed beside Cara and tucked her under his arm. She caressed their son's tiny foot and her beautiful lilting voice lifted the same song over her son she'd sung the night he first saw her.

"Who heals the broken in heart and binds up their bruises? Who determines the number of stars and calls them all by name? Great is our Lord. Great is his power. His wisdom cannot be numbered. The Lord lifts up the meek and brings the wicked down to the ground. Sing, you, to the Lord with praise..."

The baby's eyelids drooped and closed, and her voice trailed away, her own eyes shutting with sleepiness.

"I think I may know of a name that would please you, love. Eamon."

Cara's eyes remained closed, but a smile lifted her cheeks. "Like my da. And Léo. Eamon Léonid MacLean."

Hector's chest tightened and he wished with all his heart that Léo had lived to see his namesake. "Aye. Eamon Léonid MacLean."

Margaret crouched, tears dripping over her cheeks as she touched Eamon's wee fist.

"Here, take your first grandson." He placed Eamon in Margaret's arms, and she sniffed, touching his tiny curls of red hair.

"Hector, can you believe this? God has restored a grandson to me."

As he looked at his beautiful sleeping angel curled against his chest and their child in Margaret's arms, his faith became sight.

God had restored everything.


The end.

# NOTES

## PROLOGUE

1. The Rhins of Galloway - A sea peninsula in Dumfries and Galloway, Scotland.
2. Iona - (Pronounced eye - owna) A small island off the coast of the Isle of Mull. The center of Gaelic faith and monasticism.
3. Cuirass - (pronounced qwer-iss) body armor that protects the torso of the wearer.
4. Ken - Scots word meaning "know."; Uisge-beatha - (pronounced Ooshkih beh-ha) Scottish word for whisky. Hebridean peated single-malt whisky is famous for its refined potency.
5. Pontvallain - (pronounced pont-VALL-ohn) A battle during the Hundred Years' War in which French forces, led by Bertrand du Guesclin, heavily defeated an English contingent of approximately 5,200 soldiers, which had broken away from the army led by Sir Robert Knolles.
6. Bannockburn - A battle during the First Scottish War of Independence. A major turning point and decisive victory for the King of the Scots, Robert the Bruce, who faced the army of King Edward II of England.

## CHAPTER 1

1. Leman - (pronounced lee-men) meaning a mistress or lover.
2. Keening - From the Irish word *caoineadh*, a form of lamenting poetry performed by women upon the death of a loved one. The caoineadh is a series of utterances, breathed and lilted, rhymed and rhythmic, grieving the dead person, usually a man.

## CHAPTER 2

1. Estoc - French sword, from the French word meaning "thrust." This two-handed sword is long, straight, and stiff. The sword has no cutting edge, only a deadly point. The sword is useful for piercing armor, and in hand-to-hand combat practice, or as defense when the intent is to incapacitate, not kill.
2. Bon après-midi - (pronounced bun-ah-pray-mee-dee) French phrase meaning good afternoon, spoken when departing.
3. Camarade - (pronounced kam-a-rade) Early French military slang for someone who shares with someone else. A sense of close friendship, buddy.
4. Beithir - (pronounced BAY-hith) In Scottish folk-lore the beithir was the largest and most deadly of serpents. Similar to a dragon but without fiery breath or wings, the beithir is equipped with a venomous sting. When a person is stung by a beithir they must head for the nearest body of water such as a loch, before the beithir may reach it. If they reach it first, they are cured. If the beithir reaches it first, they are doomed.

5. Dord - A bronze horn, native to Ireland, with a deep, droning sound.
6. Marmousets - A group of councilors that advised the French king.
7. Tocher - Scottish term for dowry.
8. Merks or Merk land - An old unit of Scottish land measurement based on rent amounts. Twelve ounce lands equals one merk land. Based on the historical charter given to Hector MacLean by John of Islay, Hector received twenty "merks" of land on several islands and in Scotland. The point here being, that he is being given the most valuable lands on four separate territories. The charter indicates that Hector became the more prestigious chief of the two brothers. A mind-boggling amount of wealth.

## CHAPTER 3

1. Bìrlinn - (pronounced BEAR-linn) Or West Highland Galley. A Scottish sailing vessel used extensively in the highlands and in the Hebrides. A large vessel, typically with 12-18 oars.
2. Leine - (pronounced LAY-na) Traditional Gaelic gown/tunic, worn by both men and women. Men often belted it up to their waist. Women wore it to their feet.
3. Barmkin - Scots word for a fortified defensive enclosure typically around smaller tower keeps.
4. Crotal Bells - (pronounced CROW-tal bells) A cluster of bells worn on horses and horse-drawn vehicles used to worn people, and other horses and horse-drawn vehicles of approach.

## CHAPTER 4

1. Touché - (pronounced too-shay) From the French word *"tochier"* meaning touch—a reference to fencing, meaning "you get a point."
2. Berserker - A norse idea of a specific animalistic warrior. Berserkers are subject to fits of frenzy, and according to belief, a berserker would become immune to battle and make great havoc on their enemies. The term for going berserk, "hamask" means to change form. When the frenzy abated the berserker became drained, weak and tame.
3. Ç'est assez - (pronounced set-ah-say) a French phrase meaning "that's enough."

## CHAPTER 5

1. Lazybed - a traditional method of cultivation used in Scotland where banks of dirt are mounded in long rows to improve drainage and soil quality.
2. Èireannach - (pronounced AY-ren-nogh) Scottish Gaelic word meaning Irish.
3. Dhún na nGall/Donegal - (pronounced Dun-ee-gall) Ireland's northernmost county.

# CHAPTER 6

1. Sext - Midday.

# CHAPTER 7

1. Fear-taic - (pronounced fehr-taighk) Scottish Gaelic term meaning support man. The fear-taic was usually a relative of the clan chief, and was given control of the land for rent. The fear-taic then managed the collection of rents.
2. Bere barley - (pronounced bear barley) A type of moisture resistant barley typically found in Islay.
3. Arnoul d'Audrehem - A marshal of France, honored with distinction for his military service during the Hundred Years' War. Arnoul d'Audrehem summoned Guesclin back to France in 1370 and despite his age, participated in the battle at Pontvallain.

# CHAPTER 8

1. Enchanté - (pronounced on-shon-tay) meaning delighted to meet you.
2. Absolument - (pronounced ab-so-lou-mont) - meaning absolutely.

# CHAPTER 9

1. Fleurs Frites - (pronounced flurs-freets) meaning fried squash flowers; Brochet en Doucette - (pronounced bro-shay on doo-set) Soft pike. Two common medieval banqueting dishes.

# CHAPTER 11

1. Ceilidh - (pronounced KAY-lee) a social event with traditional storytelling, singing, and dancing.
2. Plaid/Tartan - A "plaid" is not always a tartan, but a "tartan" is always a plaid. The word comes from the Scottish "plaide" which means blanket, and is traditionally worn over the shoulder. Tartan comes from the Irish Gaelic "tuartan" which is described in the 8th century text *The Senchus Mór* as a material containing cloth of every color. Clans often had distinctive tartans, the earliest recorded evidence dates from the 14th century. Kilts did not exist until the 17th century.
3. Bandle - a narrow length of linen.

# CHAPTER 13

1. Ponass - a simple technique for cooking fish over a fire where the fish is butterflied, then sticks are driven into the flesh. The stakes are then driven into the base of the

fire near the embers to be slow roasted.

2. Bow Butts - An archery shooting field, usually made up of earthen mounds.

# CHAPTER 14

1. Psalter - A book of psalms. This could be a complete book of psalms or a commissioned book of specific psalms. This, along with books of hours (liturgical prayers) served as a personal Bible for nobility. Personal copies of the Bible did not exist until centuries later.
2. Cad as duit - (pronounced cod-oss-dit) meaning where are you from? With the intention of learning where where you born; Is as Bun Crannacha Dom - (pronounced iss oss Buncrana dum) meaning I am from Buncrana or I was born in Buncrana.
3. None - The ninth hour, mid-afternoon. The none hour is the holiest hour as it coincides with the hour of the death of Christ.
4. Staffa - a large uninhabited island in the Inner Hebrides. Derived from the old norse term for pillar island. It is formed of great pillars of basalt. There is a large cavern that exists upon the island called "Fingal's cave."

# CHAPTER 16

1. Ma chérie - (pronounced Mah-share-ie) a French phrase meaning "my darling."
2. Crios - (pronounced criss) a traditional Irish belt, woven by hand without a loom, and decorated with many bright colors. Similar to plaid, the stitches of the crios often were distinctive to the family.
3. Lummon - Irish outerwear. A rough, course wrap similar to a cloak.
4. Chausses - (pronounced show-s) Medieval term for leggings and leg armor, could be made of metal or leather.
5. Favor - A medieval lady would bestow a "favor" on a knight at tournament. Usually this was a sleeve, a handkerchief, or a scarf. Something that fluttered in order to make a public declaration of devotion. It was often something handmade by the lady with her colors or symbol.

# CHAPTER 18

1. Gong - Medieval slang meaning human excrement.

# CHAPTER 19

1. Sean-nós - (pronounced Shawn-nohs) Irish phrase meaning old style. A traditional form of highly ornamented singing with long melodic phrases, and lilting lines. Often performed unaccompanied or with the assistance of long droning notes. Songs sung include lullabies, laments, and love ballads. The singer and audience often closed their eyes, and the singer wound their hand, or had their hand rotated in a circle in order to unwind the song.

# NOTES

## CHAPTER 20

1. Vespers - Sunset.

## CHAPTER 25

1. Bannocks - a type of Scottish quick bread.
2. Compline - The end of the day, the entrusting of one's soul to the Almighty before sleep.

## CHAPTER 26

1. Somerled - A 12th century Gaelic-Norse lord who rose to create the Kingdom of the Isles and Argyll, and who became King of the Isles.

## CHAPTER 29

1. Dùn - (pronounced doon) Scottish Gaelic word for fortress.

## CHAPTER 33

1. Tànaiste - (pronounced tahn-ish-tehh) Scottish Gaelic term meaning heir-apparent.

## CHAPTER 34

1. Terce - The third hour, or third hour after sunrise (about 9:00 a.m.).

## CHAPTER 36

1. Frangach - (pronounced Fran-goch) Scottish Gaelic for Frenchman.

## CHAPTER 37

1. derrière - (pronounced dey-rr-iaire) French word meaning behind, rear end.
2. Clan Chattan - A confederation or community of twelve Highland clans bound under one high chief. Each Highland clan was also represented by a clan chief, but under Scottish law, they were bound to a superior chief for protection, solidarity and sustenance.
3. Monadh Liath - (pronounced monna-lia) Scottish Gaelic for "gray mountain range." A mountain range in the highlands of Scotland, near Loch Ness.

# CHAPTER 39

1. Rondet - (pronounced Ron-day) a medieval dance also known as a carole or ronde. It consists of many dancers joining hands and dancing together in a circle whilst a song is led by a singer.

# CHAPTER 40

1. Mo mhuirnín - (pronounced mu voor-neen) Irish for my darling.

# DEAR READER

Dear Reader,

Thank you for reading this tale of love & friendship. I began writing this book in 2022 at the beginning of my walk with Christ, and in sobriety. At that time, there were so many things that I'd lost I didn't know who I was anymore. I prayed to God to show me that I still had purpose, and he answered in a big way—this book.

It's the first thing I've ever written, so I hope that as you read it, you enjoy it. It's taken me 40 years to decide what I had to say to the world. And here it is— for those, who like me, struggle with their past— approach the throne of grace with confidence in Christ. You are loved and forgiven. For those who, like me, have survived traumatic pain and abuse—approach the throne of grace with confidence in Christ. You are significant, and loved beyond measure.

And dear reader (if you're still reading this) I hope you will join me as we head into book two. Be sure check out my website (www.byashley worrell.com) and follow me on instagram (@byashleyworrell) to keep up with the next book in this nine book series, *The Splendor of Fire*, which follows the story of... Léo & Aileen.

Until Then,
*Ashley*

# ACKNOWLEDGMENTS

Thank you first and foremost to God, who answered my prayer and showed me that I still had purpose.

Many thanks to my husband, Jonathan, who has given so much that I could write and create this series. If you ever want to know where the best parts of Hector came from, it's all Jonathan. I'll love you always, all my life.

Thank you to my children, Luke and Levi, for listening to all my action sequences and telling me if they stank. You are everything to me.

I could not have possibly produced this work without my friends and critique partners, Amber Saare, Cara Harris, Christine Boatwright, Kate Huff, Tema Banner, Ashley Dill, and Heidi Gray McGill. Thank you for listening, for praying, for helping me figure this out, and giving me a reality check when needed.

Thank you with all my heart to my first reader, and developmental editor Libby Reed. You gave me the confidence I needed to finish this tale. You helped me believe in myself.

Thank you to my friend and copyeditor Denise Harmer for helping me spell "whisky" and "blond" correctly about 3,000 times, and for making a silk purse out of a sow's ear. Your encouragement and help came when I needed it most.

And finally— Dad and Mom. I was the baby you weren't supposed to have. Surprise. I bet there were times you didn't think I'd make it. And I know there were times I let you down. I hope as you read these words you know how God has changed my heart and my life. And I hope I make you proud. But mostly, I hope as you read these words you know—none of this was possible without you. Love you.

# ABOUT THE AUTHOR

Ashley Worrell is a repentant HR professional, thankful to be writing adventure stories instead of disciplinary notices. Since leaving the HR world in 2021, she has become a full-time writer and 2023 ACFW Genesis Contest Semi-Finalist for her debut novel, The Radiance of the Moon. Ashley lives with her family and beloved dog Baxter in Greenville, South Carolina, at the foothills of her beloved Blue Ridge Mountains. When she is not spending time in the medieval Scottish isles, she enjoys playing traditional percussion on her bodhrán.

Made in the USA
Middletown, DE
04 October 2024

61983337R00213